MIRACULUM

MIRACULUM

STEPH POST

Copyright © 2019 by Steph Post
Cover and jacket design by Mimi Bark
Interior designed and formatted by E.M. Tippetts Book Designs
ISBN 978-1-947993-41-9
eISBN 978-1-947993-57-0
Library of Congress Control Number: 2016952315

First hardcover edition January 2019 by Polis Books, LLC
221 River St., 9th Fl., #9070
Hoboken, NJ 07030
www.PolisBooks.com

POLIS BOOKS

ALSO BY STEPH POST

A Tree Born Crooked
Lightwood
Walk in the Fire

For Twinkie and Mama C,
A Pair of Miraculous Dogs

OVERTURE

This is a story where no one wins.

Oh, they might think they do. There's always the possibility of thought. When the dust settles, when the day bleeds into dusk, when they look up into the fading light, waiting for their lives to flash before their eyes. In those last moments, they may congratulate themselves. Mourn loved ones. Their pride. Their stolen honor. Their chances at glory.

It is 1922. Half the world has been blown to bits; the other half races on in a blinding maelstrom of frivolity. There is no place for glory. There are no heroes in this new world of mirrors and man-machines.

And, to be quite honest, heroes are so very dull. All those rules. Chivalry. The dreadful speeches with ribbons snapping in the air. The promises.

I'm boring myself now just thinking about it.

No, you can keep your heroes. Give me the players. The ones who take the risks. Who beat their wings frantically against the odds, who aren't afraid to lie, to cheat, to play the game. The ones sporting a little backbone. The ones with scars and teeth. They will lose all the same, yes, but at least I will have been entertained. At least I will have had a little fun.

I do not yet know who the pieces in this game will be. But where I am going, I can hope for the best. Men and women on the fringe. Outsiders. Oddities. Those who lurk in the shadows. Those who know no better.

They are calling to me. With voices they cannot even hear, with intentions they cannot perceive. They are unafraid. They are asking me to play.

ONE

Daniel stood in the center of the midway and felt its beating heart.

"Step right up, gents! Step right up, ladies! That's right! Prepare to be astounded, confounded and utterly shocked beyond your wildest dreams!"

The carnival's pulse raced around Daniel, surging forward, parting around him like water in a cataract. He reached his long fingers into the jacket pocket of his suit and pulled out a silver cigarette case.

"Ten for one, folks! Ten wonders for the price of one. You won't believe your eyes once you've stepped inside!"

Daniel opened the case without looking at it. He was fixated on the world erupting around him, its energy rushing out in all directions, the colors erratic, the spectacles jostling and competing with one another. Jeweled bulbs strung along the tops of the tents illuminated the garishly painted banners advertising horrors and wonders, feats of inhuman strength and displays of savage humanity.

"I've got the Alligator Lady and the Lizard Man! I've got a Giant so tall he can barely fit inside the tent!"

Daniel took out a cigarette and snapped the case shut. He balanced the cigarette between his fingers and closed his eyes. Electricity was humming through the wires, sizzling along the length of the midway, encircling the towering Ferris Wheel, framing the game booths and crowning the ballooning big top tent like a ribbon cinching ever tighter and tighter. Daniel loved the sound of electricity. He loved the way it reverberated in the back of his throat.

"I've got a woman so fat she can't walk on her own, but she's got a voice like a canary and a complexion like a summer's day! You've never seen a prettier gal in all of Louisiana! Don't miss out on Jolly Marjorie!"

Daniel listened. Clicking, shuffling, screeching, laughing, stamping, scraping, fire igniting, oohing and ahhing, crying, hissing, bells tinkling, canvas flapping, clay bottles tumbling, clattering, plates shattering, ropes snapping, corn popping, crackling, metal banging, clanging and a thousand voices clamoring for a thousand wants and underneath it all, the ceaseless march of the whistling calliope.

"And don't forget, folks! When you're done with the Ten Wonders of the World, the marvels just keep on coming!"

Daniel kept his eyes closed. A fight between two men broke out next to him, but he didn't flinch. He was tasting the burnt sugar in the air. He was smelling the greasepaint and the sour perfume and the unwashed bodies.

"There's still so much more to see! We've got men who can lift a thousand pounds and swallow swords! We've got women who can charm snakes and see your future!"

Daniel fit the cigarette between his lips. He pulled out a box of matches and shook one into his hand. He struck the head, smelled the sulfur and felt the heat glinting off his shiny fingernails. He touched the match to the end of his cigarette and drew breath.

"And don't forget, gents! If you go all the way around, you'll find the ladies dancing the Dance of the Seven Veils. And let me tell you, what a dance that is!"

He tossed the match into the trampled muck and took the cigarette in his fingers again. Daniel let the smoke seep from his lips and nostrils and then he opened his eyes. The midway was still dazzling. The people were still rushing around him and the Ferris Wheel cars were still climbing high up into the night. Daniel lifted his head. The stars were still there, too. Still glittering in the night like sparks.

But there was something else.

"Prepare to be amazed, folks!"

Something more.

"Prepare to be astonished!"

An undercurrent. A ripple. Scintillant, but always in shadow. Daniel blinked slowly. It was there, flickering at the edge of his awareness. Prowling around the corners. Tantalizing, yet unseen. Unknown. Hermetic, but beckoning all the same.

"And don't forget, my ladies and gents, at nine o'clock sharp, under the big top..."

Daniel turned to the talker who had been yelling from the nearest bally. He cocked his head as he looked at the man, sweating on the small wooden stage, shaking his cane and his straw hat at the crowd of people flowing past.

"...you'll witness an acrobatic performance of daring, grace and beauty like nothing you've ever seen! Ever imagined!"

Daniel slowly shook his head. He had seen everything. He had imagined everything. Daniel had been lured to the midway in search of a distraction, driven by his all-consuming need to keep the boredom at bay. But this. A shiver darted through him. This was more than he ever could have hoped for: something new.

"Are you ready, folks? Are you ready for it tonight?"

Daniel put the cigarette back between his lips and grinned. Oh, he was ready all right. He was ready for the night. He was ready for the show to begin.

The geek crouched down in the long, wet grass at the edge of the dirt yard and dangled his hands between his knees. He cocked his head and considered the tree in the sharp moonlight. It was tall, an oak tree, with scraggly leaves and roots sunk down deep into the earth, too deep to care about a summer's drought. Too deep to know that everything else in the yard had already withered and died. It reminded the geek of a tree he had once climbed as a boy, back in a place called Missouri, on a farm whose name was escaping him. He couldn't think. He couldn't remember. He could only see the tree, surrounded by a ring of child's playthings: a cracked teacup, a spade, a dirty cloth doll in a dishtowel dress. Tattered ribbons had been tied to the base of a swing.

In the shadows, the geek thought he saw the swing move, twist slightly, the ribbons flutter for an instant, but the air was still, eerily still, as if the curving moon was crushing the night into a stupor. A whippoorwill called through the dark early morning, echoing its own song, and the geek heard it, but did not hear it. He studied the swing. He picked up the rope at his side and ran it through his hands, counting out the lengths as his eyes climbed the height of the tree to the branch arching out over the yard. There was enough for the job. The geek leaned back on the heels of his thin-soled shoes and pushed himself to standing. His bad knee, dislocated once on the ball field and once on the stage when he'd slipped in the blood of the chickens whose heads he had just bitten off, popped, but the geek did not stop to shake his leg out. He could feel the presence behind him. Watching, waiting. Expecting. He could smell the cigarette smoke.

The geek stood beneath the tree branch and looked up. He judged. He moved over, closer to the swing, and tilted his head upward again, trying to focus on the branch that kept disappearing into the darkness. He tossed the rope. Missed. Tossed again. The knotted end came down and dangled in front of the geek. He caught it and pulled it through the loop, threading the rope carefully, quietly. He did not want one of the dark eyes of the house to blink awake. He yanked the rope taut, leaned back, testing the weight, and then began to coil. When he reached thirteen, he trimmed the excess with his pocket knife. He had always been meticulous. He liked to do things right.

The geek stepped up onto the narrow board of the swing and steadied himself. He couldn't remember why he was doing this. He could barely remember who he was or once had been. The only memory that was clear in his mind was that of meeting the man on the midway. The man in the suit with the smile. A smile that, somehow, had driven him to this. The geek reached for the noose.

The swing wobbled as he struggled to get the rope over his head with one hand, but then it was around his neck, heavy, a little awkward, as he had never done this before. He tugged at the rope and thought it would hold. It wouldn't break his neck, but he figured it would strangle all right, so it would do. He angled his head backwards, looking up at the laughing sliver of moon flashing through the leaves. He didn't know why he was doing this. He only knew that he was. He only knew that he must. He squeezed his eyes shut. He was afraid. He stepped off the board and prayed it would soon be over.

Ruby knew something was amiss the moment she opened the door to her wagon and allowed the stale carnival air to wash over her. The midway was quiet, the sounds of the awakening cookhouse only reaching her as a muffled din, but she could feel it. The whisper. The urgency of news as it boiled over in the cramped, isolated confines of Pontilliar's Spectacular Star Light Miraculum. Ruby leaned on the warped wooden doorframe and raked her dark, tangled hair back away from her face. Already, the early July air was stifling, threatening to choke her if she breathed too deeply. She looked out at the lonely carousel, the garish horses frozen in mid-leap, the remnants of last night's show, paper cotton candy cones and sticky candy apple straws, strewn beneath their painted hooves.

Ruby finished braiding her hair and rubbed at her eyes with her rough palms. She pulled her hands away from her face and looked at them. The palms were like those of almost everyone else in the carnival. Callused along the base of the fingers, creases filled with the never-ending dirt that was impossible to escape. Skin, just skin. There was a thin scar on the fleshy part at the base of her right thumb and one running down the length of her middle finger, but still, it was only skin.

She turned her hands over and the tattoos flashed. Tiny stars, crosses, glyphs and other intricate symbols clustered on her fingers and swirled into the larger symbols on the backs of her hands, which spiraled around her wrists and began the covering of her entire body. Ruby flipped her hands back over. Only the palms of her hands, the soles of her feet and her face, for the most part, had been spared. The ink crept up her neck and ran along the length of her angular jaw, with a few subtle marks escaping upwards all the way to her hairline. The tattoos on her face were the most faded and now, more than ten years later from when it all began, her lucent gray eyes, like glittering chips of the sky collecting for a storm, were the brightest feature in her face.

"Flag's up!"

Jimbo's call that breakfast was ready rang out across the haphazard camp of sleeping tents, the long Ten-in-One and the wagons on the edge of the midway. Ruby hated being caught up in the morning rush for greasy biscuits and limp slabs of ham, but she knew that if she waited too long, there wouldn't even be a hot cup of coffee left. She tucked her shirt into her home-sewn trousers and rolled up the sleeves. Ruby knocked the dried mud and muck off her boots before pulling them on and jumping down into the space between the back of her wagon and the side of the illusion show tent. She trailed her fingers along the rough canvas flaps as she made her way through the backlot toward the chaos of the cookhouse.

The long tables scattered in front of the cookhouse tent were crowded with carnival workers, as usual divided into their respective tribes. The talkers, roustabouts and some of the gamesmen, mostly hungover and grumbling, shot dirty looks over at the table the freaks had congregated around. Lead by Alicia, the Alligator Lady, and Marjorie, the Fat Woman, the freak table was always a cacophony of loudly voiced opinions, complaints and observations. Timothy was banging one giant fist, nearly the size of Ruby's head, and shaking the other in the face of Henry/Henrietta. Josephine had apparently brushed some of her long, silky beard into Bernard's plate of eggs and the Half-Man was indignant, twisting around on his torso, trying to bounce a few places down on the long wooden bench. Only Linus, the browbeaten Lizard Man and husband to the screeching Alicia, had his head down, focused on his breakfast. As Ruby poured her coffee, one of the newer rousties leaned back from his table and yelled across the cookhouse yard for Marjorie to dry up already. Ruby rolled her eyes, knowing this would only make her louder.

The other rousties groaned and Ruby shook her head as she walked past with her coffee. There was a hierarchy in the carnival and the rousties knew they were at the bottom. A man pulling on a rope or driving a stake into the ground was a dime a dozen. A four hundred and fifty-seven pound woman who could also yodel was a much more precious commodity. The freaks weren't at the top of the totem pole, though. It was the performers who occupied the tables in the shade beneath the tent canopy. They were the most comfortable, and therefore the quietest, group as they made a point to display their civility in the face of barbaric conditions. The Flying Royal Russians whispered to each other in their own language and the clowns, Zero and Marco, were quietly reading the paper, searching for recent news they could parody in their act. Ruby had every right to sit with them; as Esmeralda the Serpent Enchantress, she was one of the Star Light's top performers, with her own show tent, and she had also been with the outfit longer than most. She skirted the performers just as she did the others, though, and sat by herself at one of the smaller tables at the edge of the muddy yard. The news was buzzing all around her and she wanted a moment by herself to comprehend what she was hearing and to think. She didn't get it.

"Oh my God, did you hear about the geek?"

Ruby hadn't even blown on her coffee yet to cool it. She sighed and leaned back, waiting for the svelte blonde to situate herself and her plate across the table. If it had been anyone else, Ruby most likely would have just gotten up and left. But this was January, the lead dancer in the Girl Revue and Ruby's closest friend. January wasn't even twenty-five, looked younger, and had a heart-shaped doll's face that was impossible to say no to. Ruby raised her eyebrows and carefully sipped her steaming coffee.

"I'm guessing that's what everyone is talking about."

January spoke through a mouthful of scrambled eggs.

"Oh, it's terrible. Absolutely terrible. Have you heard?"

Ruby tried to compose herself and keep her expression flat. She had known the glomming geek for a long time. She also knew, though, that it was probably better to hear the details from January than from someone else. January loved a sensation as much as anyone, but beneath her glamorous affectation was a depth of generosity and compassion. Ruby set her tin cup down and fingered the rim of it.

"What happened to the geek?"

January took another bite of eggs and then set her fork down beside her plate. She leaned forward on her elbows and whispered.

"He did himself in last night."

Ruby nodded slowly and frowned.

"Did himself in? You mean he killed himself?"

"Hung himself. Last night. That's what everyone is talking about. Tom got the details from Franklin this morning."

January looked over her shoulder toward the roustie table before continuing.

"Tom said the geek hung himself from a tree in some townie's yard. Put the noose 'round his neck and stepped off a child's swing. I mean, can you imagine? Why would someone do such a stupid thing? Even if you are a disgusting geek who bites the heads off chickens for a trade. How screwy do you got to be to just bump yourself off like that?"

Ruby didn't answer. January picked up her fork and poked at her cold eggs.

"Tom said it was the little girl who found him this morning. The geek. Woke up early and went out into the yard to get her dolly she'd left by the swing or something. Jesus Christ, poor kid. Having to see that. Tom said the geek must've been all bug-eyed, white as a ghost."

Ruby glanced across the yard at Tom, sitting at the roustie

table and shoveling ham and eggs into his mouth with a purpose. She turned back to January and snapped at her.

"And what else did Tom say? Since he seems to know everything."

January pursed her lips.

"Don't do that. Don't be ugly to me just because you don't like Tom."

Ruby dug into her shirt pocket and pulled out a box of matches and a squashed package of cigarettes.

"I could care less about Tom. Seriously. You want to spend your time with a shifty-eyed roustie who couldn't say no to a bet if his life depended on it and is probably only sweet-talking you because you make more in a blow-off than he can in a month? Go ahead. It's not my business."

Ruby held out a cigarette, but January only stared coldly back at her. Ruby shrugged her shoulders and put the cigarette to her lips. January finally sighed and pushed her plate away.

"Listen, what happened to the geek is awful. It's okay to be upset about it, but you don't got to take it out on me."

Ruby turned her head to the side and blew out a stream of smoke.

"His name was Jacob, you know. He had a name. He wasn't just a geek."

"I know."

They sat together in silence while Ruby smoked. She knew she was making January uncomfortable, but she didn't care. She smoked her cigarette and looked out across the cookhouse yard at all the people who were discussing the geek, but who were also complaining about the food and sore feet and having to sew up holes in their costumes. She closed her eyes against them. January finally forced Ruby's attention back to her.

"Do you know why he did it? Why he killed himself?"

Ruby opened her eyes and stubbed out her cigarette on the

edge of the table. She sighed and dropped it into the dirt.

"I have no idea. It's not like I talked to him all the time. I saw him yesterday before we opened and he seemed fine. Wasn't saying goodbye to people or anything."

January rested her chin in the palms of her hands.

"Tom, I mean, some people, some of the boys, are saying he owed Kensy for poker."

Ruby shook her head.

"All the guys owe Kensy money. He's a shark. But come on, how much could he owe him? No one has any real money around here."

January considered this and then glanced down at the table.

"You know, I was thinking. What if the geek got a letter from his wife? Did he have a wife?"

Ruby sipped at her coffee. It was cold.

"I think so. He's never wintered with us down in Florida. He always says he's going back home to his family. In Missouri, maybe? Somewhere out that way."

January lifted her eyes and nodded.

"So, what if he got a letter from his wife back home? And in it she said she was leaving him. Or that she'd cheated on him. Was still cheating on him and wasn't making no plans to stop. Wouldn't that kind of news make a man cash it all in?"

Ruby gave January a sad, half-smile.

"That how it happen in your magazines?"

"I'm serious. It happens all the time. People killing themselves over love. In the stories, but in real life, too. I just read in *Photoplay* about this one actress. She found out her beau was sleeping with some other girl and she walked out into a lake and drowned herself. Seriously."

"You would think people would have better things to kill themselves over."

"And you would think you're made of stone. Don't act like

you've never been heartbroken."

Ruby looked away as January stood and picked up her plate. The tables across the yard were slowly beginning to empty. Alicia and Marjorie had left and so the cookhouse was already quieter. January stepped over the bench seat.

"I got to go. Me and Darlene and Wanda got a new routine to put together. I'm going to go out of my mind if we keep doing the same damn number with those stupid fans."

Ruby nodded but didn't move.

"All right."

January sauntered away, but Ruby didn't watch her leave. She studied the woodgrain of the table in front of her and absently rubbed her finger along the rim of her empty cup. It didn't add up. If it had been the Ossified Man, whose bones were growing out of control, creating a cage of his own body, maybe she could believe it. Or the fortune teller, YaYa, with one foot in the insane asylum, the other edging toward the grave. But Jacob? He was odd, but no odder than anyone else who chose a carnival life over a normal one. Yet Ruby, better than most, knew that life wasn't supposed to make sense. It wasn't supposed to be clear or have a purpose. Sometimes, it was only about surviving. About waking up each day and taking a breath and then fighting for that breath. Maybe the geek just didn't want to fight anymore. Maybe he wanted something easier.

Ruby shook away her thoughts and started to stand up, but a heavy hand forcefully pushed down on her shoulder.

"Sit."

Ruby lowered herself back on the bench as Samuel slowly came around the table and stiffly sat across from her. She crossed her arms, waiting.

"This matter with the geek. Do you know why he did it?"

Ruby huffed.

"Why do you think I'd know?"

Samuel's eyes didn't leave hers. They were stormy, darker than his skin, and Ruby knew from their intensity that Samuel was furious. The rest of his face, however, betrayed no emotion and his voice, still stilted with the British accent he had retained in America after almost thirty years, was level and even. Almost dangerously so.

"Because you see things. You see people."

"No more than you."

"Perhaps."

Samuel finally looked away from her and they sat together awkwardly for a moment. Samuel had been with the Star Light longer than anyone save Pontilliar himself and he watched every part of it like a bird of prey. Considering. Calculating. Anyone who was new to the show, a First of May man, invariably underestimated Samuel. They assumed he was merely Pontilliar's boy, shining shoes and running errands. They found his perfect posture, branded cheeks and extreme articulation unsettling. The rumor that he had once been an English baronet's butler made his presence even more disconcerting. It was the actual truth, though, that was baffling for so many: Pontilliar's name was on the banner, yes, but it was Samuel who made sure the show stayed open, food went into their bellies and money into their pockets.

Ruby picked up her coffee cup and tapped the edge of it on the table.

"I'm guessing we're hightailing it today?"

Samuel sighed.

"As soon as Pontilliar takes care of this mess. He's in town right now, at the police station. Apparently, the citizens of Sulphur don't appreciate finding dead carnival workers hanging from their trees."

"Damn it, I didn't even think about that. How much is this going to cost him?"

"More than I'm sure Pontilliar is willing to part with. And more than we can spare."

Ruby nodded.

"Jesus. Where are we going to go? Aren't we supposed to be in Sulphur for two more nights?"

Samuel closed his eyes and pinched the bridge of his nose. Ruby realized that he wasn't irritated, so much as weary. She knew that to Samuel, Pontilliar and most others, the death of the geek was more of a frustrating inconvenience than a loss to mourn over. If Jacob had been killed by an accident on the lot, they would be holding a vigil. But suicide was a coward's way out. There would be no memorial. There would be no words. Samuel opened his eyes and stood up from the table.

"I wired Chandler early this morning, as soon as I received the news. He's already in Baton Rouge, setting up the advance. I'm hoping he can move us in early. Perhaps he can even have us open by tomorrow night. Baton Rouge is always a profitable stop and we could use the extra days. Between the advance and whatever damage Pontilliar is settling for, there will not be much left in our coffers."

Samuel turned away, but Ruby bolted up and stopped him.

"The body."

Samuel turned back to her and cocked his head, listening. Ruby came around the table.

"We need to get it back to his wife. I think he had a couple of kids, too. We need to send the body back."

Samuel frowned and the lines across his forehead deepened.

"That's not going to be easy."

Ruby raised her chin slightly.

"Jacob was with us for seven seasons."

"He took his own life."

"He was still one of us."

Samuel sighed and his shoulders slumped forward.

"All right. I'll see what I can do."

"Good."

Ruby looked around the empty cookhouse yard.

"Should we start breaking down now?"

Samuel shook his head.

"Not yet. But be ready to. Franklin is having all the rousties stand by. We don't want it to appear that we are vacating until Pontilliar has everything sorted out."

"Makes sense."

Samuel frowned again and looked away.

"There's something else. When I met with Franklin this morning, he told me some news I'm not certain you want to hear."

He paused. Ruby's eyes narrowed and she crossed her arms.

"Well?"

Samuel glanced back at her, his eyes more wary than concerned.

"I just wanted you to know before you saw him. I wasn't sure how you would react, given the circumstances of your last parting."

Ruby's face went hot and she clenched her jaw, trying to control her emotions. It could be no one else.

"Hayden's back."

TWO

Daniel clasped his hands in front of him and waited while the man who had been less than welcoming banged on the door above him.

"Pontilliar? There's someone here to see you."

The man turned around and glared at Daniel before calling through the heavy wooden door again.

"Someone who refuses to go away until you speak with him."

Daniel smiled up at the man and then turned to look around. He was standing at the base of the narrow steps leading up to a wagon marked "Office - Keep Out!" Behind him, the midway that had so captivated him the night before was being dismantled. Men in peaked caps and overalls, some stripped down to their gray undershirts in the heat, were untying ropes, prying up thick stakes and stacking wooden crates. Everywhere people were hurrying about, pushing handcarts, carrying trunks and boxes, pointing and calling out orders to one another.

Just as it had been the night before, when the carnival was in full swing, the noise was terrific. The metal cars of the Ferris Wheel clanged and screeched as they scraped against one another while being slid into the long bed of a truck with high, slatted sides. Two men carrying the booth front for the Kill the Kats game were shouting at a third who was trying to help maneuver them around a still-standing tent. A prune-faced woman in a long, full skirt and bright orange head scarf swished past the office steps, muttering loudly to herself. Her arms were piled high with blankets and strings of beads, but she slowed down to look over her shoulder and squint her one good eye at him. He flashed her a brilliant white smile and she quickly turned away, disappearing into the chaos.

And underneath the bedlam, Daniel could still feel it. The seducement he was determined to find. Its presence was quieter now, but still there. Hiding, but scratching at him from the shadows.

Daniel continued to smile, but he could feel the stony glare coming from two steps above him. The African man with the precise British accent and striped bow tie was obviously not in the mood to be dealing with him. The man raised his fist once more and knocked on the door, scowling down at Daniel as he called out again.

"Pontilliar! I said, there's someone here to see you."

"Tell him to go the hell away! For God's sake, Samuel!"

The voice coming through the door was muffled, but nothing could soften the agitation and contempt of the words. Samuel shrugged his shoulders and stepped down to the dirt beside Daniel.

"You heard the man."

Daniel looked Samuel up and down once before going around him and climbing the stairs. He put his hands in his pockets and stood solidly in front of the door. His voice was a low purr.

"Trust me, Mr. Pontilliar. You want to see me."

Daniel leaned back slightly as the door ripped open and a red-faced man, bald, sweating and with ice blue eyes about to bug out of his head, stood before him. Daniel smiled. Pontilliar looked around him and yelled down to Samuel.

"For the love of God! Get this clown out of here."

Daniel shifted his body to block Samuel and force Pontilliar to look at him. Pontilliar huffed and eyed him suspiciously while Daniel waited patiently for the man to take him in. His exquisite black suit, sharp, perfectly creased and tailored, was more expensive than anything Pontilliar had or would ever own. He watched Pontilliar's eyes as they traveled up his body, from his gleaming crocodile skin shoes to his diamond cufflinks to his black silk tie and pocket handkerchief, still crisp even in the unbelievable heat. His jet black hair was swept back with pomade and though his suit called for a homburg, Daniel refused to wear hats. He noticed Pontilliar avoided his eyes. They always did. Daniel waited a moment more and then flashed his dazzling smile to display perfect, white, even teeth.

"I have something you want."

Pontilliar crossed his thick arms and rested them on his distended paunch. He huffed.

"Unless you got either a million dollars or Clara Bow stuffed up that fancy suit of yours somewhere, I ain't interested."

At the base of the stairs, Samuel groaned, but Daniel ignored him.

"Mr. Pontilliar, I said that I have something you want. Now step back and let me inside."

Samuel lunged up the stairs and reached for Daniel, but Pontilliar held up his hand to stop him. He narrowed his piggy eyes at Daniel, but opened the door wider to let him pass.

"This better be good, stranger. You picked a hell of a day to start going door to door selling Bibles."

Hayden removed his hat and fingered the brim of the trilby. It was hot. Too hot to be wearing the hat and too hot to go without it. He stood next to the base of the mostly dismantled Ferris Wheel and stared across the midway at her wagon. The carnival was coming down all around him; the smaller tents, for the Snake Charmer show, the Wild Geek show, the Girl Revue and the Illusion and Electric Elucidation, had already been taken apart and were waiting in heaps to be packed up. The big top tent, always the first to be loaded, was completely gone and only the long, narrow Ten-in-One tent was still standing. The bally banners had already been lowered and rolled, and Hayden wondered if they were still the same ones he had painted years ago or if they had been replaced. The wagon murals were still the same and Hayden was glad of that. He'd first come to the Star Light because of those wagons, and if they were still there, he figured he might still have a place on the show.

The truck wagons had been Pontilliar's new great idea when he had split from yet another business partner during the fall of the 1916 season. America hadn't entered the war in Europe yet and though the carnival business was booming, Pontilliar's partner, McAdams, had decided to pack up and hitch himself to the Sun Brothers. McAdams had taken the circus animals, the heart of the show, and left Pontilliar stranded in Beaumont, Texas with only the contracts for the freaks and an acrobatic family of exiled Russian dissidents. And the caravan wagons.

What was left wouldn't be worth moving by train, even if Pontilliar could convince towns to let him set up his decimated show, and out of this predicament came Pontilliar's eureka moment to mount the wagons on cut-down trucks and create a motorized circus, such as America had never seen before. Pontilliar's Star Light Modern Motorized Menagerie! Instead of carting the elephants and tigers around in horse-drawn cages for the parade, Pontilliar would decorate the caravans, mostly used only as dressing rooms and sleeping quarters for the performers, with painted animals and drive the parade down Main Street. When Hayden had first met him, after skeptically answering an advertisement in the newspaper for a painter, he had thought Pontilliar was completely off his rocker. He would later learn that Pontilliar came up with a new great idea every few years and hence the Star Light was ever evolving from Wild West Show to American Exposition to Circus to Carnival to Phantasmorgia. Always a new gimmick, always a new, longer than necessary name. For Hayden, the entire concept was bizarre.

But as a twenty-one-year-old roughneck already tired of working Spindletop's oil derricks, the chance to not only paint a set of murals, but to be paid for his work, was too good an opportunity to pass up. He accepted the job and Pontilliar gave him free rein to paint whatever he liked on the wagons, as long as each scene incorporated animals of some kind. Pontilliar and what was left of his show had wintered in Beaumont that year instead of Florida, and Hayden had six months to work on his masterpieces.

No one in the boomtowns he'd drifted through since he was seventeen knew that Hayden was a secret artist. In the lull between twelve-hour shifts, he had sketched on crumpled sheets of newsprint and packing paper pulled from trash barrels. He drew everything he saw: automobiles and horses clashing in the muddy streets, the towers rising up into the gas-choked air, men coated in black grime, whores leaning on the railings of boardinghouses. Creating the murals for Pontilliar, however, allowed Hayden to slip into a different world. One of color and creatures he had seen only inside of books and his imagination. He was thoughtful about it, getting to know the occupants of each caravan before designing the mural. He painted birds on the Russian family's wagon and beautiful white horses on the one for the women of the Girl Revue. Reptiles on one and lions on another. And, of course, there was his favorite, the wagon painted with snakes: in the grass, hanging from trees and even twisted, serpentine monsters heaving up out of a turbulent ocean. He labored over that particular wagon for weeks, mainly so he could catch glimpses of the girl who lived in it, coming and going up the steps without so much as giving him a glance. Until he decided to join up and travel with the carnival that summer, painting bally banners and drawing portraits on the midway for a nickel a piece. Until he became part of her world. Until she knew him enough to trust him, to talk to him, to introduce herself not as Esmeralda the Enchantress, but as Ruby. Ruby Chole. The woman he would give his heart to. The woman whose heart he would break.

"Hey, da Vinci! You going to stand there all day with your hat in your hand or you going to get to work?"

Startled, Hayden turned around, barely dodging the long tent pole that Franklin, the Lot Man, was carrying on his shoulder. Franklin scowled at him and jutted his chin out toward the snake wagon.

"I don't think she wants to talk to you. If she did, I think she'd be over here by now. Just 'cause I brought you back on after disappearing for two seasons don't mean everyone else is going to be happy to see you. So quit lollygagging and start loading the tubs for the Whip. I got two new rousties on it already and they don't know their ass from their elbow."

Hayden nodded and squashed his hat back over his unruly, ash-brown hair. He had thought about stopping in town for a shower and a shave, but news of the geek's suicide had quickly spread across Sulphur and Hayden knew the Star Light would be on the move as soon as it could. He'd been afraid that if he didn't get there in time, he would never have the courage to follow the show to its next stop. So his vest and trousers were still covered with road dust and his moustache was as unkempt as his hair, but he supposed it didn't matter. It looked like he was going to be lifting ride tubs and packing tent canvas, not standing awkwardly in front of Ruby, trying to figure out what to say to her. Which was just as well. He'd had so much time to think, but now that he was back at the Star Light, he had no idea how to approach her. Hayden heard Franklin yelling at him again and he quickly turned on his heel toward the Whip where, indeed, the two rousties were trying to load the tubs upside down. They'd never fit that way. Hayden rolled up his sleeves and sighed. At least it felt good to be back.

"So, mister, um…"

Daniel sat down in the camp chair offered to him by Pontilliar and crossed one slim leg over the other.

"Revont. Daniel Revont."

Pontilliar slowly walked around the mammoth teak desk and sat across from Daniel. He spread his hands across a mound of yellowing papers and receipts and leaned back in his chair.

"Mr. Revont. Now, what is it you have that I need so badly? Because I mean it, this is not a good time right now."

Daniel nodded as he glanced around the cramped space of the office wagon. It looked like it had once been a traditional gypsy caravan wagon, but had been gutted completely. The preposterous desk seemed to take up most of the available space. Over Pontilliar's shoulder, Daniel could see a metal frame bed wedged into the corner and a small table with a pitcher and water basin. A faded red coat, trimmed in cheap gold ribbon, hung from a nail in the wall. He noticed that although the midway had been awash in electric light, here, only an oil lamp hung from the low ceiling.

24

Daniel found the contrast curious. He languidly brought his gaze back to Pontilliar.

"Because you need to be out of here before the sheriff of Sulphur returns from his daughter's wedding over in Beaumont, correct?"

Pontilliar leaned forward.

"How the hell…?"

"Because when the sheriff returns he's going to be asking too many questions about Jacob Darnfield, the glomming geek who killed himself on Oak Barren Street last night."

Pontilliar's face turned from ham-pink to rare steak-red. He sputtered, sending a spray of saliva across the papers.

"Are you trying to blackmail me? You think you can come in here, expecting some sort of payout just because you know what probably half the town already knows? Did you just fall off yesterday's turnip wagon or something?"

The corners of Daniel's mouth turned down and he shook his head.

"No, Mr. Pontilliar, I am not trying to blackmail you. I am not trying to do anything of the sort and I find it absurd that you would jump to such a conclusion. I said that I have something for you, not that I want something from you."

Pontilliar stood up from his chair and pulled a filthy handkerchief from his back pocket. He wiped the sheen of sweat from his face, stuffed the wadded handkerchief back in his pocket and looped his thumbs under his suspenders.

"Then why don't you tell me what it is, so you can move along and get the hell out of my office?"

Daniel remained seated.

"I have a new glomming geek for you."

Pontilliar snapped his suspenders and stomped back and forth across the short width of the wagon.

"Jesus Christ. What kind of manager are you? You think I

got time to negotiate a deal on a performer right now? How wet behind the ears are you?"

Daniel's entire body had grown still. He didn't even move his head, only followed Pontilliar with his black, glittering eyes.

"I have no idea what you are talking about. You are in need of a new geek and I have brought you one. Myself."

Pontilliar stopped in his tracks and barked out a laugh.

"You? What are you, some kind of cake eater looking for kicks? You want to get blood all over that dandy suit of yours there?"

Daniel's blank expression didn't change.

"I am a geek. You are in need of a geek. I will leave with you today and you can pay me whatever you deem appropriate."

Pontilliar snorted.

"Who do you think's getting paid around here? Aside from the pennies and nickels you can scrape up off the stage floor at the end of the show, you're not going to see much legal tender around here. Not after this fiasco, anyway."

"That's fine. Pay me what and when you can. I am a geek. You need a geek. What more is there to discuss?"

Pontilliar scratched the side of his jowly face and looked closely at Daniel again.

"Seriously. You mean to tell me that you're going to stand up on a stage, in front of a gawking crowd, and bite the heads off of live chickens?"

Daniel finally stood.

"I will bite the heads off of whatever live creatures you need me to."

He met Pontilliar's eyes and Pontilliar slowly nodded in agreement. Daniel shook the man's proffered, sweaty hand and smiled. It had been as easy as pie.

THREE

R uby shaded her eyes against the noon sun and surveyed
the caravan of cars and trucks lined up across the dusty lot,
ready to pull out as soon as the order was given. They were
leaving the vast dirt clearing pockmarked with trampled garbage
and scarred with footpaths, tire tracks and large impressions in
the earth where only hours before the heavy ride machinery had
seemed like a permanent formation of the landscape. Now all had
been bent, folded, bundled and swept into the nineteen various
vehicles that would transport the Star Light to the next location.
Every inch of space on wheels that could be used was packed tight
with every element of the carnival, from cookhouse tables to bally
banners to rousties and performers. Ruby's own truck wagon was
crammed to the arched wooden ceiling with rolls of canvas, tent
poles and, of course, her four boxes of snakes. Her ever-changing
riding companion for this jump was Sonja, one of the Russian

trapeze artists, and the sullen, petite blonde had already climbed up into the open cab of the truck and fallen asleep. It was an eight-hour drive to Baton Rouge and Ruby was relieved she would be sharing the cramped bench seat with the acrobat. Sonja was not only tiny, but refused to speak English, even though she was fluent in the language. This removed the threat of hours of idle chit-chat, something Ruby detested. The trip was going to be a long one, but at least it would be quiet. If they ever got started in the first place.

Ruby leaned against the side of her wagon and jammed her hands into the pockets of her trousers. They were all waiting for Franklin, Samuel or Pontilliar to give the signal, but the three men were still huddled in Pontilliar's office wagon, arguing over the logistics of the move. Ruby blew a stray strand of hair out of her face and hunched her shoulders, knowing there was nothing to do but wait. And think. And try not to look down the line of vehicles to the Model T with Hayden sitting idly behind the steering wheel.

She'd seen him earlier, standing like an idiot next to the base of the Ferris Wheel and staring dumbly at her wagon, the one he had painted himself. She had stayed out of sight, fearful of how she might react when she finally confronted him, still unsure of the smoldering remnants in her chest. Ruby wanted to kill Hayden. She wanted to reach inside him and burn his own heart, so he could know. She wanted to run to him and be held. She wanted to bury her face in his shoulder, smell his sweat, feel his hands on the back of her neck and his arms against her ribs and she wanted to destroy him. She wanted to surrender to him and to bruise him. To break him.

Ruby wanted answers, but she dreaded them, too. She was afraid to get close enough to Hayden to ask, so she'd not let him see her, not yet given him the chance to speak. Ruby had watched him standing in the middle of the disassembling midway and from a distance tried to judge the expression on his face, the look in his eyes, but she had been able to discern nothing. When he'd turned

28

around toward the rousties struggling at the Whip, he had set his hat back on his head and the familiarity of the gesture, the way he held the crown pinched between his fingers, the way his chin dipped slightly and the corners of his mouth came down, made her breath catch in her throat. It was such a quick, simple movement, one she'd seen him make a hundred times, and for a moment she expected him to cut his eyes over at her and wink. When he didn't, the stab she felt was as confusing and painful as when Samuel had first told her that Hayden had returned to the Star Light. She didn't know what to do; she didn't know what to want.

So she kept herself now from looking over and finding Hayden's car. She leaned her head back against the warm boards of the wagon side and kept her eyes on the head of the line, waiting for Pontilliar to emerge so they could get started. When he finally did, trailed by Franklin and Samuel, Pontilliar didn't climb into the cab and signal for everyone to crank their engines. Instead, he marched down the length of wagons until he got to Ruby. His face was dark red and she knew he was furious from the way he twisted the tight gold ring back and forth on his pinky finger as he stormed toward her. She waited until she could see the fat droplets of sweat on his forehead and then she pushed herself away from the wagon and crossed her arms.

"Yes?"

Pontilliar slowed to a waddle and then closed in on her, turning his head to the side and keeping his voice low. His words came out in a biting wheeze.

"Everyone ready to go?"

"Have been for a while."

Pontilliar's eyes darted to hers.

"Don't you pull that with me. We would've shaken out an hour ago but somebody thought it was a good idea to try to get that worthless geek's body shipped home once it's released. Are you kidding me?"

Ruby shrugged her shoulders and looked away from him.

"It's important."

Pontilliar twisted the ring on his finger and hissed at her.

"Don't you ever go to Samuel with another dumb idea like that. You want to try to make waves? Ask me. I'll shut you down so fast it'll make your head spin."

Ruby laughed.

"Since when have I ever gone to you for anything? You think I plan to start now? And I just mentioned it to Samuel. You act as if I have a say in anything."

Pontilliar shook his head and looked over to Samuel, who was waiting outside of the management wagon. His face, as usual, was an unreadable mask. Pontilliar rolled his eyes.

"Yeah, but you get ideas into his head. And then he wants to follow through on them. Next thing you know, I'm spending another goddamn hour sweating my nuts off in that outhouse this place calls a town hall, trying to bribe yet another official with money we don't have to do something that no one cares about in the first place."

Ruby narrowed her eyes at him.

"They should care. You should care. Jacob was with us. He was good at his job and he was a good person. You can't just ignore that."

"He clocked out. Craven idiot. If he wanted to kill himself so bad, he should've done it off the circuit and spared us the headache. What a waste of time, this whole mess."

Ruby's eyes flashed.

"That's all this is to you, isn't it? Just a waste of time? A waste of money?"

Pontilliar had been looking over his belly into the dirt, but now he jerked his head up and nearly spat at her.

"Hell yes, it's a waste. An inconvenience and a waste."

Ruby crossed her arms and slowly shook her head as she

ground her teeth together. Her voice came out laced with acid.

"An inconvenience? Did you really just say that?"

Pontilliar braced one arm against the side of the wagon and leaned in close, boxing Ruby in. He turned his head away from her when he spoke and his lips stretched wide in a phony smile, just in case anyone was watching them.

"Are you going to be the one to tell all those folks hoping for a sawbuck bonus that there's nothing left now? That the whole nut was blown trying to patch this mess up? This show is on its last legs and we're barely raking in enough to pay the next advance and keep some stew in the pot. You think about that?"

Ruby could smell the sweat oozing from his face and neck. She leaned away in disgust.

"The Star Light's been on its last legs for the past fifteen years. I'm pretty sure this is just one more drop in your sad little bucket of show business."

Pontilliar whipped his head around, his eyes popping. He grabbed her arm and jerked her closer.

"Now you listen to me. You may be my daughter, but that doesn't mean I won't—"

Ruby's whole body was tense, but she raised her chin defiantly, staring him down.

"What? You'll what?"

Ruby's eyes bored into his.

"What? Tell me what you'll do."

Pontilliar's mouth curled into a smirk.

"Let's just say I'm not above throwing you out on your ass."

Ruby twisted her arm away from him.

"Better than being here."

"Is that so? Because where would you go? What would you do?"

Pontilliar stepped away from Ruby and looked her up and down as if appraising her. His face was still red, still slick with sweat, but his eyes were cruel.

"I mean, look at you, for God's sake. Who would take you?"

Ruby kept her trembling down in her throat. She would never let him see that his words could touch her. She would never give him the satisfaction. Never. She tried to think of something to say, another comeback to the taunt she'd heard so many times spewed from his lips, but before she could speak, Pontilliar had turned his back on her. She could hear him puffing as he marched away and gave the signal for the drivers to move out. Ruby uncrossed her arms and shook her head, feigning disbelief. She muttered, mostly for the benefit of Sonja, in case she had been listening.

"Bastard."

Ruby climbed up into the truck's cab and gripped the steering wheel. Sonja was still curled into a tight knot, asleep, and so Ruby finally let her face fall. She and her father had been having the same standoff for over a decade, but his words, because they were true, still stung her. For all that she wanted to rage against him, Pontilliar was right. She had no future outside of the Star Light. There was no path leading her away from the midway, no refuge waiting for her on the other side. She certainly couldn't survive out in the real world, where her only fate was to be either shunned or violated. And there was no point in jumping ship, either. She was tattooed, but she wasn't a Tattooed Lady. Her markings were crude, the designs nonsensical. There was no way she could compete with women who had the Last Supper emblazoned across their chests in full color. Nor could she make it as a Snake Charmer in any other outfit; she had spent years asking around. The few sideshow managers she'd met with had given her a once-over and agreed that no, she couldn't be a Tattooed Lady. And no, they wouldn't take her on to dance with snakes either; she wasn't pretty enough, voluptuous enough, feminine enough. In other words, good enough. The last manager she had talked to before giving up completely had chomped on his cigar for a while and then offered her a job as a pit geek. Dressing like a savage and biting the snakes and frogs and rats thrown down to her by the handler. Groaning and screeching and rubbing blood on her face as the crowd looked down from above.

Ruby started the truck's engine and breathed deeply. At least at the Star Light, she had her own bally, her own show, her own tent and wagon and billing. She had her dignity. Ruby glanced at her fingers, stretched out along the curve of the steering wheel. It was because of Pontilliar that she was trapped by her own skin, imprisoned by the webbing of her own body. Ruby knew Pontilliar would never willingly admit to the damage he had caused, would never apologize for her fate, but Ruby knew, too, that he would always allow a place for her in the Star Light. Ruby and Pontilliar were tied together by guilt and necessity, each daily reminding the other of what they owed, and had taken from, each other.

Ruby didn't speak to a single soul for six months after her mother died of a rattlesnake bite. When Miranda came stumbling into the cabin, face pale and streaked with dirt and sweat, bony fingers clutching her right wrist, already crimson and swelling, Ruby's grandfather had sent her racing down the mountain to their nearest neighbors, the Wynnes, in what twelve-year-old Ruby thought was a desperate attempt to save her mother's life. She couldn't have known that her grandfather had only sent her away to spare her the cruelty of watching his daughter puff up and bloat, writhing on the dirt floor in agony. He had known she was lost from the moment he had laid eyes on the bite.

When Ruby made it back to the cabin after dark, alone, the Wynnes having deserted Jackrabbit Mountain months before, she stood outside the closed door and listened. She waited for groans.

She waited for calls for water, for screams, for quiet murmurings. The terrifying silence drove her back into the trees and she sought shelter in the crook of an oak, her legs and ankles bloody from the briars she had crashed through. Her face dry with the tears she refused to cry.

In the morning, she stood leaning against the well pump, shivering, watching the still-closed cabin door. There was a fire inside, thin blue smoke drifted up from the chimney, but she would not go in. Finally, the door creaked opened and her grandfather called out from the gloom. He told her to go find a shovel.

Ruby spent most of that winter in the woods, surviving in the ways her mother had taught her. The Chole land had been in the care of her mother's people for generations, and Ruby knew their five hundred acres of Appalachia as well as she knew her dreams. Her mother had taught her how to build snares made from delicate slips of twine and crackling branches. She knew how to find the trout still murmuring under the thin skin of creek ice and how to chew and swallow bark if she couldn't find anything else. She knew how to kindle a fire from damp, mushy wood and she knew how to sleep in the snow and stay warm. When her mother had twisted the necks of squirrels, she had forced Ruby to watch. Now, alone, Ruby looked the squirrels in their tiny black eyes and felt nothing. She crushed the skulls of muskrats and felt nothing. There was nothing left inside of her to feel.

It wasn't cold or loneliness or even pity that drove her back to the cabin, but a dull sense of duty. Her grandfather was slowly sinking into another world and Ruby, though she knew she could not save him, felt the need to at least bear witness to his descent. She brought him chunks of smoked meat and made pans of cornpone with what was left in the sack by the hearth. She stoked the fire and crouched near it, shoveling the flat bread into her mouth with greasy fingers, watching as her grandfather stared vacantly into the flames. She left food in the cast iron pan and melted snow in the bucket, but did not pull the blanket tighter around his shoulders. She did not take his hand or nudge his rocker forward or part her lips to speak. She ate and made herself warm and then went back out into the winter.

When Ruby came one evening in the spring and found her grandfather dead, she had still felt nothing. She had wrapped him in his blanket and dragged him up the mountain. He had been lighter than she expected and his body had slid easily over the slick new grass. She had dug a grave next to her mother's and added him to the long line of Choles. She had not returned to the cabin. She had known it was time for her to leave.

FOUR

The jump had been a nightmare. Baton Rouge was only a hundred and fifty miles east of Sulphur and they should have arrived at the lot on the northern outskirts of town well before midnight. Instead, here it was daybreak and they were just now pulling in. With a caravan of nineteen vehicles, twenty now that Hayden had joined up, delays were to be expected, but this debacle was an exception. Between overheated engines, closed roads and Chandler, the advance man, having painted half the follow arrows in the wrong direction, the journey had taken them into morning. Ruby's eyes were burning as she steered around recently cut tree stumps and circled her wagon in with the others. Chandler was on the ground already, trying to step out the lot and put markers down for the tents, rides and booths on the midway. Ruby could hear Franklin hollering at Chandler that he was doing it all wrong before the trucks had even slowed to a stop. She found the mark for her wagon, as always wedged between where the snake show tent and the illusion show tent were to be erected on the cul-de-sac back end of the midway, and shut the engine of her truck off. She shook Sonja awake and then tumbled out of the cab, grateful for her boots to hit the ground. All she wanted was a cup of coffee, but it would be another hour at least before the cookhouse tent was set up and Jimbo had picked up the pre-ordered provisions in town. Until the flag's-up call went out for breakfast, everyone needed to get to work.

Ruby stretched her arms and twisted her shoulders, trying to wake herself out of the travel-induced daze. Sonja had already slipped away to join the rest of her family who were lifting boxes out of the back of the acrobats' wagon. As soon as the long cargo trucks had arrived, the rousties had swung down from the piles of canvas they had ridden in on and begun to pound tent stakes. Ruby could feel the ground vibrating beneath her feet as Franklin and his crew sunk the spikes deep into the dry, packed earth.

Everyone was expected to pull their weight in setting up the carnival and no one would be allowed to rest until every tent was constructed, every bally banner hung on the line, the donikers dug, the rides bolted together and the electric lights strung up and down the length of the midway. The performers and freaks were responsible for outfitting the tents and the gamesmen for the booths, but everyone had multiple roles in bringing the show to life and everyone worked together. Augustus, the Electro-Man, dragged cables from the hot wagon generators and Timothy the Giant helped him check all the bulbs on the midway's entrance arches. The dancers unrolled canvas, the acrobats carried the long tent poles across their shoulders and even Pontilliar was on the lot, hoisting boxes and begrudgingly taking direction from Franklin.

Ruby was standing beside the snake tent, coiling up a length of rope around her shoulder, when she saw him. A man striding across the midway in an immaculate black suit. He was tugging at the cuffs of his jacket, as if he were on his way to a fancy dinner and fastidiously adjusting himself before he arrived. His skin was unnaturally white and even from a distance Ruby could tell that his eyes were glittering black. While everyone else around him was already coated with a layer of sweat and grime, his slick black hair shone in the sunlight and matched the gleam of his oiled leather shoes. Ruby stared at him, incredulous, until the man's gaze swept vaguely in her direction, passing over her like a lighthouse beam, and the world around her went black.

Ruby's eyes were open, but she could not see. Or rather, what she saw could not be there. A thousand glistering constellations, all on fire, swirled around her. Or they were her. Or she was they, moving in and out of the ether, hurtling toward an empyrean supernova that was somehow inside of her chest. Ruby could feel herself draw a breath, but as she did, her chest was pierced with an incalescent arrow and the fever blossoming from the wound shrouded her in a warmth of wings and she knew herself going backwards into millennia.

"Ruby?"

Ruby blinked.

"Hey there, Ruby. You okay?"

She looked up. Zero was standing over her, a clown wig in one hand and a wet rag in the other. Ruby stretched out her hands and became aware that she was now sitting in the dust outside the snake tent. The rope was in a tangle beside her. She shook her head and allowed Zero to help her to her feet.

"What the hell?"

Zero shrugged his bony shoulders and handed her the rag. It was cool and she pressed it to her face.

"Beats me. You was standing there one minute and then, just as sure as day, the next you was on the ground. I thought maybe the heat got to you, so I run over with some water."

Zero nudged a tin pail of water at his feet.

"To tell the truth, I was just about to drown you with it if you hadn't looked up. The way you was just sitting there like that, with your eyes open. Give me the willies. The heat must've got to you bad."

Ruby dipped the rag in the water and squeezed it over her face and neck. She took a deep breath and smiled at Zero, who was anxiously watching her every move.

"I'm fine, Zero. Thanks."

He nodded solemnly.

"It's powerful hot out here. You best find some shade and rest a spell."

"I will. Thank you. Really, I'm okay."

She smiled at him again and finally Zero nodded in satisfaction and went back to the big top. Ruby shaded her eyes as she watched the clown walk away, but she had the sinking feeling she'd just lied to him. Ruby pressed her hand to her chest, where she felt a spark still flickering. She wasn't sure she was okay at all.

January looked the chicken in the eye, waiting for it to blink. It didn't. She pushed a finger through the wire, trying to scratch one of the birds underneath its scraggly wing, but it twisted around and went for her. She yanked her finger back and instinctively wiped her hand down the front of her turquoise and cream kimono, even though she hadn't touched the animal.

"Do you like them?"

January started and whirled around, instinctively closing her kimono tighter across her chest. Underneath, she was wearing one of her costumes for the show, a short chemise barely covering her thighs. Most everyone in the carnival had seen her in far less than a slip, but she still tried to maintain an air of decency when she could. And this man was a glomming geek, lower than a doniker digger in January's opinion. She might take her clothes off night after night for strangers in a crowd, but at least she didn't bite living creatures. She'd seen a geek show only once before, as a child, and she had thrown up outside the tent. Even now, she could see the spray of blood and the discarded chickens and snakes, still twitching, their necks ripped open on the stage.

The new geek came closer, moving in a wide circle around her, as if he knew she was uncomfortable and was trying to respect that. He walked over to a wooden crate in the shade and pulled out a Coca-Cola. He pried off the cap and held it out to her.

"Want one? They're not very cold, but then, it seems difficult to keep anything cold in this heat."

His movements were languid, easy, completely unthreatening. January eyed the bottle of soda, sweating in his hand. He wasn't even looking at her, at her chest or her bare legs or even her eyes. He was just holding the bottle out, his pale face placid as he watched the chickens scuttling around in the cage behind his tent. January stepped forward and took it.

"Thanks."

"Of course."

The man took out another bottle and placed a board over the crate so he could sit down. He opened the soda, but set it, untouched, in the dirt at his feet. January came closer.

"So you're the new geek, huh?"

"I am. My name is Daniel. It's a pleasure to meet you."

Daniel held out his hand. January glanced at it before taking it. She always did this because, from her experience, people's hands said everything about them. Daniel's hand was pale, his fingernails burnished and translucent. When she shook his hand, his skin felt cool and slick, but not from sweat. It was like lightly touching the surface of a basin of water. No one who worked in a carnival for very long could have such skin.

"January. I'm over with the girly show."

She let go of her kimono and it hung open loosely, revealing the nearly sheer slip beneath. She watched his eyes. They didn't drop lower than hers. Daniel nodded.

"So, you like the chickens?"

January let her brows knit for only a moment before assuming her usual coy smile. Any newcomer, any townie, any man at all invariably said the same thing once she mentioned being in a girl show. Some variation of "I bet you are" or, "Well, I can see why" or, "Oh, so I might get to see something more when I pay my dime?" This man, sitting in his tailored suit, one leg crossed over the other, with manicured nails and pomaded hair and teeth whiter than milk, was asking her about chickens. She took a sip of her Coca-Cola and turned to the cage. The birds were cooing and ruffling their feathers as they scratched against the wire bottom.

"My uncle had chickens up in Lexington. My folks sent me up there to visit him once when I was a kid."

"You were working in the carnival then?"

January shrugged.

"Just hanging about. Helping with the washing and costumes. I think my ma was trying to get me away from the show. I wanted to be one of the acrobats under the big top. You know, doing flips in a star-spangled suit."

January stepped up to the cage again and hooked her fingers through the wire.

"But Ma knew better. She knew if I stuck around, I'd only wind up in the cootch tent, just like her."

She glanced over her shoulder at Daniel. His dark eyes were watching her intently now. Not her body, but her lips. He was listening to every word she spoke. It made her nervous, but she didn't want to stop talking to him. January turned back to the cage.

"So my uncle had chickens on his farm and it was my job to feed them. Collect the eggs. I kind of liked it."

"But you didn't stay."

January shook her head.

"There was no real work for me there. I was fourteen and too puny to be hired out as a farm hand. Too dumb to work in a shop in town. Uncle Ebert wouldn't keep me on if I wasn't bringing in any money, so I came back to the Star Light."

She looked over at Daniel. He was sitting perfectly still, with the palms of his hands resting on his legs. He hadn't touched his soda.

"Did you try to become an acrobat? As you had wanted?"

January rolled her eyes.

"No. That was just a child's dream. Kid stuff. I started on the girl show the next season. Had to. My ma and daddy were on the Corning train. Maybe you heard of it? The Independence Day Wreck? It was in all the papers back then. They made up two of the thirty-nine who didn't survive."

There was no emotion in January's voice. She watched Daniel's dark eyes and he watched her lips.

"My older sister had already gotten out by then, so she wasn't coming back to help me. Helen's living up in New York City now. Acting up on a real stage, so she says. Thinks she's the damn cat's pajamas. I get a line from her every now and then."

January leaned down and scratched the back of her bare calf.

"Christ. I got no idea why I'm telling you all this. I don't even know you."

Daniel shifted on the crate and crossed his legs again.

"Because I'm listening."

"I guess."

January turned back to the cage one last time. The chickens were settling down in the heat. This time when she poked her finger through the cage she was able to stroke one down the length of its wing. She could feel the brittle shoots at the base of its feathers.

"Are you really going to bite their heads off tonight?"

She heard Daniel stand up behind her.

"Are you really going to take your clothes off tonight?"

She twisted around to shoot him a dirty look, but there was something in his face. Something that was complicated and exposed. Maybe honest. Maybe not. He wasn't smiling. There was sadness at the corners of his mouth and January suddenly felt pity for him. She nodded.

"Yes."

Daniel nodded back.

"Well then, yes."

January gestured with the near empty bottle of soda and backed away from the cage.

"All right. Well, I got to go. We start drawing the tip in an hour and I got to get ready for the bally. Thanks for the drink."

Daniel put his hands in his pockets. He nodded again.

"You're very welcome."

If he stood at the right angle, Hayden thought he could catch a glimpse of her through a separation in the side tent flaps. Ruby. Or, as she was known when she was up on stage draped with snakes, Esmeralda the Enchantress. Hayden hadn't been sure if she was still going by that name, there had been quite a few throughout the years, but the last banner he had painted, depicting Ruby as an exotic Eastern princess with a desert in the background, was still snapping in the breeze above the talker's bally. It was a good painting, one of his best banners actually, but Hayden disliked it. It wasn't Ruby. It looked like the woman on the stage, though he supposed that was the point. Hayden moved against the side of the snake tent, trying to get a better view. He could see part of the audience and though their faces were caught up in rapture, he could recognize the fatigue as well. It was late, the last show of the night, and some of the marks must have been as exhausted as he was.

From his tiny stand, just an easel and two chairs really, wedged between the high striker and the Wheel of Chance, he had watched the faces of the townies as they ambled down the midway. Whether they were coming or going, each face had been lit up with a certain kind of light, and in drawing a patron's portrait or caricature, he could always tell whether they had just arrived or already witnessed all that the Star Light had to offer.

If it was still early in the night, he mostly drew the likeness of folks who had just hit the midway. Their faces were shining with gluttony and the expectation of more. They had played a few games of chance, knocked over a few milk bottles, maybe already won a chalkware prize. They had stuffed themselves with popcorn, with roasted peanuts and cotton candy, and were buoyant, spending their hard-earned pennies and nickels on whatever delights floated into their view. If anything, they were astonished by the colored lights, by the height of the Ferris Wheel and the speed of the Whip, by the crush of people, moving in all different directions, a disorganized herd scattering toward wonders and then realigning and bunching back into crowds. These were faces flushed with excitement, but not yet transformed. That would come later in the night.

About three hours in, Hayden had sketched his first face that he was sure had witnessed the back end of the carnival. The boy, maybe in his late teens, dressed in his cleanest pressed overalls, unruly cowlick stubbornly sticking up, had a shine in his eye that told Hayden he had already seen the first show at the big top. Hayden knew the boy had seen the Royal Russians fly through the air on invisible wings, urged on by Pontilliar in top hat and tails, calling from the center ring and pointing with his cane. The boy must have laughed at Zero and Marco, the duo clown act, chasing each other in baby doll dresses and tumbling in the dirt, and held his breath in awe as the sisters, Sonja and Zena, blindfolded and swathed in shimmering gauze, pirouetted around one another on the high wire. From the glint in his eyes and the flush of his throat, Hayden knew the boy had already visited the Ten-in-One with the freak attractions. He had set eyes on the Ossified Man, lying in pain in his straightjacket of bones, and on the Bearded Lady and the Human Blockhead and Henry/Henrietta, the He-She from Chicago. He had ducked into the cootch tent and stood with mouth open, eyes agog, as January and the girls performed the Dance of the Dragon Lady and left their costumes on the floor by the footlights.

And Hayden had been sure the boy had looked upon Ruby. With her dark hair swinging down in braids and a snake curling up around the gold cuffs on her arms. He was sure the boy had seen the sandals laced up her calves to her knees and the gauzy skirt beginning to hike up her thighs and the curve of her exposed lower ribs, more ink than bare skin flashing in the dim lights of the tent as Ruby swayed to the drumbeat and exotic whine of the sitar coming from the gramophone in the corner. Hayden had felt a stab of jealously as he filled in the shading around the boy's eyes, knowing where those eyes had been, knowing whose body they had seen and lusted after, knowing that the boy would go home and not dream of January's creamy flesh or Zena's arched back, but of Ruby's kohl-rimmed eyes, mesmerizing the serpent in her hands.

But the night had worn on and as Hayden had drawn face after face, settling back into the familiar rhythm of the midway, his jealousy had subsided. In its place, though, crept the burning shame and the presentiment that although he had returned, he might have lost Ruby forever. Hayden had avoided her all day through the carnival setup, but the longer he was away from her, the more paralyzing the fear became. Once the midway had begun to thin out, he'd closed down his stand and headed toward the snake tent. He still wasn't ready to talk to her, to try to explain himself, but he had to at least see her. Hayden's cowardice had reduced him to peeping through the gaps of the tent for a glimpse, and when he finally set eyes on her, he found that his breath had been stolen away from him.

Ruby. It made his bones ache to look at her. He could feel it in the marrow, piercing. The longing for her sucking out his pride and his disgrace simultaneously, leaving him hollow. Carved. A gutted shell. She looked the same as when he'd said goodbye to her, though then her face had been glowing with apprehension and hope, and now it was a mask of studied seduction and poise. She had never liked for him to see her performing. It wasn't her, she claimed, but Hayden knew that this side of Ruby defined her just as much as her rebellion in wearing trousers and smoking cigarettes, or her laugh, or the odd way she had of looking at people as if she were weighing their hearts in her hands. All of it was Ruby and the parts of her that he knew stuck in him like shards of glass and the parts that he didn't seemed to mock him cruelly from a distance. He wanted it all, to grasp every part of her, even if it tore him to ribbons, even if it ripped him asunder. It would be no less than he deserved.

FIVE

*et me tell you about carnivals. There was once a god named
Cronus. He had a terrible bloodlust. He killed his own father,
he married his own sister, he ate his own children. One of those
types of gods. Always raging against something. Always having to bite
the head off of something or send down thunder or start earthquakes.
The priests later said that one of his children escaped and this child
became the god Zeus, but this is not entirely true. No matter.*

*What the gods do is one thing and what humans do with the
gods' stories is another. For some reason, the Greeks looked on the
reign of Cronus as a time of idyllic delight. A golden age. And most
of the people were stupid, so maybe it was a happy time. Apparently,
all anyone did was drink and fornicate and eat fruit off of trees. They
did have to offer themselves up occasionally, human sacrifices and all
that, but that was nothing out of the ordinary. It was all very clean,
very peaceful. Just slitting throats on altars, you understand.*

A thousand years later, once Cronus had grown tired and left for the West and Zeus had come along with all of his rules, all of his many god sisters and brothers and incestuous children, the people grew nostalgic for the times of the past, as people always do. So they started up the festival of the Cronia and decided to let themselves have a little fun. For a week or so at the end of the year they turned everything upside down. Slaves became masters. Masters became slaves. Men women and women men and so on. Lines blurred, all caution was thrown to the wind and everyone was happy again. Men of no stature, criminals even, were appointed the Kings of Cronia and could do whatever they liked for those few days. Anything at all. Though, in the end, they still had to have their throats cut.

Of course, the Romans picked this up, though they added on yet more guidelines. Only one king was appointed, the Lord of Misrule, and so at the end of the gluttony, only one man had to die, which, I suppose, was a bit more humane. And since the Romans had been calling Cronus Saturn for some time, the Cronia became the Saturnalia. Do you see where this is going? Time passed, the calendar was moved around a little, empires rose and fell, the gods were given new names and the Saturnalia became the Italian Carnevale, later stolen by the French to become Mardi Gras, and next thing you know it's the twelfth century and you've got Bartholomew's Fair popping up in London like a toadstool. I'm sure you know where it leads from there. Dark ages be damned, people were going to have their fun and it just kept right on going. Different places, different names, until here you are, it's three thousand years later and not much has changed. There are electric lights and motorcars, but it's all still topsy-turvy. It's a bit more spectacle than participation, the women take their clothes off behind a tent wall, it's mostly children who gorge themselves on sweets, but the intoxication of revelry is still in the air. For a moment, on this path they call a midway, every man feels that he is a king. And while Cronus is not here, he is still slumbering in the West, I am biting the heads off of chickens to the screeches of a blood-spattered *crowd. If Cronus does one day wake to discover that his legacy has been usurped by the occupation of the glomming geek, I am sure that he will not be pleased.*

"What is your opinion of the new geek?"

Ruby looked over her shoulder at Samuel and groaned. She was right in the middle of sweeping out her wagon and he had a look on his face like he wanted something from her. Most people said they couldn't read Samuel at all, that his face was a mask carved from stone, but Ruby knew him better than most. There were slight nuances in the arch of his eyebrows or the flare of his nostrils. The turned-down corners of his mouth. Samuel was standing at the base of the wagon, waiting, and she knew that he wasn't going to go away. The small space that had been her home for the past twelve years, the place where she could sleep and read and think in peace, became coated in carnival detritus every time they made a jump. She'd gotten most everything clean again, except for the thin layer of sawdust shaken from the snake boxes that now resided underneath the stage in the tent. It was a losing battle, her wagon would be stuffed again when they moved on in the next few days, but she had to try. Ruby rested the straw broom against the doorframe and came down the steps to Samuel.

"New geek? I didn't know we had one."

Ruby wiped her palms down the front of her trousers and sat on the bottom step. She took a package of cigarettes out of the front pocket of her shirt and tapped one out. Samuel waited patiently for her to light it.

"Yes. We have a new geek. We took him on right before we left Sulphur."

"You mean, right after Jacob died."

Samuel crossed his arms and frowned.

"That's correct. Apparently, he was very convincing in his application to Pontilliar. I wasn't privy to the conversation. And so, yes, we now have a new geek."

"All right. So who is he? I guess I haven't seen him."

"If you had, you would remember. He does not resemble any geek you've ever encountered before."

Ruby blew a stream of smoke out of the side of her mouth.

"Wait a minute. Tall? Wearing a suit like he just stepped off Wall Street? The sun reflecting off his hair and teeth like to put your eyes out?"

Samuel nodded.

"So you've seen him."

She studied the ash on the end of her cigarette. Ruby had seen the man in the suit a few times now, always from a distance, and nothing had happened to her like what had occurred the first time. No swirling lights, no darkness, no burning in her chest. He still made her uneasy, but it couldn't be his fault she had seen stars and collapsed. Ruby had gone through the incident over and over in her head, though each time the details faded further into something that more resembled just a feeling. That could definitely have been brought on by the heat. And the exhaustion. A few years back, the Star Light had done a double jump across South Carolina, seventy-two hours straight with a show in the middle, and by the time they reached Charleston, half the freaks and most of the rousties were hallucinating. Seeing mirages and talking nonsense. Somewhere inside of her, in a tiny, chipped part that she kept locked away, Ruby knew she hadn't just been hallucinating. But as she had no other explanation, she kept that thought buried deep. Besides, she had one too many other things taking up space in her mind.

Ruby nodded back.

"I've seen him. The guy practically twinkles. How could I not? I guess it makes sense now. I couldn't for the life of me figure out what he was doing on the midway yesterday morning."

Samuel tilted his head slightly.

"Do you know how much that suit costs?"

Ruby flicked the ash off her cigarette and gestured with it toward Samuel's bow tie. In this heat, every man working the show, even Pontilliar, had hung up his tie and at least popped the top button of his collar. But here was Samuel, with his pressed white shirt, the sleeves down and the cuffs fastened. Not since he'd left his show days behind as Mutumbo, the Wild Man of Borneo, had he been seen in anything less. Ruby cracked a half-smile.

"No. But I'm sure you do."

Samuel's eyebrows came down in a scowl.

"And the price of that suit doesn't bother you? The fact that a man wearing such a suit is now in our midst, as a geek no less. That doesn't concern you?"

Ruby swung her legs and looked down at the dirt below her boots.

"Look, I'm busy. What do you want?"

She glanced back up at Samuel's dispassionate face and sighed.

"All right, so the guy's a fruitcake. So what? You remember that banker man Pontilliar picked up in Nashville? A few years back. Caught his wife with her skirt up over her head with the milkman or something and went a little crackers."

"Paperboy."

"What?"

"Mr. Brates. He caught his wife with the paperboy. Fourteen years old."

The sweat was pooling on the backs of Ruby's thighs. She slid off the step and pulled at her trousers.

"Of course you remember. You remember everything. You've probably still got his vitals written down on an index card somewhere."

Samuel dipped his head slightly.

"So you're making a comparison."

Ruby tossed her cigarette into the dirt and ground it out with her heel.

"I'm just saying. That guy was nuts, too. Left all his money to his cheating wife and ran off to join the circus. As a candy butcher, no less. He was out on the midway selling cotton candy in a three-piece suit and brand new homburg. He looked like more of a freak than the Rabbit Girl we had on loan that year."

"Daniel Revont is not selling candy."

"Is that the new geek's name?"

Ruby walked over to the side of the wagon and dunked her hands in a bucket of water that had been sitting out in the sun. She raised a palmful of water to her face.

"Listen, you know where we work. People join up for all sorts of bizarre reasons."

She splashed the water on her face and then wiped her face on the shoulder of her shirt. The tepid water did little to cool her off.

"Come on, Samuel, let it go. I don't like the look of the geek either, but what's that got to do with me?"

Samuel came around the steps to her. He looked disdainfully down into the bucket of water.

"I just want you to keep an eye on him. Pay attention when I can't. See things like you do. And let me know what's going on."

Ruby shook her head.

"No, thank you. You got it in for this guy because his fashion sense is better than yours, fine. But I've got better things to do."

"Such as hide from Mr. Morrow?"

Ruby's face flushed and she stepped closer to Samuel.

"Don't talk to me about Hayden."

Samuel finally uncrossed his arms.

"Fine. We won't talk about Hayden. But what if I told you that our new geek, Mr. Revont, has been seen in the company of January?"

Ruby stepped back from Samuel and narrowed her eyes.

"What kind of company? January cut all that out when Tom came along. And she never rolled with trade. Not that it's any of your business to begin with."

Samuel nodded slowly.

"Of course. But January is perhaps too nice to everyone."

"January can take care of herself."

"I'm simply letting you know."

Ruby held Samuel's eyes for a moment and then shook her head in disgust. She walked past him toward the snake tent, but then stopped and spoke over her shoulder to his back.

"Let it go, Samuel. Just let it go. And leave me out of it. Christ, as if I didn't have enough trouble already."

Hayden started with the lines of the center pole and the curve of the bale ring. The rest of the tent flared out from there, the red, blue and yellow panels swooping down to the quarter poles and then the side poles in a ripple of sun-bleached canvas. He was sketching out the high wire platform and didn't have to worry about shading in the lengths of dusty canvas that tumbled down to the dirt, enclosing the big top. A few of the smaller side panels were tied back to the poles to let in a breeze, but for the most part, the air inside the tent was stagnant and reeked of dried sweat. The carnival smell.

A whistle sang out through the stuffy air and Hayden turned his head to find it. Zena was standing on the other high wire platform and waved down to him. She was the tallest of the Russian acrobats, and standing thirty-five feet up in the air she somehow seemed even taller. The sun filtering down through the canvas panels bathed her in an ethereal light and made her long blond hair glow around her head in a luminous halo. Hayden waved back from his seat on the third tier of the grandstand benches and then glanced down at Niko, Zena's uncle and trainer. He was standing in the middle of the ring, underneath the high wire net, with his hairy, beefy arms crossed and deep scowl lines between his eyes. Hayden waved to him, too, but Niko's scowl only grew deeper.

Hayden spent the next hour in the big top tent, sketching Zena and Sonja practicing first on the wire and then the trapeze. Their brother, Mikael, joined them, tossing the girls effortlessly through the air. They sailed from one end of the big top to the other like flying fish, skimming across the surface of the ocean. When the final two Russian acrobats and Tito the Strongman showed up in the ring for warm-up, Hayden knew it was time to leave. It was early afternoon and the Star Light would be opening soon.

He closed his sketchbook and stood up. Even though none of the Russians were paying him any attention, he felt self-conscious now that they were all in the ring. Whereas years before, when he had been an almost permanent fixture in the big top before show hours, enjoying the quiet coolness where he could read or draw, Hayden now had the sense that he wasn't quite as welcome. It was only the second day of their stop in Baton Rouge and no one had said anything yet, but he knew everyone was watching him. Trying to figure out what he was doing back. Wondering what was going to happen with Ruby. Hayden was extremely taciturn about his personal life, and Ruby was even more so, but carnival life allowed for little privacy.

Hayden was starting down the grandstands when he saw her, standing in one of the tied-back tent openings, watching him. Ruby was backlit by the blinding sun, so it was hard to see her face, but it was obviously her. She was standing still, with her arms crossed tightly over her chest and her held high and erect as if she were judging him. Appraising him. Hayden froze and waited.

Just as it was impossible to have any privacy, it was near

impossible to avoid someone in the cramped quarters of a carnival, and he'd already seen Ruby that morning at the cookhouse. He had stood up from the table as soon as he saw her coming, but she had immediately turned in the opposite direction with her cup of coffee and headed back toward the wagons. They hadn't made eye contact, and he hadn't been sure whether to go after her or to let her be. The other gamesmen and rousties at the table had observed his movements carefully, and he wouldn't have been surprised if there was money on how long it would take him to talk to Ruby. Finally, Franklin had jerked at his sleeve and told him to sit down already. Give her time. Let her come to him if she wanted.

So now Hayden waited to see what Ruby was going to do. She stood there for a moment longer and then gave a slight shake of her head. She started to turn away, then stopped and looked at him again. Hayden didn't know what to do. He wanted to talk to her, had to talk to her, but he wasn't going to beseech her. He wasn't going to beg. Hayden forced himself not to reach out to her. He tucked his sketchbook under his arm and put his hands in his pockets, waiting.

Ruby turned on her heel and disappeared out into the sunlight. Hayden cast his eyes down at his shoes. He supposed she wasn't ready yet.

January stood on the bally in front of the Girl Revue tent and pouted her lips. She swayed just slightly, with one hand perched on her slim hip and the other dangling languidly at her side, and surveyed the onlookers before her.

"Yessiree, boys, you've never seen anything like our Cherry here. Other shows might promise you the wild, the exotic, but you'll get none of that here. Cherry is one hundred percent homegrown

American and as sweet as apple pie. 'Course, you'd have to find that out for yourself, gents."

Otis winked at the crowd and then pointed at January with his cane. She shifted her weight from one foot to the other and pushed her silk robe back so she could rest her hand on the waist of her slip. It was a simple gesture, and one that didn't display any more skin than she was already showing, but it always did the trick. The mothers in the crowd, who had tolerantly been standing behind their curious sons or daughters, now turned their children quickly by the shoulders and headed off across the midway. This gave the men a little more freedom to ogle, and January made sure to give each a slight, shy smile. Otis kept on beside her, banging his cane down on the wooden bally so hard that January could feel the vibrations beneath her high-heeled shoes.

"I'm going to let you fellas in on a little secret."

Otis leaned forward over his cane conspiratorially and the men in the crowd leaned forward as well.

"The secret is this, boys. I've been doing this for a long time. I've seen a lot of girls in my day. Let me tell you, a lot of girls."

January kept her smile going while Otis drew in the tip. Some of the men already had their mouths open, tongues near hanging out, and this was only the ballyhoo. It was going to be an easy night, for sure.

"A lot of girls that could do a lot of different things. But here's the God's honest truth, gentlemen. In all my travels, even in King Scheherazade's harem, not once have I ever set eyes on a woman who can top Cherry over here. Cross my heart, God's honest truth."

Otis glanced over at January and she smiled at him and winked back, signaling for him to call it already and get her the hell off the bally. Otis pointed his cane out into the crowd at a few of the men he had already marked.

"Now don't forget, boys, the next show with our Cherry here starts at seven. Don't miss out!"

January gave the crowd a last smile and then slowly closed and tied her robe shut. The men dispersed and Otis helped January down the rickety bally steps. She rolled her eyes at him once her feet hit the dirt.

"King Scheherazade? Really?"

Otis took off his straw hat and mopped the sweat from his bald head with a ratty handkerchief. He grinned at her.

"Well, it sounded good, right?"

January put her hand on Otis's broad, lumpy shoulder.

"Scheherazade was a woman, Otis. She told the stories to the Arabian king to keep from getting her head chopped off."

Otis stuffed his handkerchief back in his pocket.

"Oh, right, right. Think anyone noticed?"

January was already making her way around the back of the cootch tent to smoke, but she called over her shoulder to Otis.

"Don't think so."

She lit a cigarette and pitched the match into the dirt. Baton Rouge was a red crowd, but Pontilliar still liked to run it clean until evening. That meant doing light shows up until seven, when the afternoon big top performance let out and the Star Light really swung into gear. January left the kiddie acts to Wanda and stayed with working the bally. Once night fell, she'd be doing back-to-back sets with blow-offs until closing, so she wasn't worried about losing out on the few extra coins tossed on the day shows. The new girl could have them.

January leaned against one of the tent poles and out of the corner of her eye she could see him watching her. Not gawking, not even curious, but just standing in his dark suit, with his hands in his pockets, looking in her direction. January flicked her cigarette and called out to him.

"You don't got to stand over there, you know. You can come on by and say hi."

Daniel nodded to her and slowly made his way over. January

had forgotten how dazzling his smile was.

"I didn't realize before that our tents are set up next to one another."

January smiled back at him.

"Pontilliar likes to have the tents set up in a way that will draw the rubes around the midway. I think it's his idea that the blood from the geek show gets the boys excited and so they'll spend more when they come on over to me. Or maybe he's just trying to keep us away from the families lined up for the big top. Who knows."

"Who knows, indeed. I was going to offer you a light and a cigarette, but I see you already have one. Do you mind?"

He took a silver cigarette case out of his pocket and held it up. January shook her head.

"No, please, go ahead."

She watched with interest as he opened the case and took out a cigarette. The inside of the case was blood red and when he snapped it shut, she noticed that the outside of it was intricately engraved. When Daniel took out his lighter, January's eyes widened. He lit the cigarette between his lips and was about to put the lighter away when January reached out, almost touching his sleeve to stop him.

"Can I see it?"

"This?"

Daniel held up the lighter and January nodded.

"Of course."

He handed it to January and she took it greedily, turning it over in her hands. It was silver like the case, but inlaid with a green stone circled by diamonds. January could hardly believe her eyes. Diamonds on a lighter, for Christ's sake. She tried to act nonchalant as she handed it back to Daniel.

"What's the green stone?"

Daniel took the lighter and put it back in his pocket.

"Jade. Do you like it?"

January nodded.

"It's a Dunhill, right?"

"It is. How do you know that?"

January grinned at him.

"I've seen it in magazines. I mean, not that one exactly, but ones like it. I can't even imagine how much it cost. Makes me dizzy just thinking about it. Was it a gift?"

Daniel patted his pocket and smiled at her.

"No. I just picked it up in New York when I was last there."

January couldn't help herself.

"New York? Are you serious? You were in New York City? Did you live there? What's it like?"

January felt foolish asking, but what did it matter? Daniel already knew she had never been there herself. There was no point in acting like she was something she was not with him. Daniel raised his eyebrows, but his smile seemed genuine, if amused.

"It's thrilling. So many lights. So many interesting, delightful people. They're everywhere."

"Did you ever meet anyone famous?"

Daniel shrugged.

"I did have dinner with Marion Davies and William Hearst at Delmonico's last year."

January was breathless.

"Marion Davies?"

"She was lovely. Truly lovely. And stunning. In many ways, you look just like her. But I'm sure you hear that all the time."

January rubbed her forehead with the back of her hand. She shook her head, still in amazement.

"No. I mean, yeah, the fellas say that sometimes, but it's not true. Marion Davies, I mean, she's just spectacular. I got all her pictures from *Photoplay* and *Screenland* cut out and pasted up in the wagon."

January suddenly realized how dumb she must sound, and she tossed her cigarette to the dirt and ground it out with the toe of her shoe. She was blushing and didn't want Daniel to see her face. With her head still down, she pulled her robe tighter and crossed her arms. When she finally glanced up at Daniel, he had his head tilted and was giving her an odd look. He raised a finger to his lips.

"You know, the resemblance is actually quite remarkable. Especially when you stand just like that."

Daniel reached out and lightly touched one of the waves in her hair. January wasn't sure exactly what he was doing, but she didn't want to back away from him either. Daniel quickly put his hand in his pocket and dipped his chin.

"If you have just a moment longer, I'd like to give you something. Can you wait right here?"

January began to shrug her shoulders, but Daniel was already heading back toward the geek wagon. She could hear Otis calling the bally for Darlene now, claiming that she was a captured Indian princess and in possession of the wild secrets of love. January rolled her eyes. She lit and smoked another cigarette, trying to decide if it was worth waiting around for Daniel and having to listen Otis go on and on about Darlene. She stamped out the second cigarette and was just about to duck inside the tent to check her makeup when Daniel came around the corner with his hands behind his back.

"Thank you for waiting. It took me longer than I thought it would to find this. Close your eyes."

January pursed her lips, but Daniel was insistent and she finally closed her eyes and held out her hands.

"I thought you should have this. Considering how much the two of you are alike."

January opened her eyes when the fabric touched her fingers. It was a scarf, and when January held it up, she could see that it was pale blue silk, hand-painted with a design of birds and flowers. Tiny glass beads were embroidered around the edges. January looked up at Daniel with wonder.

"It's so beautiful."

Daniel nodded once.

"I drove Marion and William back to their hotel after dinner and she left it in my car. I sent her a note about it, but she told me to keep it. As a thank you for a lovely evening. It's yours now."

January fingered the silk, not knowing what to say. Her voice was timid.

"Are you sure?"

"Of course I'm sure. Marion was one of the finest women I've ever had the pleasure to dine with. She's full of grace and kindness. Just as you are."

Daniel put his finger under January's chin and raised it so she was looking at him. He winked at her and then abruptly turned on his heel. She held the scarf up to her face as she watched him disappear inside the geek tent. It wasn't until later in the night that she realized she hadn't even thanked him.

SIX

One of the snakes was sick. Yellow Snake. Ruby didn't give them real names. Why would she? They weren't pets; they were props. Ten years ago, when the Star Light had a true circus going on under the big top, the entire outfit had felt like a menagerie. The trained animals were more famous and received higher billing than their human counterparts. The star elephants Rosie and Fanny. Dolores, the Fire-Leaping Tiger. Wilson, the Pig Prodigy. Sarah, one of the chimps, would eat dinner alongside the performers in the cookhouse tent. She was considered family by many, though Ruby hadn't cared for her much. Once, a reporter from the *Jackson Daily Harald* came down to the lot to do a special feature on the animals. He'd cornered Ruby between two tents, determined to ask the Snake Charmer all of the names of her various snakes to prove that even the reptiles were the stars of the show. Ruby had shrugged. Black Snake. Brown Snake. Striped

Snake. Skinny Snake. Snake with the Crooked Tail. The reporter had not been impressed.

Ruby lit a cigarette and rubbed her forehead. The brass bracelets stacked all down her arm jangled, irritating her. Yellow Snake was sick. Or dying. Something. It wouldn't keep its head up, wouldn't flick its tongue. She'd had to cut the last set short because it had only hung limp around her neck like a chain. Ruby took a drag of her cigarette and leaned against the back of the snake tent, the pole digging into her shoulder blades. She only had about ten minutes between sets. Just enough time for Jasper to draw and close the tip. Ruby couldn't stop thinking about the snake, though. The lot they were set up on was next to an overgrown field and beyond that was the tree line. She'd have to take the snake out to the woods tomorrow and set it free. She didn't know anything about healing snakes. She just figured that if it was dying, it'd rather do so outside, where it belonged, and not in a wooden box in the back of a tent.

Ruby was about to grind out her cigarette on the heel of her sandal when she saw them. Just a flash between the management wagon and the cookhouse, but they were together. She heard January's laughter and shrunk back into the shadows behind the tent. Ruby crouched down and steadied herself with a hand in the dirt, watching. She could hear the crowd of people filing into the snake tent and she knew she'd get the whistle from Jasper any second. She waited, staring out into the darkness, but there was nothing. And then.

"Oh, I don't think so. I don't know about that."

January laughed again, her voice tinkling the way it did when she was flirting with someone. Ruby knew exactly the look January must have on her face. The arched eyebrow. Lips puckered into a slight pout as her hand deliberately led the eye by fingering the straps on her dress. Ruby listened and then another voice came out of the night. This one low, purring. It was a man's voice, but she couldn't make out anything he was saying. She heard Jasper's whistle from inside the tent, but ignored it.

Then she saw them again, heading back toward the midway. It was almost too dark to see them, but they were lit up from behind by the low light from the cookhouse and there was no mistaking their silhouettes. January's hair, perfectly coiffed into finger waves, and her short kimono. The way her hands moved like a dancer's. And the person beside her had to be the geek. Tall and thin. His tailored suit making his figure aquiline against the light. No one else could cut a shape like that. As she watched, January reached out and rested her hand on the geek's shoulder. Gave him a playful push. She laughed again. The geek bent his head toward January, but said nothing. Or if he did, Ruby couldn't make it out. They disappeared behind the Illusionist's wagon and were gone.

Ruby continued to stare out into the empty space where she had just seen them until Jasper poked his head through the back tent flap and asked her what the hell she was doing. She stood up, but didn't look back at him.

"None of your goddamn business."

Ruby had come down from the mountain like a wild child. Her hair was long and matted into ropes and her face and arms were brown. She had carried a knapsack containing only a circus playbill, a catch of pelts tightly rolled and a Barlow knife sharp enough to split hairs. The playbill was black and white and faded, worn soft along the creases. It depicted a cameo of a woman on the back of a leaping horse. Serious, arms raised triumphantly, streamers billowing out behind her. The scroll beneath the horse's painted hooves read: "Pontilliar's GRAND EQUESTRIAN SHOW!" And lower, in curling script: "Come See The BEAUTIFUL And ASTONISHING Horse Lady Of Pontilliar's WORLD FAMOUS

Star Light Company!" The woman on the back of the horse was indeed beautiful. The woman was Ruby's mother.

For two years, Ruby chased the Star Light. She never stayed in one place long, picking cotton in work camps or helping with washing in the small towns as she journeyed farther and farther away from the mountains. If asked, she lied about her name, her age, her parents. After two terrifying encounters, one she almost didn't get away from, she lied about her sex. She stole a pair of boy's breeches off a line and cut her hair sharply with the knife. This kept her from domestic work, but also kept her relatively safe. At every new town or camp, she took out the playbill and showed it to anyone who would look.

Some would point north, saying they heard the show had once gone through Charlotte or Rock Hill. Others shook their heads and frowned. No, it never came up this far. You had to go down to Augusta, or maybe all the way over to Charleston, if you wanted to see a circus that big. Men argued on the sloping front porches of stores about which shows they had seen go through which towns ten years back. The Great Ferari Brothers. Gaskill's. Crane's Variety. Minstrel Show. Wild West Show. Diving Exposition. Jubilee. All Girl Revue. No one could agree, no one could remember for sure where they'd been or what they'd seen. A preacher tried to take the playbill from her and baptize her on the spot for carrying it. She crept back in the night and stole everything she could from his church.

Eventually, Ruby made it to Macon and set out to wait for a show to come through. She put a dress back on and kept house for a nearly blind woman who had forty-two cats and could only pay Ruby with leftovers from her own table. The woman lived in what was left of a burned-out plantation house four miles from the edge of town. The back of the house, where there had once been a library, was open to the elements and Ruby would spend hours in the dusty sunlight, leafing through books ruined by age and weather and animals.

When a show finally did come through Georgia, in the summer of 1907, it hadn't been Pontilliar's. She had befriended a daredevil rider on Johnny Jones's Motordrome, though, and the boy began asking around. Soon, Ruby had a near complete circuit map for the Star Light and made ready to chase it. The daredevil had tried to put his hand up her skirt by way of payment and she had stabbed him in the bicep with a screwdriver as a thank you. By the time Ruby had made it to the Star Light's ticket booth in Tallahassee, at the end of the season, she was no longer the wild girl who had come down from the mountain. She had become something else entirely.

Daniel saw the spark first. Then the curve of a face in the light from the match, flickering, and then it was dark again. He stopped walking in front of the empty cookhouse and put his hands in his pockets. He turned toward where the lit cigarette was hovering in the air and waited. Her voice was biting.

"What the hell do you think you're doing?"

Daniel cocked his head. It was three in the morning and all of the electric lights had been shut off, all of the tents were quiet. The heavy, lambent moon hung over him and he didn't need to look up to know that the stars were glinting down on him like ground glass beneath his heel. He watched the lit end of the cigarette, seeming to float in the darkness on the opposite side of the yard. It dipped and then a candle flame sprung up from one of the tables. The cigarette and voice belonged to a woman. It was still too dark to tell, but he knew her eyes were fixed on him, challenging him. Daring him to come closer. So he did.

"Just going for a walk."

Daniel passed through the rows of tables in a few quick strides and stood across from the woman. She leaned back away from him slightly, but kept her chin raised, looking up at him.

"Little late for a midnight stroll."

"And midnight cigarette, I suppose."

The woman crossed her legs underneath the table, shifting her weight on the wooden bench. Daniel watched her mouth. Her lips coming down hard around the cigarette.

"I work here. I live here. I can do whatever I want in the middle of the night…"

She yanked the cigarette away from her lips and leaned forward, blowing the smoke straight at him.

"…Daniel Revont."

Daniel sat down and adjusted the cuffs on his suit. He rested his forearms on the edge of the table, as if preparing for a meal.

"I work here and live here, too. Ruby Pontilliar."

Ruby sat up straight, as if she'd been stung.

"Chole. It's Ruby Chole."

Daniel cocked his head.

"Are you not the carnival master's daughter? Is Randolph Pontilliar not your father?"

Ruby flicked the ash off her cigarette and slouched again.

"How do you know that?"

"I know lots of things. And people talk. That's one thing I've noticed about this place. Everyone is talking, all of the time. They never stop."

Ruby seemed to consider this for a moment.

"All right, fine. You know things. You live here, too, I suppose. That doesn't mean you can do whatever you want."

Daniel glanced at her cigarette.

"Maybe."

Ruby blew another stream of smoke toward him and then picked up the package of cigarettes next to the candle. She slid it toward him. He pulled one out and fit it between his lips as he glanced around the table. Ruby sighed.

"That was my last match. Here."

She picked up the candle and held it out to him. Daniel leaned forward to light his cigarette, making sure to look her in the eyes. This close, he could see that they were gray. Unusual. She didn't look away. He leaned back, relaxing into the cigarette.

"I didn't answer your question, though, did I? About what I'm doing?"

"No."

"So then, what are you really asking?"

He watched Ruby collect her thoughts. When she finally spoke, her words came out forceful, but uncertain.

"January. She's my friend. She's everybody's friend. We all care about her."

Daniel nodded slowly.

"All right."

"And for better or worse, she's Tom's girl. He makes her happy. Or something. But she's happy with him, at any rate. So what the hell are you doing?"

"With January?"

"With January."

Daniel edged back on the bench so he could cross his leg over his knee. He took a long drag on the cigarette, making her wait.

"Nothing."

"Liar."

Daniel smiled.

"No, I mean it."

Daniel wiped at the tiny bits of ash collecting on the table.

"She's not really, how would you say it? She's not really my type."

"You're lying again. I saw you two together. I saw the way she looked at you."

"Through all those shadows?"

He puffed on the cigarette, enjoying the shock on Ruby's face.

"You must have very good eyes. From where you were standing behind that tent, I'd doubt you could have seen much more than silhouettes. Heard much more than whispers."

Ruby ground out her cigarette on the edge of the table and dropped it into the dirt.

"So you know I was watching."

Daniel nodded and grinned at her.

"I told you. I know lots of things."

Ruby stood up and put her fists on the table. She leaned on her knuckles, getting close to him. From this angle, Daniel could see the tattoos running underneath her chin and down her neck. He followed the lines of symbols intersecting in the hollow of her throat and disappearing down the open collar of her shirt. He lazily looked back up toward her face and into her eyes. They were blazing.

"Stay away from her."

Daniel smirked, but said nothing. Ruby smacked her palms on the table and then pointed her finger at Daniel.

"I don't know what you're doing, but just stay away from her. She's a good kid. She's got a good thing going. Don't screw that up for her."

Daniel slowly twisted his cigarette on the top of the table, crushing it out. He kept his eyes on Ruby's.

"My dear. Who exactly do you think I am?"

Ruby pushed away from the table and stepped over the bench. Her body was stiff and Daniel noticed that her fists were clenched, nails cutting into her palms, no doubt. She suddenly leaned in close to him and her words came out low. Dangerous, but tinged with a hint of desperation.

"I don't know. And I don't care."

Daniel turned to watch her disappear into the night.

"Oh, but you should. You really should."

And then he frowned, as a new thought flitted through his mind, and he murmured into the darkness.

"I wonder…"

SEVEN

Ruby took another swig from the bottle and handed it back to January.

"This tastes like dog piss."

January hooked her arm around the horse's brass carousel pole before reaching across the space between them and grabbing the bottle back. She smirked and then giggled.

"You would know, I guess."

"Shut up."

Ruby cracked half a smile as she fumbled in her pocket for a cigarette.

"Well, you're the one who got it."

January squinted one eye and looked down into the bottle. The sickeningly sweet rum sloshed around as she started to slip off the horse's back. She pulled herself upright and hiked up her dress so she could hold the bottle between her legs.

"That fella came up out of Florida got it. I got it off him in Sulphur. Said it came straight from Cuba. He tried to trade for the bottle, but I said nothing doing."

"For a bottle? Just one bottle?"

January laughed.

"That's what I said. Even if it was back in the day, I would've held out for at least a crate. I mean, look at me."

January gestured up and down the length of her body. Ruby nodded, still digging into her pockets.

"Look at you. At least a crate."

"I made like I was all hurt at his suggestion. All pouty. And so he just gave me the bottle for free and took off. I need to start using that trick more often."

"Well, at least one of us is good for something. Even if it is just bringing in coffin varnish."

Ruby pulled out a package of cigarettes and held it up to her ear. She shook the paper box and frowned. She held it up, peered through the ripped top and then crumpled it in her fist before tossing it over her shoulder to the ground. January watched her and laughed.

"That preacher man was good for something. What'd you say his name was? Preacher Tin?"

Ruby gripped the brass pole of her own horse and leaned back, looking up at the gears in the roof of the carousel.

"The esteemed Reverend George H. Tindall. Samuel said he's some big cheese around here. Wouldn't let the mayor give Pontilliar a permit to set up unless we agreed to go dark on Sunday. Some carrying on about corrupting souls. You know he just wants to make sure the good folks put their coin in his basket and not ours."

"Well, I, for one, am thankful for the good Reverend. I needed a day off. Christ. Six, eight shows a night. Then you got all the lot lice just being damn lookie-loos. Watching the bally all day, but not forking over a dime. I know we're all trying to make the nut here, but it's just too much."

Ruby rolled her eyes and shrugged, causing January to laugh at her again. In the mirrored panels, behind January's head, Ruby could see the reflection of the carnival at dusk. It was quiet, the midway deserted. It was an eerie sight, silent and haunting. Ruby liked the carnival when it was like this. Empty and dead. As if it were her own. Being one of the freaks, she couldn't just walk the midway when it was full of people like everyone else could. She couldn't just throw on a robe between shows and walk down to Willie's grab joint and get a cone of cotton candy or a bag of peanuts. She couldn't lean across the booths and flirt with the gamesmen. She couldn't saunter through the crowd, keeping an eye out for rich gentlemen she could slip her arm around and pinch a few coins from. She wasn't January. She wasn't one of the other girls. Just showing her face was giving it away for free.

Ruby watched January swing her bare legs as they dangled over the side of the horse. The white horse for January, like snow, and the red for Ruby. It was always the same and had been since Ruby had come back to the carnival at nineteen and January had sat next to her on the edge of the carousel, no longer a child dreaming of becoming an acrobat, but a sixteen-year-old dancing the cootch. They had been drinking that night, too. Some awful whiskey Ruby had stolen from one of the talkers. It was January, of course, who had earnestly picked out the horses for them. Like in a fairy tale. That night they had laughed and drank and in the early morning hours, when Ruby held January's hair back so she could puke off the side of the carousel, their friendship had been cemented. The carnival was a man's world, and Ruby and January had just then been on the edge of discovering their place in the grand scheme of the show, but at least they had found each other.

"Hey."

January snapped her fingers at Ruby to get her attention. She held the bottle out and Ruby took it.

"What are you thinking about, all deep in your thoughts there?"

Ruby raised the bottle to her lips and took a long drink. She handed it back.

"Nothing."

"Come on."

Ruby wiped her mouth with the side of her hand.

"I was just thinking about you and Tom."

January frowned.

"Me and Tom? What the hell for?"

Ruby slipped her hands into her pockets and shrugged slightly.

"I don't know. I just wondered if things were good. If you were happy."

January arched an eyebrow.

"Oh really?"

"Yeah. You know. What's wrong with that? Why can't I ask if you're happy?"

January pursed her lips and tilted her head.

"Because that's not the kind of thing you ask. Not you. I know you, Ruby Chole. You don't care about Tom. I'm surprised you even remembered his name."

"But I care about you."

January shook her head.

"That's not the same. What are you driving at?"

Ruby reached for the bottle again. She wouldn't look at January.

"You and the geek. The new one. You two just seem kind of close."

"What are you talking about?"

There was an edge to January's voice. Ruby took a swig and then looked up, straight into January's eyes.

"Just what I said. I'm talking about you and that new geek. Daniel. I've seen you together. It's none of my business what goes on between you and Tom—"

"You're damn right it isn't."

"But there's something not right about Daniel. The way he looks, the way he talks."

"You're judging him on the way he looks? You? Really?"

Ruby gritted her teeth.

"I don't think you can see it. I don't think you can see what he really is."

"And what's that?"

Ruby looked down at the scratched wooden baseboards beneath the horses. Her voice was quiet.

"I don't know."

January narrowed her eyes and her mouth turned ugly. She leaned toward Ruby.

"Now you listen to me. There is nothing going on between me and Daniel that doesn't go on with half the men in this place. Sure, I talk to him. I talk to everybody, unlike you. I mean, what do you think I am? You think I'm screwing the geek?"

"That's not what I'm saying."

"I got a man. I'm with Tom now. Everybody knows that. Everybody respects that. Everybody but you."

Ruby shook her head.

"I'm not saying you're screwing him."

"Then what?"

Ruby bit her bottom lip, trying to figure out how to say what she needed to say. The alcohol buzz wasn't helping.

"I'm just saying that you should stay away from Daniel."

January slid off the horse.

"So now you're telling me what to do. Perfect."

Ruby jumped off her horse and stood eye to eye with January.

"Okay. Sorry. How about I think, then, if you've got any sense in that empty head of yours, you should stay away from Daniel."

January put her hands on her hips.

"And I think that you're just jealous."

"Jealous? Of some creepy guy in a suit trying to get with you?"

"Of any guy trying to get with me. Because no one is trying to get with you."

Ruby stepped back and steadied herself against one of the horses, but January kept going.

"You ran Hayden off. Probably one of the nicest fellas to ever come around here. Nice and good looking and absolutely crackers for you. Crackers. I had to hear it from him all the time. Never mind that I'm right in front of him, standing right there, but he's only got eyes for you."

Ruby shook her head, confused. Her face was beginning to burn from the rum and she couldn't understand where the conversation was going.

"This isn't about Hayden. This is about Daniel."

January swayed and caught herself. She pointed her finger at Ruby.

"No, this is about Hayden. He was crazy about you and you ran him off. Like you do everyone. Because you're too proud or too stubborn or I don't know what. And now he's back and let me guess, you haven't even spoken to him. He's been hanging around like some kind of lost dog and I bet you haven't even given him the time of day. You don't deserve him. You really don't."

Ruby closed her eyes and ground her teeth together. Everything was rising up inside her and she held her breath to push it back down. She forced herself to stay calm and remember where the conversation had started.

"You can say that and think that all you like about me. But stay away from Daniel, okay?"

Ruby opened her eyes, but January was already stepping down off the carousel, walking away, stumbling every few steps. Ruby yelled at her.

"Okay?!"

Ruby watched January's back as she disappeared around the

Ferris Wheel. She gripped one of the carousel poles, trying to clear her head, and then stepped down into the dirt. The sky had bled from a burnt orange into a dark blue and a few stars had already broken through on the horizon. Ruby took another drink from the bottle still in her hand and then hurled it across the midway. She wanted to hear the glass smash, but it only landed and rolled unsatisfyingly. Ruby clenched her fists. She had tried with January. Now it was time for Hayden.

Ruby pushed aside the tent flap and peered inside. The smell of new sweat, old sweat and the rush of winning and losing hit her immediately. She ducked inside and stood in the fog of layered smoke, the dim light from the two oil lamps hanging from the side poles barely cutting through the murk. Technically, this was a communal tent for the rousties and gamesmen who didn't own their own private sleeping tents, but everyone knew its real purpose: it was the place where what little money the men had shifted from hand to hand, night to night, in an endless circle of elation and dejection. Ruby squinted her eyes against the smoke and glanced around the tent. Five of the men were sitting around a large overturned wooden spool with greasy, limp cards held close to their chests or flattened against the makeshift table. More men hung back in the shadows, making bets of their own, some whispering, some laughing loudly. Most were drunk already. Ruby watched Tom swigging from a ceramic jug of hooch before passing it over to the roustie next to him. She narrowed her eyes at him, but he only returned the look with a smirk.

"He ain't in the G-top."

Ruby jumped and turned to the voice at her shoulder. Franklin was at her elbow, holding out a badly rolled cigarette. Ruby shook her head at the offer.

"Who?"

Franklin grinned and leered at her slightly, but Ruby didn't step back. She had known Franklin since she was nineteen years old and she could handle him. She could handle any man in the show and they all knew that. They all knew better than to mess with her, and not just because she was Pontilliar's daughter. Franklin took a long drag off his cigarette, but blew the smoke away from Ruby's face.

"You're looking for Hayden, right?"

Ruby's eyes scanned the tent again.

"Maybe."

Franklin laughed and the sound caught like thick phlegm in his throat.

"Well, he's out looking for you."

Ruby turned back to Franklin.

"What?"

Franklin hacked and spit along the side of the tent wall. He wiped his mouth with the back of his hand and then wiped his hand down the front of his shirt.

"Sure. Tried getting him in a game, but he wasn't having none. Hasn't played yet since he's been back. Used to pull a good hand, too. I don't know if he's smart or just turned chicken. Lucky bastard though."

Franklin leaned in toward Ruby again, his mouth twisted in a sneer around the limp cigarette. His breath caught Ruby in the face and she grabbed him by the front of his shirt. She jerked him back firmly and the jolt made his eyes widen slightly. Ruby didn't let go of him.

"Where did he go?"

Franklin mumbled something and Ruby grabbed him by the shoulders. Franklin didn't have a height advantage, but he did have about eighty extra pounds of muscle on her. Still, in the smoky darkness, with her tattoos and that savage look in her wild eyes, Franklin would never have laid a hand back on her. Ruby knew this, knew the uneasiness she could cause in people, and wasn't afraid to use this to her advantage. She brought her face in close and leveled her eyes with his. Franklin raised his hands in front of him.

"I told you. He said something about ponying up and going to talk to you. He was half in the bag, just said something about needing to find you right away and he ducked out. Just took off."

"When?"

Franklin shook his head.

"I don't know, an hour ago? What, he already find you and piss you off that bad? That what this is about?"

Ruby let him go. Franklin stepped back and dramatically brushed off the front of his shirt, as if Ruby could have gotten it anymore dirty than it already was.

"Thank you."

Ruby opened the tent flap behind her and was turning to leave when she saw him. As far back in the shadows as a man could get, in the opposite corner of the tent. He was still in his suit, though the air was stifling and most of the men had their collars open and sleeves rolled up or had already stripped down to their undershirts. He stood leaning against one of the tent poles with a cigarette raised to his lips. His black eyes were locked on hers and she couldn't read his expression at all. No one in the tent seemed to notice him. Or how out of place he appeared in the midst of all the squalor.

She gripped the edge of the tent flap and stared back at Daniel. He inhaled and then blew a stream of smoke out, directly toward her. His mouth curled and Ruby's eyes narrowed in disgust. She shook her head slightly at him and he laughed. She couldn't hear him over the shouting from the men at the table, a hand had been called and someone was raking in the pot, but she knew he was laughing at her. She saw the snarl of his lips and the flash of his brilliant white teeth. They locked eyes again and she could feel her throat tightening. She involuntarily pressed her hand against her chest as the memory of that blazing arrow reverberated through her mind. Then Daniel's eyes narrowed and he dipped his head at her, a strange nod of acknowledgment, and Ruby forced herself to turn away. Hayden. She had to find Hayden.

Ruby finally came upon him at the far edge of the lot where the vehicles were parked, sitting alone with his legs dangling off the end of one of the empty cargo trucks used for transporting the rides. Ruby approached Hayden in the bright moonlight and though he saw her coming toward him through the high grass, he said nothing. She watched Hayden raise first a jar, then a cigarette, to his lips. Ruby had never seen him like this before. She knew Hayden to be a fighter, as stubborn as he was charming. He was an outsider to the carnival just as she was an outsider to the rest of the world, but whereas Ruby had built up walls, Hayden crashed through the walls of others. He had always been so confident, so sure of himself, even to the point of being cocky. She'd watched him with other women, and she knew they loved his swagger, but Ruby was drawn to what was underneath. The hard-edged honesty. The ability to throw himself at life and take whatever it had to offer. To trust that he would land on his feet.

This man, however, was a different Hayden. One with red-rimmed eyes and an impassive stare. One who was broken. He followed her with his eyes, but didn't turn to her as she hoisted herself up onto the truck bed and sat down beside him.

Ruby hadn't been sure of what she was going to do when she finally came face-to-face with him. Up until four days ago, she hadn't thought she ever would. Part of her still wanted to scream at him, but the other part had finally won out. She wanted the answer. She just wanted to know. Ruby tried to think of what to say, but only the obvious came to mind.

"I thought you were looking for me."

Hayden passed Ruby the glass jar, still without turning to her. She tasted it. Some sort of moonshine. Apple. It was better than the rum had been. She took another sip and felt the zing, and then the quick wave of heat, flush through her. She set the moonshine between them and stared down at the jar. When he finally spoke, Hayden's voice was raw and cracked in his throat.

"I was. Looking for you, I mean."

Ruby waited for him to continue, but he slipped back into silence. She looked out across the field at the glow coming from behind the midway. Ruby could hear the sounds of the night getting wilder. Shouts coming from the poker tent. Someone picking out a tune on a guitar. A woman's high-pitched squeal of laughter. Ruby frowned.

"It's not exactly hard to find someone in a place like this. Not a whole lot of ground to cover."

Hayden flicked the ash off his cigarette.

"I got distracted."

"Distracted? Or scared?"

Ruby turned to look at him. In the shadows, his eyes were sunken, his mouth drawn tightly. She realized that she was going to have to take the lead and draw him out, as he had with her so many times before. She wasn't sure if he was worth it. But her head had become clear with the jolt of moonshine and she was determined. Maybe he wasn't worth it, but she was. Ruby sat up straight and threw her shoulders back.

"How about we start with a cigarette? I've been out all night."

Hayden reached for the package next to him in the dark and wordlessly handed it to Ruby. She pulled one out.

"Matches?"

He handed her the box. She struck a match and lit the cigarette.

"I need to know."

Ruby waved out the match and pitched it into the darkness. She blew out a stream of smoke and turned to him, holding her cigarette close and raising her head defiantly. Hayden turned to her and the dullness in his eyes frightened her. She kept going, though.

"I need to know what happened. I need to know why you didn't come back. Or send for me. Or something. I need to know why you broke your promise."

Hayden tilted his head and shook it.

"Ruby. I don't even know how to explain."

She took another drag from the cigarette, shielding herself with the action, with the smoke. Her movements were jarring and forced, giving her courage.

"Find a way. You owe me."

He looked up at her with eyes that were pleading, pathetic. The look sent a bolt of anger through her and Ruby held his eyes, unrelenting. Challenging.

"I've never known you to be a coward. Never. So, is that what you've become now?"

The words tumbled from her.

"If you didn't come back for me, then what the hell are you doing here anyway?"

Hayden looked away from her. She stared hard at the side of his face, waiting. He picked up the jar, but only held it, turning it in his hands.

"I'm afraid you'll hate me. I'm afraid you won't forgive me."

"Tell me now. Or I'm leaving you here alone in the dark. And I'm never coming back. Then you'll never know if I could have forgiven you or not."

"Ruby."

She kept staring at him.

"And it will mean that none of it mattered."

Hayden turned to her sharply.

"Of course it mattered. It was everything. You were everything."

He looked down at the jar in his lap and his voice changed.

"Are everything."

Hayden took a deep drink and handed the jar to Ruby. She set it down away from her and crossed her arms. Hayden finally sighed and looked up at the sky.

"Two summers ago, when I left, I meant every word I said. I promise you, Ruby, I swear. I meant it all."

Ruby didn't blink. Two summers ago when he had left. After they had finally broken down and given in to what had been in front of them for years, building, interlacing, a dance back and forth, aggressing, receding, and finally, reckoning. After three months of something Ruby had never known before. A passion outside of herself, an ease with her body, with her thoughts. Three months of letting go, of allowing herself to fall into something she believed she could trust. Of catching a glimpse of something else on the horizon. Something resembling hope. After he had held her face in his hands and promised to write as soon as he got back to Texas. Promised to meet her in Florida, at the Star Light's winter quarters, as soon as he'd put things in order back home. If not that winter, then at least by the start of the season in May. He promised they wouldn't be separated for long. And Ruby had believed him.

Hayden was waiting for her to say something, but this was on him. He sighed again.

"When I got back to Beaumont, there was someone waiting for me. Someone I wasn't expecting."

Ruby's breath caught in her throat.

"Her name was Eileen. I met her the spring before I jumped on the circuit the last time. Meet's not even the right word. I was in a roughneck saloon on Merchant Street. I don't even know what I was doing there. I certainly don't know what the hell she was doing there. Trying to be something she wasn't, I guess. She looked older. The way she was dressed. The way she acted. I didn't know. I was drunk, I barely remember it. I didn't even think twice about it later. I mean, I just thought it was what it was. I had forgotten her name. I had forgotten her completely. And then there was you and me."

Hayden sat up straighter and threw his shoulders back.

"Eileen was there, waiting for me when I got back into town. It'd been six, seven months. She was pregnant. She said it was mine."

Hayden paused and lit a cigarette. Ruby watched his hands. Her head was buzzing as she tried to process what he was saying.

"Turns out she was seventeen. Christ, seventeen. Her parents were some big shots. Landowners. They were talking charges, jail, but she wouldn't let them. She wanted to marry me. Told me she loved me. I think maybe she did, though I don't know how. She thought she was all grown up or something. She didn't know nothing about me. Nothing."

Ruby couldn't help herself.

"You tell her about me?"

Hayden shook his head.

"How could I? This girl standing in front of me, belly out to here. Goddamnit, she was just a kid. I told her I'd marry her. I did. Marry her."

Hayden looked up at Ruby, finally meeting her eyes directly.

"So that's why I couldn't write."

Married. Ruby reached for the jar.

"I see."

Hayden looked down at his cigarette.

"I didn't know what I could put in a letter. You and me. And then me and her. What would I have said?"

Ruby took a long swig of moonshine and then carefully set the jar back down between them. She took a hard drag on her cigarette and looked away at the carnival glow.

"I thought you had just run off. Or were dead."

"I thought I was dead. I felt dead. I married her and two weeks later I was back at Spindletop. The baby was born while I was off working the derricks. A girl. Cora. I tried to make a go of it, I guess, but it was no good. Being a husband. Being a father. I couldn't come back here, of course. But I couldn't make myself stay in Beaumont with Eileen and the baby. I hadn't even gotten them a house. They were living with her family. I traveled to different oil towns, working as much as I could so I could send her money for things. And to get away."

Ruby's mouth twisted around her cigarette.

"I looked for you. At every stop on the whole circuit. I didn't want to give up. I was so stupid. I felt so stupid, standing there on the empty lot, not wanting to get in the truck, not wanting to leave in case you were going to show up. Everyone giving me looks of pity. Poor Ruby. I was so stupid. "

Hayden's hand found hers. He gripped it hard.

"Ruby, I'm so sorry."

She looked down at his hand warily, as if she'd never seen it before. She started to pull away, but he wouldn't let her go. She looked up at him, her jaw tight, eyes wide and blinking, still refusing to cry. Her voice was a biting whisper.

"Why are you here?"

Hayden released her hand. He took his hat off and ran his hands through his hair, messing it up even further. He scrubbed at his forehead with his palm and then put his hat back on.

"Last fall. I was working Goose Creek and I got a telegram. There had been an accident. Eileen had been in Houston visiting a cousin. She wanted us to move there. I think she was trying to find us a place. A house. But there was a streetcar accident. Something happened, she fell, I don't know. They said she was still alive when they got her out from underneath it, but she didn't make it."

Hayden took a long drag on his cigarette.

"Damn it, she was just a kid. I didn't love her, but she was a good girl. She tried so hard. She wanted things I couldn't give her, she wanted me to be something to her that I couldn't be. She didn't deserve to go out like that. "

This time, Ruby reached for him. She laced her fingers with his, but didn't say anything. He shook his head and flicked away his cigarette with his other hand.

"After the funeral, her folks told me to stay away. They said I had ruined Eileen's life, ruined everything for her. But I still went out to their place, to see Cora. She'd just turned two. Hardly recognized me. Eileen's parents wouldn't even let me in the house. Said they'd decided to raise Cora. They'd pretty much been doing it all along, anyway. They told me it was for the best. I said I'd write, send money, whatever she needed. They said to get the hell off their porch. They looked at Cora and told her I was the man that had killed her mother. Pointed right at me and made the girl cry. So I got off their porch. I got out of town."

Hayden looked down at Ruby's hand in his. She followed his eyes. The tiny stars and spirals. The tattoos climbing up her wrist. She hadn't had another person's skin against hers since he had left.

"I went back up to Goose Creek and kept working. I thought about writing you. Hell, I'd thought about writing every day. But still, what would I say? How could I explain? You deserved better. Eileen and Cora, they deserved better."

Ruby's voice was very quiet. She was trying to figure out what it all meant now that he was back. After he had put her through so much, but also endured so much himself. There had been nothing but misery for them both.

"Maybe you deserved better."

Hayden let go of her hand.

"So I kept working. Goose Creek, Burkburnett. I sent money for Cora, even though she probably didn't need it. And when summer came, I thought about it and thought about it. About you. About coming back here to you. I didn't know if you'd want to see me. I didn't even know if you'd still be on the circuit. But I had to try. And so, that's the answer to your question. That's why I'm here. I couldn't let you go. I had to try."

Ruby looked at him hard for a long while in the moonlight. He had been someone else's husband. He had a daughter out in the world. She could see it in his face now. The lines of guilt. The ravages of living with despondency and regret. The weariness of it. They were both older now and wiser to the risks of falling in love. They had hardened their hearts to survive.

Ruby slid down from the truck bed. She could walk away from him forever. She knew she could. She had her answers. She had gotten what she wanted. Ruby looked out across the field at the carnival. The lights were few, but they were brilliant against the backdrop of darkness. Ruby turned around.

"You came back."

Hayden looked down at her, his mouth still twisted, his eyes still wary. He slowly nodded.

"I came back."

She could walk away. Or she could take a chance again. Ruby took a deep breath before reaching out and pulling Hayden down to her.

EIGHT

Tom had thought he'd made up his mind on the other side of the midway, when he'd been left alone after the poker game had finally broken up. An extra ace had been discovered, a short brawl had ensued, and the Alligator Lady had been sent for to sew a line of stiches into Ricardo's head. Alicia had not been happy about being woken up at two in the morning to take care of drunken rousties and the game had fallen apart shortly after. A few of the gamesmen had their own small tents to burrow into, but most of the rousties stumbled back to the sleeping areas they had previously claimed for themselves: dugouts underneath the cargo trucks or canvas pallets behind the cookhouse tent. No one had wanted to stay in the damp, fetid G-top and Franklin had rolled up the canvas sides to help air it out before morning.

As everyone had fallen away around him, only Tom had remained, alone outside the poker tent, unsteady on his feet as he tried to decide what to do. The smartest thing would have been to finish the bottle of rotgut still clutched in his hand and make his way across the field to the sleeping bag he had stowed beneath the front tires of a truck. That would have been smart. The easiest thing to do would be to head across the midway to the back line of wagons and tumble into January's bed. She shared one of the wagons with the two other dancing girls, and though Wanda and Darlene didn't care much for Tom, if he pounded on the door long enough, January would let him in and lead him back to her bunk, despite the glares from the other girls. He would wake up in January's bed, with the deep pillows and the faux gilt mirror hanging over his head and the smell of perfume spilled across every surface. The smell of women all around him.

But then he would hear it from January before he had even opened his eyes. Tom had been promising for a month to get them their own tent. He would hear it about that and about losing the two dollars she'd loaned him and about drinking himself sick. At least Tom wasn't a fighter. Still, he would have a headache from her before he even had a chance to have a headache from the liquor. Tom had finished the bottle and let it fall from his hand while he tried to navigate the haze in his brain and decide what to do. Sleep under the truck. Or with January.

January. The more he had thought about her, the more his head had burned and his stomach roiled. He hadn't seen her all night. Maybe she wasn't asleep in her wagon at all. Maybe she was with that tattooed freak, Ruby, the one who always gave him the shifty eye. The one he knew tried to poison January against him. Tried to convince her that he wasn't good enough for her. The bitch. The tents began to spin around Tom and he leaned over, hands on his knees, trying to clear his head. Maybe it was worse. Maybe January was with the tall man, the bastard in the fancy black suit that was worth more money than Tom would ever see in a lifetime. The geek. The sick man who bit the heads off of chickens. He couldn't imagine January getting anywhere near him, and yet he'd heard the rumors, the other men sniggering behind his back. He had seen January's face when the geek walked through the cookhouse yard and grinned like a cat at her. She hadn't been disgusted. She'd smiled back. He was sure he had seen her smile back.

Tom had stood up abruptly and quickly realized that it was the wrong thing to do. He had taken a few steps in the direction of the doniker, but knew he wouldn't make it. He managed at least a few feet, though, before kneeling over and vomiting into the dirt. January. If there had been men before Tom had joined the show, there could be men after, too. Even if she promised there were not. Men who gave her money or men she might care for and give herself to for free. Men who stood in the pit of the Girl Revue, staring up with their fat mouths hanging open, nearly drooling down the front of their shirts, as January whipped around in fake surprise, breasts bouncing, a Chinese fan the only covering for what rightfully belonged to him. Men gawking and jeering and grabbing themselves and sweating and lusting. Tom had seen it only once and had threatened to kill every man in the audience before Franklin had hauled him outside and given him a choice: stay far away from January when the girly show was on or get the hell off the lot altogether. Tom had needed the money. And January. He had needed her, too. So he stayed on and stayed away when the crowds lined up outside the bally to watch his girl take everything off.

Tom had braced himself against the dirt and retched and retched until his body was empty and his head burning and heavy. January. And other men. And the geek. The geek. With his suit and his teeth and that smug look of ownership in his black eyes when he walked past January. The rumors and the whispers. People had seen them together. Behind the tents, talking, laughing. Daniel's hand on her waist. On her waist and who knows where else. On his girl. His girl. Tom had pushed himself up and wiped his mouth against the sleeve of his shirt. He had known exactly what he needed to do. His head had felt clear and he'd marched purposefully across the empty midway to the wagons on the far side.

Now Tom was standing in front of the wagon decorated with a mural of chickens and rodents and snakes, all struggling against each other in the painted grass, and he felt sick again. He clenched his fists and forced himself to climb the steps. He wiped his mouth and raised his hand to pound on the door, but it opened before he could touch it. From the darkness inside, a voice purred at him.

"Come in, Tom Given. I've been waiting for you."

Tom didn't move. His instincts told him to run, but then a light bloomed inside the wagon and Tom felt compelled to step through the doorway. The door closed gently behind him and Tom stepped farther inside. The only other wagon he'd ever spent time in was January's and it was always a mess of costumes, clothes, dime novels and magazines. With three bunks and two dressing tables all crammed together, divided by swooping curtains, there was barely space to turn around. He had helped unload some of the other wagons and they were all relatively the same. Living spaces and sleeping spaces, the wood walls and floors scratched and gouged from being packed with tent materials during the jumps. He'd even helped to unload the geek wagon once, and it had appeared the same as all the others. Even sparser than most since Jacob had lived alone.

The geek wagon now was nothing like it had been before. The wooden walls were a slick, blood red and seemed to shimmer slightly in the candlelight. Faded tapestries woven with scenes of mythical beasts fighting one another hung on the walls and between these were tacked long scrolls, painted with complicated designs and symbols. There was a lacquered wooden bench running down the length of the wagon and it was strewn with the sorts of small trinkets and artifacts that Tom had once seen in a dime museum. Animal skulls and lengths of twisted branches and glass jars half filled with cloudy liquid. Thick books with leather covers were stacked along the wall, but Tom was sure the titles weren't written in English. A long row of small statues carved into monsters and human figures with ugly, twisted faces was lined up along the very edge of the bench. There was no bunk or bed of any kind, but a large round table, inlaid with gleaming squares of white and black, occupied the center of the wagon. And at the table sat the man in the dark suit, his back straight, hands clasped before him, long white fingers interlocked beneath his sharp chin and flashing smile. Daniel was indeed waiting for him and Tom could do nothing at first but stand there stupidly, trying to remember what had brought him to the geek in the first place. Daniel raised one arched, black eyebrow and helped him.

"I assume you're here about the girl. About January."

Tom caught his breath and pushed his hair off his forehead. He was sweating. He licked his lips and nodded. Daniel leaned back and shifted in his high-backed chair. He crossed his legs and knit his fingers over his knee. Tom could see the sharp crease in the trouser fabric creating a shadow in the flickering candle light. That crease alone cost more than Tom would make in a year and suddenly his anger overtook his astonishment and he balled up his fists again.

"I know what you're doing, glommer. I know what you're doing with my woman."

Daniel blinked his eyes slowly, calmly.

"No, you don't."

Tom stepped forward, the lanky muscles in his forearms taut. He wasn't a big man, he did more running from brawls than fighting in them, but he could hold his own if he had to.

"Now listen to me. I know what you're doing. I know what you're doing with January. Or what you're trying to do. And I ain't allowing it. So, I'm only going to give you one chance. You back off from her, you hear me?"

"Or what?"

There was a chill in Daniel's voice that almost made Tom falter. A chill and an unnerving certainty. But then Tom remembered the way January had smiled at the geek. And Daniel's knowing smirk back. The rage came up in him again like bile.

"Or I will mess you up, pretty boy."

Daniel laughed. Not like a man with bravado, but like a man hearing a truly ridiculous notion. A joke. Tom might as well have said that he just stepped down from the moon. Daniel brought his lips together in that smug smile again and Tom felt his stomach twist. Something about that smile was wrong. Something about the wagon was wrong and Tom felt a disorienting buzz between his ears that wasn't coming from the liquor. Daniel sighed.

"Oh, Tom. You don't even know what those words mean. You don't even understand the language that you speak. I doubt you even feel the emotions behind them. You are an ape trying to make sense of the shapes and colors around you. You are clay. You are a speck."

Daniel flicked his fingers at Tom and Tom narrowed his eyes.

"What the hell are you talking about?"

Daniel shook his head and his smile grew wider.

"Never mind. It is too much. You want to fight me, don't you?"

Tom dipped his chin, glaring, trying to conjure the anger again.

"Are you man enough?"

Daniel pursed his lips and cocked his head.

"No."

Tom's eyes widened in surprise.

"No?"

Tom looked around the wagon, grasping to figure out what was going on. The situation just seemed to keep turning for him. Daniel put his chin in his hands.

"No. I will not fight you. I will play you."

"Play me?"

"Play you. A game. A bet. I hear you are a betting man, Tom."

Daniel reached into his pocket and pulled out a pair of sleek black dice. He set them precisely in the center of the table.

"Will you roll the bones with me?"

Tom looked intently at the dice. He had never been able to walk past a pair of dice. He had never backed away from a bet, whether it be cards or horses or how many drinks or whether or not it would rain. He eyed the dice on the table, double sixes staring straight up at him, and felt his rage replaced by the burning itch, the need to play, the need to be a part of the odds. To win. His fingers trembled.

"What are we playing for?"

Tom looked up at Daniel. He wasn't smiling now, but there was a curious glint to his eyes. Tom recognized it. The junkie look for a game of chance.

"For January, of course."

Tom stepped back.

"Are you kidding me?"

"No. I'm serious. One game. Dead Man All In. You know it?"

Tom nodded silently.

"Good. If I win, I get January. No questions. No interference. She'll belong to me."

Tom swallowed.

"And if I win?"

"You win and I disappear. Leave this place. You'll never have to worry about me again."

Daniel reached out and fingered the dice.

"So?"

Tom licked his lips. His forehead was slick with sweat again, but he didn't wipe it away. He stared at Daniel's hand. Daniel cupped the dice and rattled them softly.

"Are you in?"

Hayden stared up at the roof of Ruby's wagon. They had left one of the lamps flickering on the table and its small glow came through the carved panels at the head and foot of the bed and illuminated the painted ceiling above him. Hayden had forgotten he'd painted it for her that summer. Ruby had curled up against him and told him how much she hated the curved brown ceiling arching over her every night. He had taken an evening off and crept into her wagon, painting it for her while she performed. A celestial ocean with fish made out of stars and clouds blowing ballooning airships through forests of seagrass. It was completely fantastical, the sort of painting that came from dreams, and Ruby's eyes had flashed and her lips had trembled and she had thrown her arms around him. It was underneath his painting, cocooned in the high dormer bed, that he'd spoken so many promises to her. Promises he knew she had hesitated to believe, but had wanted to. Promises he hadn't kept.

Ruby shifted against him and he gently put his fingers against her temple, touching her warm face and cloud of tangled hair. He could tell by her breathing that she had finally fallen asleep. They hadn't spoken much after she led him back to her wagon. It was almost as if she trusted her body, but didn't trust her voice. Or perhaps she just didn't know what to say. He had told her the truth and hadn't expected this in return. But he hadn't expected it before, when one summer had suddenly become different than the rest. She had possessed him for years, since he'd first seen her with Pontilliar in Beaumont, standing with her arms crossed and hip cocked out, arguing with her father about his grand idea for the painted wagons. He'd tried to win her that first season, using every trick he knew for women, failing at them all. She ignored his teasing and flirtations with the other girls. He couldn't seem to interest her or make her angry or jealous. She looked right through him, walked past him as if he were a ghost. He had been dumbfounded, and then frustrated, and finally fed up. He'd come back the next summer, though, and the next and the next.

Each season she seemed to warm a little more toward him. By his third summer with the Star Light, Ruby was laughing, drinking cheap wine with him behind the big top and telling him stories. He'd tried to kiss her, but she had socked him so hard his jaw hurt for a week. The summer after was a rollercoaster between them. One night he put his arm around her waist and she leaned into him. The next morning, she insulted him in front of the entire cookhouse. She would smile at him and then ignore him for days. That season, Ruby had made his head spin. Hayden had fallen for her to the point of hating her, telling himself over and over just to leave her alone. There were so many other women, both at home and on the midway, and yet he had wanted only her. When he was apart from her, he understood her. He understood why she pushed him away, why she built up the walls, why she was constantly battling against him and against herself. But standing next to her, he was bewildered. Hayden was overcome and he raged, tormenting them both. He had left at the end of that season swearing never to go back.

But, of course, he had. And it had been different that year, from the moment the Star Light came through and he had jumped on the circuit. There had been something in the air, something in the way her eyes were always on him. He halfway thought she was going to kill him. Two weeks in, he had followed her back to her wagon, arguing with her, challenging her about the way she was acting toward him. He'd said terrible things to her and she'd returned them and it reached a point where he wouldn't have been surprised if she had knifed him. Instead, she had crashed into him with an inconceivable force and everything between them had changed. He'd later held her in his arms, as he held her now, and asked her why. Ruby could give him no explanation, only herself.

He didn't dare ask her now. Hayden bent his head and put his face in her hair. He closed his eyes against the painted ceiling, against the wavering lamp glow, and breathed in the moment.

Tom ran his sweaty palms down the length of his trousers and eyed the dice in front of him. Dead Man All In was simple. The winner of each round was determined by the highest roll. The winner of two out of three rounds was called the Dead Man and set the bar for the final round. The loser of the first rounds had to play against the bar and roll higher than it three times in order to turn the tables and be declared the winner. It was easy, though Tom knew the odds could shift in the blink of an eye. The chair he was sitting on was hard and uncomfortable, and the air in the wagon seemed to become even more stifling as the seconds ticked by, but Tom was only focused on the game. He picked up the dice and blew on them. He rattled once in his right hand, switched to his left, blew again, back to his right and rolled. He had never been able to toss a pair of dice without this routine, just as he had never been able to draw a card without licking his index finger first or place a bet on a horse without crossing himself three times. The dice rolled to a stop. A four and a two. Low, but not too low. Daniel's long fingers encircled the dice and Tom heard the rattle, but he did not look up at the man across from him. He kept his eyes on the checkerboard pattern of the table. Waiting. Tom held his breath as the dice clattered across the surface. Double twos. Round one was Tom's.

Tom slung his arm over the back of his chair and grinned at Daniel. The man still had a smirk on his face, but Tom thought it was wavering just a bit. Tom wished he still had the bottle of liquor and could take a celebratory swig, but Daniel didn't appear to be drinking. He glanced around the room, just to see if there was anything to drink nearby, but there wasn't. Only those strange jars and skulls and the red walls and the flicker of the candles on the bench. Tom turned back to the table. Winning the first round also won him the privilege of rolling first again in the second. He picked up the dice, rattled and blew on them.

"Well, here we go, partner. You ready for this?"

Tom rolled. A six and a five. He couldn't help himself and he smacked the edge of the table with the palm of his hand.

"Beat that, sucker! I hope you got a trunk big enough to pack up this fancy-ass wagon of yours, because it looks like you're going to be leaving in a hurry."

Daniel didn't say anything. Tom watched his face, thrilled to see that Daniel's smile had continued to fade. He wished they were playing in the G-top and that the other rousties could see what he was doing to the geek in the rich suit with the greasy hair and the perfect teeth. Daniel reached for the dice. His hand was like a claw, not casually scooping the dice up, but enclosing them fully before letting his fingers part from the table. Tom clicked his tongue as Daniel rolled and watched intently as the dice settled. Snake eyes. Tom had won both rounds and could set the bar for the final. He smacked his thighs and hooted.

"Whew-ew! We didn't even need to go for three. You throw any lower there and somebody's going to have to make a special pair of dice just for you."

"There is still the final round, Tom Given."

Tom snorted and rocked back in his chair.

"I know the rules. But with the run of luck you're having, you sure you don't want to just throw in the towel now? I won't make a fuss. Hell, I'll even give you 'til morning to pack it in, seeing as you got all your little toys and dolls to wrap up before you go."

Tom gestured at the row of statues and laughed. His head was spinning, but he felt good. For a moment, the room seemed to grow even hotter and the red walls seemed to ripple, almost as if the wagon had taken a breath and exhaled. The sensation was unnerving. He could no longer read Daniel's expression, it seemed neither superior nor concerned, but the man's black eyes seemed larger than before and his skin appeared almost translucent in the candle glow. Tom quickly looked away from Daniel and down at the dice in his hand. He had this; he knew he did. Tom blew, rattled, right, left, right and rolled. A three and a six came to a halt in the center of the table. Nine. Tom almost couldn't stay in his seat.

"Ha! Now that's what I call a Dead Man roll! Three times, mister. Beat that three times. Let's see you do it."

Daniel had to roll the dice three more times. If any roll came up nine or below, Tom won. The only way the geek could trump him now was to throw three rolls coming up higher. Tom had it in the bag. He watched Daniel's expression to see if it had changed again, but it hadn't. Daniel silently reached for the dice and Tom couldn't help himself.

"Come on, let's see you do it. Hot damn! I should've staked more than January on this game."

Daniel rolled. Double sixes. Tom was unfazed.

"I guess if you're going to go out, you might as well start with a bang."

Tom had the sense again that the walls had quivered. Wherever he looked they were still, but he had the feeling that something had shifted in the air. He was suddenly ready to end the game and leave the geek's wagon. Daniel picked up the dice and rolled. Double sixes. Tom stopped smiling.

"Well, the harder they fall, they say. You going be able to pull that one off again?"

The smirk had returned to Daniel's face and his eyes were not only larger now, but shining. Tom felt the room grow hotter once more and this time he was sure he saw the walls pulse. He felt the floor roll underneath his feet in a wave and tried to tell himself that it was just the hooch catching up with him. He shifted in his chair and leaned his elbows on the table to steady himself. Daniel grinned, showing his teeth.

"Yes, Tom Given. I am."

Daniel picked up the dice and rolled. Tom watched them settle. His stomach churned and a rush of heat flared up around him. Tom closed his eyes and opened them again, just to be sure. Double sixes. He couldn't look up at Daniel, but the geek's voice floated to him from across the table.

"That was fun. Perhaps we should do it again sometime."

Tom stood up, knocking the chair over with his clenched fists, but a bet was a bet. Tom had never reneged on one before. He didn't think about his job at the carnival. He didn't think about January. He only thought of those double sixes. The impossible luck of it. The absurdity. But he himself had never figured out a way to cheat at Dead Man All In, so the rolls had to be true. Tom looked down at his boots and heard Daniel's voice again.

"Or perhaps not."

Tom stumbled out of the wagon to the sound of Daniel's crackling laughter behind him. He stood out on the midway with his head in his hands, trying to comprehend what he had just done.

NINE

Ruby could hear the screams in her sleep. She jolted awake, fighting with the sheets twisted around her hips. The early morning light was barely penetrating through the two small wagon windows, but in the gloom she could see Hayden turning around in the narrow space, searching the floor for his clothes. Ruby scrubbed at her face with her hands, trying to wake up. The screaming had stopped, but now she could hear movement and muffled shouting as people ran past the wagon on their way to the center of the midway. In the dim light, Ruby found Hayden's eyes and whispered.

"What the hell?"

Hayden leaned over the dresser and peered through one of the windows as he yanked up his suspenders.

"There's a mess of folks on the midway. At the Wheel."

Ruby kicked away the sheets and slid off the bed. She clawed her hair away from her face and reached for a robe hanging on the back of a chair. She slipped her arms into it and wrapped it tightly around her waist. Hayden was already on the wagon steps and he called over his shoulder to her.

"One of the rousties just ran by. Said something about someone being killed on the midway."

Ruby didn't bother with her boots.

"Oh my God."

Hayden turned to her, his mouth set in a grim line, his hair wild and sticking up. He reached out his hand to her.

"Come on."

From the steps, Ruby could see the crowd gathered beneath the Ferris Wheel. She followed Hayden down and headed toward the very heart of the midway, where the great wheel rose like the crown jewel of the carnival, outshining even the big top. The crowd had formed a tight ring around something on the ground and Hayden and Ruby began to push their way in. As faces met hers, the circle slowly opened up, letting Ruby through. In the very center, she found him. A broken man, legs going in unnatural directions, brown blood crusted across part of his face, the neck of a smashed bottle still in the clutches of his curled fingers. Hayden came up beside Ruby, but she couldn't take her eyes from the body.

"Jesus Christ. It's Tom."

The rest of the crowd was as shocked as Ruby. It didn't seem as if anyone had yet disturbed the scene. Two rousties stood closer, shaking their heads as they looked at the body from different angles, and Zena and Sonja were sobbing quietly in each other's arms, but most everyone was standing like Ruby, with helpless hands and stunned expressions. Ruby scanned the crowd for Samuel or Pontilliar, but she didn't see them. Someone was fighting their way through the wall of people behind her, though, and Ruby spun around just in time to catch January in her arms. She was hysterical.

"Is it Tom? Tom? Let me see him! Get off me! Let me see him!"

Ruby tried to hold January, but she was clawing at her eyes, clawing at anything and everything she could, and Ruby had to let her go. January stumbled past her and collapsed on Tom's body, screaming and trying to turn his smashed head so she could see his face. Ruby moved toward her, but Hayden put his hand on her shoulder and stopped her.

"Let them."

Hayden moved aside, letting Wanda and Darlene rush past him and fall on January. The two dancers were able to drag her a few feet away from Tom's body and hold her. January was sobbing into Darlene's shoulder and the women held her in a protective embrace, letting her keen and rock against them. Ruby turned to Hayden, confused and hurt that he would try to keep her from going to January. She tried to pull away, but Hayden squeezed her shoulder and nodded toward another disturbance in the crowd.

"Let the girls be with January right now. You need to deal with him."

Ruby warily looked across the circle of shocked faces and whispers, but she heard Pontilliar before she saw him.

"What the hell is going on here? Why is everyone standing around the chump heister like a bunch of lollygaggers? Jesus Christ, if I find another one of you lepers passed out on the midway again…"

Pontilliar broke through the crowd, but pulled himself up short when he saw the huddle of women and Tom's body beside them. Darlene looked over January's bent head and gave Pontilliar a vicious, protective look and he took an uneasy step back. A few of the rousties in the crowd shook their heads and scowled. Ruby left Hayden and crossed over to Pontilliar. She grabbed him sharply by the elbow and turned him around, steering him back through the crowd. She hissed in his ear as she pushed him through.

"What the hell is wrong with you?"

Pontilliar sputtered as they broke out into the open.

"I didn't know. Jesus, I didn't know."

Ruby saw Samuel standing alone beside the Whip and she shoved Pontilliar in that direction. Samuel slowly shook his head as they approached.

"Another dark, dark day for us."

Pontilliar smoothed his palms down the front of his striped vest. Unlike most everyone else in the crowd, he'd taken the time to get fully dressed before responding to the screams and commotion. Even Samuel looked slightly disheveled with his shirt untucked and his cuffs open. Ruby cinched her robe tighter and turned from Pontilliar to Samuel. She raised her eyebrows.

"What happened, Samuel? Did he fall?"

Samuel dipped his chin a moment.

"Zena and Sonja found him like that. Just like that. I was here shortly after I heard the first scream."

"So he fell."

"I believe he fell."

Pontilliar craned his neck to look back toward the Ferris Wheel. The large crowd was beginning to break up and small loose groups of onlookers had formed, some crying, some whispering, a few just lighting cigarettes and kicking at the dirt, already grumbling about the heat. Pontilliar turned back to Samuel.

"He fell? From the Wheel? What the hell was he doing on the Wheel?"

Ruby's eyes rose to the top of the fifty-foot Ferris Wheel. Then she looked back to Tom's body. Someone had covered it with a quilt and Darlene and Wanda were again trying to pull January away from it. Ruby set her gaze directly upwards from the body. Tom would have had to fall from one of the top outside cars. High, but not too impossibly high to survive a fall. She turned to Samuel and saw that he had followed her eyes.

"Yes, he must have fallen from a car only forty feet up."

Pontilliar pulled out his handkerchief and wiped his upper lip. "And that killed him? Wouldn't it just, break his legs or something?"

Samuel closed his eyes and spoke slowly.

"I've seen many men die under strange circumstances. Unexplainable. Without a scratch on them. It is not unheard of for men to die in unnatural ways."

Pontilliar huffed impatiently.

"Yes, but this man?"

Samuel opened his eyes.

"This man, I believe, fell."

"And it killed him."

"It killed him. He might have fallen backwards out of the car, hit one of the spokes or the drive rim on the way down and mangled his legs. I don't know. I suppose Tom could have been beaten and killed somewhere else and then dragged beneath the Wheel, but I saw no evidence of the body having been moved. I can't be sure until I look closer, but I believe, from the angle, that his neck was snapped. He most likely hit the ground head first."

"Holy Mother Mary."

Pontilliar stuffed his handkerchief back in his pocket.

"But what was he doing up there in the goddamn first place?"

Ruby shook her head. She suddenly felt dizzy and was reminded of the events of the night before. The rum, the moonshine. Hayden. Ruby pushed back the swell of nausea and tried to focus.

"There was glass smashed around him. Part of a bottle still in his hand."

Pontilliar scowled at her.

"So he was drunk? Did you see him drinking last night?"

Ruby rolled her eyes.

"The show was dark last night. Of course he was drunk. Everyone was drunk."

Pontilliar frowned and turned back to Samuel.

"So, what, he's drunk? Climbs the Wheel and loses his balance?"

"Maybe."

Pontilliar's eyes popped and he turned from Samuel to Ruby. Ruby shrugged and looked away. Hayden was still standing where she'd left him. He wasn't looking toward the covered body, though. He was staring intently across the midway at something she couldn't see. She leaned to the side, trying to follow Hayden's line of sight, but Pontilliar's screech snapped her back to attention.

"Maybe? For God's sake, what does 'maybe' mean?"

Samuel sighed.

"It means that maybe he climbed up the Wheel, lost his balance and accidentally fell. Or maybe he climbed up with the intention of falling."

Pontilliar stepped back a moment and then stabbed his finger into Samuel's chest.

"No."

Samuel glared at him, but Pontilliar continued.

"No, we are not doing that again. Absolutely not. First the geek decides to go off and count worms and now this? Not in my carnival. No way."

Ruby stepped closer, trying to get Pontilliar to lower his voice. A few of the bystanders were beginning to look over at them with concern. Samuel's voice remained perfectly level.

"It's just an idea."

Ruby turned to Samuel.

"But a plausible one? You think Tom could've killed himself? Fallen on purpose?"

Samuel shook his head and raised his hands in defense.

"I have no idea. He could have been pushed for all we know. I'm just remarking that it is a peculiar death. We shouldn't rule out any possibilities until we know for certain. That is all."

Pontilliar closed in on Samuel, his voice grinding into a whisper.

"Pushed? Now you're talking murder? You're saying someone murdered that roustie on my goddamn Ferris Wheel?"

Ruby tried to get between them.

"No one is saying anything about anything. Stop jumping to conclusions. Both of you."

Pontilliar stepped back and pulled his vest down tighter over his bulging stomach. He looked around and glared at the rousties standing idly nearby. They quickly ducked their heads and returned to their cigarettes. Pontilliar pointed at Samuel again.

"You. Clean this up. Figure this out. I want to know what happened. And I don't want anyone talking. You hear me? We open the show at two today and I do not want word of this hitting town. You make sure all these half-wit gazoonies keep their flaps shut, you understand?"

Samuel's eyes were dark and his face stiff.

"I understand."

Pontilliar turned on Ruby.

"And you."

She glared back at him.

"Don't even start."

Pontilliar looked back and forth between Samuel and Ruby and then pushed between them, huffing and stomping toward the office wagon. Ruby turned, looking around for Hayden. He was still in the same spot, his head bent strangely as he looked across the midway. Ruby started toward him, but froze when she finally saw what he was looking at. He was staring at the geek, standing alone in front of the big top tent with his eyes riveted on the covered mound of Tom's body. Even at the distance, Ruby could see that Daniel's eyes were narrowed and his mouth twisted. His shoulders rose in a sigh and then he turned his back and slowly walked away.

Some of my brethren feared the King Gods. Odin and Dyaus and Zeus. Odomankoma and Ta'aroa. Re-Horakhty and Chernobog. Even now, those closest to me, my allies, if you will, still cast their eyes down if Bondye or The Great Spirit come strolling into town. It's pathetic. I did not fear Esus so long ago and I do not fear El now. No, the only thing I will run from, the only thing I truly abhor, is boredom.

When I left the ruined forest of Verdun it wasn't due to the stench of the piled bodies or the sucking sickness of the mud or the matchstick trees exploding like confetti against the snow. I was disgusted, yes, but not from the blood and pus and rain. Not from a death toll or a loss of humanity, whatever that may be. No, I was repulsed by the complete and total lassitude of the spectacle. Here we are, in the modern age. Men are no longer covered in blue paint, waving pointy sticks at one another. There are no swords and shields, no catapults, no buckets of burning tar. This war, The Great War, had tanks! Fortresses on wheels and guns the size of cattle and chlorine gas floating across the land like morning mist, ready to drown men without a drop of water to be seen. Such promise of a smash-up! Yet what did these men do? They dug lines in the mud and sat, pouting like children, cradling their automatic rifles in their arms like dolls. I once witnessed the siege of a Norman castle and thought it could never get any duller than that. Men sitting around, eating rats and peering through the turrets, just waiting for their walls to crumble around them. And they did eventually, of course, but, oh, at what cost to my sanity?

This new war was far worse, though. Boring, boring, boring. Give me men with only sticks and tar, as long as they are using them. As long as they are running and shouting and causing some commotion.

For there is nothing so terrible as inertia. As complacency. As the static coming and going of lives, parading past on an endless loop, over and over, the same, the same. Technology accelerates and atrophies, morals loosen and tighten with the fashions, but the trials of men never change. It's always the same. The same chessboard pieces of lust, pride and possessiveness, moving around each other like magnets caught in a spiral, never drifting too far off course. Even when half of the world has just exploded in the name of some sort of politics, the pieces will never spin off the board.

I apologize. I digress. I admit, I have only myself to blame for this petulant mood. I've been doing this for long enough, you'd think I would know better. When I stood upon the tawdry midway and felt the promise of something new steal into my heart, I had hope. I was galvanized by the possibilities. I let myself salivate in anticipation. But I was tempted, only to be jilted. I have combed the corners and felt along the cracks to no avail. There is nothing here but more remnants of the same. I tried to assuage my disappointment with a distraction, a momentary, if mundane, high. Girl loves boy. Boy gambles girl. Girl loses boy. Pandemonium beneath the Wheel. Chaos! Disruption and disorder, my bread and butter. And yet. The rush behind my lungs lasted less than a second, the spark of intrigue fizzled before it could even flare. This endless monotony stretches on for all time and I can do nothing but sit here and grumble.

TEN

Hayden was just finishing the caricature of a woman who almost didn't need one when he caught sight of Samuel weaving through the bustling midway crowd toward him. Though Samuel was at the heart of every affair, every concern, of the Star Light's, he rarely strode down the center of the carnival during the day, in full view of the rubes. Samuel wasn't a freak or performer, wary of giving the show away for free, it had been years since he'd stooped to the role of Mutumbo, the Wild Man of Borneo, but he was still liable to cause a stir. A dark African man, well dressed, with tribal scarring on his face, always raised eyebrows, if not insults or worse, from the townsfolk. Oftentimes, the marks thought he was part of a minstrel show and tried to heckle him back into a tent. On more than one occasion, Hayden had witnessed a man take a swing at Samuel, simply for being present on the midway. This never turned out well, though, as two

or three rousties were always immediately on the scene, calling a
Hey Rube. The rousties certainly harbored their own prejudices
and didn't enjoy taking orders from Samuel, but they never forgot
who was responsible for them having a job in the first place.

Samuel skirted around a cluster of barefoot children,
whispering and pointing, and came up beside the woman sitting
for her portrait. Her eyes bulged even farther out of her head when
she glimpsed who was sharing space with her and her cheeks
began to puff up in complaint. Hayden grimaced and finished
adding a third chin to the lady's profile. He signed the paper
quickly and swept it off his easel. Normally he had a little spiel
when he presented the finished product, in the hopes that the sitter
would bring back a few friends, but Hayden didn't even bother this
time. He handed her the drawing and wiped the charcoal from his
fingers with a rag before turning to Samuel and sighing.

"What do you want?"

Samuel waited for the woman to squeeze her bulk past them
and then he took a step closer, bowing his head slightly. His dark
brown eyes and ramrod posture had always been unreadable to
Hayden and he didn't know if the news he was about to receive was
good or bad. Samuel's voice was low and sharp in his ear.

"My wagon. Now."

Hayden stepped back and looked around for a customer who
might be headed his way. He gestured toward his easel and chair.

"And what about this? I've got a livelihood to make here, in
case you hadn't noticed."

"Your silly pictures can wait."

Samuel continued on down the midway. Hayden turned to
watch him disappear between Alicia and Linus's reptile wagon and
the Ten-In-One tent. He tried to remind himself that Samuel was
one of Ruby's oldest friends, but he'd never gotten along with the
man. Hayden knew he didn't have much of a choice, though, and
signaled to Casper at the Toss-A-Ring game to keep an eye on his

spot. He tugged on the bottom of his vest and reluctantly followed in Samuel's wake.

Samuel's wagon wasn't marked with a sign, as Pontilliar's was, but everyone working the show knew that it was where all of the real management decisions issued from. It was where the money went in and out, the circuit route was adjusted in the event off storm blowdowns and delays and the bribes for Chandler to take to the town bag men calculated. Samuel came to Pontilliar's office wagon on petty errands; Pontilliar came to Samuel's management wagon to do business. Hayden approached it, noticing that, unlike the other wagons, the side of Samuel's had been repainted. The scrolling banner for the Modern Motorized Menagerie had been whitewashed and the mural now proclaimed the arrival of RANDOLPH PONTILLIAR'S SPECTACULAR STAR LIGHT MIRACULUM! Hayden frowned at the shoddy paint job as he climbed up the rickety steps and pushed through the door without knocking.

Samuel was already sitting behind a mahogany, kidney-shaped desk, scratching away at papers as if he hadn't just arrived a moment before Hayden. He gestured for Hayden to sit down, but Hayden remained standing in the doorway while he glanced around. From the outside, the wagon was the same size as the others, but inside there seemed to only be half the space, and most of it was taken up by the imposing desk. There was a lamp hanging above Samuel's head, but he hadn't lit it, and the only light came filtering in through the one dusty window. The wagon walls were cluttered: old circus playbills hung alongside framed oil portraits of white men in powdered wigs and carved African masks with elongated, animal-like features. Hayden had only been in Samuel's wagon once before and he noted that nothing seemed to have changed in the years since.

Hayden pinched the crown of his hat and removed it before easing himself into the chair across the desk from Samuel. He decided to just go ahead and get it over with.

"So, is this about Ruby? Or is this about Tom?"

Samuel pulled out his watch and glanced at it. He frowned before tucking it back into his pocket.

"Now why would you say either of those?"

"Because you don't like the fact that I'm back and especially don't like the fact that I could be back spending time with Ruby. And Tom, well, Jesus Christ, if you aren't the tenth person today to insinuate I killed him."

Samuel picked up a pen and signed one of the many papers scattered across the oxblood leather inset on top of his desk. Hayden knew he was doing it for effect. Taking his time, trying to make Hayden squirm. It was one of the reasons he couldn't come to terms with Samuel, even though he understood how important he was to the Star Light. Hayden considered himself a patient man, but of the few things he couldn't stand, putting on airs was at the top of his list. And in his eyes, Samuel was the very epitome of pretension. He waited silently, though, for Samuel to quit showing off and get to the point. Samuel set the pen down, carefully folded up the paper he had just signed and then slid it underneath a thick leather ledger on the corner of his desk. He cut his eyes up at Hayden and frowned.

"Ruby. No."

Samuel finally raised his head and sat up straight, squaring his shoulders back.

"No, I don't like you with Ruby. That girl has been through enough without having to consider your vacillating decisions."

"Last I checked, Ruby wasn't a girl. She's a woman, and she can make her own choices about who she wants in her company."

"And Eileen? Was she a woman as well? Or just a girl? Would you like to enlighten me on the facts of that situation?"

Hayden clenched his jaw, but kept his eyes on Samuel.

"Ruby tell you that?"

Samuel was returning the stare.

"God, no. Do you think she would tell me a thing like that? She'd most likely go to the ends of the earth to protect your sorry little secret. Though I am glad to hear that you've told her. It was going to have been a very awkward conversation if I had been forced to broach the subject myself."

Hayden tossed his hat on the desk and leaned back in the chair.

"Then how do you know?"

"I make it my business to know."

Samuel looked down at the spread of papers in front of him.

"But right now, whatever is going on between you and Ruby is not my concern."

Hayden crossed his arms.

"So this is about Tom."

"Yes."

"And you think I killed him?"

Samuel frowned.

"Why would I think that?"

Hayden leaned forward.

"Because everybody else seems to think so. One of the splinterheads outright accused me of it. Said that I had showed back up so I could have a go at January and then murdered Tom to get him out of the way. Biggest load I ever heard. I would've rattled his teeth for him if he wasn't already a half-wit. And now I guess you've hauled me in here to accuse me of the same ridiculous thing."

"No."

"I mean, everyone in the whole damn carnival knows I only ever had eyes for Ruby. Me being jealous of someone with January? Come on. And who even said Tom was murdered? One minute everyone is saying he got drunk and fell. Then it's that he offed himself like the geek on the swing. And then all of a sudden, no, somebody killed him. And that somebody could've been me."

Samuel shook his head slowly.

"Everyone is just excited. Two shocking deaths in the span of a week. They're just trying to make sense of it all. Some of the new hands don't know you, so they're lashing out because you're unfamiliar to them. That sentiment will pass quickly."

"But you know me. You think I did this?"

Samuel gave what for him passed as a smile, a narrowing of the eyes without a frown.

"Of course not."

Hayden picked up his hat and tapped the brim on the edge of the desk.

"Then what the hell am I doing in here, Samuel? I need to get back on the midway."

"I want to know what you think."

Hayden groaned.

"What I think? About Tom?"

"Yes."

"Why?"

Samuel sighed and folded his hands on the desk.

"Because I saw you looking at the scene this morning. Everyone else was staring at Tom, but you were looking up at the Wheel. I saw the cogs in your mind turning as you measured angles, considered possibilities."

Hayden put his hat on his head and gave Samuel a sly smile.

"You could tell all that just from looking at me, huh? Or is it maybe that no one else wants to talk to you about Tom's death, but you just can't resist harassing me. And though you think you know everything that goes on, everywhere, all the time, you don't."

Samuel didn't blink.

"I know that Franklin did not want to take you up in the Wheel before we opened today, but you convinced him to. So you were looking for something. Unlike most of the others, you're not overreacting and you're not sticking your head in the sand. You're working the problem. Now tell me what you're thinking."

Hayden reached into his pocket and pulled out his package of cigarettes. He removed one and held it up for Samuel to see. Hayden knew Samuel detested smoking and wouldn't allow it in his wagon. He raised his eyebrow at Samuel and Samuel looked from the cigarette to Hayden and then nodded in irritation. Hayden grinned.

"All right then."

Hayden lit the cigarette and blew out a stream of smoke.

"The show was dark and we were all half-under last night. I saw Tom early on and he was bent even then. So I think he was drunk and stupid, decided to climb up the Wheel and then he fell. That body wasn't moved there, it landed there."

"So you don't think there was any foul play."

"I didn't say that."

Hayden tapped the top of the desk with the hand holding the cigarette.

"I think he fell. But you saw the angles. He had to have fallen from one of the cars, not while climbing up the spokes. So, if he was sober enough to be able to climb near to the top of the Wheel and make it safely into one of the cars, I don't think he would've been so flush that he just toppled out by accident."

"You think he was pushed."

"I don't know."

Hayden squinted through the smoke.

"I mean, I don't see someone climbing up there with him. I think if someone did, and tried to push him or what have you, they both would have gone over. It's a Wheel tub, they're not stable if you stand up in one, let alone have a struggle."

Samuel frowned.

"You think it was suicide, then?"

Hayden tapped a lump of ash from his cigarette onto the floor.

"See, I just don't know about that either. I mean, come on. He's got a job, got a girl. I didn't know Tom from Adam, but he didn't seem like the theatrical type."

"Then what?"

Hayden leaned forward.

"Look, Samuel, I wasn't there, I don't know what happened. You asked me what I thought. So that's it. I think he fell, but I don't think it was an accident. Something just isn't right about the whole picture. When I went up in the Wheel, I was just trying to get a feel for it. The car he was in, the height, that sort of thing."

"Yes?"

"But when I was up there, just looking around, I noticed something odd. If you're looking straight out ahead, you can clearly see the woods behind the truck lot. Well, dead ahead of the Wheel, it looked as if the tops of the trees had been broken off. Just the very tops. And just in that one spot, almost like a corridor going back through the woods. I'm not certain, though. It could've been a trick of the light. That's not how wind usually works, going in just a streak like that."

"So you think Tom might have been knocked out of his seat by a gust of wind?"

Hayden shook his head.

"It was a perfectly still night last night. Not a breath of air moving. How could one gust, strong enough to break tree branches, come out of nowhere? Wouldn't other folks have noticed it? Heard it?"

"So you don't think it was the wind."

"Jesus Christ, Samuel. I have no idea. Didn't I just say that about a half-dozen times? I just think it's an unusual death. It doesn't add up. That's all."

Hayden stood up and flicked his cigarette. Samuel stood up as well.

"That's not all you think."

Hayden was turning to leave, but stopped. Samuel came slowly around the side of the desk.

"You were also staring at a man this morning. You couldn't take your eyes from him."

Hayden nodded cautiously.

"The geek. Daniel."

"Yes. Why were you staring at him?"

Hayden glared at Samuel and then dropped his cigarette on the wagon floor and ground it out with the toe of his boot.

"Listen. The only thing I know is that something isn't right about the whole picture. First the geek, Jacob, hanging himself. Killing himself out of nowhere. No note, no reason that anyone can think of. I mean, are we even sure he wasn't strung up by someone else?"

Samuel narrowed his eyes.

"The coroner called it a suicide."

"Okay, but it's still an unexplained suicide. Don't tell me you think Jacob's death was cut and dry."

Samuel shook his head.

"No."

"And now this with Tom. Another death that doesn't make sense, only this one with even stranger circumstances. Are you telling me it's just a coincidence?"

"I'm not telling you anything."

Hayden jammed his hands in his pockets and rocked back on his heels.

"Oh, right, right. You want to pick my brain, but you want to keep your secret theories to yourself. Well, go ahead. All I can say is that there's something about Daniel being here that just doesn't sit right with me. I haven't shared two words with the man, and I'm not throwing the blame around yet, especially when my name is still first on everybody's tongue, but I just have a feeling that Daniel's got something to do with it all. Everyone said he was chasing January right in front of Tom, so maybe that was it."

"But you don't think that was it."

"Look, Samuel. I'm done talking about this. Something's just off with the Star Light this go 'round. Something doesn't feel right. You don't have to say it, but I know you feel it, too. And whatever it is, I know it has to do with that new geek."

Hayden touched the brim of his hat and opened the wagon's door. The low evening sunlight hit him directly in the eyes and he flinched. As he banged down the steps, he knew that everything he had said to Samuel was true. He might not have even realized it before, but now he was certain: it all went back to Daniel. He could feel it. He just couldn't begin to explain it.

Ruby carefully untangled herself from Hayden and slipped off the edge of the bed. She was pulling her boots on when she heard Hayden's breathing change. She knew he was awake, listening to her in the dark. Ruby stood up from tying her laces and whispered.

"I'm just going for a walk. I need to think."

She heard the sheets rustle as Hayden turned over. His voice was a sandy mumble.

"You want me to come with you?"

"No."

She reached out and groped across the bed for Hayden's hand. Ruby touched his warm, curled fingers and then stepped outside onto the wagon steps and quietly shut the door. The silent midway was lit up by moonlight and the towering Ferris Wheel cast long, spidery shadows across the trampled earth. The carnival only slept during the very depths of night, the quiet space a few hours after the last show had ended and a few hours before dawn broke and the earliest risers straggled to the cookhouse tent in the hopes that Jimbo had water boiling for coffee. It was during this brief respite, when the Star Light paused for breath, that Ruby loved to roam the carnival grounds. Tonight, though, she wanted to be far away from the midway and the enveloping tents and the monstrous Wheel. She headed for the far side of the lot, beyond the row of empty cargo trucks, to the field and the woods beyond.

Pontilliar had insisted on running the Ferris Wheel, even though Franklin had warned him it was bad luck to operate a ride immediately after a death. Even Samuel had suggested they shut it down for at least one day, but Pontilliar had refused. The Baton Rouge crowd was the largest they'd had in a month and they were playing it out until the end of the week. To keep the townsfolk coming back night after night they needed the brilliantly lit Ferris Wheel spinning over their heads, enticing them to shell out for just one more ride.

Once Tom's broken body had been removed and the site swept over, Pontilliar had also made it clear that if anyone else on his crew felt like dying they'd better let him know so he could kill them first. Tom was a First of May man and had only been with the show since the opening of the season when he'd joined up in Georgia. Pontilliar wouldn't have remembered Tom's name if it hadn't been on everyone's tongue and he was unmoved by the effect his death was having on the rest of the Star Light. He couldn't see that the unease trickling through the show had nothing to do with who Tom was. It was the circumstances of his unnatural death and the discovery of his body, splayed out for all to see. It brought Jacob's death into a new light, now that it wasn't the only one, and it stirred questions in the minds of the carnival workers. There were whispers of madness. And of murderers.

Ruby had spent the day avoiding the knots of speculation that congregated at the cookhouse and behind the show tents. The apprehension was gnawing at her, too, but she didn't want to talk about it. Despite Pontilliar's protestations, the cootch tent had gone dark and there was nothing he could do about it. The dancers had secluded themselves in their wagon, creating a quiet place for January to grieve, and no one, not even Ruby, was welcome inside. She had only been able to send word of her condolences through Wanda at the wagon threshold. Ruby had gone through the motions of her show like always, but her heart was in it even less than usual. She'd been relieved when the night was finally over and she could put the snakes back in their boxes. Ruby had found Hayden sitting on her wagon steps, waiting for her, and she had let herself fall into him.

Ruby waited until she reached the long, dew-soaked grass of the field to light a cigarette. She had to cup the match against the slight breeze that had stirred up, but the shift in the wind felt delicious. She threw back her head and felt the cool air on her neck and throat. There was too much to think about. Tom's death, yes, but also now Hayden. Hayden's return. She didn't know if she could trust it, but she wanted to. And there had been an ease now, too, knowing he had already hurt her once so badly; he would never be able to do it again. Before, she had felt almost helpless, bound by the sudden realization of her need for him. She'd been drunk on Hayden that summer, staggered and reeling in the fever she'd discovered with him. She had been floating then, but now was grounded solidly by the doubt and disappointment she'd endured. The past two years had given her strength. She wanted Hayden, yes, but she no longer needed him, and there was a power in that knowledge. Ruby stood in the middle of the field, cigarette in hand, the breeze shifting long tendrils of hair around her face, and felt free.

And then she saw the eyes. Ruby froze. They were low to the ground, belonging to a wild dog perhaps, but luminous, with a strange reddish glow. Ruby took a long drag on her cigarette and slowly started walking toward the edge of the woods. The eyes moved, coming out of the shadows, and now Ruby could see the outline of a fox, skulking along the perimeter of the field. She stopped again, waiting to see what the animal would do. The eyes disappeared as the fox turned and she could barely make out its shape, just movement through the long grass. Ruby couldn't tell if the fox was coming closer or moving farther away. She strained to see in the darkness, scanning the field, and then the eyes reappeared again, this time much closer.

The fox was big, the largest one she had ever seen, but she could tell by the narrow head and the large brush of its tail that it wasn't a dog or a wolf. It was unusually tall with long, spindly legs and high, pointed ears. She wasn't frightened, but the animal's strange, garnet eyes held her. They seemed to flicker, and Ruby took a step closer, bristling with the odd sensation that the animal wasn't just watching her, but had recognized her. Just as she was not afraid of it, the fox did not appear to be afraid of her and this was contrary to everything she knew about the creatures. She kept her gaze fixed on the fox, but suddenly it bounded away, rustling through the grass. Ruby thought she saw it disappear back into the woods, but it might as well have disappeared into the ether. Her cigarette had gone out and she dropped it into the grass. The night was suddenly stifling and Ruby gathered her hair and held it up off her neck. She continued to look out at the tree line of the woods, but the fox had vanished.

When his estranged fourteen-year-old daughter had finally found and confronted him, Pontilliar had only shrugged his shoulders. Ruby had held out the proof, the circus playbill she had carried all the way from the mountains, but Pontilliar hadn't bothered to question the validity of her claim. He also hadn't been impressed by the arrival of his only offspring. Pontilliar had simply asked her what she could do. What skills. What talents. How she could contribute to the show. When she had answered that she could hunt and trap, he had laughed at her. What useful skills? She was a pretty good thief when she needed to be, so Pontilliar had set her up as a picker: she picked up the trash on the midway and picked the pockets of the rich gentlemen and ladies who had been marked by a chalky hand patting them on the back as they passed through the ticket booths.

Ruby had no illusions about her father. She had not really expected him to love her and so was not disappointed by his coldness. Ruby had found her family; the Star Light accepted her as one of its own and became her home. No one even seemed to know that she was Pontilliar's daughter, although eventually rumor spread, and if they did know, only a few appeared to care. She had seen Zero, the clown, frown when Pontilliar scolded her as he would any other employee and she often caught Samuel Mtangoo, grandson of a captured Wagogo chief and son of Sir Richard Grimthal's head butler, staring at her from across the midway. Samuel bothered her, he seemed always to be watching her, at times she was sure he was following her, but Ruby knew better than to complain. The Star Light had become her touchstone and she clung to her place within it with a fierce desperation.

In truth, Samuel was the keeper of the one secret which, if she discovered it, would have driven Ruby away from the carnival forever. Ruby's mother had been both the queen of the Star Light and Pontilliar's young wife. Miranda had been everyone's darling, the heart of the show, and had taken the circus to a new height of glamor, but Pontilliar's ambition couldn't be contained. He wanted more than a big top arena. The new public fad was for sideshow freaks, but Pontilliar was having trouble paying for them. He had read about Dr. Christopher Fillini and his proposed chemical and psychometric dysgenic experiments for aiding Francis Galton's new eugenic research. Pontilliar decided to conduct these experiments himself and began to slowly and secretly poison Miranda when she was pregnant with their first child. He began with drops of an atropine solution in her coffee every morning. She miscarried in the middle of a show, blood smeared down the side of her white horse, the clowns quickly closing in to distract the crowd and carry her away. Pontilliar had insisted on examining the fetus. Normal. No tail. No lobster claws.

The second baby was a stillborn, the birth agonizing, the only indication of Pontilliar's endeavors was a slight webbing between two toes. He considered putting the body in a jar for the pickled punk show, but Miranda wouldn't let him. The baby boy was buried; Miranda heartbroken beyond solace. Pontilliar was frustrated and redoubled his efforts, varying his chemicals. When Ruby was born, perfect and healthy, Pontilliar gave up on subterfuge. He needed Miranda's help. He needed to try more combinations at higher doses, and for that Miranda needed to be a willing participant. When Pontilliar explained to her what he had been attempting to do over the past four years, Miranda became hysterical. She had taken her daughter and left her married name, her career, her stardom, and returned home to the sanctuary of the mountains. The only other person who had been aware of Pontilliar's diabolic experiments had been Samuel and, though he was sworn to secrecy and would never renege on an oath, he took it upon himself to protect Ruby as penance for his silence.

After two years of watching his daughter dip into pockets and collect trash, Pontilliar approached Ruby with a proposition. She didn't have a talent, either in skill or physical features, and had basically proven herself useless to him. He would be willing, however, in light of their filial relationship, to invest in her carnival career. If she was willing to go on a journey. If she was willing to transform. If she had what it took to become a star like her mother.

Ruby did not know then about Pontilliar's diabolical scientific proclivities. She was unaware of her unborn siblings, of the thin, wailing voices that had haunted Miranda's every step. She knew

Pontilliar felt no true affection for her, but she was dazzled by his promises of ballys and billings, his exuberance for her future success. He put his arm around her shoulder, touching her for the first time in months, and wrote her name in the air before them. One day, he enthused, her name would be written in lights. And she would have done her mother proud.

Samuel had sought her out, cautioning Ruby not to trust Pontilliar, but Ruby did not trust Samuel and so his warnings went unheard. She was only sixteen, a girl who had spent so much of her life with a tattered playbill clenched inside her fist, and the father she had spent years seeking was asking if he could give her the moon. Of course, she said yes.

ELEVEN

Ruby threw her cigarette to the dirt and ground it out with the toe of her sandal. She stretched her neck back and forth and then felt the back of it. Sweat. There was nowhere to go to escape the heat, but inside the snake tent was hotter than behind it. Every now and then a breeze funneled through the backside of the midway, shuffling the hot air around. It was the Star Light's sixth night in Baton Rouge and even though it was only Tuesday, it was the biggest crowd they'd had all summer. The midway was jammed shoulder to shoulder and there were lines queued up outside of the Ten-In-One, waiting to push their way through and gawk at the freaks. The grandstands in the big top were full and the Ferris Wheel and the carousel were whirring non-stop. Jasper was turning the tip so fast outside of the snake show that he had to call in one of the rousties to help force people away. There was a feverish energy in the air, as if the townsfolk were fearful that when the carnival went away, they'd never see another one. Perhaps it was the truth. Reverend Tindall had set up about a hundred yards beyond the Star Light's gates and was damning the carnival to the depths of hell. Pontilliar was making so much money that he didn't even care.

Halfway through the evening, word had come down the tent line that Beaner, the talker for the electric show, was puking up his guts in the doniker. There was no else to call the bally on Augustus's show and he was having a fit. Jasper had asked Ruby if she minded taking a two-show break so he could fill in and she'd agreed before he even finished the question. She hung the closed sign on the bally herself and retreated behind the tent where at least there wasn't a crush of people and a body could breathe a little.

She leaned back against one of the tent poles and was about to shut her eyes for a moment when she saw a familiar figure wrapped in a pink silk kimono coming slowly toward her from the cookhouse. Ruby hadn't seen January since the previous morning, when she had tried to hold her back from Tom's body, and she hoped January was coming to see her. January paused, unsmiling, and raised her hand to her hair to check it. Her normally perfect finger waves were frizzy and limp, matted on one side of her head. Her lips were pale without the usual stain of bright red and her face was sallow and waxy. Dark shadows hung under her eyes. She pointed to one of the empty camp chairs set up at the back of the tent, surrounded by a ring of burned cigarette ends.

"You mind?"

January pulled her kimono tighter and sunk down into the chair. Ruby watched her cautiously and then quietly came over to the chair next to her, not sure of what to say. The two women sat together in silence, scuffing their heels in the dirt and staring aimlessly at the ground until finally Ruby spoke. Her voice was halting, timid.

"I tried to see you. I wanted to be there for you."

January threw back her head and sighed.

"I know. The girls told me."

Ruby chewed on the inside of her cheek and tapped her nails on the narrow arm of the chair.

"I mean, I am here for you. Anything. Whatever you need."

"I know."

Ruby picked at the wooden arm of the chair, trying to pry up a splinter.

"And I know you don't want to hear it right now, but I'm sorry about Tom. Really."

January loosened her kimono and then pulled it across her chest even tighter. She looked about as awkward as Ruby felt.

"I know that, too. Thanks. But I don't want to talk about it."

"Okay."

"That's all everyone wants to do, talk about it. Tell me what they think happened. He fell, he jumped, he was pushed. This reason, that reason. I don't care the reason. He's gone. He's dead. And talking about it won't bring him back and it won't make it better, so I don't want to."

Ruby nodded.

"Okay."

January looked down at her chewed nails. The paint was chipped and her cuticles were red and raw. She jerked her head up and caught Ruby staring at her hands. Ruby had never seen January without a manicure. Even in a carnival, where everything a person touched was covered in a layer of dust and dirt, January had always maintained the illusion of glamor. Her inability to keep the façade going was what hurt Ruby the most. If January couldn't, how could any of them? January finally shoved her hands between her knees and looked over at Ruby.

"At least Tom's death has been deemed an accident and everyone can lay off their theories. Pontilliar came to the wagon and told me himself. So I guess that lets Hayden off the hook."

"Hayden's not important here."

January shook her head.

"No, it's good. I mean, at least it wasn't a suicide like in Sulphur. And we don't got to worry about somebody having killed him. I can live with an accident. I can bear that. I don't think I could bear the others."

January stared down at her hands again and sighed loudly.

"And no one ever really thought Hayden had anything to do with it in the first place. I was looking out the window this morning and I saw you two walking together. You looked happy. I guess you worked things out."

Ruby realized that January needed this. To talk about something other than Tom, other than her own grief. Ruby dug out the splinter of wood and twisted it between her fingers.

"Yeah."

"You're not going to give me any details, are you?"

Ruby glanced up at January. She wasn't smiling, but there was just the tiniest hint of light behind her eyes. Ruby shook her head.

"Nope."

"Figures."

Silence fell between them again until January finally stood up and brushed off her kimono.

"Well, I should get out of here. Don't you got a show going on?"

"Jasper's calling for Electro for a couple sets. He's probably on his way back over now. You're not working, are you?"

January shook her head.

"No. Maybe after the next jump. I just want to get the hell away from this whole place, you know?"

January was looking over at the Ferris Wheel, blazing and spinning high above the tents. The rumors of Tom's death beneath it had quickly made their way into town, but it didn't stop the rubes. There was still a line coiling around the base of the Ferris

Wheel as the townsfolk waited to be taken up into the sky. January turned back to Ruby.

"By the way, Samuel's looking for you or something. He said he needs to talk to you."

Ruby stood up and groaned.

"I swear to God, that man is going to kill me."

"What's he want?"

Ruby grimaced and wiped her palm across her forehead, skinning away the sweat.

"I'm sure it's about the new geek. Samuel's got it in for him."

January frowned.

"Daniel?"

Ruby shook her head.

"Don't worry about it."

January narrowed her eyes and put her hands on her hips.

"I know what everyone is whispering. But it isn't true."

Ruby wished she had never said anything at all about the geek. She turned back to the snake tent.

"Don't worry about it, January."

"No, listen."

January snapped and Ruby was forced to turn around.

"I've got ears, you know. I may be sad, but I'm not stupid. I know what everyone is saying. That there was something going on between me and the new geek."

Ruby tried to interrupt, but January held out her hand to stop her.

"I talked to Daniel maybe three times. Said hello, being nice. That's it. Being decent. And next thing you know, I've got my skirt up. Because apparently that's what everyone thinks I do. Oh look, there goes January the floozy. Just talk to her once and she'll take you to bed."

"No one's saying that about you."

"Oh, yes, they are. No matter what you do, you can't catch a break in this place. I never once stepped out on Tom. Not once. Why is that so hard for people to believe?"

Ruby tried to reach for January, but she stepped away, angry tears burning in her eyes.

"And everyone that's talking about Daniel should just stuff it, too. I'm probably the only one who's even spoken to him. The only one who gave him a chance. And look where that got me."

January threw her arms out wide. There was an ugly smile on her face.

"God, this place. We're all a mess and yet everyone is judging everyone else. Gossiping behind their backs, thinking the worst. Everyone biting at everyone else's heels. Who needs to worry about tripping over a rope and getting a stake bite? We're hurting ourselves worse just by beating our gums. As if we don't have all the rubes on that side trying to gnaw away whatever pride we might try to carry, we've got to chew each other up and spit each other out for the dogs. What's wrong with us?"

Ruby knew January was hurting, but she was still shocked. She hadn't seen this side of her in a long time. January looked like she was going to continue, but when she saw Ruby's face, she just laughed. A haunting, hollow laugh. January shook her head, turned her back and walked away, and Ruby could only look after her, not knowing what to do. Then she heard the voices behind her, the crowd packing into the tent, shoulder to shoulder in the heat, waiting for Esmeralda the Enchantress to Tame the Serpents of the East! She heard Jasper calling for her, frustrated that she wasn't ready to go, but she didn't move. Ruby looked up at the Ferris Wheel, looming overhead, winking its brilliant lights against the sky, and felt nothing but emptiness.

Daniel sat at the table in his wagon and sullenly moved the pieces around. Of course, pieces was the wrong word, as was table. The only person who had been inside the geek wagon since Daniel had taken it over was Tom, and he knew what the drunkard had thought about the carved figures lined up like sentinels along the bench. Dolls. Toys. Statues for collecting along with those ridiculous Dresden figurines the Vanderbilts couldn't seem to get enough of. Daniel leaned forward and edged one of the Osud Zrcadla back onto its square. Fate Mirrors. Daniel had picked up the set on one of his journeys across the Carpathians. The table was a Deska Kosti, a Board of Bones, and it usually amused him. The figures, intricately carved into representations of men, women, priests and spirits, had chips of mirror affixed to their bottoms and could slide easily across the onyx and ivory surface of the table. The figures of the Thracian Rider and the Domovoy house spirit were Daniel's favorites. He had no idea what the Deska Kosti was supposed to be able to do or tell him, and he didn't care. Arranging the pieces in various patterns and groupings often helped him to think. He picked up a figure of a woman with her rosewood arms outstretched and her head flung back, mouth open wide in a howl. He rolled the figure back and forth between his palms and sighed.

He had wanted to leave. The carnival had no place for him; it was not the adventure he had thought it would be. But where would he go? What would he do? It was always the same, so much of the same. Daniel sighed. He tapped the figure on the rim of the table and then carefully set it down on a white square. Then he moved it to a black one. He rested his chin on his hand and cocked his head. No, back to the white one. Daniel closed his eyes, listening intently to the Chopin nocturne playing on the gramophone behind him, and tried to decide what to do.

The woman, Ruby, with the wild hair and fierce eyes and strange tattoos, was complicating things. He couldn't seem to stop thinking about her. She had no fear of him. It seemed she lacked fear for a great many things, what with her affronting stares and her cigarettes. Her absurd trousers. But it was more than simple brazenness. Nothing could shock Daniel, no, but he found her lack of trepidation unnerving. When he had looked at her, hard, she had not turned away, and yet, she had not been drawn into him. She had held her own, meeting him as some sort of equal, at least in her own mind. Who the hell did she think she was?

Daniel opened his eyes and rested his elbows on the table. His gaze roamed across the scattered figures and he began to knock the pieces down one by one, smiling to himself as the wood struck ivory with a pinging sound. He toppled all twelve pieces and then stared at the woman with the outstretched arms, the lone standing figure, still on the square of white. She was curious, this Ruby. And tempting. She could perhaps be more than a mere amusing diversion, as the other one had been. She could be a point of intrigue. This one had backbone and an uncanny appeal, as well as something else he couldn't quite put his finger on. Something rustling beneath the surface that he couldn't place, but couldn't turn away from either. He wanted to know more. Perhaps this was the first move in a new sort of game. Perhaps this could be fun.

The Chopin recording ended and Daniel's shoulders slumped. But perhaps not. After all, she was only a woman in a dirty little carnival. He couldn't expect to hope for too much. The silence in the wagon began to grate on Daniel's nerves and he quickly stood up. He needed to get out in the open, away from the close walls and the warm flicker of the candle. Daniel extinguished the wick with his bare fingers on the way to the door and then paused to look behind him. There was only one window on the side of the wagon and it let in a faint glow of moonlight. He could see the solitary Osud Zrcadla, still upright on the table with its back to him. He took a step forward, with his finger outstretched to topple it, but then caught himself and held his hands behind his back. He grinned in the darkness. He would leave the woman standing for now. He would see what her fate would bring her.

Ruby gripped the back of his head and pressed the knife to his throat. One slip and a line of blood would blossom beneath the blade. She snarled her fingers in his hair and leaned in close.

"Who are you?"

The man didn't even bother to raise his hands in defense.

"My name is Daniel Revont."

Ruby leaned in closer, her face only inches from his.

"Who are you?"

Daniel's black eyes were locked on hers, but there was no fear present in them. Neither was there outrage or even calculation. He wasn't trying to get away from her.

"The geek your father took on in Sulphur."

Ruby adjusted her grip on the knife. She pushed in even closer and spoke slowly, choking out each word from behind her gritted teeth. She was so close she could have bitten him. Or kissed him.

"Who the hell are you?"

"The man with a knife to his throat."

Ruby consider this for a moment. Considered his black eyes and pale skin in the moonlight. He didn't look the same without the customary smirk on his face. He looked vulnerable, but that might have been because of the knife. Still, he could have fought back, could have defended himself. He had come up behind her while she was sitting out in the field, legs drawn up to her chest, head tilted up toward the stars, and so she was holding him at an odd angle. He could have twisted, broken her hold, slipped out from under the knife, kicked her in the stomach. All of these scenarios were running through her head, but Daniel only stood there, his head pulled back awkwardly, his eyes wide and his hands limp at his sides. Ruby let him go.

"You shouldn't do that."

She pushed him back and he easily caught his balance. Now he raised his hands up to show her that he was unarmed. Ruby sheathed the small knife back into her boot.

"Don't ever do that. Sneak up on me like that. Next time, I might not be able to catch myself before I slit your throat."

Daniel smoothed down the front of his suit and then put his hands in his pockets. Ruby noticed that his jacket wasn't buttoned. It hung slightly open, a sliver of white showing through. He didn't fix it.

"You were in control. I trust you."

Ruby wiped her hands on the thighs of her trousers and turned away from him.

"What do you want, geek? What are you doing out here?"

Daniel came up to stand beside her. The night sky was resplendent over the field, the moon full and the stars dazzling. It was past two and the carnival was dark and asleep. The sky was wide open and clear. Inviting. Daniel looked upward.

"I couldn't sleep."

Ruby was closely watching his face. The curve of his cheekbones made sharp shadows across his lips and jaw. This was the first time she had been this close to him. She could see his eyelashes and noticed that they were long. He tilted his head slightly and glanced over at her.

"Forgive me, though, for startling you. It wasn't my intention."

He looked back up at the stars, his mouth turning down slightly.

"In case you hadn't noticed, I'm not always the best with

people. I don't always…"

Daniel paused and Ruby watched him swallow. She watched the skin against his high, tight collar contract. She had never seen him with the top button undone or his black silk tie loosened. She wondered if he felt as if he was choking all of the time. He continued.

"…I don't always understand other people. I don't know how to interact with other people in the proper way."

"What, is that an understatement?"

"It's an apology."

Ruby looked hard at him for a moment and then pulled her cigarettes out of her pocket. She put two between her lips and lit them both. When she handed the cigarette to Daniel, their fingers touched. Ruby blew out a stream of smoke and stepped away from him.

"Well, you know, people are crazy. Especially in this place."

She gestured over her shoulder back at the carnival.

"I mean, I think you've got to be to wind up in this joint."

Daniel smoked his cigarette and shook his head.

"Maybe. But that's not what I'm trying to say."

Ruby turned on him.

"Well, then what are you trying to say?"

Daniel looked down at his cigarette, turning it between his fingers.

"It's an apology to you."

Ruby closed her eyes and rubbed her forehead with the palm of her hand. The smoke trailed over her head.

"Look, mister. It's late. You're disrupting the one time of peace that I get out here. And let's just get to the point while we're at it."

Ruby opened her eyes and looked at him hard.

"I don't like you and I don't trust you. I don't know who you are, for real, and if you're not going to tell me at knife point, then I might as well pass that one up. So why don't you go ahead and tell me what you want. Stop speaking in riddles and be on your way."

Daniel looked as if he was about to hand his half-smoked cigarette back, but then raised it to his lips again. He looked away from her.

"I'm not speaking in riddles. I couldn't sleep. I was out here, just the same as you. I came out to see the stars, same as you. To look up and wonder."

"Don't presume to know what I'm doing out here."

Daniel bit his lip. He waited another moment before continuing.

"I saw you and wanted to apologize. See, everything I've been saying makes sense."

Ruby crossed her arms.

"Apologize for what?"

"For myself, I suppose. For making you uncomfortable with my presence in the carnival."

"You make everyone uncomfortable."

"Maybe."

Daniel threw his cigarette down into the long grass and stamped it out.

"But everyone else doesn't seem to care. It rolls right off of them. My being here bothers you in a deeper way. I see you watching me. You're angry and you're wary. I thought it had to do with me speaking to your friend. To January."

"You leave her out of this."

Daniel paused again. He put his hands back in his pockets and looked down at the ground.

"All right."

He took a step back, still not looking at her.

"But now I think it is simply me that disturbs you. And though I can't do anything to change that, to change how you see me or how I make you feel, I wanted to apologize. We've started off at such odds with each other, and I'd rather it wasn't that way."

Ruby took a last drag on her cigarette and pitched it into the grass. She watched it smoke for a moment and then die out. She laughed harshly.

"If I thought you were off your nuts before, well then."

"Well then."

They didn't look at one another. Finally, Daniel turned to leave. He was a few feet behind Ruby when he stopped and called back to her.

"You're not going to return the apology, for pulling a knife on me?"

Ruby turned around and met his eyes.

"No. I'm not."

"Good. I would expect no less from you."

Ruby raised an eyebrow, but didn't say anything. There was a disconcerting half-smile on Daniel's lips.

"And thank you for the cigarette. That was kind of you. Good night."

TWELVE

Daniel was waiting. He sat on a crate behind the Ten-In-One, one leg crossed over the other, and folded his hands in his lap. It was early afternoon and the sun was blazing in the hazy white sky, but Daniel was not sweating. His pale skin was as clear and cool as ever, though he did wish he had a pair of dark sunglasses like the kind he had bought and left back in New York. He had no magnesium flashbulbs to hide from, but he liked the sunglasses' expense. Their extravagance. And he liked to take them off at appropriate moments in conversations like the one he knew he was about to have. He liked to twirl them around in his long fingers. It was like smoking a cigarette. He couldn't feel the smoke in his lungs, couldn't feel any sort of nicotine rush, but he liked to have something in his hand. He liked to strike a match or flick a lighter; he liked the simple ritual of it. And it made people much more comfortable around him for some reason.

Daniel didn't have his sunglasses and he didn't have any cigarettes, so he simply clasped his hands and waited. He had made a decision after his last encounter with the woman in the night and now things needed to be set in motion. The midway would open soon and a few of the gamesmen and the rousties trudged past him on their way from the cookhouse. One man spat a wad of tobacco in Daniel's direction but, of course, it missed his gleaming shoes. Daniel didn't flinch. He looked at the man, a candy butcher, and winked. In a few hours, the man would leap back from the edge of the hot sugar cauldron with an angry red line burned into his forearm.

Finally, Daniel spotted the man he was waiting for, heading toward the midway with a sketchbook under one arm. Daniel didn't move. Hayden looked up from underneath the brim of his hat to glance at him and Daniel smiled. Hayden scowled and started to walk past him, but then slowed, stopped and turned around just as Daniel had known he would. Hayden eyed him for a moment and then came closer. Daniel had never spoken to this man before, had never had cause to, but he could tell that his presence was unnerving to Hayden. Good. Daniel continued to wait in silence, forcing Hayden to speak first.

"I thought you were leaving."

Daniel stood up and faced Hayden.

"Whoever told you that?"

"It's just what I heard last night. Some of the men talking, saying the geek was packing it in. Hayden, by the way."

Hayden tucked his sketchbook under his left arm and extended his hand. Daniel dipped his chin slightly and stared down at it. He didn't take it.

"Yes. I had thought to leave this place. It seemed as if there was nothing left for me here."

Hayden pulled his hand back and shook his head in disgust.

"Why am I not surprised? And now?"

"Now."

Daniel paused. He tilted his head and looked past Hayden's shoulder at the snake tent. He slowly brought his eyes back to Hayden.

"Now, I believe that I've discovered something I was looking for. Something unexpected, yes, but which might prove worth waiting around a bit."

"Plus, it would've looked pretty damn suspicious, you leaving out of the blue like that."

Daniel blinked.

"Do you think so?"

"I think anyone running off right now is going to look suspicious. Just because Tom's death has been declared an accident, doesn't make it true."

"And yet."

Daniel stepped closer to Hayden. He watched Hayden's light brown eyes shifting back and forth, trying to take in the measure of him. So foolish. So futile.

"You are leaving yourself, are you not?"

Hayden stepped back.

"What the hell?"

Daniel smiled and shrugged his shoulders.

"Just a thought. You leaving. I staying. It could make things interesting."

Hayden shook his head and tried to force a laugh, but Daniel could see the confusion in his eyes. It was a little added thrill he hadn't expected and it delighted him. Hayden stepped forward.

"Listen here, geek. I don't know you and even then, I don't like you. Personally, I think you're just as cracked in the head as everyone says you are. That and more."

"Cracked in the head?"

"Yeah, a looney. A nut job. If we weren't in a goddamn carnival, they'd probably lock you up. Maybe that's why you came here in the first place, I don't know. I swear, I'd forgotten how crazy everyone is in this place."

"Including your Ruby?"

Hayden leaned forward and grabbed for Daniel's shirt front. Daniel easily stepped out of reach.

"Struck a nerve there, did I?"

"You keep her name out of your mouth, you understand?"

Daniel cocked his head.

"Why?"

Hayden threw his sketchbook down on the crate and balled his fists. Two rousties who had been walking past them, giving them a wide berth, paused to watch.

"You aiming for a fight?"

Daniel looked Hayden in the eye. His voice was completely level.

"Not really, no."

"Then you stay away from me."

Daniel smiled.

"Oh, I don't think I'll have any trouble with that."

"And you stay away from Ruby."

Daniel grinned, showing his teeth

"That might prove a trifle more difficult."

Hayden pointed at him. His face was red.

"I mean it."

Daniel dipped his head slightly, still keeping his eyes on Hayden's. Such a fool. He needed nothing more than a little nudge. It was hardly even fair. Daniel put his hands in his pockets.

"Is that all, then?"

Hayden wiped his face and picked up his sketchbook.

"That's all. Just stay away, you hear?"

Hayden pushed past Daniel and headed toward the midway. The two rousties who had stopped to watch the potential fight shook their heads and continued on their way. Daniel just smiled and looked toward the snake show tent. It was so easy. So, so easy. It would happen exactly as he knew it would and now there would be one less thing to have to bother about. Ruby would be much more fun on her own. Daniel sighed and headed back to the geek wagon to find his cigarette case.

Ruby stopped dancing when Hayden burst through the drawn front flaps of the tent. The space was empty save for herself and the heavy black snake she had draped around her shoulders. The snake was new and though it wasn't venomous, she wasn't quite sure about its willingness to be paraded around the stage. She was also trying out a new routine to a different song, this one a little more modern. Esmeralda the Enchantress could listen to jazz music, too, couldn't she? She had been planning to ask Hayden for his opinion of the song, but she thought better of it when she saw the look on his face.

Hayden came across the tent to the edge of the stage and ripped the needle off the record. The silence in the tent suddenly became very loud and Ruby crouched down, being careful with the snake still around her shoulders. Hayden's eyes were wild.

"I have to talk to you. Now. Right now."

Ruby ran her hands over the snake's smooth skin and then lifted him over her neck.

"Hold on."

She stood up and ducked through the half-raised curtain to put the snake in its box. When she returned, Hayden was sitting on the edge of the stage with his back to her and Ruby sat down beside him. Hayden was staring down at his boots, almost as if he'd forgotten her. It was dim in the tent, but cool with only the one side flap open to let in the small breeze. Ruby's chest began to constrict and she wanted to take his hand, but didn't. Hayden finally turned to her and his voice was a little less frantic, a little more firm.

"We need to leave."

"What?"

Ruby stared at him, confused. She had been expecting to hear some terrible news. Another death. But this? Suddenly, Hayden leapt down from the edge of the stage and stood in front of her. He slid his hands up her hips and drew her in close to him. His face was bright, his eyes shining with a mix of determination and desperation.

"We're leaving. Tonight. We have to."

Ruby didn't know what to say. Her mouth opened, but she had no words. She didn't even know how to respond. Hayden gripped her tighter.

"Don't look at me like that, just listen."

Ruby's face had twisted into a question. A fearful one. She leaned away from him, but Hayden only pulled her closer.

"Things are crazy here. Crazy. The first geek hanging himself. And then Tom. And everyone thinking I had something to do with it."

Ruby frowned.

"No one thinks you killed Tom."

Hayden shook his head vigorously.

"That doesn't matter. That's not what I'm talking about. You're not listening to me!"

Ruby tried to pull away from him, but Hayden grabbed her tight. He was speaking so fast, she could barely understand him.

"Something's wrong here, can't you see it? The deaths. And then that crazy new geek, Daniel. Skulking around. Going after January the way he did. I can't make heads or tails of this place, but I know it's not right. This place is different now. The Star Light Miraculum is different than the Star Light Menagerie. It's all wrong now. Wrong. It has a cloud over it. Maybe you can't see it, maybe no one else can, but I can. We need to leave. We need to leave now. Now!"

Ruby's eyes widened.

"Hayden, what's going on?"

Hayden took a deep breath and for a moment the maniacal sheen disappeared from his eyes.

"The only reason I returned to the Star Light was for you."

Ruby bit her bottom lip and nodded.

"And I'm here. I'm right here."

Hayden shook his head. He let go of her and took a few steps back, throwing his hands in the air.

"No, you don't understand! You're not listening to me. The past is over. We have to only focus on the future."

"The future? You're not making any sense, Hayden. What's going on with you?"

Hayden tilted his head and took a step closer. Ruby almost braced herself against him. His eyes were wild again.

"What's going on with me? Aren't you hearing what I'm saying, Ruby? I'm saying I want to take you away from here. From the Star Light. From Pontilliar and Samuel and the rousties and the freaks. From the dirt and the dust and the tents. From the snake show. From that hell-sent geek. From it all."

Ruby started to speak, but Hayden held out his hand to stop her.

"No, stop questioning me. I'm serious. I can give you the life you deserve. Far away from here. You can forget this place and come away with me and never have to set foot in a carnival again."

Ruby slid off the edge of the stage.

"You want me to leave the Star Light with you?"

Hayden nodded emphatically.

"Yes! Finally, you're listening to me."

"And then what?"

"What do you mean?"

"And then what do we do? Where do we go? Where do we live?"

Ruby realized that Hayden couldn't see what was so obvious to her. She had thought, for a moment there, they were back in sync with one another. That they had come to a new understanding. And now this. Hayden threw his hands up in the air.

"We go anywhere you want! Anywhere at all. I can find work wherever we go. We can make it happen."

Ruby walked a few feet away from him and held out her arms. She was wearing part of one of her costumes. A thin, short dress that left her arms and legs bare. She spun around slowly and then lowered her arms.

"And me? What am I going to do? Go live in a town somewhere with you? Where I can never go anywhere without being covered up every inch, including a veil? Where I'll be ridiculed and mocked and asked on the street how much to take my clothes off so a man can see my tattoos. You ever stop and think about that for a second?"

Hayden shook his head.

"No. It won't be like that. I promise."

Ruby crossed her arms.

"Oh, it will. You can come and go between worlds, between the carnival and…"

Ruby gestured toward the tent opening.

"…whatever's out there. But I can't. And you know that. And now you get some harebrained idea that we're just going to go join the folks in the real world and live happily ever after? What the hell's gotten into you? I knew you had changed when you came back, but I didn't think you'd lost your mind."

"So you won't leave with me."

Ruby was taken aback. He wasn't seeing where she was coming from at all. Not even trying to. Hayden could be stubborn, but she had never known him to be selfish.

"No, I won't leave with you."

Hayden looked toward the tent opening and set his jaw.

"Fine. But I'm going without you. I have to leave this place. I want you to come with me, but if you can't, so be it."

Ruby spat at him like her words were poison.

"To hell with you."

Hayden shook his head.

"To hell with you, too, Ruby."

Hayden tipped his hat to her and then turned on his heel and marched out of the tent. Ruby didn't go after him. She turned around and kicked the stage as hard as she could with the heel of her sandal. He was infuriating. And obstinate. And now egotistical and stupid. She couldn't understand what had come over him, but it wasn't the first time they had fought. Nor would it be the last. Ruby wasn't worried; she knew he wouldn't leave her again.

THIRTEEN

Ruby sat at a table by herself and stared into her cold coffee. It was early, too early, and the sun was already beating down on her mercilessly. Most of the freaks had chosen to cash-in on their marginal performer status and had settled down to breakfast under the shade of the cookhouse tent, albeit at the edge. That left only the rousties and gamesmen out in the uncovered area, sweating into their eggs and bacon. And Ruby, of course. She flicked the ash off her cigarette, but kept her eyes on the full cup in front of her. She didn't want to look at anyone; she didn't want to talk to anyone. Everyone, it seemed, already knew.

Hayden had actually left. Sometime in the late afternoon of the day before, according to Franklin, and only hours after they had argued. Hayden hadn't stopped to think or reconsider. He hadn't taken time to cool down, walk it off. He hadn't come to her again, trying a different approach, offering a compromise, talking it through reasonably. He hadn't even said goodbye. Hayden had been so desperate to leave the Star Light that he'd let their fight be the last words between them. He had abandoned her again.

No one had said anything to her yet, but she could tell from the sideways glances that word had traveled fast and everyone was aware Hayden had left. She didn't think he would have spoken to anyone about why he was leaving, but secrets traveled like wildfire in a carnival. Ruby was ready for someone to come up to her and ask her about it, hoping to collect a choice piece of gossip. She had been through it all before. Ruby didn't want to talk about it, but she did want to bite someone's head off. Fortunately, she didn't have long to wait.

"I heard that Hayden left us sometime yesterday afternoon."

Samuel sat down in the chair across from Ruby and rested his hands in his lap. She flicked her cigarette and looked up at him.

"Really? You don't say. I wasn't sure I had noticed."

Samuel sighed. He started to reach across the table, but drew back.

"Ruby. I'm sorry. I know that I'm not very good at expressing…"

Samuel paused, trying to find the right word. He traced his thumbnail along a woodgrain vein in the top of the table. Ruby gave him no encouragement.

"…sentiments. But I wanted to tell you that I'm sorry."

Ruby crossed her legs and leaned back in her chair.

"Why? I thought you'd be glad. Throwing a party to celebrate by now."

Ruby stubbed her cigarette out on the table and pitched it into the dirt.

"And Jesus Christ, what is there to be sorry about? So Hayden left. He came back a week ago. And now he's left. A man fell off the Wheel a few days ago, but I guess that bit of news has lost its shine. Is everyone so tired of pitying January that now they're turning to me?"

"Ruby."

"And you know, maybe Hayden is the smart one around here. Getting out while he could. Before this place sucks him down into the muck again."

Samuel frowned.

"Is that how you see it?"

Ruby slung her arm over the back of her chair.

"How I see it is none of your business. But come to think of it, anyone who stays on here when they don't have to is a fool. And anyone who has the sense to get out, who's got something better going for them than this, should be applauded."

"You don't believe that."

Ruby jutted her chin out.

"Maybe I do."

The Electro-Man and one of his assistants, who were hurrying out from underneath the tent, slowed and looked over, questioning. Three of the rousties at the closest table turned and one grunted his agreement. Ruby had made sure her voice was loud enough for anyone in the surrounding area to hear. Samuel's expression had faded back into his usual mask of stoic practicality. He kept his voice low.

"Well, it's good to know you feel that way. And that you are undeterred by recent personal events. With that in mind, I have a favor to ask."

Ruby stood up and slung the full contents of her coffee cup to the ground.

"Nope, not interested. Whatever you need, whatever it is you want to know, find someone else."

"That's not exactly the attitude I was commending."

Ruby leaned one hand on the table and spoke very slowly.

"I don't care. Find someone else."

Ruby pushed away from the table and marched across the yard without looking back at Samuel. The tables had become silent and she knew everyone was watching her, but she didn't care. She kept her jaw clenched and her eyes straight ahead. Let them stare. Let them talk. It wasn't her job to fix problems or boost morale. It was her job to give a good Snake Charmer performance. That was all. She swung around the corner of the cookhouse tent and saw the geek coming through the line of wagons. Daniel stopped and bent his head slightly with his eyes fixed on her. He nodded once, slowly. The usual smug smile on his face had been replaced by an uncharacteristic look of concern. Not of pity, but of commiseration, perhaps. It was unnerving, and Ruby's eyes narrowed as they met his. Then, without knowing why exactly, she nodded back to him before disappearing among the tents.

Pontilliar's vision for Ruby had been as a Tattooed Lady. It was 1909 and though the Star Light had been doing well that year, he couldn't attract someone like Nora Hildebrandt or Irene Woodward, and he couldn't have afforded to pay for them anyway. The animals for the big top circus show were literally eating all his profits and Pontilliar had been racking up more than his fair share of debts. He had decided to call in on a debt of his own and had sent a telegram down to New Orleans. He had to wait six months for a reply, but it was worth it. Madame Celeste had agreed to take Ruby. Pontilliar had been thrilled; he would be rid of Ruby and her frustrating uselessness for a year and gain a new freak attraction for free. As soon as Ruby had assented, Pontilliar had her packed on a train heading west.

When Ruby arrived in New Orleans, she was sixteen with empty pockets and only one suitcase to her name. She waited at the train station for six hours until twilight began to set in and a dark-skinned man with jaundiced eyes approached her on the platform. She was to get into his wagon and he would take her to the Madame. When she asked how long the journey would take, his reply was only "bajou kase." About an hour outside of the city he handed her a long silk scarf. She spent the night sitting bolt upright and blindfolded on the buckboard seat next to the driver, clutching her Barlow knife in the folds of her skirt, as the mule wagon carried them west and then south, deeper and deeper into the bayou.

When the man finally helped Ruby down, she could feel the warmth of early daylight on her skin, but she still wasn't permitted to unwind the scarf from her eyes. She could hear birds trilling all around her, then a woodpecker hammering into a tree and a barred owl hooting in the distance. The man tied a rope around her wrist and started walking. She stumbled along behind him, tripping over stumpy cypress knees and splashing into thick, warm water that oozed into her shoes. She carried her suitcase in one hand and gripped the rope with the other until she began to hear the sounds of civilization. People's voices, roosters crowing, the thud of an axe hitting a plank of wood. The canopy of shading trees opened up and she could feel the sun beating down on her, suffocating.

When the man finally yanked her to a stop, Ruby knew that she was in some sort of town or village, and she could sense the crush of people crowding around her. The man had told her what he would do to her if she removed the blindfold on her own and so Ruby stood still, her legs and dress caked in drying muck, the suitcase handle in her fingers slippery with sweat, and wondered whether it was better to die with your eyes open or closed. She did not die that day, but she did meet Madame Celeste Fontaine Laveau, who would change the course of her life forever.

The inhabitants of the place Ruby came to know as Vilaj La Nan Pèdi A, or The Village of the Lost, said that Madame Celeste was over a hundred years old and the sister of Marie Laveau, the famed voodoun priestess from Bayou St. John and St. Ann Street. Some said she was Marie and Doctor John's daughter, known as the Widow Paris, and some said she was Marie herself. Regardless, they all called her Madame Celeste during the day and Manbo Celeste at night and during the ceremonies. Madame Celeste welcomed the mystery about her identity. She claimed to be a quarter white, a quarter African, a quarter Comanche and a quarter Maori, from the other side of the world. She was fine-boned with yellow eyes housing enormous dark irises. She wore a long, sweeping skirt and kept her glossy black hair underneath a blue, seven-pointed tignon. Like a few of the elders, her right arm and the right side of her neck were pocked with small circular and linear tattoos. Everyone in The Village was terrified of her and she ruled the hidden bayou settlement with absolute power.

Ruby's given name disappeared the moment she first stood before Madame Celeste in the center of The Village market. Madame Celeste had removed the blindfold and spat at Ruby's feet, laughing. The woman looked her up and down and pointed at Ruby's arms, neck and chest, festering with mosquito bites, some angry red and fresh, some already oozing and crusting over. Madame Celeste had taken Ruby by the shoulders, turned her this way and that, and stood back to laugh again. "You are nothing but a feast for the moustik." The old woman had then frowned. "But you are also nothing but a white woman lost. A ghost. You are Fet Wairua now. Like the story from the far island. That spirit did not survive. Maybe you will. Maybe you won't. It matters not to me." And so Ruby became Ghost Feast and took on a new life.

It didn't take long for Ruby to realize that Madame Celeste had no intention of turning her into a Tattooed Lady and sending her back to Pontilliar. At first she was kept in the garconniere of Madame Celeste's Acadian house and was not permitted to leave. She sat on a pallet in her attic room and sewed gris-gris bags for Madame Celeste to fill and sell when she journeyed north to New

Orleans in the winter. After two months of sewing in the dark with no complaints, Ruby was allowed to climb down the side stairs and run errands for Madame Celeste. The Village was larger than she had imagined and more spread out. The houses, mostly made of stripped logs and palmetto fronds, radiated out from the central market in a sort of spiral and were connected to one another by paths made of rough cypress planks pressed down into the mud. Only one straight street ran through the village, starting at Madame Celeste's front door and cutting directly through the market. It ended abruptly at the edge of the wild bayou, with no indication of where to go from there. Ruby delivered Johnny the Conqueror roots and collected alligator skin payments; she learned to select the best ropes of rattlesnake meat from the stalls at the edge of the market and to bargain shrewdly with the beads and packets of tinted powder Madame Celeste had sent her with. No one in The Village liked her, but she traveled safely because she was Madame Celeste's Wairua. Ruby kept her head down and her eyes open as she mapped out as much territory as she could. Exactly five months after she had first arrived, Ruby silently climbed down the stairs and fled.

Ruby had threaded her way through The Village in the darkness of the new moon and headed north. She had no idea where she was in relation to any other towns, or even to any roads, but she had decided that traveling north, away from the water, was her safest bet. She had taken only her knife, her mother's playbill and the clothes on her back as she disappeared into the thickets of arching cypress trees cloaked in Spanish moss. She had moved swiftly, trying to put as much distance as possible between herself and the scouts she knew would be out looking for her soon. Madame Celeste had warned her of what would happen if she tried to leave. She would become more than just a feast for mosquitos. Ruby could navigate mountain terrain in pitch darkness, but the bayou, with its quick mud and canals filled with glowing-eyed alligators, had been a different story. About two hours before sunrise, a bank of peat moss had given out beneath her and she had slid down into a dried-up canal bed. She had heard the snakes before she felt them, writhing and coiling over her trapped body, and Ruby had known it was the end. In the black confusion, she had felt the force of the bites and in a strange moment of lucidity, Ruby had realized that she was going to die as her mother had done. Ruby had felt a wave of comfort wash over her, and soon the world was gone.

FOURTEEN

Ruby could taste it in the air; something was wrong with the town. With the light, with the shadows, with the soil. With the subdued crowd that walked along the midway timidly, nervous to try the cotton candy and put a nickel on red and spin the chance wheel. Chandler had gone ahead as usual and set up the advance, greased the right palms and plastered playbills up and down Main Street, but still the turnout was weak. The Star Light had skipped around Napoleon the past five years due to rumors passed along the circuit that the town was fading away. It had once been a thriving logging town, home to two of the largest and most prosperous sawmills in Mississippi, but the coming of the railroad had changed everything. The logs didn't need to roll down the Pearl River to the Gulf when they could ride safely in shipping cars along the iron rails of the newly laid Southern Railroad Line. The tracks bypassed Napoleon by too many miles and its habitants had slowly crept away to the new rail towns springing up across the bottom of the state. It was a testament to Pontilliar's determination to turn a buck that the Star Light was now set up in the shadow of the abandoned Western Pearl Sawmill.

The morning after the first quiet, unsettling night in Napoleon, January approached Ruby on the midway. One of the gamesmen, Gig, and his wife, Linda, had come up with a new game for their booth and were testing it out before the gates opened. They had built a circular trough in front of their stand and filled it with water and small wooden fish that floated on the surface of the continuous current. The object of the game was to use a short cane pole and line to loop one of the fish, each of which had a number painted on the bottom. The number corresponded to the prizes arranged on the back shelves of the booth. Linda and Gig were arguing over the logistics of the game, the speed of the water, the length of the line, and Ruby had wandered over to see the new game before the townsfolk arrived. She was bent over the metal rim of the trough, trailing her fingers in the water absentmindedly, when January appeared next to her and snatched up one of the brightly colored fish. She looked over at Ruby coyly.

"So, are you coming tonight?"

Ruby stood up and shook the water from her hand. January was dusted with powder and made up with lipstick and rouge, even though the Girl Revue wouldn't begin its first show until late afternoon at the earliest. Underneath the thick makeup, January's face was blotchy and puffy. Ruby tried not to notice.

"What's tonight?"

January dropped the fish back in the water and sighed.

"How do you not know what goes on around here? You used to be on top of everything. This town is a dump."

"Well, I know that."

January picked up another fish floating by and flipped it over. Number seven.

"Lucky me."

Ruby took the fish from her and plunked it back in the water.

"What's going on tonight?"

January's hair was pinned tightly to make finger waves and she felt along the back of her head, checking for loose strands.

"I mean it, this stop's a real blue one. Napoleon is like a ghost's haunt. We had to call off the final show last night because there weren't more than three guys in the tip at a time and even when we could get them inside the tent, none of them were willing to pay the extra dime for the blow-off. I mean, what kind of town is this where the men don't want to watch a girl dance the cootch?"

Ruby nodded, her eyes on the fish bobbing along.

"We're only here because no other show will come through. Pontilliar thought we could make it because these folks haven't seen a carnival in years. But you're right, there's something off about this place. It's more than just the sawmills closing down and folks moving away to Picayune and Santa Rosa. There's something odd about the marks who are still here. They're walking around in a trance. It's as if all of the life has been sucked from the land and the people. Even the air."

"It's like everyone here is afraid to have fun. Or maybe they just don't know how. Normally, I'd be mad about having to go dark, but at this rate, who cares? It's not like I'm missing out on any big daddy spenders."

Ruby looked up, startled.

"Going dark?"

January groaned.

"Where have you been? Yes, we're going dark tonight. On a Monday, for Christ's sake. Last call for the gates is at six. Six! I'm only going to get one show in, if that. You'd think we could just run a Sunday school show and keep everything else going, but Pontilliar's come head to head with yet another preacher. Some sort of revivalist. Damn sky grifter."

January put her hands on her hips.

"What's wrong with you? How do I know this and you don't?"

Ruby looked away, down the mostly empty midway. A few of the gamesmen were arranging chalkware figurines and boxes of Cracker Jack on the shelves of their booths. McCleary was tossing coins at the rack of his own pitch game to kill time and Willie was just beginning to heat up the cotton candy cauldron. Ruby ran her hands through her loose hair and coiled the length of it around her wrist. Willie sneered at her and she closed her eyes and pursed her lips in frustration. What was wrong with her? Since they had pulled out of Baton Rouge two nights ago, with still no sign of Hayden, she'd been walking around as if in a dream. A nightmare. Where nothing made sense and the people around her were shadows, alternately chasing her and drifting away. Samuel had tried to talk to her yet again about Daniel and she barely remembered the conversation. She did remember slamming the door in his face and then collapsing behind it while she banged her fists against the floor of her wagon. How could Samuel not understand? Pontilliar, too, had tried to discuss carnival business with her, as if everything was still the same. He'd tried to complain to her about the laziness of the rousties and the wastefulness of Jimbo in his cooking. She had simply turned and walked away from him, leaving him spitting and red-faced outside his wagon. At least everyone was too embarrassed for her to try broaching the subject of Hayden in her company. There were still whispers of his possible involvement in Tom's death, but for the most part that thinking had died down. Ruby was grateful for that and grateful no one wanted to talk to her about Hayden. But she was also alone.

January splashed her hand in the water to get Ruby's attention.

"Hey! So now you know we're dropping the awnings early tonight. Does that mean yes or no that you're coming?"

Ruby opened her eyes and swallowed the bitterness rising up in her throat like bile. She knew January was doing her a favor, trying to keep her from sinking down into the mire. Ruby forced herself to smile.

"You just love doing this, don't you?"

January cocked her head and batted her eyelashes.

"It's not every day that I know a secret about the Star Light and you don't. I might as well savor the moment. Hell, maybe Samuel will start wanting to have special conferences with me now."

Ruby groaned.

"Please, I hope so. Anything to get him off my back. You can take Pontilliar, too, while you're at it."

January rolled her eyes.

"Never."

Ruby waited for January to continue, but January just smirked at her. Ruby finally threw her hands up in the air.

"Fine. For the love of God, I'll bite. Will you please tell me what is happening tonight?"

January looked over her shoulder and then leaned in close, her voice a whisper.

"We're going into town tonight. To the picture show. And you got to come."

Ruby frowned and stepped back. She had never seen a full-length motion picture. The closest she'd come was sneaking into a nickelodeon show when she was thirteen. Ruby started to shake her head, but January held out her hands and stopped her.

"Don't. I know what you're going to say. But you got to. We're going dark because the whole town of Napoleon is heading off to some big camp revival over in Gallsville. I heard Franklin tell one of the rousties that Pontilliar had given in and agreed to shut us down tonight so there'd be no competition. No chance of the marks coming down here and enjoying a ride and a show when they could be rolling around on the ground, praising Jesus and barking like dogs. So you see? Everyone in town will be gone, hopping and hollering for the Lord, and no one's going to be watching *Robin*

Hood at The Rainbow. And if there are rubes at the theater, who cares? We're going to take it over tonight."

Ruby looked down at the ground and shook her head.

"We?"

January grabbed Ruby's arm and her eyes lit up.

"Well, not everyone. Only the folks I'm asking to come. Half the Ten-in-One has already said they're game. We're going to get all dolled up, make a real night of it. It'll be fun."

It was the first time Ruby had seen January excited, or even happy, since Tom had died. Still. Going into town? Going out into the real world?

"I don't know."

January crossed her arms over her chest.

"Come on, if Marjorie can haul all four hundred pounds of herself down there, then you can, too. No veils, no covering up. Glad rags only. Just going into town to see a show. Like ordinary folk."

"So we're going to be ordinary?"

January put her hands on her hips again and held her head up high.

"We're going to be extraordinary."

Ruby shook her head and laughed. She was surprised at how good it felt.

"All right, all right. What the hell."

"Perfect."

January smiled. It was worth agreeing just to see her smile again. To realize there was a chance of them both making it through the darkness and coming out on the other side. Ruby turned back to the trough of fish and January turned to leave, but then stopped. She had a mischievous look on her face that suddenly reminded Ruby of a different January. The January before Tom had died, before Tom had even come to the carnival in the first place. Ruby raised her eyebrows in question.

"There something else?"

January gave Ruby a sly, knowing look.

"Daniel's already said he's coming. Said he's looking forward to it. I just thought you might want to know."

January winked and whirled around to leave, but Ruby reached out and caught her arm.

"Why would I want to know?"

January shrugged.

"Oh, you know. Fish in the sea."

January twisted out of Ruby's grasp and turned her back, sauntering slowly away. Ruby's face clouded over and she slapped her hand down in the water hard enough for Gig and Linda to stop arguing and look over. Ruby didn't apologize.

January had been right. Everyone was coming. Or rather, everyone who had been invited. Apparently, January had made a point of asking the freaks and performers to come and of leaving the rousties and the gamesmen out. January had only commented that the men could go into town anytime they wanted for a blow-out, and that was true. But Ruby also knew January was looking to make an impression. She wanted to be reckless, to break the rules and shock any marks they came across, as well as Pontilliar. Her attitude was contagious and the large group, twenty-one souls in all, couldn't help but become infected with January's adventurous spirit.

There was a festive air to the group as they began to walk along the muddy, curving road toward town. A sense of topsy-turvy fun. The girls looped arms around one another and a jar of 'shine was passed from hand-to-hand as they all tried to get at least tipsy before showing up at The Rainbow Theater. Bernard had donned a tuxedo jacket and top hat. The gloves he wore were white with gold buttons and not as durable as the leather ones he used as shoes every day, but he did look dashing. Timothy had a length of gold satin wrapped around his gigantic cowboy hat and Josephine did not wear a veil to conceal her beard, but rather a gigantic bonnet crested with ostrich plumes and a tight-fighting dress of bright pink organza. Only Daniel, hanging in the back, wore his usual black suit. January had been disappointed with his appearance and had slipped a white fabric rose through his buttonhole and draped a white silk scarf around his neck. He had begrudgingly let her.

At first, Ruby had been unsure about the dress. When she'd returned to her wagon after the final show, a package wrapped in brown paper had been waiting for her. An attached note, scrawled in January's childish handwriting, proclaimed "No Excuses" and Ruby had wondered what the hell she'd gotten herself into as she ripped open the paper. The dress was a dark gray sheath, cut high in front, low in the back, and falling just below the knees. When Ruby held the material up to the window, the fading light made it shimmer. Ruby had never worn anything like it and she wasn't sure she wanted to. Underneath the folded dress were a pair of heeled shoes with silver straps. Ruby had held those shoes in her hands and known there was no getting out of it. She had left the dark kohl on her eyes from the snake show and loosely pinned up her hair. Ruby had felt awkward and self-conscious when she joined the group meeting in secret behind the cargo trucks, but January had beamed her approval and Ruby supposed that was all that mattered. It was worth it to see January smiling, flitting from one person to another, straightening ties and smoothing down fringe, just as she would have a year before.

They had almost reached the pavement of Main Street when Daniel quietly came up to walk beside her. Ruby had done her best to avoid him as the group had whooped and sashayed toward the town. Like her, he was more reserved than the rest. He drank when the jar came his way and he had skipped a few paces with Alicia when she'd tackled him and thrown her scaly arm around his shoulders, but mostly he was quiet, only watching, with a strange curl at the corner of his lips. Ruby stiffened when he appeared beside her, but then thought about the knife and the darkness and let her shoulders drop and her body relax. They walked together in silence for a moment before he turned his head slightly toward her.

"Hello."

Ruby didn't look at him.

"Hello."

"You look…"

Daniel paused and glanced down at the road. The evening had grown into late twilight as they had walked, but his shoes still glinted in the half-light.

"…different."

Ruby turned to him and raised her eyebrows. She could feel the warm night air on her back and legs. She suddenly realized Daniel had never seen so much of her skin. She quickly looked away from him, keeping her eyes on the road. The first lamp marking the beginning of Main Street was only a hundred yards away. Ruby couldn't see anyone on the street.

"Different? Is that some sort of veiled attempt at a compliment?"

"An attempt, yes. Do you mind if I walk alongside you?"

"Suit yourself."

Their shoes clicked when they hit the paved road. Behind them, Timothy and Marjorie had broken out into an off-key rendition of "The Little Red School House." Ruby could feel Daniel's eyes on her.

"It's been three months, at least, since I've seen a film. It was something with Buster Keaton, a short one. I wish I could remember the name of it. I love going to the pictures."

Ruby nodded, keeping her eyes ahead.

"It's been a while for me. When I was a kid, I saw that one

about the men taking a ship up to the moon. It was so strange and beautiful. Like a dream."

Daniel's eyes lit up and he clasped his hands together.

"*Le Voyage dans la Lune! A Trip to the Moon*. It's my favorite."

Ruby turned to Daniel and tried to contain her smile.

"Really? The ship hits the man in the moon when it lands and the moon makes an awful face. I remember that part."

They were now walking down the middle of Main Street and the group had become more subdued. The shops that weren't already boarded up were closed and the sidewalks deserted. A restaurant on the corner was open, but there didn't appear to be anyone sitting at the tables alongside the window. It was, as January had said, a ghost town. Ruby could see the sign for The Rainbow Theater up ahead, lit up in colored lights against the blue-black sky. Daniel moved closer to her and she could see that his pale cheeks were slightly flushed.

"*A Trip to the Moon* is beautiful, yes, but Melies made so many excellent films. The Cinemagician they called him."

"Now that's a title."

"So much of his work seems impossible to find in this country. *Under the Seas. The Conquest of the Pole*. You should really see that one. With the snow giant. It's quite fantastic."

Daniel turned to her with his eyes bright and flashing. For a moment, she thought he was going to touch her arm in his excitement and she looked at his long, white fingers sailing through the air as he gestured. She suddenly realized how beautiful his hands were. Immediately, she pushed the thought from her mind and turned back to the road, grappling for something to say.

"So, you've been outside of America?"

"Oh, yes!"

Daniel flung his arms out to the side.

"I have traveled all over the world. Everywhere. Mountains, deserts, I've sailed on the high seas. I love the big cities the most, though, I must admit. Those that are filled with people and music, art and ideas. New inventions. Progress, moving ever forward. The hallowed grounds of the future. Cities so vast, thronged with people from so many cultures, that judgement has no place and even those such as myself can fit in without incurring a second glance."

"Those such as yourself?"

Daniel lowered his eyes to the ground and hesitated before answering.

"Those that are not always understood. Who may not always find themselves welcome in average company. Perhaps you know."

Ruby pursed her lips and nodded.

"I know."

Daniel stood up straighter and smiled at her.

"Who knows? Perhaps one day I'll take you with me. We can find the films of Melies still playing somewhere in France and I can show them to you."

Daniel's eyes were no longer as bright, but had taken on a strange gleam. There seemed to be a sadness there, a curious longing, and Ruby's face went hot with confusion. She quickly looked away and was relieved when January suddenly came up between them and threw her arms around them both. The group had grown even quieter and more compact. They passed a drugstore and Ruby could see a man standing behind the counter, next to the soda fountain. He was wiping out an ice cream dish and shaking his head in either disbelief or disgust. Ruby could smell the liquor on January's breath as she laughed.

"What are you two jabbering on about?"

Daniel shrugged his shoulders. Ruby couldn't help but notice that he seemed uncomfortable with January touching him.

"Daniel was just telling me about big cities. Places to visit one day."

January turned to Daniel.

"How about Atlanta? Biggest city in the South, they say. I went there once with my folks, but that was when I was just a kid. They say now it's one of the most modern places in America. All lit up like a Christmas tree and almost as fine as your New York City. Have you ever been?"

Daniel shook his head, but then leaned forward and winked at Ruby.

"No, I've never been. Though I suppose I'll have to go now."

January nodded emphatically.

"Oh, you really should. In the last issue of *Photoplay*, they had a whole piece on Atlanta on account of Gloria Swanson possibly buying a house there. Could you imagine? They called it the City of the Future or something like that."

They were less than a block away from The Rainbow Theater and January dropped her voice. Ruby felt January's nails digging into her shoulder.

"Now listen. We're going in there, no matter what. They can't refuse our money. They can't refuse to let us in."

Ruby was sure they could, but didn't say anything. Daniel shrugged out from underneath January's arm and smiled at her.

"If they give us any trouble, let me handle it."

"What are you going to do? Bite their heads off?"

January laughed at her own joke, but then grew silent as they approached the ticket window of the theater. The entire group had grown tense, their revelry now subdued into anxiety. Ruby realized that everyone was expecting to be turned away. To be laughed at and told to go back to the circus show. To get back in their cages and back on stage. Even January. Ruby knew how many times January had gone into a shop, dressed and acting respectable, and was met with nothing but leers and jeers. The never-ending question of "how much?"

Still, as the group bunched around the ticket window, January tossed her head back with confidence and peered at the startled cashier on the other side of the glass. Ruby held her breath as January spoke.

"*Robin Hood*. The nine o'clock showing."

The man seemed to twitch behind the window as he sat up straight. He wore a maroon bow tie and his thin gray hair was parted down the middle and plastered on either side of his head with too much pomade. He clearly hadn't been expecting anyone to arrive at the theater that night. He looked at the crowd hanging back behind January and combed his nail-bitten fingers down through his bristling mustache.

"I don't think we're showing that one tonight."

January took a step back and looked up at the marquee, bright beneath the electric Rainbow sign. She put her hands on her hips.

"Looks like you are. Sign says so, anyway. *Robin Hood* with Douglas Fairbanks and Enid Bennett. Nine o'clock."

The cashier narrowed his eyes. He let his gaze roam across the faces of the Giant and the Bearded Lady. The Alligator Lady and Zero the Clown. And Ruby. When his gaze returned to January, leaning against the counter, he was scowling.

"Listen, lady. I don't want no trouble. But I don't think you want to be here tonight."

Daniel stepped forward and rested his elbows on the counter. He clasped his hands and met the cashier's gaze directly.

"Yes. We do."

January stepped back slightly. She looked over her shoulder with concern at Ruby and Ruby shook her head warily. The man scratched his mustache and looked down at the empty counter in front of him, as if searching for a piece of paper that might indicate something different. He spoke slowly.

"You know, with that revival going on and all, I don't think I'm even supposed to be open tonight."

Daniel didn't flinch. His voice was deep and steady.

"Yes. You are."

The cashier looked up at Daniel and suddenly seemed nervous. He began to stutter something, but Daniel leaned closer to the glass.

"Now, it is almost nine o'clock. You are going to sell every one of us a ticket. And then you are going to let us into the theater. And you are going to sell us popcorn and Coca-Colas if we want them. And you are going to go up into your little projection booth and you are going to put *Robin Hood* with Douglas Fairbanks and Enid Bennett on the film reel and we are going to watch it."

The cashier looked back down at the counter and nodded quickly. Daniel reached into his pocket and pulled out a dollar bill. He passed it through the window to the man.

"Three. Myself and these two ladies."

Daniel gestured back at Ruby and January. Ruby started to protest, but January pinched her and whispered.

"Just enjoy it, for God's sake."

Ruby looked at January, confused, but January only tilted her head and widened her eyes, giving her a knowing look. Daniel collected his change and turned around. He held out both his arms for them to take, but he was looking only at Ruby.

"Shall we?"

FIFTEEN

The Rainbow Theater was not much of a picture palace. The popcorn was stale and cold, the seats reeked from years of sweaty mill workers and the man who usually played the Mighty Wurlitzer was busy giving his soul up to God at the revival. Still, it was one of the best times the performers and freaks from the Star Light had ever had. Zero and Marco took control of the theater organ so the film had some sort of soundtrack. Linus began reading the intertitles out loud and soon Bernard took on the role of King Richard, making up the dialogue as he went along. Soon everyone took parts with Zena as Lady Marian, Timothy as the Earl of Huntington and Josephine as the evil Prince John. As the story progressed and the moonshine jar rolled empty along the floor, the performance became more raucous with most of the audience standing on their seats to act out their parts. Timothy soon began leaping from chair to chair, mimicking Robin Hood's acrobatic feats on the castle turrets and Josephine rose to the challenge of battling him wall to wall across the theater with her invisible sword. Ruby, content with her role as Will Scarlet, one of Robin Hood's Merry Men, had never seen anything like it.

Near the end of the film, when endless pageantry takes over the swashbuckling scenes, the group began to quiet down. There was less shouting and more conversation. Popcorn was still being thrown at the screen, but now it was cutting through a heavy cloud of cigarette smoke. During their antics, and being the only occupants, the group had spread out across the theater. Ruby was now sitting in the back corner with empty seats all around her. She stretched her arms out on the wooden armrests, leaned her head back against the seat and closed her eyes, enjoying the warm glow spreading across her body from the moonshine.

The seat next to her creaked as someone sat down beside her and Ruby's eyes snapped open. It was Daniel, but he wasn't looking at her, didn't even seem to notice her. His eyes were trained on the screen before him, his mouth slightly open in rapt attention. Ruby didn't move. She watched the side of his face, but it didn't seem as if he was going to turn to her and Ruby hesitantly closed her eyes again. She could hear Daniel breathing next to her and she could smell him. He smelled like cedar. She heard the rustle of his suit as he shifted in the seat and then she felt it. Very light at first, but then with a warm pressure, she felt Daniel's hand on hers.

Ruby didn't open her eyes. Daniel moved his fingers ever so slightly so they curled under hers. She heard him shift and then she felt his suit jacket grazing her bare shoulder as he moved to lean against her. There was timidity in the way he guarded his movements, but also a certain boldness. Daniel had come to her, though she wasn't even sure she had wanted him to. He was reaching for her in a quiet, assured way that was completely foreign to Ruby and both troubled and excited her. She was afraid that if she moved toward him herself, or even opened her eyes, the spell would be broken and the moment would disappear. She didn't know if she wanted this or not, but she didn't want it to end.

But then the theater was filled with clapping and cheering and Ruby knew the film was over. She heard the seat next to her creak again and when she opened her eyes, she was alone. She stood up, clapping along with everyone else as the lights came on, and searched the theater for Daniel. He was walking toward the exit with his shoulders hunched and his hands deep in his pockets. Ruby watched his back as he ignored the calls of January and Alicia and quietly slipped through the door.

Daniel stood underneath the streetlamp and waited. He watched The Rainbow Theater slowly empty as the freaks and performers spilled out onto the sidewalk, arguing loudly about the film and reliving their own swordfights. Daniel pulled the silver case from his jacket pocket and lit a cigarette. He snapped the arm on the lighter down, extinguishing the flame, and pocketed it. Daniel knew that if he stood in the pool of light just so, eliciting both mystery and vulnerability, she would come to him. Of course she would. He smoked his cigarette and watched Ruby leave the theater, nodding at something Zero was saying to her. The clown was miming drawing back a bow and arrow, and Daniel could see that Ruby's lips weren't moving, but she was smiling slightly while scanning the sidewalk. January had turned around and was waving her forward impatiently, but Daniel knew Ruby was looking for him. He watched Ruby glance over her shoulder and when his eyes met hers, he gave her his most brooding look. Then she was telling January she'd catch up in just a second and January was looking in his direction and smiling her coy, coquettish smile and Ruby was walking alone across the street to meet him. Bingo.

Daniel took out his case and offered Ruby a cigarette. She shook her head and he snapped the case shut with a loud click. He smiled at her.

"So, what did you think?"

He watched her eyes. She was looking everywhere but at him.

"Of *Robin Hood*? I liked it. I read the story in a book somewhere once. And, of course, the performance in the theater was better than any picture show."

"Of course."

She glanced down the street. Two men had come out of the diner and were watching the group pass. They were shaking their heads and one pointed at the Half-Man with disgust.

"We're going to hear it tomorrow, though."

"From who?"

Ruby shrugged.

"Samuel. Pontilliar. For coming out here like this. Causing a disturbance in the town and giving it away for free. I'm sure that'll be Pontilliar's biggest worry. That he lost a buck because someone saw us without paying first."

Daniel took a small step closer to her.

"You don't have much regard for Pontilliar, do you?"

He watched Ruby scuffing the heel of her shoe against the edge of the sidewalk. She kept looking down, away from him, but there was a smirk on her lips.

"Is it that obvious?"

"Even though he's your father. And your employer. Why?"

She shook her head.

"It could take a lifetime to explain. And even then, I'd rather not."

Daniel didn't reply and they stood in silence beneath the streetlamp while he smoked. Daniel decided it was time. She was here now and he needed to do this. He needed to know for sure that what he had felt when she had held the blade to his throat, and just now in the theater, when he had taken her hand, was real. He had to be certain. For the first time that he could remember, Daniel was unsure of trusting himself. His voice cracked.

"Who are you?"

She finally looked up at him. There was something audacious in her eyes. Defiant. Even dangerous. Daniel frowned, finding himself on unfamiliar ground. Ruby tilted her head slightly.

"I thought that was my question to ask."

Her eyes were still on him, still blazing in an almost preternatural way. Challenging him. He couldn't understand it.

"I don't know what to make of you."

It was the first truly honest thing he had said out loud in a while and it felt strange. Like a scratching at the back of his throat. Or deep in his chest somewhere. Like a cough that wouldn't come out. He let his eyes drift down to her lips. She was halfway smiling now.

"Do you have to know?"

Daniel brought the cigarette up to his lips.

"No. I suppose not."

He reached for her.

"Ruby."

Daniel took both of her hands in his. He ran his thumbs down the back of her hands, along the bones, and then gently turned her palms upward. Her skin was warm. He traced his thumbs along the lines in her palms. The sun line, the heart line, the fate line. He slowly raised his eyes, let them rest first on her slightly parted lips and then on her eyes, wide and shining in the streetlamp glow. He waited a moment and then jabbed his thumbs into her palms as hard as he could.

They both gasped at the same time and Ruby tried to snatch her hands away from him. He held fast and pressed deeper, searching harder. When she struggled again, he quickly released her and dropped his arms at his sides.

"What the hell? What's wrong with you?"

Ruby held her hands up to her chest protectively as Daniel slowly took the cigarette from his lips and dropped it on the pavement.

"I'm sorry."

Ruby stepped away from him and rubbed her palms together. Her face was livid.

"You're sorry? What are you, crazy? Are you trying to crucify me or something?"

Daniel shook his head. He needed time to think and didn't have the energy to be charming.

"No. It wasn't my intention to hurt you."

He looked down Main Street at the group, now several blocks away from them.

"We should go."

Ruby crossed her arms in front of her chest.

"Seriously? You're not even going to try to explain yourself?"

Daniel bit his lip and dipped his chin.

"I will. I promise. It's all too much right now. You. You're too much right now."

He walked past her, not letting himself look up at her eyes. He waited until he was a few feet away and then stopped. She was still behind him, unmoving. He raised his head and called back to her.

"And, Ruby…"

He looked over his shoulder to see that she had done the same. He gave her a small, dejected smile.

"…you really do look beautiful tonight."

Madame Celeste never explained to Ruby how she had been found and how she had survived falling into a nest of cottonmouths.

When she woke, it had been in a proper bedroom in the back of Madame Celeste's house, and once Ruby was coherent enough to drink some five finger tea, Madame Celeste had put it to her plainly. No more chicanery, no more servitude and no punishment for running away. She would tattoo Ruby as asked, temple to ankle, and send her back to New Orleans when her body was complete. Madame Celeste had taken Ruby's hands and performed the binding ritual, giving her a new name as well: Vwayaje Wairua. Ghost Traveler. Madame Celeste had refused to explain, however, what had made her change her mind and uphold her agreement with Pontilliar. She had said only that the sky had told her she must. Madame Celeste had waited until Ruby's snakebites had healed and then began the ordeal.

Ruby spent the next two and a half years in Madame Celeste's house, plucking chickens, grinding roots, molding conjure balls and laying under the tap-tapping of the Uhi chisel and mallet grinding ink into her skin. She asked about the strange designs accumulating across her body, but was met only with silence and the occasional bizarre tale of spirits and monsters that came to her through the pain like a fever dream. At times, while she lay dazed and sweating on the rough cypress floor, she was sure she saw shadows crouching all around Madame Celeste as she worked. Once, as the hours of dull pain dragged on, she saw Rohe, wife of Maui, the trickster god from the far islands, and half-goddess of death. When she had later explained to Madame Celeste how Rohe had come to her with a bird on her hand and touched Ruby's forehead, the old woman had thrashed her across the face. Ruby could listen to the stories of the gods from across both oceans, but she could not dare pretend that the Iwa would ever visit her.

Even though Ruby was no longer considered a slave in The Village, she was still not allowed to take part in any of the numerous festivals and ceremonies held throughout the year. Whenever a Night Fire took place, whether its cause was for celebrating a manje, warding off bakas spirits or calling to the lemo from the grave,

Ruby was barred inside Madame Celeste's house and guarded by Hetako, her mute servant. No matter that she had cheated death and was undergoing a transformation. She was not one of the Pedi Moun Ki. She was still an outsider. She was still a ghost.

At times, though, she was just a young woman, growing up with the other children of The Village. She quickly picked up their language, a unique amalgamation of English, Creole and Maori, though she was often chided for her pitiful accent. She understood it was taboo for her to wear a skirt when she was unmarried and she sewed herself a pair of wide, loose trousers as the other women her age wore. She learned to play Boul Gayan and that she could run faster after the ball if she went barefoot, with her toes digging into the mud. She braided white spider lilies into her hair and wore turtle shell bangles on her arms and attracted the attentions of a few of the eligible Mohoao, even though it was forbidden. At the start of her third summer in The Village, she found herself to be happy.

Ruby had not been prepared, then, to be dismissed by Madame Celeste. She had just turned nineteen when the last tattoo, in the center of her chest, had healed and she was told that it was time for her to go. Ruby argued with Madame Celeste, but the old woman had been adamant. It didn't matter that Ruby had spent more time in The Village than she had with the Star Light; she had to leave. Madame Celeste didn't even care if Ruby returned to Pontilliar or not. But she could no longer stay in The Village and she would never be allowed to come back. Everyone had a place in life, Madame Celeste had told her, and Ruby's place was not in the bayou. She had an Iku'anga to fulfill. Her charge would be to create a Toenga Lespri in the world. Ruby didn't understand and she didn't care about the world outside of The Village, but she had no choice. Madame Celeste herself had tied the blindfold around Ruby's eyes and guided her back through the swamp until they reached the road and the waiting mule wagon. Ruby's time as a Wairua was over.

SIXTEEN

Ruby leaned against one of the tent poles and pushed her sleeves up higher. Even though it was just past midnight, it was still sweltering, and it was even hotter in the geek tent. She had unbuttoned her shirt an extra button and pinned her hair, still coiled into braids, high up on her head to keep her neck cool. She watched Daniel, slowly and methodically folding and putting the chairs in the pit away. He was wearing his suit, of course, but Ruby could see that he wasn't sweating. She watched him work, waiting for him to acknowledge her. Finally, he stood up straight and nodded.

"I'm glad to see I haven't run you off for good."

Ruby didn't know whether to be angry with Daniel, or to pity him. Or something else entirely. She arched an eyebrow.

"Not yet, anyhow. Though I think it's fair to say that you owe me an explanation."

Ruby held out her hands to him. In the center of each palm was a thin, red crescent. Daniel looked at her hands, but said nothing. His mouth was drawn tight and his eyes were hooded. He appeared to be regarding her more with regret than with remorse. Ruby shoved her hands in her pockets.

"I mean, I don't know if you've got some strange idea of being The Sheik, but let me just go ahead and break it to you. You're no Rudolph Valentino."

Daniel stood completely still, with his hands behind his back and his eyes cast down. His voice was very quiet.

"No. I suppose not."

Daniel raised his head and finally met Ruby's eyes.

"I don't know how to act around you. You're not like other women."

Ruby stepped away from the tent pole.

"Well, you've made that clear. I get it, I'm different. You didn't need to cut off my circulation to tell me."

"You're remarkable."

Daniel took a few quick steps toward her.

"That's what you are. Remarkable. I've traveled the world. I've met so many people, so many women. But no one like you. No one who brings out in me what you do."

"No one who makes you want to hurt them? Or whatever you were trying to do to me last night?"

Though she could see the intensity in his eyes, Ruby couldn't help herself. She didn't know how else to respond. Daniel wasn't deterred.

"No one who unsettles me so. No one who makes me feel as if I've been flayed of my superficiality."

Ruby shook her head.

"I don't even know what that means."

Daniel tilted his head. Finally, there was a small smile on his lips.

"It means I like you. How about we start there?"

Ruby bit her bottom lip as she tried to figure Daniel out. She had never met someone who was at once so vulnerable and so self-assured. He was an enigma, a sphinx of sorts. Perhaps, then, Ruby was the same to him. That was something she could understand, at least. Ruby finally smiled back at him.

"All right, we'll start there."

"Good."

Daniel began to fold up the last row of chairs as Ruby slowly walked around the tent. When she came up to the bloodstained stage, she turned back to him.

"You know, I don't think I've even seen a geek show before. Not all of the way through."

Daniel shrugged.

"There's really not much to see. That man who talks for me tells the crowd a ridiculous story about how I have some sort of blood lust, how I can't control myself and how no small creature is safe around me. I just stand on stage while he talks and then when it's time, he procures a chicken and lets it flap around for a bit and then I bite its neck and the crowd screams. I have no idea why people find it entertaining."

Daniel had left two chairs in front of the stage and he sat down in one of them. Ruby crossed her arms and stayed where she was.

"How do you keep from getting blood all over your suit? Don't most geeks wear some sort of tribal get-up anyhow?"

Daniel cocked his head and seemed to think about it a moment.

"I suppose so. That loud man on stage with me has suggested as much."

Ruby shook her head and smiled.

"Lloyd. His name is Lloyd. He's one of the best talkers we've got."

Daniel nodded.

"Well, Lloyd has tried several times to get me to wear some

180

atrocious costume with leather fringe and bones around my neck. I told him I'd bite him in the neck if he so much as mentioned the idea to me again."

Ruby realized Daniel wasn't joking and she laughed.

"This is your first time being a geek, isn't it?"

"Yes."

Ruby nudged a wad of melted cotton candy with the toe of her boot.

"So why do you do it, then?"

"Pardon?"

Ruby sat down and crossed her legs. She rested her elbow on her knee and her chin in her palm as she looked at him intently.

"I don't understand you."

Daniel's face didn't change.

"In what way?"

"Every way. But this geek deal. Come on, let's be honest. Your suit alone is worth more than you'd make here in ten seasons. You've been all over the world. You know about French films and cities, God knows what else. Sure, you're not the best at expressing your feelings or blending in, but in the grand scheme of things, I mean, it just doesn't add up. Even if you were on the run from someone or hiding out, why the Star Light? Why be a geek?"

"Why do you do it?"

Ruby uncrossed her legs and leaned forward.

"Do what?"

Daniel leaned forward as well. Their knees were almost touching.

"Ruby, people like you and I have secrets. Secrets maybe no one else understands. But that doesn't mean we have to explain ourselves to each other. I don't want to know why you are a Snake Charmer, just as I don't think you really want to know why I am a geek. Those things about us don't matter. They are inconsequential to who we are."

Ruby's breath caught in her throat.

"And who are we?"

Daniel slid off the edge of the chair. He was on his knees before her and Ruby could see that his hands were trembling slightly. His eyes were locked on hers.

"We are two strangers who have found one another."

He raised his arms and gently rested his hands on her shoulders. Ruby was holding herself taut, afraid to give in and afraid not to. His fingers were so light against her skin as they moved to trace her collarbone. Daniel's eyes were on her lips now and then on the bridge of exposed tattoos across her chest.

"I promise you, Ruby."

He drew his fingers up the side of her neck and cupped her jaw in his hands. She closed her eyes.

"I won't hurt you."

She let go. And everything happened in a flash.

"That's not possible!"

Ruby's eyes snapped open as Daniel roared at her. For a brief moment, she saw his eyes flicker red and then he wrenched his hands away from her as if he'd been burned. Ruby was too dazed by the unexplainable, overwhelming sensation that had crashed into her like a wave to comprehend Daniel's movements. He rose and careened away from her, thrashing against the empty chair and then gripping it and throwing it across the tent. Ruby remained where she was, stunned.

"Get out!"

Ruby slowly stood up, shaking her head. Daniel was pacing back and forth across the length of the pit and she couldn't understand why. He was incensed. She took a few steps toward him, but he shrank away from her in revulsion.

"Get out now!"

He stopped pacing long enough for her to focus on his face. There was nothing there for her but raw abhorrence. And underneath that, a glint of terror. Ruby's head began to pound as she stumbled toward the front of the tent. She took the canvas flap in hand, but turned around. Daniel was standing with his back against the stage and his hands covering his face. He raised his head suddenly and fixed his eyes on her. Not on her face, but on her chest. On her tattoos. Then a strong wind came out of nowhere and ripped the canvas from her hand as it blew the tent flap wide open. Through clenched teeth, Daniel repeated himself one last time.

"For the love of God! Get out!"

These are things I have done. In 1663, I sank a Spanish Galleon off the coast of Tortuga. This sparked a minor skirmish with the French near Port Royal, which in turn resulted in the keelhauling of Pierre Le Grand, which in turn allowed for a trade agreement with the East India Company, which was certainly not my intention because it made the islands altogether so much less interesting. I was only playing pirate that year and things had gotten a bit out of hand.

A century or so later, I had fun with King George III and drove him mad. But only bit by bit, so his subjects still believed in his rule despite the ridiculous decisions coming from the throne room. Such decisions inevitability led to the traitors in the colonies getting the upper hand and winning the country of America. Again, that hadn't been my intention. I can't really see the future, you know, but I'm glad it worked out that way. I'm enjoying this new country of motorcars and modern ideas.

Most of the things I have done over the ages had far less drastic consequences than causing the birth of a nation. I have instigated complicated love affairs that toppled aristocratic families and I have ignited petty, tribal wars and then sabotaged both sides just to even the odds. I once made it rain fish for a week straight, creating a minor religious cult in a remote corner of southern France that lasted for almost seventy years. I got into a bit of trouble over that one, though. It's one thing to create a new country, yet another to introduce a new god. I was so vexed by the whole fiasco that I went to sleep for most of the third and fourth centuries, which, in hindsight, was probably a good thing. According to the history books, not much was happening during those years and I tend to get restless very easily and create earthquakes just to spice things up.

Because, you see, I can create earthquakes. I could shake one out right now. But they're mostly useless and harder to control than one might think. But I could, is what I'm saying, if I chose to do so. Or whip up a tornado, a sinkhole, a pillar of fire. I could flatten all of the buildings in this silly little place and I could rip the trees from their roots and I could set the townsfolk out to baying at the moon like a pack of loonies. I could make it rain pigs, though again, I must be careful when I start doing things that are too unnatural. It's not like it was, back in the day, when people were stupid and simple and one could construct Stonehenge in a night, just to see the looks on their faces. I have to be careful now of doing anything that might be misconstrued as a miracle. I have more power in this new country of believers, but there are those with even more and I'm not going to be castigated again. Such a bore, such a bore.

I can do all of these things. I can't make a man's heart stop just by looking at him, yes, I've tried, but I can topple a house on him or swerve a locomotive off the tracks to run him over or even just convince him that the voices inside his head want him to slit his own throat. And he'll do it, of course. Child's play. Sometimes this constraint is annoying, say, when you want to wipe out an entire invading army in one go, but it just forces one to get a little more creative and I like that. Just bring in a tidal wave and it creates the same death toll with just a little more effort and sometimes the necessity of a raincoat.

You think, perhaps, I am showing off a little here? Oh, you have no idea. If you let me keep going, I could go on for ages. I am trying to make a point, though, and the point is this: I can do all of these things, and yes, you'd better believe that I can, and no one has ever been able to stop me or resist me. Until now.

For here is what I saw. Here is what I sensed. Here is what came to me when I reached behind that woman's eyes, into her skull, into the very fabric of her composition, the sinews and the synapses and the breath of her being. Here is what I felt.

Nothing.

Yet here, too, is what I felt. Everything.

It cannot be.

SEVENTEEN

Daniel didn't bother to knock. He banged open the door to the office wagon and stood squarely in the frame of the mid-morning sunlight streaming in behind him. Daniel frowned at Samuel, bent over a spread of papers at the side of Pontilliar's desk, but then dismissed him. He turned to Pontilliar, with his suspenders hanging off his sides and a tin cup of coffee halfway to his lips, and got straight to the point.

"I need to talk to you."

Pontilliar sputtered.

"What in the hell do you think you're doing? Did you see the sign on the door? In case you can't read, it says 'Keep Out!' Jesus Christ."

Daniel actually looked back at the sign on the door and then slammed it behind him. In one quick stride, he was sitting down across the desk from Pontilliar, with his long fingers folded neatly in front of him. Pontilliar stood up and thumped his cup down, sloshing coffee over the desk blotter. His face was crimson.

"Are you serious?"

"I said that I needed to speak with you. Now."

Daniel looked over at Samuel. He was standing up straight with a sheaf of papers in his hand. His normally unreadable face had deep lines between his eyes. Daniel nodded at him.

"You can go."

Samuel tilted his head.

"Excuse me?"

Daniel waved his hand at him.

"Go. You can go. Go away. I don't want you as part of this conversation. Leave."

Samuel turned to Pontilliar in outrage. Pontilliar just closed his eyes and shook his head. He slowly sat back down at the desk and rested his forehead in the palms of his hands. He was already sweating.

"Samuel, give us a moment."

Daniel turned to Samuel with wide eyes, waiting for him to leave. He raised his eyebrows expectantly and flicked his fingers. Samuel tightened his jaw, but dropped the papers on the desk and quickly left. When the door closed, Pontilliar lifted his head and pulled out a handkerchief. He swabbed at his forehead and then began dabbing up the coffee spilt across his desk.

"Well now. Happy? Is this suitable for you?"

Daniel leaned back in his chair, more relaxed.

"Yes."

"So then, why don't you tell me what is so goddamn important that you need to come bursting in here before I've even had my second cup of coffee? You know, if anyone else did what you just did, I'd probably leave them by the side of the road."

Daniel almost rolled his eyes. It was so easy with him. Like slipping into a warm bath. There was no resistance whatsoever.

"But I'm not anyone else, am I?"

Pontilliar was looking down at his small, dirty fingernails.

"No."

"I need you to tell me about your daughter's tattoos."

Pontilliar looked up, confused.

"Ruby? Her tattoos? What for?"

Daniel sighed and crossed one leg over the other.

"Does it matter? Do I ask you why you wake up every day and breathe? Do I ask you why you haven't done the world a service and jumped off a bridge? Maybe I should. Maybe I should just have you jump off a bridge."

"What?"

Daniel closed his eyes and pinched the bridge of his nose.

"Never mind. I need to know about your daughter and her tattoos. When did she get them? Where? Why?"

Pontilliar's mouth was open slightly. It was easy, yes, but it also made them slightly stupid. It was much easier to just drive one insane or get one to drink poison or fall in love. It was harder to do this when he needed information. When he needed them to think. Daniel tried to be patient as Pontilliar worked back through his memories.

"When? I think it was, well, it was a couple of years after she first showed up. She'd been living with her mother and I guess her mother died and she came and joined up with me. I didn't know what to do with her, just set her about doing odd jobs, staying out of the way. I guess I felt I owed it to her. Then it occurred to me one day that maybe she could be useful. So I told her I'd set her up as a Tattooed Lady."

Daniel nodded.

"When was this?"

"I don't know, 1908 maybe? We were still a pretty primitive outfit then, didn't have so many lights and rides. More circus acts, animals and such. Ruby must have been, I don't know, fifteen, sixteen?"

Daniel considered this.

"All right. Who gave her the tattoos? Was it someone who was part of your carnival?"

Pontilliar groaned.

"God, but I wish it had been. I mean, look at her, she came back ruined. Ruined. Have you ever seen a real Tattooed Lady? They have pictures on them. Portraits, flowers, landscapes. Presidents. Bright colors. Easy for people to see what they're looking at. Electric inking had already been around for years and in this business, you've got to get the jump on things. Tattooed women were becoming popular and people had expectations. They'd never pay to see Ruby. All those mumbo jumbo designs. I already had a Wild Man in the Ten-In-One then, I didn't need another tribal bally. I needed someone to compete with Irene Woodward and look what I got."

Pontilliar paused and drained what was left of his coffee. He stared down into the empty cup as if waiting for it to refill itself. Daniel snapped his fingers at him.

"I don't care about your petty ambitions. Who gave her the tattoos?"

Pontilliar set the cup down and held it between his hands.

"This cuckoo woman I met in New Orleans once. Back in the late '90s. I got caught up in the dens around Storyville during the off season for a few years. I wasn't at my best then. Anyway, this woman called herself Madame Celeste. I tried to get her to join up with the Star Light, actually. People said she was some kind of hoodoo or voodoo priestess down in the swamps. I don't go in for any of that abracadabra funny business, of course, but I thought she'd make a terrific act. I saw her a few times around the Ma-Jong tables and I stood her once or twice when I was trying to snag her for the show. When I left New Orleans, she owed me, but I never thought I'd have a chance to call it in. Until this Tattooed Lady business came around. And I remembered she'd said something about inking her people."

Daniel nodded slowly.

"So, a Madame Celeste in New Orleans is responsible?"

Pontilliar huffed and leaned back in his chair.

"Responsible is the right word. Ruby was supposed to join back up with us at the start of the season a year later. A year later. But she stayed with that old witch for three years and when she came back, she wasn't the same girl. Not just those awful tattoos, but her hair, her eyes, something about her. Like she'd been living in the wild for those years. Like she came back as something else."

Daniel leaned forward anxiously.

"Where exactly in the wild?"

"Don't know. She wouldn't tell me anything. Just showed back up one day, ready to be a Tattooed Lady. I laughed in her face. I didn't know what to do with her. I ran through several different ideas, but the only one she was game for was the snakes. So now I have a Snake Charmer instead of a Tattooed Lady. It doesn't quite pay the same, but what are you going to do? Folks think the tattoos are just part of her costume."

"She didn't say where, though?"

Pontilliar scratched the back of his head.

"Never said. Refused to answer when asked, so I left it alone. To be honest, I was too hot under the collar to care."

Daniel narrowed his eyes, but Pontilliar was telling the truth. He had told Daniel all that he knew. Daniel stood up, irritated and disgusted. He thrust his hands into his trouser pockets.

"Has it ever occurred to you that money doesn't really matter? Not in the scheme of things. That the moment of your birth and the moment of your death have absolutely nothing to do with the price of an admission ticket?"

Pontilliar looked up at him blankly.

"Why, no."

Daniel glared at him and then with a flourish, waved his hand over the desk. The papers littering it went flying in all directions, some ripping themselves in half and exploding into pieces. At this, Daniel grinned and left Pontilliar sitting alone at his desk, astonished.

A small crowd had gathered outside the entrance to the G-top and though Ruby wanted not to care, wanted to stay out of any roustie drama and head straight to the cookhouse for a basin of clean water, she stopped when she saw January at the edge of the circle. She had her hands on her hips and was nodding along with the others, so Ruby sighed and headed over. She had spent the morning in the woods, with the excuse of hunting for snakes, although she didn't really need to acquire any more. She had just needed to be alone.

When she came up to stand next to January, she knew from the look she was given that she must appear as dirty and disheveled as she felt. She tried to smooth her tangled hair back and shrugged.

"Snake hunting."

January pursed her lips.

"Were you hunting snakes or slithering through the dirt yourself?"

Ruby wiped her face with the side of her hand but figured she'd only made it worse. She put her hands in her pockets. Franklin ducked back inside the tent and a few of the rousties followed him.

"What's going on?"

The rest of the crowd broke up and January turned aside as well. She and Ruby began to walk toward the cookhouse.

"Franklin just got word from Samuel. We're heading out tonight."

"Why?"

"Hell if I know. I'm not asking questions, though."

January stopped for a moment. The blue scarf pinned over her hair was coming loose and she paused to re-tie it. She hadn't done her makeup yet, though, and Ruby could see the dark circles under her eyes, deep, like bruises. Ruby shook her head.

"Thank God."

"You're telling me. I thought we weren't making a dime here before the revival. Yesterday, there might as well have been cobwebs in the girly tent. I always thought that confessing all their sins gave folks leeway to commit more."

"Catholics."

"What?"

Ruby shaded her eyes and looked toward the cookhouse. She saw no sign of Daniel.

"You're thinking of Catholics. It doesn't work that way with Bible-thumpers. They get off so much at these revivals that they don't even need us."

"Well, that explains things."

January finished with her scarf and they kept walking.

"So Samuel or Pontilliar didn't tell you anything about shoving off a day early?"

Ruby shook her head.

"I don't think they're speaking to me. They're still riled up about us going into town. About The Rainbow."

January grinned and bumped her shoulder into Ruby's.

"Well, they can be angry all they want. It was worth it. Although, I got to say, Ruby, you're running them off faster than I used to. How many hearts are you going to break in a month?"

Ruby froze.

"What are you talking about?"

January touched Ruby's arm, picking at her shirtsleeve. She was suddenly serious.

"I'm sorry. That was mean. I don't know why I said that. I don't know why I have to turn everything into a joke."

"No, what did you mean by that?"

January sighed. She looked away from Ruby.

"I just meant Daniel leaving this morning. I'm sorry, that was cruel. I know you two sort of had something there for a minute. At the picture show, I could tell something was going on. And I hoped it was. After Hayden taking off like that, you deserved to have someone paying attention to you. I thought, maybe you two had hit it off."

Ruby's eyes widened.

"Daniel left this morning?"

January raised her hand to her mouth.

"Oh my God, I was right. And you didn't know he left? Jesus, Ruby, I'm going to hell. I'm going straight to hell."

Ruby licked her lips and collected herself. Then she scowled at January, who was watching her anxiously.

"Quit it. Don't worry, there was nothing. Absolutely nothing. I don't care if he's coming or going. I just didn't know. I guess we'll have to find another geek. Again."

January fidgeted with the lace collar of her dress.

"He was asking about you, you know. Daniel was."

Ruby was silent for a moment and then slowly spoke.

"What was he asking?"

"It was sort of odd, really. I only found out he was leaving after he came to me to ask some questions about you."

"What sort of questions?"

"About your tattoos. Where you got them, how you got them. I don't remember exactly. I don't know why he was asking. He was just curious, I think."

Ruby clenched her fists at her sides.

"Curious? You think he was just curious?"

January looked confused.

"I don't know. He was just asking."

"What did you tell him?"

"I didn't tell him anything. I don't know anything. I told him that if it was that important, he should go talk to Pontilliar. That he was probably the only one who would know, but I didn't think he knew, either. You're so damn secretive about it."

Ruby wiped her forehead with the back of her hand, creating another smear of dirt. January grabbed her elbow and shook her.

"Ruby, what is the big deal? What did I do? What's going on?"

Ruby stood up straight and threw her shoulders back. Her jaw was set, but she tried to smile at January. It didn't come out very well.

"Nothing. It doesn't matter. Except that he's gone. That matters. That's all that matters. We can just forget about him. With any luck, we'll never see him again."

EIGHTEEN

It took Daniel less than a day to find her. Getting to New Orleans was easy, but from there it took some work. He had stood on the corner of Basin and Canal, closed his eyes, raised his head and sent out feelers. He knew this Madame Celeste was real, he could sense traces of her in the cobblestones and the twisted iron railings, but he knew he would have to get out of the city. It took a few hours, but by late afternoon, with the long summer sun slithering through the bald cypress trees and disappearing into the bayou murk, Daniel came upon The Village of the Lost.

He strolled out of the curtains of Spanish moss, out of the grasping creepers and the peeling cypress knees and the fog of dusk mosquitos, as if he were just stepping out on the sidewalk in front of the Metropolitan Opera. There wasn't a single scratch on his face or hands, not a tear in his suit, not a scuff of mud on his shoes. His skin was glowing, his black suit was smoldering and his teeth and his nails and his slicked back, pomaded hair glistened in the fading light. The Pedi Moun Ki trailed behind him through the market, gawking at this strange white man sauntering through the center of their lives. Daniel did not even look at them. He put his hands in his pockets and leisurely meandered through The Village, heading for the largest house, marking the end of the road. Unlike the others, it was built up on bricks and had wooden shingles cascading down the slanted roof of the garconniere. An old woman, dark and wrinkled, was hunched into a cane-bottomed rocking chair on the front gallery. She stood up and frowned around the long stem of her pipe as Daniel came up the mud walkway. Her voice was a frog's croak.

"I knew you were coming. Tonight. And in the past I knew. And before that I knew and I knew and I knew. I have been waiting for you all this time."

Daniel narrowed his eyes. He was standing on the porch steps, looking up at her.

"Well, Madame Celeste. If I had known that, I might have arrived sooner."

The old woman threw back her head and laughed a long and terrifying laugh. Daniel waited patiently until she had finished and stumped her way across the porch to him. She was so small that upon reaching Daniel, standing on the bottom step, their faces were level with one another. He looked into her yellow, watery eyes with unnaturally large, black irises and began to have some idea of who he was dealing with. He smiled, but kept himself from laughing. He needed to humor her because he needed information. She spat at his shoes, but missed.

"Come with me."

She hobbled down the stairs, clenching the pipe between her teeth, but didn't reach out to Daniel for help and he didn't extend his hand. She followed the muddy walkway and then turned down a path framed by clumps of palmettos and wax-myrtle, leading

Daniel away from the main part of The Village. Madame Celeste walked slowly and deliberately, and Daniel kept an even pace beside her. He walked with his hands clasped behind his back, occasionally looking up into the thick canopy as if he were sightseeing. An extremely tall man with a grizzled beard and a machete stopped them at one point, and the man glowered at Daniel and bared his filed, pointed teeth. Madame Celeste waved her hand and the man begrudgingly stepped aside, allowing Daniel to pass.

Madame Celeste took him through a thick stand of tupelo and swamp cottonwood, ducking under wide nets of spider webs, until they emerged into a gloomy clearing. A squat, round lodge had been built in the middle, surrounded by a low, intermittent wall of rocks and what appeared to be rib and pelvic bones. The walls of the lodge were paneled with dried rushes and painted with primitive symbols Daniel halfway recognized from centuries before. Strange crosses and spirals, contorted shapes with eyes and teeth swirling fluidly into one another. A large copper bowl filled with smoldering bricks of peat moss guarded the low door and Madame Celeste leaned over it. She pulled out a small leather bag from inside the front of her shirt and dipped her fingers into it, procuring a pinch of what looked to Daniel like sand. She sprinkled it into the bowl and a green flame leapt up, shooting sparks high into the air, and then died down just as suddenly. Daniel watched Madame Celeste with curiosity as she then took out a thin, curving knife and hitched up her long skirt. Her legs were spindly and webbed with brittle skin and her long-toed feet were bare and caked in mud. She flicked the knife just below her ankle bone and then tapped the blood from the knife into the bowl. The flame flared up again and turned blue, then green, and then died back down to a glow. Madame Celeste fixed her skirt and turned to Daniel, still waiting.

"Tuath De. I know you. Will you come inside with me?"

Daniel grinned and pointed to the bowl at her feet.

"Are you going to tell me what's in the fire?"

Madame Celeste cackled.

"No. That wouldn't be playing fair. Or rather, that wouldn't be playing at all. And I know you love your games."

Daniel nodded and stepped inside the circle of rock and bone. Madame Celeste picked up a torch and dipped it into the bowl, setting it aflame. She pushed open the door to the lodge and disappeared. Daniel ducked low and followed her. The space seemed smaller inside than it had appeared outside and Daniel had to stoop as he watched Madame Celeste lighting the fire in the center of the lodge. The blaze sprung to life, only this fire was made from black alder branches and was surrounded by a ring of sharp antlers, bound together by thin strips of leather and adorned with long, scraggly heron feathers. Once the fire was going, Madame Celeste put out the torch and turned to the door. Daniel watched with interest as she put something into her mouth, chewed vigorously and then spit a stream of white powder across the face of the door. She mumbled something low as she wiped a drip of saliva from her chin.

The close walls of the lodge were alternately lined with shelves made of raw cypress boards and hung with grotesque masks painted red and black. These Daniel recognized and he smiled. He also recognized the Asons, wooden rattles filled with beads and painted red that hung down in heavy clusters like grapes. The shelves were crammed with jars clouded over with soot and wooden boxes inlaid with Veve calling symbols. Madame Celeste removed three short black sticks from a box on the lowest shelf and then arranged herself on a stool across the fire from Daniel. She drove the sticks into the dirt floor, two beside her and one behind her, and then made a complicated sign that ended by crossing herself. Finally, she appeared to be settled and gestured for Daniel to take the stool opposite her. When he sat, she put her hands on her thighs to brace herself and leaned over the fire.

"You came to Vilaj La Nan Pèdi A on your black crow wings,

this I know. I looked to the heavens and I saw you circling as you searched for me. You've found me, yes, but you're in my realm now."

Daniel couldn't help but smirk.

"I don't think you really understand how this works, Madame Celeste. Do you mind?"

He took out his silver cigarette case and held it up. Madame Celeste leaned back from the fire and glowered at him. Daniel struck a match and lit the cigarette, being careful to put the used match back in his pocket. He inhaled deeply and crossed his legs to the side. He sighed and examined the burning end of the cigarette.

"You know, it's become such a habit now. Of course, I can't feel anything, but I've sort of gotten used to it over the past few years. It always seems to make others more comfortable, but I think I've taken a liking to it myself. And it's so much easier than having to pretend to eat. Would you like one?"

He reached into his pocket for the case, but Madame Celeste had already taken out her pipe. She packed it slowly and then fit the long stem into her the wide gap between her front teeth. She puffed slowly, her yellow eyes glowing above the fire, and scowled at Daniel. They smoked in silence for a moment until Madame Celeste made the first move.

"All right. You are here. What did you come for?"

Daniel rested his elbow on his knee and flicked his wrist out.

"Well, it's not you, if that's what you're thinking. So you can dispense with the chalk lines and gris-gris nonsense. Do you know who I am?"

Madame Celeste's eyes burned.

"I have been waiting for you for longer than you know. Since the trees grew inside out and the snakes shed their skin into their own mouths. My people, my true people, servants of Bondye in the old country, we have been waiting a long time. We have kept the watch. Kept the time."

She paused and looked into the fire, studying it.

"Coyote was the first to leave this land."

Daniel puffed on his cigarette.

"Well, yes. He was never the strongest."

"He was one of the oldest. This is his land. My people are only intruders. You, you are only a parasite."

The corner of Daniel's lip curled around his cigarette.

"Did you just call me a parasite?"

Madame Celeste was looking deep into the fire now, lost in the hypnotic coil of the flames.

"Coyote was here, but then his people tired of his tricks. And they tired of the Great Spirit and Grandmother Spider. The old ways. And so Coyote has all but left this world entirely."

Daniel ground his cigarette out on the bottom of his shoe and put the remainder of it in his pocket. He was getting annoyed.

"I need to ask you about a girl who came here once."

Madame Celeste ignored him.

"And there was Legba, who came over with Bondye and Oshun on the boats and crept up here through the plantations."

Daniel grinned.

"Yes, and how is Papa Legba? I've been looking for him since I heard he came up to America from the southern lands. Did he get scared and pack up his macoute? Run away again to the jungle?"

Madame Celeste pulled a stick from the fire and held it glowing white hot between the palms of her hands.

"Iwa Legba. Keeper of the gates to Ginen. Carrier of our destinies. Bridge to the Grand Master and the lemo. Connecting us to our dead. Opening doors. Protecting us from—"

Daniel held out his hand, interrupting her.

"Oh, come now. He's just a trickster. Just like me. Just like Coyote and Loki and Hermes and goddamn Ea if you want to go back that far. I understand that he's your god and all, but you don't have to make Legba out to be more than he is. He'll get a big head.

As if he doesn't have one already."

Madame Celeste suddenly bared her teeth.

"You dare to insult Iwa Legba?"

Daniel laughed.

"Of course I do, you ridiculous old crone."

Madame Celeste's shoulders dropped. She pushed the stick back into the fire and sighed. Her voice returned to its sing-song, storyteller lilt.

"And though Legba acquired the followers of the new Voudou in the Americas, those ways did not last this far above the equator and he has begun to retreat as well. To the islands and the southern wilderness."

Daniel leaned forward and nodded.

"Which is where he belongs."

"And now here you are. In Coyote's place. In Legba's place. You, who have been around since the beginning. Who should have journeyed to the West long, long ago."

"Ah, but I learned. I adapted. When the old ways were being driven out of Britannia by the Romans, I changed. No one had thought the new upstart religion would go anywhere. Christianity. Ha! Odin and Woden said that no one would follow it. A monotheistic ideology? It'll never spread. It'll never last. And where would a trickster find a place in such a system? Everyone had overlooked the obvious. Christianity is no more monotheistic than your silly hoodoo cult."

Madame Celeste rested her hands on her knees, palms upwards. She spoke around her pipe, still clenched in her teeth.

"And so we have Light Bringer. The Morning Star, the Wailing Yell. In this part of the world, Devil."

Daniel stood up, though he had to keep his head bent to avoid hitting the ceiling of the lodge. He bowed extravagantly.

"And so you have me."

Daniel sat down and took out another cigarette.

"And this grand country of America. With its cars and lights and restlessness and speed and energy. I love it. Where the old religions are leaving faster than rats on a sinking ship and Christianity reigns supreme. It couldn't be better. I may never have to retreat and settle in the West."

Madame Celeste nodded slowly.

"But you want to know about the girl?"

Daniel lit his cigarette.

"Yes, I do. I think we've spent enough time posturing. You really are lovely to talk to, it's been so long since I've spoken to one who keeps the old ways and can chat with the gods. That is something we're sadly missing over in my neck of the woods. But enough of this. I need to know about the girl you tattooed and I need to know about her right..."

Daniel leaned far over the fire. The smoke curved around him, not touching him, and the flames flared away.

"...now."

Madame Celeste pulled her pipe from her mouth and set it on the floor next to her. She glanced at the sticks on either side of her and then pursed her lips. Her bony knuckles cracked as she folded her hands in the dip of her skirt between her knees. She spat into the fire and then sighed.

"What do you want to know? How I tattooed her? Why I tattooed her?"

"I could care less about that."

Madame Celeste raised her eyes.

"You should care."

Daniel shook his head.

"I want to know what the tattoos mean. The one on the woman's chest. With the eye and the wings. And the others like it. Do they do something, can they do something? What's their purpose?"

Madame Celeste cocked her head to the side like a bird and then her mouth opened wide again, exposing her brown teeth, and she laughed until there were tears in her eyes.

"So, you've seen the Eye of Kakarauri. You've met her already, haven't you? The white woman from the mountains. My Wairua. You haven't just heard of her or sensed her. You've met her. I bet you've actually touched her, haven't you?"

Madame Celeste looked down again at the stick in the dirt next to her and then cut her eyes back at Daniel.

"Were you surprised?"

Daniel threw his cigarette into the fire and the flames immediately rose to the ceiling of the lodge, scorching it black. A rush of wind came through the room and circled into a vortex around Daniel and his eyes glowed red. Madame Celeste watched all of this happening around her without fear. A moment later, the flames died down and the wind ceased and Daniel calmly straightened the cuffs of his suit. Madame Celeste grinned.

"You can kill me, sure. I know about you, Daniel Revont, kin to Bondye and Legba. I know what you can do and I know what you can't. But if you kill me, you'll never know about the tattooed one. And try as you might, you can't just pull the information straight out of my head. Oh, don't bother, you don't have to trick me or convince me. I'll tell you freely. I've been waiting years to tell you this."

Daniel narrowed his eyes, but kept his temper in check.

"Go on."

"We've known about you for a long time. About you coming and taking what wasn't rightfully yours. About your ambition. Your limitless, fickle appetite. We Manbos are only human, yes, but you are only a trickster. Existing in the twilight between man and god, between here and there, this world and the next. When all others would choose to hide in the heavens or under the sea, you are cursed to be out among the mortals. Forever one of us, but not us. And so I knew about you and when the time was ready, when the moment was right, I received the sign."

"What the hell are you babbling about?"

Madame Celeste grinned.

"The girl was sent to me by her father. To become a carnival attraction. A stupid, useless girl. What was I to do with her but make her knit trinkets for me to sell to the blind believers in the city? Then she ran away one night and I found her the next morning in a nest of serpents. A hundred of them. She was not dead, she had slipped away, unaware. The snakes had bitten her, but she had not died. She was in the land of Kakarauri. The between world. The twilight. I looked up and the sun went black and there was a roar in my ears from my Manbo ancestors and I knew it was time. I knew she was the one to carry out the Toenga Lespri. I took her home and called her back to this world. And then I did to her what I had not dared to do to another before. I protected her. I opened the door for her, though she may never step through it."

"Hogwash."

Madame Celeste leaned forward suddenly.

"And yet, you have been around her and cannot enter her mind. You have touched her and cannot feel her, cannot control her. This is so, or you wouldn't be here. You would not need to know."

Daniel frowned. A strange, anxious feeling had taken hold of him and he fidgeted with his diamond cufflinks.

"That's ludicrous. Preposterous. And to what end did you, as you say, protect Ruby? For what purpose?"

Madame Celeste shook her head.

"I do not know exactly where her Iku'anga will take her. She does not even know her power. She suspects nothing. I do not know what she will do when she discovers it. And discovers you. But there is a need in this world for her. A need for one us to stand up to one of you. Protecting her was a way of creating a balance, of putting a little weight on our side of the scales, evening things out against the power of the gods. Toenga Lespri."

Daniel stood up suddenly. The door behind him blew open and the fire in the bowl extinguished itself. Pale moonlight dimly lit up the lodge.

"That's pathetic."

Only Madame Celeste's yellow eyes could be discerned in the gloom.

"It is true."

"You have no idea what you have done, old woman. You have created a pawn and set her down in the middle of a dangerous, dangerous game."

"Pawns can become queens."

Daniel's eyes glowed red. His skin began to shimmer and turn silver and his bones began to elongate. They stretched up out of the skin on his face and curved out of the sleeves of his suit. His shoulder bones rose up over his head like an arc of wings and a swirl of dust came around him, drawing his bones out ever farther. The shadow of Daniel's monstrous skeleton filled the lodge and the wind came roaring through and the dust blasted every surface. When it settled, Daniel's appearance did as well. He stood up and straightened his cuffs as he leveled his gaze at Madame Celeste, cowering behind the fire, grasping at her sticks in the dirt.

"Not in my game, you fool. Not in my house, not in my game. You are trying to play with the gods and, my dear Madame Celeste, the gods don't lose."

Ruby dropped the sack of ticket stubs on Samuel's desk and crossed her arms.

"I'm not your errand boy, you know."

Samuel carefully set the stub of his pencil down and looked up from the ledger in front of him.

"I would call you a lot of things, Ruby Chole. But I certainly wouldn't call you an errand boy."

"Then why am I collecting stubs for you? Are you just that busy?"

"Are you?"

Samuel closed the ledger in front of him and smoothed his palms down the front of it. He gestured for Ruby to sit down, but she remained standing. She still had her arms crossed and her chin jutted forward.

"Is that it, then?"

Samuel opened his mouth twice to speak, but bit back his words each time. Finally, he sighed and slumped in his chair.

"We're leaving Napoleon tonight, after the last show."

Ruby nodded.

"I heard. The news has already done the rounds. Are we going to be able to set up and open in Alabama tomorrow?"

"I'm waiting on a telegram from Chandler. We're hoping to open tomorrow night, ahead of schedule, and he's trying to make it happen. Monroeville should be a turn out. Better than we've had here."

"Anything would be better than here."

Samuel stood up.

"Ruby. I need to show you something."

Ruby already had her hand on the door handle. She turned halfway around and rolled her eyes. Samuel suddenly banged his fists down onto the desk, shaking it all the way to the floor of the wagon.

"Goddamnit, Ruby!"

Ruby froze. Samuel outwardly demonstrated his frustration about once every ten years and cursed even less than that. He seemed to collect himself as he sidled around the desk and his tone was gentler when he approached her.

"I know you're upset about Hayden. And I know that you're

upset about Daniel leaving as well."

Ruby backed away from him.

"Whoa, whoa. I'm not upset about Daniel. Who said I was upset about Daniel? January? Jesus Christ, the only thing I'm upset about is everybody being in my business."

Samuel leveled her with a steady gaze.

"Ruby, I've known you a long time..."

Ruby threw her hands up in the air. It was too much, all of it too much, and the last person on earth she wanted to hear it from was Samuel. She remembered when Hayden had left the first time and how Samuel had tried to console her and offer her advice. It had been a disaster and they hadn't spoken for the remainder of the season. Ruby was already too exhausted to go through that again.

"Stop worrying about my feelings."

Samuel snapped at her.

"I could care less about your feelings right now. Truly. But I do care about you. And I need to show you something. So put aside your anger and your self-pity and your ridiculous, childish querulousness and come with me."

Ruby started to protest, but Samuel had already turned away and was lifting up the knotted tapestry hanging behind his desk. He hooked it to the ceiling, exposing a small door cut into the wall. Ruby watched him with curiosity as he inserted a long, brass key and opened the door. Suddenly, the mystery as to why Samuel's office seemed so small made sense. Ruby was still frustrated, but there was no way she couldn't follow him. She ducked through the low door into the hidden back room of the wagon.

"Be careful, there is not a lot of space."

She was immediately confronted with a wall of carnival odds and ends stacked almost to the ceiling and made up of broken chairs, old marquees with peeling paint, rolled up playbills, and the front part of a broken carousel horse. Ruby barely had room to turn around. She looked over to Samuel, but he had disappeared, edging around an upended leather trunk stacked high with folded maps and molding account ledgers. Suddenly, a glow came over the top of the wall in front of her and Ruby realized there was yet another area behind the collection of junk. She followed Samuel's lead and squeezed into the opening between the trunk and the wall.

Samuel adjusted the flame of the lamp before sitting on the narrow cot pushed against the back wall of the wagon. The space was immaculate, the bed made with precision, the small table next to it lacquered to a high shine. A tower of books and a collection of carved ivory elephants were lined up exactly along the edge. Ruby turned in wonder and realized that all of the carnival detritus in the front part of the room was backed up against a massive bookcase, rising to the ceiling and spanning almost the entire width of the wagon. She started to reach out and run her hand along the leather spines, but caught herself. The books were lined up to the edge of the shelf perfectly and though many of them looked ancient, not one had a spot of dust or mildew on it. Ruby turned to Samuel, her mouth agape in amazement.

"What is this place?"

Samuel moved one of the elephants on the table and then straightened it back. He shrugged.

"This is my room. This is where I live."

"I thought..."

Samuel smiled sadly.

"What? That I slept curled up under my desk?"

Ruby raised her eyebrows.

"That was the rumor. Ever since you quit Mutumbo."

Samuel shook his head and pointed to the books.

"Those were mine even then. I didn't have them with me while we traveled, but they were mine. Most of them belonged to my father and many of them were from Sir Richard's private collection. When my father died, I brought them over here from Brightwall

Hall in Suffolk. Fortunately, by then I had a wagon to put them in."

He cut his eyes at Ruby.

"I don't think it would be wise for others to know about these. Even here, even in a carnival, where freaks are more common than not."

Ruby looked back at the books.

"Why? Half the folks here can't read, anyway."

"Exactly."

Ruby sat down next to Samuel on the cot. He sighed.

"And wouldn't want to know about someone like me having something like this. Books, words, knowledge, they are power. And people are terrified of power in the hands of someone who looks like me. It just makes things even more complicated."

Ruby leaned back on her hands and nodded.

"All right, I understand. Now what did you want to show me?"

"This."

He pulled a ring of keys out of his pocket, smaller than the giant ring he was known to always have on him. He selected a long, curving key and unlocked a cabinet that had been built into the bottom corner of the bookcase. Samuel had to perform a complicated set of jerks and twists with the key until finally the wooden door popped opened. He looked over his shoulder, not at Ruby, but just as if it were habit, and slid out a large, thick book. He closed the cabinet and locked it before bringing the book over to Ruby and setting it carefully on the table where she could see it. Samuel nodded to her.

"Look."

Ruby stood up and bent over the table. The book was square and bound in a dark red leather cover. There was no writing on the front of it.

"What am I looking at?"

Samuel opened the book and began to quickly turn the pages. A sharp, sour smell filled the air. Some of the pages were thicker than others and stained from liquid and colored powders. They crinkled in Samuel's hands and some pages emitted puffs of talc when he flipped them. Ruby could see that they were filled with bizarre words in strange languages and curious ink drawings.

She reached out to touch the pages.

"Wait, what is this? You're going too fast."

Samuel slapped her hand.

"Don't. This is not for you to touch and these pages are not for you to see."

Ruby frowned.

"Why do some of the pages look like they're not made of paper?"

"Because they are not. Most are made of vellum. Like thin sheets of leather. Buffalo skin mostly. Antelope. A few are human."

"You're joking."

Samuel abruptly stopped turning the pages.

"Let me tell you what this is. This is a Laleritha. Some call it The Book of the Forgotten. I have always known it as The Book of Others. There are three or four that I have heard of existing in the world, though I have never seen them and never will. They are all different. They are collections of a sort. Nothing is replicated. As far as I am aware, this one began in the lost city of Mtakatifu Nyota Mji on the shores of Lake Tanganyika."

Ruby looked down at the page Samuel had stopped on. One side of it contained a faint map drawn on a brown, fraying piece of cloth. The cloth had been sewn onto the page with thick stiches of horsehair. The other page was inked with crude symbols made mostly out of lines and triangles. Samuel looked down.

"That is okay for you to see. That doesn't matter anymore."

"Is it writing? What does it say?"

Samuel began to flip through the pages again.

"It is writing, though I have no idea what it says. Most of this book was put together before written language came to us. Some of the ink is blood, some a mixture derived from plants. Some, I would dare not dwell on the composition. This book has been around for thousands and thousands of years and been through more wars, seen more things, than we will ever be able to imagine. Whole tribes have given their lives to protect it. It is a history. A chronicle. A definition of civilization at each stage."

Ruby nodded.

"Like Herodotus?"

Samuel shook his head.

"No. Not like Herodotus. It is not concerned with what can be seen, but rather with what cannot."

"I don't understand."

"You don't need to understand."

Ruby crossed her arms.

"Well, how did you get it?"

Samuel sighed.

"It has been in my family since before the Europeans ever set foot on our coasts. Before that, I do not know. It has traveled from the Mediterranean to the Cape and back again many times. Now quit asking about the origins of the book and look at this."

Samuel flipped another page and turned the book toward her. It took Ruby a moment to comprehend what she was looking at, but then she gasped.

"Oh my God."

"Now do you see? This is what I had to show you."

Ruby covered her mouth with her hands and stared at the pages in front of her. One was inconsequential, filled with tally marks and rows of antlered animals. It was the other page. A crudely drawn human figure, sexless and faceless. Its hands and feet were black and in the middle of the figure was a strange design: a half-lidded eye surrounded by three wings, spiraling in around it and themselves. The figure was circumscribed by a thick oval line and there were other small, strange symbols scrawled across the bottom of the page.

"Samuel?"

He put his hand on her shoulder.

"That symbol. With the eye and the wings. It's on you, isn't it?"

Ruby nodded, still stunned, and undid the top button of her shirt. In the center of her chest, about three inches below the base of her throat, was the symbol from the book. Samuel nodded.

"I thought so."

Ruby quickly buttoned her shirt and pulled her collar tightly closed. She wrapped her arms around herself and shook her head in disbelief.

"It's all over me, the eye with the wings. Different versions of it, too, but still the same. I've never seen a picture of it anywhere, though. I thought all my tattoos were just nonsense. Crazy things made up."

"I don't think that symbol exists anywhere else, Ruby. I've gone through most of my books. There's no other picture of it. No other description in history that I can find. Only here."

Samuel tapped the page.

"And on you."

Ruby turned to him.

"Well, what does it mean?"

"I don't know."

Ruby pointed to the bottom of the page.

"Those markings there. Do you know what they mean?"

"I recognize them. They are an ancient form of writing. Pictographic, from somewhere in the Kalahari, I believe. I was able to compare them to a drawing of petroglyphs in another book."

Ruby shook her head.

"I have no idea what you're talking about."

"Never mind. I was able to decipher one of them. Each symbol is a word, you see."

"Okay. What's the word?"

Samuel frowned.

"Hila Mtu."

"What?"

Samuel traced his fingers over the page.

"It roughly translates to a type of trick. But it's a sort of person as well. A Kivuli Mungu, a shadow god. It's hard to explain, exactly."

"Sounds like it."

Ruby took a deep breath and lifted her shoulders.

"All right, so what is all this?"

Samuel slammed the book closed.

"I don't have the answers, Ruby. I think the symbol is supposed to be some sort of totem. Like a protection charm. The ring around the figure. Maybe that goes with it. I don't know. You don't know anything about what your tattoos mean?"

Ruby shook her head. She had never told Samuel about her time at The Village. She had told no one.

"No more than you. The woman who gave them to me would never tell me what they meant."

"Did she tell you anything? About being protected? Or about what you were supposed to do out in the world with the tattoos?"

Ruby huffed. He was pushing her too far. She wasn't going to talk about her time at Vilaj La Nan Pèdi A. When Madame Celeste had performed the binding ritual between them, before the tattooing began, that had been one of the requirements. The Village was a secret and had been for three hundred years. It had to remain that way.

"You mean, besides not become a Tattooed Lady?"

Samuel shook his head.

"Ruby, this is not a joke."

"I didn't think it was. Finding my tattoo in a creepy book like that and all."

"Is there anything at all you can think to tell me?"

Ruby crossed her arms and sighed.

"The only thing the woman ever said to me about going out into the world was that I had something called an Iku'anga to complete. And no, I don't know what that means. She never told me anything else. Just kicked me out and sent me back to Pontilliar."

"An Iku'anga?"

Ruby raised her eyebrows.

"You know what the word means?"

Samuel rubbed his forehead with the palm of his hand and then looked up toward the ceiling of the wagon.

"It's sort of like a direction. A task. Something you'll need to accomplish, but which is intrinsically bound up with who you are. It cannot be separated from you. A more dramatic person might call it a destiny."

Samuel rested his hand on The Book of Others and his shoulders dropped.

"Maybe I shouldn't have shown this to you."

Ruby looked up at him.

"Wait, how long have you known about this?"

Samuel raised his hands in defense.

"Only a few days. I promise. I had never seen it in the book before. It's not the sort of book one just peruses through. There are things in there I haven't put my eyes on yet. Things I would not want to. I was looking for something else, though, and I found the drawing."

Ruby narrowed her eyes.

"What were you looking for?"

Samuel started to shake his head, but then changed his mind and met her gaze.

"I thought Daniel would be in the book. Though I don't know how or where or why. I don't think he is just a geek and I don't think he is a businessman or a banker or any of the other things the rumors have proclaimed him to be. I think he is something else. Something unnatural."

Ruby turned away, but the mention of Daniel's name jarred

her. The symbol in the book. And the way Daniel had looked at her tattoo in the geek tent. The arrow to her chest when she'd first seen him, sauntering across the midway in his glittering suit. Ruby understood now. They were all connected, like stars bridging a constellation, like the very constellations she had seen when the world had turned black and the heavens had spiraled above her and, for a moment, Ruby felt a surge inside of her as if taken over by something greater than herself.

But then she remembered, too, the horror on Daniel's face when he had ordered her from the tent. None of it mattered. Symbols and feelings, destiny, magic charms and hocus-pocus mojo. The typical carnival fare. There was no point in searching for meaning; it was all just smoke and mirrors in the end. And in the end, she was still left empty and alone. Always alone. As always she would be. Ruby stubbornly shook her head.

"Daniel is gone."

Samuel grabbed her wrist, forcing her to look at him.

"Is he?"

"Leave it alone, Samuel. He was strange, you didn't like him, but now he's gone. Left. Like people do around here. Those who have any sense, anyway."

"I think you are clouded in your judgement of Daniel. I think he made you feel something and it made you vulnerable. Daniel is chimerical."

Ruby pushed him away from her and he crashed back into the table, knocking over the carefully stacked pile of books.

"Maybe Daniel was smart."

Samuel began to restack the books. He wouldn't look at her. Ruby threw her hands up in the air.

"We've had women with three arms, men with four legs, we had a child who looked and walked like a crab. Remember Crab Girl? That was unnatural. Why don't you look that up in your fancy book?"

Samuel's voice was very quiet and he still wouldn't look at her. "I'm not talking about physical natures."

Ruby spun in a circle and slapped her hands down on her thighs.

"And the man who was afraid of the color yellow? The talker? Remember him? Or the clown who tried to legally marry his goat? That clown wasn't physically unnatural. He was just crazy."

"And you think Daniel is just crazy?"

"I don't think he's anything. I think he's someone who came along, saw what this damn place was all about and got the hell out as fast as he could."

"You believe that?"

"I believe that!"

Ruby knew she didn't. But she also knew she couldn't let Samuel win. She couldn't let him shame her with the truth: she had let her guard down with Daniel. Just as she had with Hayden. And, just as before, she had been deceived. It made her feel foolish. Degraded. No one could know she had failed yet again. That, once more, she was undeserving of love. Samuel finished arranging the books and stood up. He brushed off the legs of his trousers, even though the floor was spotless.

"And everything with Jacob and Tom was a coincidence?"

"Jesus Christ, now we're back to that."

Ruby's hair was falling down and she yanked the pins out and let it swing down her back. She ran her hands over her head to push the stray strands out of her eyes and then pointed her finger in Samuel's face.

"I mean it. Leave it alone, Samuel. Leave it alone, leave me alone. Don't show me anymore of your secret books, don't talk to me anymore about your mumbo jumbo. Don't follow me, don't give me those looks, don't ask me to do a thing. I'm sick of it. From all of you. All of you trying to mess with my head."

Ruby drew an invisible line between them on the floor of the wagon with the toe of her boot.

"There's you and there's me. Got it?"

Samuel clasped his hands in front of him and looked down his nose at her.

"I'm just trying to help you. To protect you."

Ruby laughed, hoarsely and cruelly.

"Oh, because you're real good at that, aren't you?"

She couldn't read his expression and she didn't care to. Ruby slammed her hand against the wagon wall on her way out just so she could feel the sting.

Two months after she had returned to the Star Light, disoriented, uncivilized, a woman now, but more lost than the feral girl who had come down off the mountain, Ruby had discovered the truth. The venom of that secret had also been spat at her from the pages of a dusty book.

Ruby had been cleaning out old baggage trunks, trying to find one she could drill holes in, one that would be suitable for snakes, when she found Pontilliar's journal. Ruby was not sure she wanted to be a Snake Charmer. She was not sure of anything. Ruby had not seen white faces for three years and here they were, everywhere, gawking at her, contorting in smirks and sneers, hiding behind hands to whisper. Ruby knew that more than her skin had changed since she has last called the Star Light home. She dressed differently now and refused to exchange her worn trousers for skirts. English words felt like gravel in her mouth, so she barely spoke. She wove flowers into her knotted hair when she could find them. Ruby became another kind of Wairua, a wandering ghost with no people at all.

Pontilliar had been disgusted with her appearance and did not keep his revulsion to himself. He could not bill her as a Tattooed Lady and did not know what to do with her. Ruby had suspected that it would be the case, but made no move to leave the carnival. The Star Light was the only mooring she had left. It was Samuel who suggested the snakes, those creatures whose destines seemed always to coil around her and consume her. Ruby had mutely assented; she would be the Snake Enchantress. She would do her best to put on a show.

The journal she found was at the bottom of a red steamer trunk, buried underneath the detritus of rotting ledgers and crumbling, misprinted playbills. She fluttered the pages before tossing it aside, but was arrested by a word inked in a scrawling, faded hand. Miranda. It took her a while to decipher the alchemical names, some of the poisons she recognized, others only stood out as glaringly sinister, but gradually she began to understand. There were ounces and dates listed, observations of reactions. And there was a drawing, a crude sketch of a baby, its eyes closed, its toes webbed. A thick arrow pointed toward the child's feet. There was a question mark. There was the word "Dead." And following it, "Try Again."

Of all people, it had been Samuel who held her tight around the waist as she kicked and thrashed, screaming at Pontilliar, threatening to cut his eyes out. Threatening to murder him where he stood. She flung the journal at Pontilliar's feet, its pages snapping like the broken wings of a bird, and howled until her throat bled. Throughout the episode, carried out in the dust behind the cookhouse tent as an August twilight descended, Pontilliar had remained calm. He gave Ruby explanations. He gave her rationales. He talked about time passing and water under the bridge. Spilt milk. Pontilliar did not give into shame; he did not apologize.

Samuel had most likely saved Pontilliar's life that day, though it took years for Ruby to forgive him for intervening. And for keeping Pontilliar's secret. When she finally broke free from Samuel, she was too exhausted to do anything but spit at Pontilliar's feet and announce that she was leaving the Star Light. Pontilliar wished her good luck and Godspeed. Ruby walked in a daze through the labyrinth of tents and found herself in the center of the midway, surrounded by a crowd of townies, startled to see a freak off the bally. A tight circle quickly formed around her, grubby children and gaping mothers. Teenage boys whistling, calling for a free show. A man with a waxed mustache reached his hand out and tried to touch her face. It was slick with tears, but, of course, he wanted only to prod at her tattoos.

And that was when she had known for sure. There was no place for her in the real world. She had seen it in the faces of the crowd; she was no longer one of them. Her fate was tied to the carnival as surely as the ink was etched into her skin and she could not escape it. The mob around her had turned rough as more hands shot out to touch her and Ruby had begun to push back. She had panicked, but soon rousties were at her side, breaking up the crowd, and Samuel, yet again, had his arm around her waist. She had hated him and she had hated her father, and the Star Light and all the world and herself. But at that moment, she had no more rage to expend. Ruby had let her head drop onto Samuel's shoulder and had allowed him to lead her away to safety.

NINETEEN

Daniel came forth when he heard the drums. He stood at the edge of the large clearing, back in the shadows of the cypress trees, and watched. As he had watched Jacob step off a little girl's swing and hang himself. As he had watched Tom, blindly climbing the Ferris Wheel, not knowing why he was doing what he was doing, and certainly not anticipating a high wind with the force of a gale on an otherwise perfectly still night. As he had watched Ruby, her profile lit by the flickering stream of light and dust motes and put his hand over hers in the theater darkness. Ruby. He could have left the Star Light after Tom. He should have. The carnival had already become tedious for him. It was filthy and miserable and, in too many ways, honest. He should have gone back to Chicago, where every woman was devious and every man a cutthroat. Where every moment popped and sizzled and the streets were filled with so much vice that it fell from the air like confetti. But as he had been loping away, determined to put his little dalliance with the Star Light behind him, he had seen her in that field, with the moonlight burnishing her hair and a cigarette held between her fingers just so and her wide eyes that were so devoid of fear, and he had changed his mind. He had encountered a thousand raven-haired tragedies in his time and his travels, some who had inspired a generation of weepy literature and some who had brought kingdoms to their knees. How could this woman be any different? But he had stayed. He had not been able to resist the game, and look where it had gotten him. Seeking answers to questions that only bred more questions. Wasting his time with a swampland crone. All because of what he had felt for a few seconds inside a foul-smelling geek tent. All because of her.

The drums were increasing in intensity and Daniel turned his attention to the circle that had formed in the ceremonial ground just outside of The Village. He was bored already, but he needed to know more. Had to know more. Daniel lit a cigarette in the darkness and smoked it with his hands in his pockets, leaning against a tree, as he watched the ceremony unfold.

For the moment, Madame Celeste was nowhere to be seen. A younger woman, lighter-skinned, her hair coming loose from a purple tignon, seemed to be presiding over the rite. The tempo of the drums increased as the woman twirled around a heaping bonfire in the center of the circle, her long hair and skirt swirling around her in a dervish and coming dangerously close to the flames. The circle had been made up only of men, each beating a drum with the palms of both hands, but now a string of women entered the clearing, stamping their bare feet hard into the ground. Each one carried a rattle in one hand and a lit candle in the other. The line of women, shaking the rattles in tempo with the drums, formed an outer circle to the men. The woman in the center hadn't stopped spinning, but now she slowed and untied a blue cord from around her waist. She held it aloft over her head with both hands and the drums beat even faster. Finally, she threw the cord at a low altar constructed of crumbling bricks and cypress planks and collapsed. The drums and rattles ceased immediately and two of the women broke through the line of men and dragged the woman away. She had fallen too close to the fire and the hem of her skirt had begun to smoke. Daniel rolled his eyes and lit another cigarette.

In the silence that followed, Madame Celeste appeared in the circle. She looked the same as before, only now she wore a long purple dress and had heavy gold hoops dangling from her ears. She wore a tricorne hat with a plume of heron feathers streaming down the back and carried two bottles of tafia. Daniel smiled to himself. She looked like a damn pirate. Madame Celeste walked slowly around the fire three times in a counterclockwise direction and then took a swig of the raw, sugary rum. She blew it onto the fire and the flames leapt higher. The men began to chant "boudoum, boudoum" and the women behind them echoed with "canga moune." Madame Celeste hobbled over to the altar and sprinkled tafia at each corner. A man, Daniel recognized him as the man who had blocked his path on the way to the lodge, entered the circle carrying a silver bowl and placed it on the altar. Madame Celeste crossed herself six times and then pulled a burning branch from the flames. She used it to light the liquid in the bowl and then she stood behind the altar and the drumming began again. Daniel yawned.

The ceremony went on for another half hour as each villager brought forth an offering to the bowl. Most brought food, candied fruit twisted up in paper or dishes of rice and vegetables. Each offering was held over the flaming bowl while Madame Celeste made signs and spoke, sometimes screamed, words into the flames. Then the offering was flung to the ground inside the circle, the burning paper sparking through the air and smoldering in the dirt. Some villagers brought bouquets of dried reeds dusted with orris powder and these flamed spectacularly. Three women wearing blue cords around their waists brought a live chicken each to the bowl and Madame Celeste used a golden knife to cut their throats. The birds, still twitching, were thrown to the ground with the rest. After each offering, the villager was free to break from the circle and begin dancing themselves, so that by the end the clearing was filled with men and women whirling around the fire, pounding drums and shaking rattles and trampling the gifts, sometimes still burning, into the ground beneath them.

More tafia appeared and the men and women raised the bottles to each other's lips as they danced. When the last offering had been made, Madame Celeste raised both her hands over her head and the villagers suddenly froze and dropped to the ground. The bearded man who had been standing behind the altar with Madame Celeste now procured a wooden box and held it out before her. She dipped her ancient hands into it and pulled out a heavy black snake that when stretched out must have been as long as she was tall. She held it out for the villagers to see and they all began to make a guttural, thrumming noise as Madame Celeste rhythmically twisted her hips, swinging the snake over her head. Daniel liked snakes and he frowned at what he knew was coming. Madame Celeste suddenly gripped the snake behind its head with one hand and took up the golden knife with the other. The snake was writhing and twisting in her hand as its tail kept slipping into the flaming bowl, and then Madame Celeste cut it in half and it was over. She slung both halves of the snake into the clearing and shrieked an unintelligible sound that made Daniel wince. The villagers raised their hands over their heads and cheered, and the drinking and dancing continued. Madame Celeste's shoulders slumped and she receded away from the flames, back into the swamp.

Daniel watched the revelers, for now that's what they had become, and waited. The smell of wood smoke rising up in the heavy, still air masked the sulfur of the swamp and reminded

Daniel of the wicker giant sacrifices at home, so many centuries ago. The dancers were drenched in sweat, from the heat, the fire, the liquor and their continuous movement, but when Madame Celeste came up through the trees behind Daniel and stood next to him, she appeared as calm and cool as he was. She wasn't surprised to see him.

"You came back. Or didn't leave."

Her voice was flat and resigned. Daniel jutted his chin out toward the dancers.

"Quite a party. It's a little late in the year for St. John's Eve, isn't it?"

"I'm sure they will be glad to know you were here. It was a special ceremony for you."

"Oh, really?"

Daniel turned toward her and smiled. He was enjoying himself now as he tried to decide what to do with Madame Celeste and her little village. Madame Celeste sighed.

"When they saw you walk through the market yesterday, they thought you were Doctor Jin."

"Doctor Jin? I hadn't heard of that one."

Madame Celeste's face was sour, as if she could hardly keep her distaste for the conversation back behind her teeth.

"Cousin to Doctor John. Doctor Jin is a ghost. A white man who can walk through walls, whose feet never touch the ground. How else could they explain you? Your arrival is supposed to bring them great luck and wealth. That's what the Night Fire was for."

"You should have told them I was Papa La Bas."

Madame Celeste grimaced.

"What, was the ceremony not to your taste?"

Daniel shrugged.

"I've seen better."

Madame Celeste slowly began to shake her head.

"We are a strange group here. This place was built by runaway slaves. Exiled quadroon mistresses. Mixed blood Comanche and Choctaws, run down from the north and the west. Two centuries ago, a ship was commandeered as it was entering the delta and the slaves escaped. They were from the East Indies, not the West, and they came here. They introduced the tattoo needle and many other traditions to us."

"I had wondered about that."

"Some follow the ways as I do. They are mostly as old as I am. The rest have been influenced by the hoodoo nonsense coming out of New Orleans. Gris-gris and love potions and get-together-drops. They believe courage can be bought in a vial and evil warded off from a bag of cat excrement. They do not know Bondye and the Iwa. They do not know Legba. And they do not want to know."

Madame Celeste swept her arm out toward the clearing. Many of the dancers had ceased moving and were now standing still, only swaying slightly, as they ate plates of cold rice and chicken. Those that weren't eating were passing around the tafia.

"They want this. As you said, a party. They want the fire and the drums and the creature sacrifices, but more for the show of it. Not all, but for many, the old ways are…"

Daniel turned to her.

"Old? You said it yourself, woman. Papa Legba has left you."

Madame Celeste folded her arms over her chest. She continued to watch her people in the clearing.

"And you have arrived. To take his place?"

Daniel pushed himself away from the tree and stretched.

"Well, the music isn't really to my taste, but I do love a party."

"It's true, what you are wondering. What I told you yesterday was not a lie. I did it."

Something had changed in Madame Celeste's voice and Daniel slowly turned around to face her.

"Did what?"

"The girl. The white woman. I did it. I turned her body into a

225

shield. I used the Wanla and the Omi. I used bloods, I used minerals from the other side of the world, left to me by my ancestors across the ocean. Needle magic you know not of."

Daniel shrugged.

"So?"

Madame Celeste's yellow eyes began to blaze. Her lips were trembling, but she kept speaking.

"So, there are some things in this world that even you cannot combat."

Daniel laughed, but she kept speaking. Her entire body was shaking now.

"There are things that are still unknown to you. You gods who eat time. You never look back. Never under, but always over. A century to us is but a blink of an eye to you, yes, but we still have centuries. We still have hidden power."

"You have the power to give someone a tattoo? I'd hardly say that's a mythical accomplishment."

"But it worked."

Celeste's throat vibrated and her voice crackled.

"It worked. I know it worked. And you have found her. And she will know. And she will haunt you for the rest of her days. I can see it now. I can see where her path will take her."

Daniel clenched his fists. He didn't have time for this babble, for this pretense. He drew himself up to his full height and pushed his face close to Celeste's.

"You hag. You witch doctor. You conjurer. You have no power."

He grabbed her by the throat and lifted her up so that she was barely standing on her toes. Her eyes were bulging slightly. Her pointed tongue came through her lips as she laughed at him.

"But she does. And she will use it. It has come to me now. I have seen it. In the sky, in the whorls of the trees, in the sun on the skin of the water. She is a mirror. She is the reflection and the pieces you will shatter. Sharp as a razor's edge."

"Liar!"

Daniel roared and released her. Madame Celeste dropped to the ground. She was coughing and gurgling in the mud, breathing with difficulty and unable to lift herself up. Daniel kicked her like a dog, but she kept laughing.

"I have seen it! And you have seen it, too!"

"You lie!"

Madame Celeste lay on her side, holding her ribs, her face still a grotesque mask of mockery.

"You came back tonight because you thought I was counterfeit. That the tattoos on the girl were only charms. You watched this ceremony and you think yourself safe. But you know. Oh, you know, you know, you know it in your dusty ghost bones."

He kicked her again, but she only laughed louder, her words garbled between the wheezing and cackling.

"You knew it when you first saw her. You knew it when you touched her. You knew, you knew, you have seen it in your dreams, as I have."

Daniel stepped back from her.

"I don't dream, old woman. I don't dream, because I don't sleep. Because I am a god."

Madame Celeste spat out a clot. She grinned up at Daniel, with blood smeared across her lips and chin. She caught her breath between every word, but her message was clear.

"Then why are you arguing with me?"

She rolled over on her back and howled. Daniel backed away from her in disgust. He looked over his shoulder at the dancers. No one could hear Madame Celeste's maniacal laughter over the din of the resumed drums and rattles, the shouts and squeals and occasional smash as empty bottles and plates were thrown into the fire. Daniel looked at the villagers and then looked at Madame Celeste and the fury rose and rose in him like a tempest. It filled his body and his brain and the air around him, swirling like a maelstrom of unrefined rage. He faced the dancers head on and sent all of his wrath out toward them. Then his eyes glowed red as he wrapped himself in black feathers and ascended to the trees to watch.

The first one to react was a woman, who took the glass bottle she had been drinking from and smashed it into the face of the man dancing next to her. He reeled and tried to grab her wrist while feeling for the shards of glass in his face, but the woman dug the edge of the broken bottle into his throat and it was over. Or rather, it had begun. The villagers began to turn on one another, crashing into each other with bottles, plates, rattles, drums and then using their fists, their feet, their nails, their teeth. One of the men picked up one of the wooden benches that had been brought out with the food and wielded it like a club. They knocked each other into the fire and the smoke turned oily as the woods began to fill with the smell of singed hair and roasting flesh. When less than ten of the dancers were still standing they collectively turned toward the trees and found Madame Celeste, still rolling in the mud. They fell on her and tore her apart with their teeth. As her laughter morphed into screams, Daniel climbed up higher into the sky. He didn't need to see anymore. It would be over in a few minutes. They would continue like this until there was only one left and he or she would throw themselves on the flames. The air grew colder around him and Daniel closed his eyes. He didn't have time to bother with a silly swamp village. He had bigger fish to fry.

Down on the midway, a little boy in his best pressed shirt and only pair of shoes is staring up at me. He is pointing to the pinnacle of the big top tent. The boy tells his mother that a man is holding fire in his hands. He whimpers. He is the only one who sees it coming.

The crowd heard the screams before Ruby did. Their heads began to turn as they looked around at one another, wondering if the sounds were part of the snake show or another show, farther down the midway. Ruby watched their faces and slowed down her dance. Then the screams became louder, the word "fire" discernable, and a stampede broke out. Ruby froze on stage with a snake still around her neck and looked to Jasper, sitting behind the gramophone. Their eyes met for a moment and then Ruby dropped the snake on the ground and leapt off the stage, following the crush of people as they bottlenecked through the front of the tent. She stumbled behind them out onto the midway and into the path of chaos.

At first, it was hard to tell what was happening. The townsfolk appeared to be running in one direction and the carnival workers in the other, and everyone was colliding, pushing and shoving and forcing each other out of the way. Children were howling over the screams and shouts and she could smell smoke in the air, but couldn't tell where it was coming from. A woman went down in front of her and Ruby grabbed her and dragged her against the side of the tent to keep her from being trampled. Ruby braced the woman by the shoulders and shook her.

"What's going on?"

There was a terror in the woman's eyes such as Ruby had never seen before. A blind terror of pure panic.

"My boy is in there, my boy is in there!"

Ruby spun around to see where the woman was pointing and she gasped. The big top. The big top tent was on fire, its roof blazing, the flames crawling down the sides of the tent. Ruby barely noticed that the woman had darted away beneath her hands as Jasper came up beside her.

"Holy hell. Holy mother of hell."

His eyes had a wild glaze to them and already his face was beginning to darken with the soot and ash wafting through the air. Jasper pushed her hard.

"Get out of here, Ruby. Go!"

Rousties and gamesmen were rushing past her, swinging buckets of water at their sides. For a moment there was the possibility, the hope that it could be saved, that it wasn't all over, that the fire could be put out, but in the blink of an eye Ruby realized that hope was futile. The fire was too big and moving too fast. A few men were wrapping cloths around their faces and dumping the buckets of water over their heads, but it was soon clear that no one was going in or getting out of the big top tent. The fire had come down like a curtain, sealing the canvas walls. The soaking men couldn't get near it.

The crowd suddenly grew thicker around her and Ruby realized that the townspeople who had been running down the midway to get away were now running back toward the fire. They were pooling in the corral created by the circle of show tents and were too confused to think of darting behind the wagons to get out to the open field. Ruby caught Gig by the elbow as he raced by.

"Why is everyone coming back? Why aren't they getting out?"

Gig was carrying a small tin pail filled with water from the fishing game. His face was darkly streaked with ash.

"The gates. The arches. It's all on fire. It's all on fire, too. I don't know how."

He caught his breath for a moment and gripped the pail tighter. Ruby looked around her, overwhelmed by the maelstrom swirling beneath the Ferris Wheel as people crowded against it. Gig grabbed her shoulder and shook her.

"What are you still doing here? Get out! Go through the field. What's wrong with you?"

He shoved her and tottered toward the big top, wobbling against the weight of the bucket. Ruby whirled around, but Jasper had disappeared. She looked out into the stampeding crowd, still stunned, but then she heard the creak of the big top as one side of it crumpled to the ground and suddenly her head cleared. She didn't turn back and run for the field, but charged across the midway toward the cootch tent, pushing people already smelling of singed hair and cotton out of her way. The Girl Revue was on the opposite side of the midway, past the Ferris Wheel and the Whip, and as she ran she tried not to look up at the tower of flames that had once been the big top tent as it collapsed in on itself.

Then everything went still for a moment, as if all of the sound had been sucked out of the air. Ruby looked around, seeing only terrified faces, eyes rolling back like horses, skin already blistered by the heat, buckets, bodies, a useless hose underfoot, and then came the wind. An impossible, raging wind came tunneling down the midway and Ruby dropped and clung to the ground, closing her eyes against the grit and the heat. It howled over her head and Ruby knew that it couldn't be real, it couldn't be natural, and in that instant, with the wind ripping at her skin, she remembered the fox eyes in the darkness.

Just as fast as it came, the wind disappeared, but the entire midway was now lost in the blaze. Ruby dug her toes into the dirt and pushed herself up, disoriented by the surrounding flames. Every tent and wagon was burning now and she couldn't even see the big top, it was only a tower of fire. No one was running with buckets to douse the fire, they were all running away. Only there was nowhere to run. Ruby turned in circles, trying to determine the direction of the cootch tent amidst the pandemonium, still thinking that's where she needed to go. Still with only one purpose in mind. People were streaming past her, flailing in circles, careening into the ride machinery or each other. Their hair and clothes were on fire, their eyes aflame in white terror against their

STEPH POST

blackened skin, and their mouths were open and uttering inhuman screams. One of these demons was January.

She fell against Ruby and Ruby caught her and flung her to the ground, beating her chest and head to put out the flames. As soon as she rolled January over, though, she knew it was too late. The skin on half of her face and the right side of her body was sliding off. What was left of her gauzy costume had melted and her voice was bubbling in her throat as she tried to speak. Ruby didn't know if January could see or hear her, but she held January's head in her lap and kept calling her name, trying to save her with her voice and her presence. It only took seconds for the light to leave January's eyes and Ruby threw back her head and wailed like an animal, clutching what was left of her friend to her chest.

And then, through the smoke and the dirt and the tears and the heat and the flames, she saw him. Standing in the center of the midway, with his black suit and his red eyes, with what looked like bones rising up out of his back and arching over his head. His fists were clenched and his jaw so tight it seemed the bones of his face were coming through the shimmering skin. A cloud of sparks swirled around him, but did not touch him. It was Daniel and not Daniel. He was spectral. Ruby saw him and he saw her and though the bodies falling around them both were in flames and the sounds coming from them were bestial and the smell was of burning flesh and hair and dreams, neither Ruby nor Daniel looked away from one another. She cradled January's head and matched the intensity of Daniel's stare with her own and she knew and knew and knew. She felt the wind again, whipping, unnatural, and heavy with the same hatred now burning in her core. She closed her eyes against it and the world was filled with fire.

232

TWENTY

"**P**iece of pie?"

Hayden finished stirring sugar into his coffee before looking up. He carefully set the spoon down next to his cup and smiled cautiously at the woman standing behind the counter with the coffeepot still in her hand. Hayden shook his head and removed his hat. She tucked a pudgy hand into her apron and grinned at him.

"You sure? We got banana cream. My daughter made it herself."

The woman tilted her head toward a red-haired girl with near translucent skin and a swath of freckles across her cheekbones who was standing idly behind the cash register, picking at her nails. The girl blushed and hid her hands behind her back when she saw her mother and Hayden watching her. She edged around the wooden counter and began furiously wiping off one of the three tables alongside the window with a dirty rag. Hayden turned back to his coffee and shook his head again.

"No pie, thanks. Coffee's fine."

The woman put her hands on her broad hips and considered her daughter.

"She's shy, poor thing. Even working here, there's not too much of a chance to meet folks. Not too many travelers coming this way no more. For a minute there, this place was jumping. Folks headed down to Mobile and Biloxi. Up to Jackson. Going through Napoleon on mill business. People started buying cars and they came whizzing up to the door, scaring the mule teams half to death. I opened this place up after my husband passed some years back. People talked about my meatloaf halfway across Mississippi and into Alabama. And my pie. 'You got to stop by and try Pam's pie.' Everyone said that. Then the Southern Line connected across the state and the mills around here dried up. Anyone going anywhere takes the railroad now and we got no one but the locals stopping by."

Pam shook her head and finally set the coffeepot back on the stove. She smoothed down her apron and fingered the dark ringlets of hair framing her face. Hayden wrapped his hands around his cup and blew on it. The air in the cramped roadside restaurant was almost as hot as the steam rising up from the coffee. It was just mid-morning, though, and he still had a ways to go. He tasted the coffee. Even with the sugar it was strong and bitter and Hayden hoped it would keep him going. It had been a long week and a half. Pam leaned on the counter and chewed the inside of her cheek for a moment.

"Yeah, Deborah takes after her father. Quiet like. I don't know how she's ever going to find a husband."

Hayden kept his eyes on his coffee, but Pam didn't seem to notice. She stood up straight and crossed her arms over her chest, sizing Hayden up.

"You got yourself a wife?"

Deborah made a small gasping sound and ran behind the counter and into the small kitchen. Hayden could just imagine her cowering in the corner, scarlet red in the face from her mother's brazenness. Hayden wiped his mouth with the back of his hand and rested his elbows on the counter.

"No, ma'am."

Eileen's face flickered briefly in front of him. He'd never considered himself a widower and would never willingly tell anyone about Eileen and Cora. But the word "wife" struck a chord with him. It connoted only shame and regret. It would never mean anything but sorrow for Hayden. He studied the greasy film across the top of his coffee while Pam thought about his response a moment.

"Let me guess, though. You got yourself a sweetheart somewhere, waiting on you."

Hayden dropped his eyes. He fumbled in his pocket for his cigarettes.

"I wouldn't say she's waiting for me any longer."

He started to put a cigarette to his lips, but Pam shook her head.

"Sorry, fella. Can't smoke in here. Irritates Deborah's asthma something fierce."

Hayden quickly tucked the cigarette back into the package. Pam lowered her head and cut her eyes at Hayden.

"So, what'd you do?"

"Pardon?"

"What'd you do? To make her quit waiting on you?"

Pam had the gleeful look of someone leaning across a fence, just waiting to hear the worst. Hayden drained his coffee.

"I wish I knew. I mean, I know what I did. I just wish I knew why I did it."

Pam nodded knowingly.

"You and every man walking around God's green earth. She's a strong-willed girl, too, I bet."

"And stubborn."

"She pretty?"

Hayden's chest visibly rose and fell.

"She's the most beautiful woman I've ever seen."

Hayden heard the door open behind him. A man in overalls came in and sat at the end of the counter, two stools away. Pam nodded at the man, but didn't move. Her mouth was hanging open slightly as she listened to Hayden.

"And then I ruined things before they even had a chance to start. Yet again. I was such a fool."

Pam absently refilled his cup. Hayden sat up straight and fidgeted with the brim of his hat.

"But I'm going to try again anyway. I'll do whatever it takes. Drag myself through the mud if I have to. Whether she wants to see me again or not, I've got to talk to her. I have to at least tell her I'm sorry for being such an ass, excuse my language. I have to try to explain, even though I'm not exactly sure what happened myself. I don't think she's going to want me back, but I don't know what else to do."

Pam seemed to be intently thinking about what he was saying. She walked over to the man who had just sat down and placed a cup of coffee and a glass of water in front of him. Then she came back over to Hayden and leaned on the counter, staring hard at him.

"You love her?"

Hayden was taken by surprise at the woman's directness.

"What's that supposed to mean?"

"It's a pretty straightforward question."

Hayden glanced at the man in overalls. He was reading a newspaper, ignoring them both. Hayden looked back at Pam, who was still staring at him. He shook his head.

"I'd say it's actually a pretty complicated one."

The only other time someone had put it to him was when Eileen's father had demanded to know his intentions. The enormous man, pipe clenched between his teeth as he paced across his oak-paneled study, had railed at Hayden, alternately threatening and berating him. He'd wanted to know how Hayden could be so base, so foul and irresponsible. Hayden had taken the castigation with his head down, wondering the exact same things. Then Eileen's father had asked him about love. Eileen loved him, he had said with disgust, and was begging him not to go to the police. Or take him out back and shoot him with his Winchester. Did Hayden, then, love his daughter in return?

For the first time since he had seen Eileen's swollen belly, Hayden's head had become clear. Hayden had stood his ground and admitted that no, he did not love Eileen. He never had. He didn't think he ever would. And yet, he had conceded to marrying her and her father had let the matter rest with that.

But Ruby. Pam was still waiting on him. She shook her head.

"It doesn't have to be. Life is complicated. All of the things involved with loving or not loving a person are complicated. But love itself, well now, mister, it's a sin to complicate it. It's a kernel. It's a core. There are no shady areas. You either can't breathe without someone or you can. So, you love her or not?"

His Ruby. Hayden nodded slowly.

"I do."

"And she loves you?"

"I thought so, yes. Before."

Pam shook her head again.

"Before don't exist no more. It goes down with the sun and don't come back up with the moon. You think she can love you again?"

Hayden swallowed and bent his head over his coffee.

"I hope so."

Pam clapped her hands together.

"Then it will work out. It's as simple as that. You young folk are always making mountains out of molehills. Trust yourself. Trust her. It'll work out, you'll see."

She winked at Hayden and patted the counter in front of him before going back to the man reading the newspaper. He and Hayden were the only two people in the restaurant and Hayden was glad to have the attention shifted away from him. It was his fourth day back on the road as he tried to retrace his route east from Galveston back to Baton Rouge and then from there to Monroeville, Alabama, where he believed the carnival's route had taken it. He had a purpose and a direction now, but in some ways it felt like he'd been lost at sea ever since he had walked out of the snake tent, with the blind determination of leaving the Star Light, and Ruby, forever. Hayden still wasn't sure why he'd felt such a desperate need to leave the carnival. He couldn't comprehend it. He had driven west from Baton Rouge down to the Texas coast in a frenzied, sleepless haze, stopping only to fill up the tank of his Model T.

As he'd gotten farther and farther away from the Star Light, strange moments of clarity alighted on him like falling leaves and he would have to yank the steering wheel and screech to a stop, idling the car on the shoulder of the road. The fog surrounding him would lift for a few brief seconds and he would suddenly realize what he'd done. And then realize that he could still go back. He could apologize to Ruby; he could attempt to explain things to her, even though he wasn't sure what he would be explaining. She would understand that he had been impetuous and rash, she would forgive him. But now Ruby would forever be expecting him to take flight whenever the mood suited him. He had whispered to her in the darkness of her wagon that he would be a constant for her. He had promised that she could depend on him now, that he would be her touchstone. It had taken him less than forty-eight hours to break that promise.

Then there had been the horrible tightening in his chest and stomach that came over him whenever he thought of standing on the midway again. He couldn't account for it, except that he felt an almost physical revulsion whenever he imagined himself at the Star Light. The fog would creep over him and he would become nauseous until he was driving again, heading away from the carnival. When he had finally arrived in Galveston, he couldn't remember how he'd gotten there, only that it was where he needed to be. It was in Galveston that Ruby's look became his obsession.

It wasn't the look Ruby had given him right before he stormed away from the snake tent. Then, her face had been defiant, proud. She'd been furious with him, her eyes cruel, her mouth twisted in anger. He had seen that expression on her face dozens of times as they had fought throughout the years. No, the look that began to haunt him was the one he had seen on Ruby's face when he'd left her at the end of the circuit, three years before. He'd not yet bought the Ford and was taking the train back to Beaumont to set his plans for their life together in motion. He had wanted her to accompany him to the station, but she'd only gone as far as the edge of the carnival lot. They hadn't spoken much, all that there was to say had already been said the night before, but he had rested his chin on her shoulder and she had held him with a fierceness that was almost frightening. He'd made a joke about her acting like she would never see him again. A joke. He'd kissed her and she had stepped away from him with a look of such wise despondency. As if she knew all of the hope he'd impressed upon her would fail. And it had, then and now, once again.

When he'd arrived in Galveston and stood on Post Office Street in front of the only boardinghouse he could afford, Hayden had seen that look. And when he ventured to one of the blind tigers at the south end of Seawall Boulevard and drank the rum poured down his throat by the dock workers, pounding on his back and encouraging him to rid himself of his love sicknesses, he had seen that look. When a woman had sat down in his lap, giggling and spilling out of the front of her dress, everything had finally blurred and he'd thrown up all over the woman's cleavage. Hayden had woken up on the seawall, with two gulls using his body as a perch, and seen that look in the cloudless sky, going in and out of focus above him.

He'd stayed stone drunk for the next five days. Mostly he wallowed in the lice-infested bed, swilling rum from a bottle on the floor and staring up at the rotting crossbeams above him. He knew he was pathetic. He could hear Ruby's voice telling him so. Telling him he stank, that he was being a waste. Ordering him to pull it together. To stumble downstairs to the washroom and soak his head in cold water and put on a clean shirt. Whenever he thought of returning to the Star Light, though, the haze came down over him and he became disoriented and confused. He didn't want to stay in the boardinghouse, he didn't want to drink, but something kept him in a suffocating torpor. The fog had become a boulder on his chest, insistently pressing down on him, so he'd remained in bed with a bottle within reach and watched the cockroaches skittering up and down the walls.

A week after he arrived in Galveston, the sullen woman who owned the boardinghouse flung the door to his room open and told him to get out. She wasn't going to have a man die in her residence and she couldn't see what else he was doing save drinking himself to death. Hayden had wandered down to the docks and dried out, sitting with the gulls all day and watching the boats sail in and out of the harbor. When he finally sobered up that evening, he'd pulled his sketchbook out of his duffle bag and tried to draw the ships against the sunset. In all the lines on the page, he'd seen only Ruby's eyes. Only that look. And then, suddenly, the haze had been blown from him and the fog inside his head had cleared. Hayden had stood, blinking as if just emerging from a cave into daylight, and he'd hurled the sketchbook into the water. He had yelled at the top of his lungs, startling the swarm of birds around him. Then he had picked up his bag, returned to the garage where he'd left his car and headed east into the night, determined to return to the Star Light.

Hayden was slowly surfacing from the depths of his thoughts when he heard the word "circus" come from the man in the overalls sitting at the counter. Hayden shook his head and turned to the man, who was shoveling fried eggs into his mouth and talking across the counter to Pam.

"What were you just saying now, about a circus?"

The man swallowed the mush in his mouth and then slurped his coffee.

"The circus that was over in Monroeville. Over in Alabama. Star Miracle something or other. One of those names ties up your tongue. You ain't heard about that?"

The man tapped the newspaper next to his plate and Pam clicked her tongue and shook her head. Hayden swiveled on his stool toward them. His heart was pounding and his voice came out stretched and thin.

"No. What happened?"

The man pointed to the newspaper with his fork.

"The fire? Geeze, it's been in every newspaper this side of the Mississippi. Probably all the way to Georgia. Haven't had a tragedy like that 'round these parts in some time."

Pam fidgeted with the collar of her shirt.

"Such a shame. It's bad enough the way those poor carnie folk have to live. Then to have a fire like that. Just terrible."

Hayden's ears were ringing. He wanted to reach for the newspaper on the counter, but couldn't move.

"How bad? I mean, when, how? What happened?"

The man slurped his coffee again and began cutting into a hunk of ham on his plate.

"Happened end of last week. Paper today said they still didn't know how it started. I guess the inquiry's just beginning."

Pam shook her head again.

"And all those poor souls in Monroeville. Just hundreds. Probably half the town was there when it happened. Paper said it was the first night of the carnival and everybody had gone."

She turned to the man.

"Or was it a circus?"

The man spoke through his ham.

"Paper's calling it a circus. Don't know there's a difference. Is there a difference?"

Pam opened her mouth to reply, but then saw the look on Hayden's face.

"Why, honey, you all right? You're white as a sheet. Did you have people over in Monroeville? Oh Lord, I hope you didn't have family out that way. Did you?"

Hayden opened his mouth to speak, but nothing came out. He swallowed a few times and then raised his hand slightly toward the newspaper. The man stopped chewing and pointed his fork toward Hayden.

"You okay there, fella?"

Hayden coughed and cleared his throat. His voice still came out in a choked whisper.

"Survivors? How many, I mean, did they..."

His voice trailed off. The man stuck another piece of ham in his mouth and pushed the newspaper over to Hayden with the edge of his hand.

"Here. I don't know nothing more than what's already printed."

Hayden snatched up the paper. In large bold letters the headline proclaimed CIRCUS FIRE CAUSE STILL UNKNOWN. Underneath it were two long articles, the first of which was an interview with a man who had been on his way to the Star Light to pick up his wife and daughter. Hayden only caught some of the words as he read. Smoke. Flames. Screams. Death. Inferno. The second article included the names of twelve survivors, all

Monroeville residents who had been either just entering or just leaving the Star Light. There was no mention of any surviving carnival workers. Hayden carefully folded the paper and pressed it down on the counter next to his empty cup. He was vaguely aware that Pam and the man were watching him. He looked up with glassy eyes and firmly set both hands on the edge on the counter.

"I think I need to pay for my coffee. I think I need to go now."

He stood up from his stool. Pam leaned over the counter and touched his arm.

"Oh, honey, I'm so sorry."

It was Biblical, the destruction. Hayden sat behind the steering wheel of his car, looking out at the roped-off wreckage that had once been the Monroeville Fairground, that had once been the Star Light Miraculum, his home, Ruby's home, and was reminded of a print he knew from a copy of John Martin's *Illustrations to the Bible*. The piece was titled "The Destruction of the Pharaoh's Host" and Hayden had always been both fascinated and terrified by it. And now, here was the aftermath of the print come to life. Hayden wasn't sure he had the courage to stand before it.

The fire had burned itself out and the residual smoke had ceased to rise, but a faint cloud still hung over the ruins as any stray breeze lifted and carried ash up into the air. All of the show tents were gone, exposing what was left of their charred stages. One of high wire platforms still stood and a few other pieces of scorched metal rose from the wreckage: sets of wagon bases and wheels, some of the banner frames, a support bar for the entrance arches. The Ferris Wheel was mostly in one piece, though the metal had been blackened, and the core of the carousel could be seen next to it. The horses had mostly been burned away. The office and management wagons, away from the midway, were still standing, although both had been blasted so hard that their windows had been blown out and the doors were now only charred splinters. The cookhouse tent had caught fire and burned away, but the heavy iron stove had been left untouched. Most of the vehicles had been spared, too.

It seemed as though the fire had been completely concentrated on the midway and hadn't spread through the field. Most everything that comprised the heart of the carnival, though, the striped canvas tents, the bally banners, the game booths, was gone, dissolved into heaps of ash, smears of soot that had once been people's entire livelihoods. That had once been people. Hayden slowly climbed out of the Model T and stepped to the ground. The smell had already hit him when he'd driven up, but as he walked closer to the wreckage, the acrid stench grew stronger. He stood at the edge of what would have once been the brightly lit midway and wanted to cry, wanted to vomit, wanted to yell, but he could do nothing. He had begun to duck under the rope when he realized he wasn't alone.

"Hey, you there! Sir, stop! Stop!"

Hayden slowly stood back up and turned around. Two sheriff's deputies were running clumsily toward him, one with his hand outstretched, and now Hayden became aware of a caged car marked Police Patrol parked at the crossroads in front of the western side of the lot. The deputies slowed as they approached him and one bent over, wheezing.

"Sir, you can't go in there. Cordoned off. Illegal to tamper with arson evidence."

Hayden stiffened.

"Arson?"

The other deputy hiked up his trousers and caught his breath. He glared at Hayden suspiciously.

"What are you doing here? You come to scavenge? Make off

with something? There ain't much to steal, but we'll arrest you just the same."

Hayden narrowed his eyes. Nothing about the deputies intimidated him. He opened his mouth to speak, to explain, but he froze when he heard another voice coming from behind him.

"Gentlemen, it's all right. I know this man."

Hayden whirled around and saw Samuel walking toward him from another group of cars that had maps and papers spread across the hoods. Three men in suits were studying the papers, though they looked up and watched Samuel cross over to the lot. The first deputy put out a hand and stopped Samuel before he could get too close. He jerked his head back toward Hayden and frowned.

"Whoa, now. He a carnie? He work here or something?"

The relief spread through Hayden like a warm flush. If Samuel was alive that meant others could be alive. She could be alive. He started to speak again, but Samuel firmly cut him off.

"No. He has never worked for the carnival. I believe he knew some of the men who worked there, though. If it's all right with you, I'll talk to him and explain the situation. There will be no trouble."

"All right, then. Don't be too long, you hear? We ain't wanting no funny business coming from you."

The deputy spat a thick stream of tobacco juice near Samuel's boots, but let him pass. Though Samuel's face was its usual unreadable, frowning mask, Hayden broke out into a childish grin and went to shake his hand. Samuel quickly turned to avoid it.

"Walk."

Hayden cautiously drew his hand back and fell in beside Samuel.

"Samuel, I need to know. Ruby, is she alive? Did she make it?"

"Keep walking."

Hayden jammed his hands in his pockets and walked a few more yards with Samuel before turning his head around to look at the scene behind them. Samuel kept his head straight forward, his hands behind his back and snapped at Hayden when he turned.

"Don't look back. Don't turn around, just keep walking for God's sake."

"What's going on here?"

Samuel wouldn't answer him until they had gotten nearly halfway around the blistered fairground. Hayden had been doing his best not to look over at the lot. Finally, Samuel stopped and turned sharply to face him. Hayden couldn't read him. He couldn't understand why Samuel was being so evasive.

"Ruby. I need to know if she's alive."

"I don't know for certain."

Hayden took a step back.

"You don't know? Well, you made it out, right? Why couldn't she? I mean, have they, have you, seen anything otherwise? Do you have any proof that she's not alive?"

Samuel sighed and looked over Hayden's shoulder at where the big top tent had stood.

"No. I have some reason to believe that she is alive, actually, but you need to give me a moment to explain why we are standing all the way out here."

Hayden nodded slowly.

"Okay, but you think she's alive."

"I think she could be alive. I wasn't here when it happened. There were a few problems with the altered route and I was already on my way with Chandler to Tuscaloosa to see about working out the advance. I didn't find out about the fire until the next morning. I have an alibi, though. We were at a filling station in Camden and thank God so was the Wilcox County sheriff's son. He already admitted to seeing me there with Chandler at the time of the fire. For once in my life, it has proved useful that I am a hard man to forget."

Hayden shook his head.

"I don't understand. Alibi?"

"Yes, I have an alibi. I obviously could not have started the fire if I was in Camden. And again, thankfully, the sheriff and the investigators could not imagine any man doing it on my orders. You, however, do not have an alibi. Which is why you have never worked for the Star Light, you have never met Pontilliar, or his daughter, or anyone of any importance in the show. You are simply a country bumpkin whose cousin guessed people's weight or something of that nature. Understood?"

Hayden balled his hands into fists.

"You don't think I did this?"

"Of course not."

Hayden relaxed, but Samuel was still looking at him sternly.

"But this is about to turn into a nightmare of accusations and motives and guilt and so on. There are creditors already coming in, debts, the insurance. The bloody insurance."

Samuel put his head in his hands. Hayden had never once seen Samuel hide his face. He assumed this was the strongest way he knew how to express emotion.

"I don't care about the insurance. I need to know about Ruby. Now."

Samuel slowly raised his head and stood straight and tall again, his face returned to its stoic countenance.

"Someone has to care. Someone has to bring this to order. I spent thirty-five years with Pontilliar. More than half my life. This situation has to be brought to heel. Everything he built cannot be lost in chaos. It cannot be devoured by the vultures. Do you see?"

"You're talking about justice?"

"I'm talking about order. There is nothing I can do about justice."

Samuel started walking again.

"I can't go up against him. But she can."

Hayden jogged to catch up.

"Him? She? Are you talking about Ruby? What are you saying?"

Samuel kept walking and Hayden threw his hands up in the air and yelled loud enough to make Samuel cringe and stop.

"God Almighty, stop speaking in riddles!"

Samuel stopped, but still didn't turn around.

"I believe Ruby is alive because something is missing from my wagon that only she knew about. I am going to show you. And I am going to give you something. Then, you must find her and give it to her. Do you understand?"

Hayden sank to his knees, pressing his hands into the warm dirt to hold himself up. The certainty in Samuel's voice. The plain directive of the task. Ruby was alive. She had to be.

TWENTY-ONE

I'm going to tell you a story. A nursery rhyme, really. For a time in the middle of the fourteenth century, when I was feeling particularly tired, I stayed in a little village in Germany, right on the edge of the Black Forest. It was charming, if that's the sort of thing you go in for. It was the kind of place where the wolves really did come out of the forest to eat small children, which made it authentic and I liked that.

Anyway, the village children used to sing this nursery rhyme in the street:

There once was a man with no eyes.

And since he had no eyes, he had no windows to his soul.

So the people thought he had no soul.

And they tried to kill him to prove it, but could not.

Children were so much more interesting back then. When the threat of monsters and murderous stepmothers lurked around every corner. When stories were true and full of nonsense. Now everything is so rational. So shiny and clean. It's disappointing, really.

I used to walk the cobblestone streets of that little village and the children would follow me and sing this story. For some reason, the children thought it was about me. I've always had my eyes, so they were wrong there, but they were onto something about the soul. Children can do that, you know. See things. Understand things. Draw aside the curtain and peek behind it. That's why I don't like them. In their make-believe and their sing-songs they are often right.

I do not have a soul. And many have tried to kill me, baited by me, of course. They have challenged me to duels. Condemned me for seducing their sons or daughters. Rounded me up as a prisoner of war. I like to play along with it sometimes, just to see what will happen. It's always the same. I have no soul. I'll never die. There is no other way around it.

I cannot help but wonder if you hate me now. The past is one thing, but the village in the swamp? The carnival? I haven't even told you about the church steeple I toppled onto a congregation just this past Sunday morning on my drive over here. Why did I do it? I had the wind in my hair, cigarette between my teeth, lambskin driving gloves gripping the wheel, the engine of my Duesenberg Model A roaring beneath me, not a care in the world. The sun was shining. Why?

Because at the end of the day, of the year, of the century, of the millennium, what else is there? I will tell you. There is nothing. Nothing.

The inside of Samuel's wagon was coated with ash. The floor was littered with glass, charred paper, scraps of fabric, and odd remnants of the midway that had been swept in by the strange wind that was now said by the few survivors to have accompanied the raging fire. Hayden stepped over a once white, patent leather baby shoe and a collection of balloons tied together and now punctured to shreds. A woman's straw hat. A Chinese paper lantern that was a prize from the ring toss game. A bouquet of silk flowers with a gold wedding band attached by a purple ribbon. Hayden picked up the flowers and set them on the edge of Samuel's desk. What had people been doing the moment the fire came sweeping down the midway? What had Ruby been doing? What had she thought? Felt? Hayden closed his eyes and shook his head. She could be alive. She had to be alive. He didn't have time to think about anything else now but finding her.

Samuel frowned at the flowers on the edge of his desk, now blown clear of papers for the first time since he'd moved into the management wagon. He stepped over a fallen tapestry bunched on the floor and unlocked a door behind his desk. Hayden was sure he had never seen the door before. Samuel waved his hand for Hayden to hurry up.

"Come on. The deputies and investigators will be back from lunch soon. If they find us here, it's one more reason to suspect us of foul play. Nothing is supposed to be touched until a conclusion is reached concerning who could have started the fire."

Hayden followed Samuel into the dim, cramped space. Except for a fine layer of ash that had blown underneath the door, the room had been untouched by the fire. It became almost pitch black as they edged against the wall and went farther back.

"Any ideas on who did start the fire?"

"Yes."

Samuel lit a lamp and the dark area Hayden was standing in came to light. It was a bedroom. Or, as Hayden turned to the wall of books, a library. Books were also strewn across the cot and stacked in piles on the table. The floor was littered with splintered wood and Hayden could see that a cabinet in the corner of the bookcase had been battered and pried apart into pieces. It looked like someone had taken a crowbar or a clawed hammer to it.

"What is this place?"

Samuel gestured around him.

"This was my room. My home. No one but Pontilliar knew about it. And Ruby. I brought her here the day before the fire. And she was the only one, absolutely the only one, who knew what was in that cabinet."

Samuel pointed to the shards of wood on the floor.

"What was in there is now gone. Do you see? She took it. She must have survived the fire and come here afterwards to take it. She's alive, Hayden. She has to be."

Hayden looked up at the shelves of books.

"The entire carnival, her entire world, is burned to the ground. She survives and she comes here to steal something from you? Why? What was in the box? Money? Your savings?"

"A book."

"That doesn't make any sense."

Samuel turned sharply to Hayden.

"I am about to tell you some things that don't make a lot of sense, and I am going to tell them to you very quickly and I need you to listen. Just listen, don't comment, don't ask questions."

Hayden was about to argue, but all he wanted was to be back on the road, searching for Ruby. The sooner he could do that, the better. He ran his hand over a row of leather bound books and nodded. Samuel bowed his head, collecting his thoughts.

"I said I knew who set the fire. I do. I'm almost positive. The man who came to us in Sulphur, posing as a geek. Daniel Revont. He started the fire, which wasn't a natural fire at all. I think he started it for Ruby."

Hayden couldn't help himself.

"Wait, what? Not a natural fire?"

Samuel slammed the palm of his hand down on the table and

a stack of books slid to the floor.

"Will you just listen to me? I have never been a man who wastes words and I don't intend to start now!"

Hayden sighed deeply and adjusted his hat, waiting for Samuel to continue.

"That man Daniel is no man at all. I still can't figure out what exactly he is. Ghost. Demon. Jinn."

Hayden's mouth hung open, but he kept himself in check, letting Samuel continue.

"He is something not of this world. Not human. The book Ruby took, the one that I showed her, I had thought it would tell me what Daniel was. Instead, it told me something about her. I found a drawing in it, and inside it was a depiction of one of the tattoos that repeats itself across her body. The eye surrounded by three wings. The drawing, I believe, insinuates that the symbol, and hence her tattoos, protects her from something."

Samuel closed his eyes and pinched the bridge of his nose.

"Hayden, no one from the back end of the midway could have survived the fire. I walked through there with the inspectors yesterday. The big top, the small show tents, they got the worst of it. There's nothing left of the snake show tent. Nothing. It is a graveyard out there."

Samuel picked up one of the books that had fallen to the floor and held it in his hands.

"I think the fire came from Daniel. And I think she survived it because she was protected from him. Her tattoos saved her."

Hayden put his hands in his pockets and rocked back on his heels.

"You know you sound crazy, right?"

"Yes. But if I am right, then Ruby is alive. The fire didn't kill her. Couldn't kill her. Even if you do not believe anything else I am saying, please believe this much."

Hayden nodded.

"I can do that."

Samuel ran his hand over the cover of the book he was holding and then held it out to Hayden.

"Go and find her. And give her this."

Hayden took the book and looked at the spine. There was no title and the pages were bound by brown leather. It looked ancient.

"Another book?"

Hayden started to lift the cover, but Samuel smacked it closed.

"Do not open it until you are with Ruby. She is seeking. Looking for answers now as to who she is and who Daniel is and why he has committed this atrocity. I'm sure of it. That is why she took The Book of Others. I don't think it will help her any further, but I believe this one might. This is The Book of Knowns."

Samuel pointed to the book.

"I had been trying to pin down Daniel since he first arrived, but I was looking in the wrong places. He has hidden from us by appearing right before our eyes. Daniel is no Mwenembago or Amazimu, he is a wolf in sheep's clothing. He is neither us nor them. I believe he lives in a liminal state that has thus far shielded him from the prying eyes of seers and shamans, but perhaps not certain scribes. Those he would not bother with. I did not realize this before. I think The Book of Knowns will help and so you must get it to Ruby. I don't have time to explain more. And for heaven's sake, quit looking at me like a gaping goldfish."

Hayden shook his head and gathered himself together. He tucked the book under his arm.

"I'll take the book with me, but I don't understand why you're not coming with me to find Ruby."

"Someone must take care of the ruin here."

"And that's more important than her?"

Samuel slowly shook his head.

"Ruby has an Iku'anga, a path I cannot walk with her. She must be her own guide, her own shadow. But that does not mean we do not have a role to play. Mine was supplying the knowledge. Yours will be to deliver it. Perhaps more. But in the end, whatever it is Ruby must do, she must do alone."

Hayden lifted his hat and set it squarely back on his head.

"That makes about as much sense as everything else you've said in the past ten minutes. But I'll find Ruby. After this, the fire, do you think she's hiding from Daniel?"

Samuel frowned and looked once all around the room before settling his gaze back on Hayden.

"I have no idea where she is. But I can tell you one thing. I don't think Ruby is running away from Daniel. I think she is running straight for him."

Hayden put his hands in his pockets and eyed the door in front of him. It looked old and heavy and was carved with a pattern of fleur-de-lis. He focused on the design and tried to think of what he would say if the door opened to him. He could hear footsteps creaking on the hall floorboards above him and the cackle of laughter coming from the downstairs parlor. He could hear his heartbeat pounding in his ears. Hayden set his jaw and raised his fist, ready to knock.

Immediately after leaving Samuel, Hayden had gone to the nearest filling station and bought a map. Outside of eastern Texas and some parts of Louisiana and Oklahoma, Hayden was lost. He knew the towns in the usual circuit of the Star Light, but not intimately. Hayden had spread the map of Alabama out on the hood of his car and tried to think like Ruby. It hadn't been easy. He could go anywhere, do anything, blend in. She was a woman traveling on her own. A woman covered from head to toe in tattoos, who couldn't walk into a store and buy a stick of gum without being stared at, questioned or worse. And a woman trying to keep a low profile. Someone had just set a match to her entire life.

Hayden had been so focused on Ruby, on knowing whether she was alive or not, that he hadn't let the destruction of the carnival fully hit him until then. As he stared at the spidery lines on the map, he had realized with a sudden stab in his chest that he would never see January's smile again. She would never tilt her head over her shoulder and wink. He would never again hear one of Pontilliar's blustery speeches or play cards with Franklin or trade barbs with the gamesmen and the rousties or ever walk down the midway of the Star Light feeling like it was home. It was gone. It was all gone.

Hayden had pulled the stub of a pencil out of his pocket and forced himself back to the map. He found Monroeville, low in the state, and starred it. There wasn't much along the coast aside from small towns, and he knew Ruby would have avoided those places as much as possible. The only way for her to really hide was in a crowd. In a place where there were enough people, enough going on, for her to negotiate her way around suspicious and inquiring eyes. That left only two cities: Montgomery and Birmingham. He circled them and then shook his head. What was he going to do, go to each city and walk up and down every street shouting her name, hoping she would hear him and pop out of a window? No, he had to get into her head. He made his hands into fists and leaned on his knuckles, staring at the two circled cities and trying to remember if he'd ever heard anyone in the carnival say anything about either of the places. When it hit him, he had almost jumped. He circled Birmingham a few more times and then swept the map off the hood and threw himself behind the wheel. He'd made it there in eight hours.

When morning broke over the wall of textile mills in the city, Hayden began his search. He soon realized it would be a lot harder than he'd first thought. Hayden didn't even have the name of the place to go on, just the proprietors. People had laughed at him when he described a hotel owned and run by a pair of Siamese twins. A place that welcomed freaks and catered to them. No one had heard of such a thing. Armed with the only name he could remember from a long-ago conversation with a traveling Lobster Man, Hayden had ducked into shops and restaurants, asking about May-May. He was met with blank stares and Hayden quickly became aware that he was looking on the wrong side of the tracks. By late afternoon, with the dun haze from the steel factories already blotting out the sun, Hayden had found himself in a backroom bar with a backroom cellar housing a pit of opium smokers and their consorts. When Hayden had finally found the man he'd been directed to by a Chinese cook outside of a brothel, he had been in a cloudy dream of pleasure and pain. Hayden had been dolling out money all day and this encounter was no exception. The opium smoker, scarred with a strange branding across his face and hands, had finally given up the address for the Hotel Mensonges.

The dusky streetlamps were just turning on when Hayden stood outside the row house and banged as hard as he could on the door for number 114. After five minutes, it had jarred open and a man had peered at him through the crack. Using the name May-May and his story of how he'd found the place, he was begrudgingly admitted into a dim foyer with a single gas sconce flickering against the dark green and gold wallpaper. The man, who Hayden immediately noticed had a thin third leg growing out of his side, would not answer his questions about a woman with tattoos being in the house. The man refused to even speak to him at all. Finally, he'd been summoned by a high-pitched voice and he had edged past the three-legged man and gone into the parlor. May-May was sitting on a green velvet settee beneath the curtained window and gestured for Hayden to sit opposite her.

Hayden hadn't been sure if he should be addressing one or two women. Most Siamese twins he had met on the circuit were two distinctly different people. In his search, everyone who had heard of May-May referred to her only as "she." May-May had four legs, two arms and two necks and heads. As Hayden slid into the chair in the corner, though, he didn't care if the person he was talking to was one or twenty. He only cared about Ruby.

At first May-May had laughed, a shrill cackle, when Hayden had asked about Ruby and described her. Both sets of eyes had then scrutinized him and both mouths spoke at the same time, belittling him and interrogating him on how he knew about the Hotel Mensonges. He had described Ruby again and begged May-May to give him the answer he needed. Finally, she had narrowed all of her eyes and conceded that, yes, there was a tattooed woman staying there. May-May couldn't guarantee it was Ruby, the woman had not given a name and had been scarce since she'd arrived, but if he wanted to find out he could go upstairs and try the third door on the left. Hayden had leapt out of his seat, trailed by piercing laughter, and taken the stairs two at a time. It was only when faced with the door in front of him that he hesitated. What if it wasn't her? What if she didn't want to be found? What if she never wanted to see him again after what he had done, how he had left her? What if all he saw was that haunting look, the one he could never make up for?

Hayden raised his fist, closed his eyes and knocked.

TWENTY-TWO

uby froze when she heard the knock. It was her third night at the Hotel Mensonges and so far no one had approached her door. As far as she could figure, no one aside from May-May, and the few guests on her floor whom she had passed in the dark hallway on the way to the washroom, even knew she was there. Ruby had been sitting on the narrow, iron-frame bed, flipping through The Book of Others for the hundredth time, and now she quietly slid her hand under the pillow and grasped the handle of her knife. The knocking ceased and she sat in the silence of its echo, waiting. The keys to the rooms in May-May's house had long ago been lost and consequently the locks were useless. If it were Daniel, though, and she couldn't imagine it would be anyone else, a mere locked door wasn't going to stop him, regardless. The knocking started up again and Ruby edged off the bed and crept across the room. She pressed herself against the wall and held her breath. She didn't open the door, but stood beside it, knife in hand, up against her chest, ready to strike. Ruby knew the only advantage she could hope for was surprise.

There was no sound coming from the other side now, but she watched the knob jiggle and turn. She steeled herself to spring as the door opened. The handle of the knife was sweaty in her hand and she moved her fingers slightly, firming up her grip. Ruby closed her eyes and then twisted, knife out, just as the door swung open. It was only his voice that stopped her.

"Ruby?"

She stared at Hayden with wide eyes and trembling mouth, her body still shaking. He looked as terrified as she was, but he hadn't stepped back, though the blade was only inches from his chest. He looked from the knife up into her eyes and didn't speak again. Hayden's hands cautiously came up and found hers and she released the knife as he took it. And then she was in his arms, her nails digging into his back, pressing herself to him as hard as she could. His voice came to her muffled.

"It's me, Ruby. It's me, it's me, it's me."

Hayden held her until she stepped away from him and then he came inside and closed the door behind him. Ruby watched him warily while he glanced around, getting his bearings in the tiny, dark room, and when his eyes came back to her and he smiled, she couldn't stop herself. Her palm landed hard across his cheekbone. His head turned with the force, but he didn't stumble back. The smile on his face disappeared.

"I guess I deserve that."

Ruby balled her fists up at her sides.

"You guess?"

Hayden rubbed at his cheek and the red splotch blooming across it.

"I suppose I deserve a whole hell of a lot more."

"You have no idea."

Hayden walked over to the small table and two chairs crammed against the wall and set the knife down. He tossed his hat on the table and then lowered himself into one of the chairs. Ruby stood with her arms crossed, swaying on her feet, trying to decide what to do. It suddenly felt hard to breathe.

"You left me. Again. You left me again."

Ruby sat down at the table across from him. She didn't even know where to start, where to begin. In the time since Hayden had disappeared, everything had changed.

"Ruby, I'm so sorry."

He reached for her hand across the table, but she jerked away from him.

"And what does that even matter now? It's all gone, Hayden. Everything. Everyone. January, she was right in front of me. She was in my arms. And she's gone. Pontilliar. Samuel. The show. Everyone I cared about. Everything that was my life. It's all gone."

Hayden grabbed her hand and held it tightly, even though she was half-heartedly trying to pull away. Ruby realized she was shaking and she looked up into Hayden's eyes. He squeezed her hand.

"No, it's not."

Ruby twisted out of his grip. How could Hayden possibly understand? It wasn't just the fire. It wasn't just what had disappeared beneath the flames. She was gone. Who she thought she had been was gone.

"You don't get it. Everyone burned up but me. I was there and I saw him and he couldn't hurt me. He could destroy everything around me, but not me. I don't know what I am, Hayden. I don't know what I can do."

She held up her hands.

"I don't know what these turned me into. I don't know if I'm like him. I don't know—"

Hayden grabbed her hand in the air and interrupted her.

"Samuel told me about your tattoos. About the drawing in the book. About Daniel. You're something all right, but you're not like him."

Ruby's eyes went wide and her hand went limp in Hayden's.

"Samuel?"

"He's not dead. He had left already with Chandler. Samuel wasn't in the fire. I found him on the lot when I went there looking for you."

"Samuel's alive?"

Hayden nodded.

"He's alive. He gave me something to give you. Something he thinks will help you do whatever it is he thinks you're going to do. Your Iku'anga or whatever. And I'm here to help you, too."

Ruby swallowed hard and gripped Hayden's hand.

"And you're alive."

Hayden gave her a half-smile.

"I'm alive. I'm here. I was coming back to you before I even heard about the fire. I was on my way. I want you to know that. I was coming back to find you and to apologize. I'm not even sure what happened, why I left. I can't explain it. But that's no excuse. I'm sorry. "

Ruby shook her head.

"None of that matters now. Everything's different. Everything's changed."

Ruby looked across the room at the bed. The Book of Others was still lying open on the blanket. Ruby frowned.

"I don't know if you should be here with me, Hayden."

"Now there you're wrong."

Ruby turned back to him. Hayden was frowning and his eyes were serious. There was a flash of anger behind them, but it wasn't directed toward her.

"Listen to me, Ruby. You don't have to believe me right now, but you'd better know. I'm not going anywhere. And if you leave, I'm following you. Wherever you go. Whatever you do. I have walked away from you twice. There won't be a third time. I promise."

"So first I can't get you to stay and now I won't be able to get you to leave?"

Hayden took both of her hands in his.

"That's right. Bad things happen to me when I'm not with you. I lose sight of who I am. I falter. I came here to help you in any way that I can. But the God's honest truth, Ruby, is that I may need you more than you need me."

Ruby looked down.

"I don't know. With where I'm going, what I'm going to try to do. There are so many questions, so many uncertainties. Being with me is going to be dangerous. It's going to be a risk."

"I'm taking it."

Ruby shook her head.

"I want to do this alone, but I'm not sure I can."

Hayden dipped his head so that she was forced to look into his eyes.

"So we need each other."

Ruby licked her lips and nodded slowly.

"We need each other."

Hayden squeezed her hands and then released her.

"Good, because I have something to give you."

Hayden pulled a piece of tobacco off of his tongue and squinted at it. His eyes were beginning to burn. He leaned back in the uncomfortable chair and smoked his cigarette in the small pool of light from the lamp on the table while he considered the book before him. The Book of Knowns was unlike any book Hayden had ever seen before. For one, the pages weren't separated, but folded out concertina style in accordion-like sections. Each section, when completely extended, was about three feet in length, and though Hayden was pretty sure the words were all in the same language, the handwriting and size of the lettering changed for each piece of the book. Weaving in and out among the text were bizarre illustrations of people, animals and unearthly creatures and the style of these, too, changed in each different section. In the front part of the book the drawings were mostly crude, one-dimensional figures with no coloring, but the last section contained full panels with looping scrollwork and bright red, blue and gold inked images depicting men and women in lavish settings. Hayden could tell that the book had not been put together by one author, but was made up of pieces covering eras of time. It was all very interesting and beautiful to look at, but Hayden couldn't make heads or tails of what any of it meant.

The most infuriating part was that Hayden was sure there was some way to read The Book of Knowns. Ruby had shown him the book she'd taken from Samuel's wagon, The Book of Others, and aside from recognizing the eerie symbol that was most certainly one of Ruby's tattoos, Hayden knew the book could never truly be understood. It spanned too much time and contained too many languages. But whereas the first book was more of a collection of artifacts, a hodgepodge of ancient memorabilia, Hayden felt that The Book of Knowns was a linear record. In the corner of each extended section there were groups of letters that Hayden eventually recognized as Roman numerals. The ink was brighter here and Hayden assumed someone had gone back and added in the numbers. The first section was marked DCLXXX and the last was MCCCXLV. Hayden wasn't certain, but he thought they might be dates. And then there were the pencil notations all in strange symbols. Hayden pushed the book away from him in frustration and glanced across the tiny room at the rumpled bed. Ruby was still deeply asleep, twisted up in the sheets, scowling in her dreams.

She had told him about the fire. Ruby had lain on his chest and he had run his fingers through her tangled hair as she'd told him about January's face and how it had no longer been there. She told him about the running, the chaos, the screaming, the wind, January and then about seeing Daniel on the midway, watching her. How he had looked different, with the bones coming out of his back and his eyes blazing red. And then how the fire became darkness and when it was over there was nothing but a smoking wasteland of wreckage and a charred skeleton crushed beneath her. The entire carnival had been consumed and she hadn't been touched.

She had kept her face away from him while she told him this, the story of the fire and then stealing the book and making her way to Birmingham. He'd been afraid she would be unreachable, closed off, her voice dead, the way she became whenever she spoke about the past, but there was a glinting spark in her words. A spark of resolve. Of determination. Of revenge. She was going after Daniel no matter the price. He'd had to ask. Why couldn't they just run? They had each other now and nothing they could do would bring back January or Pontilliar or the Star Light. They could join up with another show. Or travel out to California and grow oranges. Or Argentina. Alaska. Anywhere. She'd shaken her head and refused. She was unwavering. Nothing he could say could convince her otherwise and he saw it very plainly in the sheen of her eyes: she would go after Daniel alone if need be. She would leave him behind in her single-minded pursuit and not look back. This was who she had become and he could walk beside her or not at all. He could help her or he could lose her. There were no other choices.

Hayden stubbed out the cigarette and rubbed at his eyes with the palms of his hands. He blinked a few times and then pulled the book back to him. It was the markings in pencil that were driving him crazy, for they had obviously been made in the book long after the last section had been completed. Maybe it was the same person who had added in the dates, maybe not, but whoever it was, they hadn't been writing in Latin, English or any other language that used recognizable letters. Instead, in the margins and blank spaces running between the chunks of text, there were strings of geometric symbols. Crosses and triangles and diamonds, some with dots inside and outside of them. Unlike the strange markings in The Book of Others, though, these were uniform all the way through. Hayden turned the sections this way and that, trying to find a pattern. On a hunch, he took out paper and pencil and copied down each individual symbol he could find. Once he had carefully gone through the entire book, he counted up the symbols on his paper. He'd been right. There were twenty-six. It was a code.

As a boy, Hayden had played spies and war, cowboys and Indians, and he and his friends had often used a Caesar shift cipher to pass along secret messages. The two sliding wheels were easy to make and the code was always breakable, but it added some mystery to an otherwise monotonous existence of growing up in the cotton fields. Whatever code this was it wouldn't be nearly as easy to break, but if he could figure out the cipher, it would be simple. Hayden closed the book and rested his forehead on the leather cover. He was no code breaker.

Hayden lit another cigarette and sat for a while, smoking and staring at the shadows created on the wall from the flickering lamp flame. He idly ran his hand over and over the cover, trying to come up with a solution. He had to be able to do this for Ruby. Hayden ground his teeth and drummed his fingers against the leather. It was golden brown and completely blank, no writing, no illustrations, just a piece of leather. He slowly ran his fingers over the minute ripples and imperfections in the skin and an idea began to form in his mind.

He clamped his lips around his cigarette and reached again for the pad of paper. He ripped off a thin sheet and placed it on top of the book's cover and then began to rub over it with his pencil.

Immediately, Hayden was able to recognize letters. He continued with the rubbing, covering the entire page with a fine sheen of lead. When he finally tossed the pencil down and ground out his cigarette, the entire cipher was laid out before him in negative relief. Someone had created or copied it, using the book cover as a hard surface behind the paper. The key to the code had gone through.

Hayden almost stood up and whooped in excitement, but he caught himself before waking Ruby. Just because he'd discovered the code didn't mean he was any closer to understanding the book. Or Daniel. With the copy of the cipher in hand, however, he thought he had a chance. He still couldn't read Latin, but he could read the annotations, and those had to be just as important as the original text. He opened the book and stretched out the first section, starting on a block of penciled symbols in the upper left corner. Like a Masonic pigpen cipher, the letters were laid out in different grids, with each part of the grid breaking off into a symbol that corresponded to a letter. After staring at the grids long enough, Hayden realized they were six different variations on the Maltese cross, with a simple cross mark standing in for the letter N. In using the cipher, the triangles, arrows and diamonds became letters and, put together, they became words and sentences. It took Hayden a while to get the hang of it, but soon he had his first translation: WHITBY ABBEY NORTHUMBRIA POSSIBLY BEDE SEVENTH CENTURY. Hayden had no idea what that was supposed to mean, except that The Book of Knowns was old. Very old. Not as old as the first book, with the blood and stains and human skin parchment, but still pretty damn ancient. Hayden scanned over the section pulled out across the table. It had maybe twenty annotations, some of which could have been at least five hundred symbols long. It would take him all night just to translate the first section. And there were twelve sections after it. Hayden put his head in his hands. It was too much. It would take too long.

He pushed the pencil, paper and cipher away from him and leaned back in the chair. He braced himself with his palms against the edge of the table and looked hard at the creased length of vellum. There had to be another way than starting at the beginning.

Hayden stared at the section in a bleary daze. The script, even in this early part of the book, had been inked beautifully. The letters were all either in black, red, or black surrounded with tiny red dots. The rows of text were perfectly straight and in some parts of the book, Hayden had been able to see the faint lines underneath the letters, guiding the scribe's hand. Though Hayden had been concentrating on deciphering the text, he was most fascinated by the artwork that took up almost as much space as the words. In the first section, the drawings mostly depicted strange animals. Birds with long necks and human arms and legs. Hares playing pipes or pushing wheelbarrows along the branches of a tree as if it were a road. Deer with their antlers on fire. In a way, the images reminded him of the dream world he had painted on the ceiling of Ruby's wagon with the fish made out of stars. Hayden frowned as he remembered that the painting had been consumed by the fire. So, too, had all of the murals on the sides of the truck wagons. And the people who had slept behind his murals every night, some for years and years, they were gone as well. Daniel had destroyed them all.

Hayden pulled out another section, and then another. The artwork became intricate and the scenes more complex as time had passed. There were images of kings, maidens and dancing skeletons. The landscapes behind the figures were detailed, with trees, gardens, hills and castle walls depicted under blue starry skies. The pictures were more realistic as they became more polished, but still there were oddities. A woman with bat wings trapped inside a bottle with a gaggle of men holding books and standing around her. A great sea monster with a swallowed ship visible in its belly, the sailors' eyes and mouths open in torment as they clung to the rigging beneath the creature's spine. Without understanding the accompanying text, Hayden could only guess at the stories these images illustrated.

"What the hell is that supposed to be?"

Hayden started, his heart pounding furiously in his chest. He had been so absorbed in the book that he hadn't heard Ruby get out of bed and come over to him. Hayden rubbed his face and stood up, stretching his back out. He'd been hunched over in the chair for hours. Ruby was still pointing at one of the images and Hayden glanced over at it as he lit yet another cigarette.

"I think it's a snail."

"It looks like it has a sword. And is fighting a man. How can a snail have a sword?"

Hayden waved out the match and tossed it into the overflowing ashtray. He shook his head.

"That book makes anything you've ever seen in a sideshow look dull."

Ruby leaned on the table and flipped over some of the extended sections.

"This is incredible, really. Can you read any of it?"

"No. It's Latin, I think. But I did figure this out."

Hayden showed her the page of cipher and the penciled notes throughout the book.

"This is like a maze, Ruby. We don't even know what we're looking for. I bet some scholar somewhere spent his whole life trying to figure this book out and maybe got nowhere. And here I'm trying to do it in a night."

Ruby held the page with the cipher code in her hands.

"But if the key translates to English, why wouldn't whoever made it, and made the notes in the book, just have written in English? What was the point of writing in code?"

Hayden took the paper from her.

"I guess whoever made this didn't want anyone else to know

what the notes said? I couldn't tell you, Ruby. This book is like one of these."

Hayden pointed to a drawing of an ouroboros at the top of one of the sections.

"It's like a snake eating its own tail, a never-ending mystery. Even if we had all the time in the world, I don't think we could solve it."

"And we don't have all the time in the world."

"No."

Ruby sat down in the chair and turned over another section. Hayden walked to the wall next to the bed and leaned his back against it, shutting his eyes. He heard Ruby rustle another page.

"What's wrong with this picture?"

Hayden didn't bother to open his eyes; frustration had given way to exhaustion.

"I have no idea, Ruby."

He stood against the wall with the cigarette slowly burning between his fingers and felt a wave of sleep creeping toward him.

"No, really, Hayden. There's something wrong with this one."

Hayden sighed and only managed to mumble.

"Have you seen the pictures in there? There's something wrong with all of them. It's like a dream. Or a nightmare."

Ruby was silent for a moment, but then the insistency in her voice forced Hayden to open his eyes.

"No, this one is different. I'm telling you. Look at this."

Hayden pushed himself away from the wall in irritation. He'd been looking at the book for hours. If there was a picture different than the rest, he would have noticed it. Hayden looked over Ruby's shoulder at the drawing she had her finger on.

"It's just a man. That's nothing compared to most of them."

Ruby shook her head and jabbed at the page with her finger.

"No, look at it. Not what it is, but how it's been drawn. Half of the picture is missing. See? Look."

Ruby stood up so Hayden could take the chair and look closer at the image. He'd already glanced at it a dozen times. It was just a man, pointing up at an abstract design of black lines and red squiggles. There was nothing bizarre about it and so Hayden hadn't paid it any attention. But now that he looked closer, he realized that Ruby was right. It did seem to be half-finished. The man only had one eye and many of the lines making up his figure had gaps in them. The lines and squiggles that the man was pointing to seemed arbitrary.

"Eye!"

Ruby pointed to a drawing in the opposite corner of the section. Hayden looked over at an image he'd previously thought was just a design. It was a scattering of red and black lines and dots that didn't make up a picture. But Ruby was right. One of the marks could definitely be an eye, now that he was looking for it. He went back and forth between the two images, certain there was some sort of connection. Then it hit him.

"Hold the book up to the light."

Ruby turned to him, confused.

"What?"

Hayden stubbed out his cigarette in excitement.

"Hold the book up. There, just like that."

Ruby lifted the book and Hayden folded the section in half in front of the lamp. He had been right. The two unfinished drawings completed one another and with the light coming through the vellum, the full image unveiled itself.

"It's him. Oh my God, Hayden, it's him."

Ruby almost dropped the book and Hayden had to steady her hand to bring the image back into the light. He nodded.

"It's Daniel. It has to be. All those years ago. Wherever this book is from. And he was there."

It was clear now what the man in the first picture was pointing at. There was a hill before him and on the top of the hill was a tall, thin man with black hair and red eyes. With bones growing out of his back. Fire was coming out of his hands and streaming down the hill, enveloping tiny figures on horseback. The man on the hill was smiling.

They carefully set the book back on the table and Hayden unfolded the section again. The Latin text next to the man pointing in the air had penciled notes beneath the lines. Hayden looked to Ruby, staring at him with wide eyes. He nodded to her slowly.

"Give me some time."

Ruby went back to sit on the bed and left him alone. It took him the better part of an hour and when he was finished, he leaned back in the chair, stunned. He looked over his shoulder at Ruby, who had been sitting up in the bed, smoking and watching him the entire time. He gestured for her to come over and then pointed down at the page of text he'd laboriously written out on the pad of paper. Ruby chewed on her bottom lip.

"Well?"

Hayden wasn't sure where to begin. He tapped the section from The Book of Knowns.

"There's two parts. The notes under the Latin text, that's a direct translation I think. And then there's this part over here."

He pointed to the annotation in the margin.

"Whoever wrote the notes, the code, this is what they had to say about it. It's the commentary."

Ruby nodded.

"Start with the actual text from the book. What does it say?"

Hayden turned back to the page he had copied out.

"It's sort of a story, I guess."

Hayden took a deep breath and began to read out loud, his voice shaking slightly.

"This I did not hear, but saw with my own eyes. A man came to us, but he was no man. We welcomed him, but knew not why. A sleep had come upon us, but we did not sleep. We were ourselves and not ourselves."

"What does it mean?"

Ruby looked at him questioningly, but Hayden shook his head and kept reading.

"An army came to us. It came for the man. The man stood on the hilltop and fire came forth from his hands and ran down the hill like a river. There was a great storm of wind and fire. And then the army was no more. There were only ashes and bone."

Hayden paused, but didn't look at Ruby. He didn't want to see her face yet. He took another deep breath and finished.

"The man left us and we awoke from the sleep. Some had forgotten him, but I had not. I knew. This man had been known to us in shadow before. We were the tricked ones. He was the trick. He will come again one day. He is known before and after in time."

Hayden slowly looked over. Ruby's face was pale and her voice was a whisper.

"When was this written?"

"Let me read you the note from the margin."

Hayden turned back to the page.

"Eleventh century sighting. Army could be Normans. Fire and wind from a man mimics ninth century destruction in Gwynedd. Also earlier with water in Halogaland. Earlier still with fire at Hadrian's Wall. This is the one. The trick is real. No one will believe me. He is real. He will go on forever."

Hayden flipped the paper over. He couldn't look at it any longer. It was finally Ruby who broke the silence.

"They welcomed him, but knew not why. That's what Pontilliar did. He hired Daniel, a man with no carnival experience, and could never explain to me why. Said he couldn't remember when I asked him. And January. And Tom falling from the Wheel. Oh my God, how many other things. How many things did he do in the Star Light, even before the fire?"

And finally Hayden knew. He understood. Hayden jumped up

from the table, knocking the chair over.

"Ruby! The day I felt I had to leave the carnival, I had words with Daniel. I don't even know what we talked about, I couldn't tell you, but it was heated and after I left him, I just knew I had to leave the Star Light, no matter what. That's when I went and found you and told you I was going. The whole time I was gone, I felt as if I were in a fog. Every time I thought about coming back to you, I felt sick and this fever, this haze would come down over me."

Ruby frowned.

"You think Daniel made you leave against your will?"

Hayden picked up the chair and pushed it under the table.

"I think he can get inside peoples' heads. Make them do what he wants. Me. Pontilliar. Whoever. I think Daniel sent me away. I don't know why, but he put it in my head to leave and I had to go. What if he's like a snake oil man? A con man, but one who always makes his mark."

He watched Ruby taking it in, figuring it out. She had been with Daniel a week longer than he had. She'd most likely seen him do other things. Her lips parted slowly, but it took her a moment longer to speak. She seemed unsure of herself, not quite caught up in the excitement as much as he was.

"But what do you think he is?"

Hayden shrugged.

"Hell, Ruby. I couldn't tell you. Samuel was talking about demons. Ghosts. Other things I couldn't understand. But who knows what Daniel really is."

Ruby was staring hard at the book on the table, but Hayden could tell her thoughts were elsewhere.

"Come on, what are you thinking?"

She crossed her arms.

"Why say trick?"

"What do you mean?"

Ruby shook her head.

"The person who made the notes. They said the trick was real. And in the story it says the man was the trick. Why a trick? Why doesn't it say destroyer? Or something like that? In this instance, Daniel took out a whole army. That's more than just a trick."

Hayden's eyes were burning. Now that he'd found Daniel in the book, his frenzy was ebbing. And the knowledge they had discovered was too much, too overwhelming, to even think about. All Hayden wanted to do now was sleep.

"I don't know. Maybe it's not talking about a trick like we think of."

"Maybe it's calling Daniel a trickster? Like one of those creatures who plays tricks on humans? In the fables and stories. Up in the mountains, people told tales of the Brer animals. And I've heard of Indians talking about Coyote and Raven tricking mankind. Destroying villages, causing fires and floods. But they were gods."

Hayden shrugged again.

"Sure. I don't think it matters what Daniel is exactly. We can call him a trickster. A god. A slick man in a suit who's been around thousands of years. Whatever. The only thing that matters is what he can do. And what you're going to do. Your tattoos might protect you from his fire or wind or whatever, but he can control peoples' minds, Ruby. Control them. Like a puppeteer. I mean, we might just be better off running."

He could see it; she was thinking hard again. Remembering. He didn't like the look on her face as she spoke.

"Other people, yes. But I don't think he can control me."

Hayden cocked his head.

"You think your tattoos protect you from that, too? How do you know?"

She spoke very slowly, as if choosing her words carefully. Hayden got the sense she was hiding something from him.

"I think he might have tried. And I think it didn't work. So, my mind is protected from him, too."

She didn't offer any more and Hayden didn't think it was the right time to push her. He turned to look at the book on the table. He felt like he had found something tremendous, but didn't know what to do with it. Suddenly, the weight of what Ruby wanted to do settled on him. It was impossible. If gods were even real, people didn't go up against them. Hayden turned back to Ruby, but now her face was lit up, her eyes shining in the lamplight.

"What is it?"

Ruby licked her lips and looked up at him. She was so beautiful. And for a moment, with that crazed look on her face, so terrifying.

"I know what we have to do."

Hayden shook his head.

"Ruby. Just stop and think for a moment. Daniel burned up the carnival. Almost a thousand years ago, he took down an army. Who knows what he can do. Who knows how much destruction you might set off. Did you consider that?"

The expression on Ruby's face didn't change.

"Yes."

Hayden couldn't stop himself. He had to make one last effort to pull her away from this madness.

"Everyone in that carnival died but you. You do this, you go after him because you're angry or you need revenge or whatever it is that's driving you toward him, and you're putting other people in danger. Your selfishness could get more people killed. Me. Did you think about that? And innocent people, who don't need to get caught up in this. People like January. Think about it. You don't have to do this."

He looked into her gray eyes, now burning silver. The crazed look had been replaced by one of resignation.

"Yes, I do. And this isn't what you think. I didn't tell Samuel this, I've never told anyone this, but the woman who tattooed me, Madame Celeste, she said something else to me when she spoke about my Iku'anga. She said I had to create a Toenga Lespri."

Hayden was exasperated. He could tell Ruby wasn't going to relent.

"A what?"

"It didn't make sense at the time, though I knew what the words meant. A Toenga Lespri is a kind of spirit balance. In the stories that Madame Celeste would tell me while she was tattooing me, men and women were always going up against the gods, trying to create a Toenga Lespri. Trying to humble the powers and spirits on the other side, so as to create balance in the world."

"Between humans and gods?"

Ruby nodded.

"Yes. I thought they were just stories. I heard them like dreams. But I've been sitting in this room thinking for days and the pieces have been slowly falling into place. And now this, with discovering what Daniel really is. Don't you see? This isn't about me. It isn't about you. Or January or the Star Light. It's bigger than all that. It's bigger than any of us. I'm not doing this because I want to, Hayden. I'm doing it because I have to. Do you understand?"

Hayden did. He didn't want to, he still wanted to take Ruby far away from Daniel and forget that any of it had ever happened, but he understood. He slowly nodded his head.

"Yes. All right. So what is it that we have to do?"

No matter what she said, he would be a part of it. He would follow her. He would. Ruby put her hands on his shoulders and looked him in the eyes.

"All we have to do is trick the trickster."

TWENTY-THREE

It was obvious to Ruby that none of the occupants of the Hotel Mensonges liked Hayden. They didn't trust him. Even though he'd spent half a dozen summers on the midway and was keeping company with a tattooed Snake Charmer, he wasn't of their kind. He wasn't a freak. He was on the other side.

Many of those sitting around the long breakfast table that morning, passing down bowls of grits and platters of biscuits and bacon, had been at May-May's for years. The Hotel Mensonges was their home, a sort of communal house that sheltered them and which occasional sideshow refugees, such as Ruby, passed through. They were a family, and though they lived in the midst of one of the largest cities in the South, they were still closed off from the outside world. They no longer interacted with rousties, marks or, even worse, handlers.

As soon as Ruby and Hayden sat down in the dining room, the

heckling began. The hulking woman carrying out plates of food from the kitchen had two bony, claw-like hands protruding from the back of her collar. She smacked a dish of butter down between Ruby and Hayden and turned to him sharply.

"What? You've never seen a woman with a parasitic twin?"

Ruby rolled her eyes and reached for a biscuit. The woman's ugly mouth twisted before she moved on down the table. Hayden called after her.

"Of course I have."

Ruby knew this was a lie. Even she had never seen a woman with a twin still embedded inside her body. She glanced over at Hayden, who was crunching on a piece of bacon. He winked at her, but she could tell he was uncomfortable. The man sitting across from her, his face hidden behind a downy coat of auburn hair and his watery blue eyes magnified by thick spectacles, pointed his butter knife at Hayden and sniffed.

"And what is your moniker?"

Hayden swallowed the bacon and reached for his coffee.

"My moniker?"

It was hard to tell if the man was smirking or not behind the fall of hair hanging down over his lips, but his voice suggested it. He had a thick German accent compounded by a lisp and he gestured with the knife again.

"Your performance title. Your stage name. What are you proclaimed to be on your pitch card?"

Hayden leaned back in his chair and blew on his steaming cup of coffee.

"Don't have one."

A dwarf sitting on a stack of Montgomery Ward catalogues at the end of the table snickered. Ruby saw what was happening and wanted to intervene, but she figured Hayden could handle himself. The hairy man leaned forward, peering intently at Hayden.

"For example, I was with Phineas Barnum for seventeen years.

I was known as Lionar, the Magnificent Lion Man. I was very popular. I made a fortune and traveled the country in my own private railway carriage. This is true."

Lionar pointed with the knife to the dwarf and then began going around the table, identifying the guests.

"This here is Major Mite from New York. He also worked for Mr. Barnum in the American Museum on Broadway. Billed as a Human Miracle. And this is the Monkey Girl. I don't know her so well and she doesn't like me, but, eh, what are you going to do?"

The Monkey Girl scowled at Lionar, but Lionar merely shrugged and kept going.

"Then we have Jolly Jack and Amora the Armless Wonder. Kreno the Missing Link, the Skeleton Man and the Human Torso. And you have probably already met Victor, the Three-Legged Marvel, as he tends to hang around the foyer, guarding the door. Miss May-May doesn't come down for breakfast and we're missing a handful more, maybe. Oh, and the Witch Woman. With the hands."

Lionar stretched his neck trying to look down to the end of the table. The Witch Woman had just brought out the last platter and was sitting down now, shoveling grits into her mouth. The clawed hands twitched as she ate. Lionar pointed at himself with the knife.

"And then, as I said, there's me. The Lion Man. Now your turn."

Lionar set the butter knife down and folded his hands in his lap. Hayden sipped his coffee and spoke over the steam.

"Hayden. Just Hayden."

Major Mite snickered again and Lionar pretended to be stunned.

"Why, that's all? So, then, Just Hayden, what is your gift? What were you known for? What wonder did the playbills announce?"

Ruby glared across the table at Lionar, but he ignored her. Hayden took another sip of coffee.

"If you're asking what I did on the midway, I drew portraits."

Lionar clapped his hands together.

"An artist! And did you, I suppose, hold the pencil with your toes? Or maybe your teeth?"

Hayden shook his head.

"Nope. Just the regular old way. With my hands."

"Oh. How dull."

Lionar began cutting up a link of sausage with his fork and knife. Ruby was tired of it. She wiped her hand on her trousers and then extended it across the table.

"My name is Ruby, by the way. And what's yours?"

Lionar looked at her hand for a moment and then set down his utensils. He cautiously extended his own and shook her hand.

"I told you."

Ruby didn't let go.

"No, I mean your name."

Ruby glanced sideways at Hayden.

"For example, this is Hayden. I'm Ruby. And you are?"

The side conversations that had been going on at either end of the table suddenly came to a halt, as everyone had their eyes on the middle. Lionar tilted his head and looked over his spectacles at Ruby, but finally conceded.

"My name is Hans. Hans Vogel."

"It's a pleasure to meet you, Hans."

Ruby released his hand and then deliberately turned away from him. Out of the corner of her eye she caught the Monkey Girl grinning at her. She heard Hans loudly asking Major Mite about a book he had loaned him and the conversations around the table picked back up again. Ruby pushed her plate away and turned to Hayden, being careful to keep her voice down.

"Atlanta."

Hayden spoke through a mouthful of biscuit.

"Atlanta? Why?"

Ruby leaned in closer to him.

"I just know. Bright lights. Big city. I remembered something last night that January had said to Daniel. It makes the most sense to me."

Hayden swallowed and then pushed his plate away as well. He turned in his chair.

"It makes the least sense to me. If he's a…"

Hayden glanced around the table to make sure no one was paying attention to them. Luckily, the novelty of Hayden had quickly worn off and everyone was busy with their newspaper or their gossip or their breakfast.

"…if he's, well, whatever he is, wouldn't he be in, like, a forest or something? Hiding in the woods? Like a, I don't know, a fairy? Or an elf?"

"I'd say he's pretty far from helping people make shoes."

"You know what I mean."

Ruby smiled.

"I know. But I think he went to Atlanta."

Hayden raised his eyebrow. Ruby hadn't told him about any of her dealings with Daniel. Not about what had happened at the theater or in the geek tent. And she didn't intend to. Hayden gave her a half-smile.

"Are you trying to think like him now or something?"

Ruby gave him a disgusted look. Hayden sighed and touched her arm.

"Hey, that's not what I meant. I was just kidding."

Ruby looked away from him. She didn't know how to say what she wanted to say, how to express everything that was roiling around inside of her. She'd been trying to just focus on the plan, the next step. She hadn't had time yet to process what was actually happening.

"I know. I just, I'm not like you, Hayden."

She cut her eyes at the freaks around her.

"And I'm not even like them. I'm something else entirely."

She held out her hands, turning them over.

"These tattoos. They make me different from everyone. Absolutely everyone."

Hayden snatched one of her hands and gripped it tightly, almost crushing her fingers.

"You're not like him, though. Don't start to get that in your head. You're nothing like him. Understand?"

He gripped her tighter.

"We don't have time for that kind of thinking. We've got something to take care of. A job to do. We need to get to Atlanta. If we leave now, we can make it by late tonight. All right?"

The pain in her hand made her focus. Ruby nodded at him and he loosened his grip. She took a deep breath and tried to smile. She was looking right at Hayden, but all she could see was Daniel.

The man with an expressionless face and crisp white jacket placed a glass of iced tea in the center of the table and gave a short bow.

"Can I get you anything else, sir?"

Daniel glanced at the tea. A white orchid trailed over the lip of the glass, pinned down by an ornately cut lemon. The ice cubes were perfectly square. Daniel sighed and crossed one leg over the other.

"No."

He waved the man away.

"Very good, sir."

The waiter disappeared into the cloud of small tables on the promenade, all filled with couples perched across from one another on high-backed bistro chairs, sipping teas and iced lemonades and spooning sherbet into their mouths. Mothers and daughters, husbands and wives, illicit lovers. All gossiping or arguing under their breaths or staring vacantly at one another with a precisely studied disinterest. Daniel turned away from them and looked over the balcony railing, down into the lobby of the hotel. He sipped the tea. It tasted the way it cost and Daniel smiled. Finally, he was back in his element.

He had never stayed at the Grand Plaza Hotel in Atlanta, but he liked it already. When he had first come over to America, he had hovered between New York and Chicago, marveling at the skyscrapers popping up around him at every turn and causing havoc with the gin runners and the strikebreakers. Nothing extraordinary or noticeable, just a fix of chaos every now and then. Mostly he had immersed himself in the new world that had risen out of the ashes of Europe's hubris. France had been a wasteland, but New York was a heartbeat on cocaine. The lights, the sounds, cars, trains, the windows the size of whole walls, women with cropped hair and crimson lips, men spilling drinks and cash all over the tables, music roaring in the hotels and in clubs and on the street, no one caring, everyone living only for the next lark, the next cigarette. For the first time in decades, Daniel had entire nights go by where he never felt bored once.

Chicago was fun, too, but darker. The women were harder, the men more serious. Energy pumped through the city's heart and veins as well, but there was less laughing and more brooding. If New York was the glittering butterfly, flitting in all directions without a care, Chicago was the frantic moth, bashing itself against the window, trying to get in to the light. He had enjoyed them both, and St. Paul, too, though he had detested Boston and found Washington to be little more than a festering swamp. Atlanta didn't have quite the pulse of his beloved cities in the North, but it was fresh and clean, opening in new buds all around him. And the Plaza was its jewel.

The ground floor was a froth of women in pale silk dresses,

men in pastel linen jackets and bellhops in starched uniforms, all dashing about, meeting one another, posing and posturing, moving luggage and palming tips and showing off to the world. Everything in the lobby was bathed in sunlight, streaming down through the tremendous domed skylight high above, and everything was white. The flowers, the sculptures, the leather sofas and armchairs, the fluted columns, the carved wood paneling, the gleaming marble floor echoing upwards with every click and clack of heel steps and cart wheels and even little puffy dogs' nails. In the afternoon glaze of this high society, only Daniel stood out in contrast with his striking black suit that seemed to sparkle in the wash of sunlight.

Daniel turned back to the table and picked up the heavy paper menu that had been placed before him. The gold letters spelled out an array of finger sandwiches and cucumber salads, sorbets and ices and delicate trays of cut meat, all described in some bastardized form of French. Daniel didn't need to eat, of course, but sometimes he ordered dishes just to look at them. He was sure anything he ordered would come served on crystal and be garnished with edible flowers. He flippantly tossed the menu back on the starched white tablecloth and out of the corner of his eye he could see a waiter drifting toward him. Daniel held up his hand before the man could get to him.

"No."

Daniel sighed and slipped a cigarette out of his case. Again the waiter started to come forth with a light, but Daniel turned to him and glared, baring his teeth around the cigarette. He lit it himself and turned his back to the bustling promenade. Daniel looked up toward the glass ceiling and smoked. All these people. All the same. Mothers trying to marry off their daughters, daughters rebelling against their fathers, fathers trying to intimidate their sons, lovers fighting, strangers flirting, people moving forwards and backwards, consumed only by their small, narrow needs. So dull. So mundane. So utterly, irrefutably insipid. It pained him to think about it.

He had journeyed south from Chicago to find something different, something new. An experience that was raw yet beautiful. Something that was gritty like the War, but bright and scandalous, too. He had thought he might find it in the oil boomtowns of Texas, but those had been nothing but a bore. When he stumbled upon a playbill for the Star Light, he thought it might be just the diversion he was looking for. Daniel had spent several years during the middle of the eighteenth century attending the Carnevale festivities in Venice, before the Austrians brought it all down. He had thought joining up with a traveling carnival would be akin to those times: seductive, enchanting, a place to prey on people's most instinctual passions. Daniel started the whole experience off with a bang, getting rid of the geek so he could take his place. Yet, it had been such a disappointment. He'd found only dirt and disillusionment, everything cheap, painted up for show. The people were tired, the mood of revelry lasted only a few hours and the performers were the worst. What should have been ecstasy, what should have been glamor, was nothing more than complaining about sore feet and scrabbling over pennies. They weren't even depraved. Just downtrodden. His little experiment with the Star Light Miraculum had been a waste.

Daniel quickly stubbed his cigarette out in irritation, smearing the gilt tray with ash. There had also been the matter with the woman. The one with the tattoos. Ruby. She was like a mosquito, buzzing around his ear, her memory refusing to leave him in peace. It wasn't so much that had he allowed himself to lose his temper over her, he most likely would have burned the wretched little place to the ground anyway, just on principle. And it wasn't that he feared her. In fact, he smiled to himself when he thought of Madame Celeste and her pathetic little attempt to challenge him. Where did she even get the idea from? If he ever ran into Legba again, he would ask. It would be just like his fellow trickster to send him a parting gift as he scurried back to the jungle.

No, he wasn't afraid of Ruby. If she had survived the fire, and he wasn't exactly sure if she had, time would take care of her eventually. Or maybe she would turn all melodramatic and throw herself into a river, though she didn't seem quite the type for that. And there was that buzz in his ear again, when he thought about her in that way. Her type. Her thoughts. Her, of all ridiculous things, her feelings. Her mind and heart that were the blank spaces on a map for him. Terra Incognita. An unending void.

Daniel twisted his cufflinks in irritation. And yet. When he had touched her, when he had put his hands on her and pressed into her, falling only into a lacuna he could not bridge, it was as though the sky had split open for a moment and he had felt something he had never, never felt. Not once in all of his thousands of years roaming the earth. Something he had shamefully and secretly thirsted for, knowing full well it could never be attained. Perhaps coveting it only for that reason. Daniel had felt mortal.

He banged his fist down on the table, clattering the silverware. A few women gasped and then there was the hush of whispers and side glances in his direction. Daniel stood up and calmly slipped his cigarette case into his pocket. He straightened his cuffs and smoothed back his hair. Then he picked up the glass of iced tea and hurled it across the tables at the curved, mirrored wall.

"Oh, piss off!"

Daniel stalked away, leaving a gaping silence in his wake. When he got to the staircase he turned, resting one hand on the scrolled brass railing, and concentrated for a second. No one would remember having seen him at that table. No one would remember him at all. He grinned to himself and sauntered down the stairs.

Ruby drew her knees up to her chest and leaned her head against the dusty windowpane. She was grateful to May-May for taking her in, but the two days and nights she'd spent suffocating in the tiny, windowless hotel room, pouring over The Book of Others had been a nightmare. All she had done was alternately try to find clues about Daniel in the book and relive the fire over and over in her head. She'd berated herself for not comprehending what had happened to her in the geek tent, even though she still wasn't exactly sure what had taken place between Daniel and herself. But Ruby was sure she could have seen the fire coming if she had tried. If she hadn't been taken in by Daniel in the first place. And she was positive that the destruction of the Star Light was her fault. Ruby had meant what she'd said about the Toenga Lespri, but she also knew that she was going after Daniel out of guilt. It wasn't revenge; it was penance. Yet she understood, too, what Hayden had said about her selfishness and about putting even more people in danger. There were so many thoughts, so many sides to consider, but the only path Ruby could believe in was the one that led her face-to-face with Daniel. Coming to terms with that had been overwhelming, but she felt that, in some regard, leaving The Hotel Mensonges meant leaving all that doubt behind. She had made her decision. She had a purpose now, and a plan.

It had felt odd, walking up the steps of The Anchor and standing before the front desk on Hayden's arm, as if they were any other couple. May-May had given Ruby the name and address of the hotel and promised her that it was a place where questions wouldn't be asked. The Anchor's proprietor, a sour-faced man with a stringy cat in one arm, had eyed her tattoos, but said nothing. Hayden checked them in under Mr. and Mrs. Jones and the sour man had only grunted, handed them a key and glanced upwards, indicating the second floor. Though it was shabby by most standards, Ruby had still been impressed with the room. There was a wide bed and an overstuffed wingback chair in the corner next to an oak dresser and mirror. An electric pendant light hung from the ceiling, instantly illuminating the room with just a quick pull on the drop cord. And there was a window with an upholstered seat. The electric lights of Atlanta were dimmer in this part of the city and at least she had been able to lean out the window and pick out a few stars.

Ruby had been astonished, though, as they'd driven into the city and were accosted by a blaze of dazzling light from all directions. She'd been with the Star Light since before they had the generators to supply power, when pan lamps and torches were the only source of lighting on the midway. Even up until its last day, the use of electricity in the carnival was reserved for shows only. In the wagons, sleeping tents and cookhouse, oil lamps were still necessary. For many of the rubes, electricity was one of the most exciting marvels of the Star Light. The jeweled electric bulbs, strung from end to end down the midway, and the brilliant entrance arches, lit up like beacons, drew the townsfolk from miles around. Sometimes, if Ruby was working the bally and looking out into the midway crowd, she could see it in their faces, that wonderment at a brilliant new age. Many of the farmers and their families had spent their entire lives in the warm, dim glow of gas or oil light and were startled beyond words at the stark brilliance of the electric world. Ruby understood how they felt. When she had left for New Orleans, the Star Light had still been a show constructed around the power of flame. When she had returned, and the blaze of those electric arches had welcomed her back into the fold, she'd felt as if she had stepped into an alien world.

It was not only the scintillating lights of Atlanta that overwhelmed Ruby, it was the skyscrapers, the streetcars and the people, flooding in every which direction like ants escaping from a drowned nest. Ruby angled herself against the window so she could better see Groton Avenue below. Merchants and shoppers were bustling about, some resembling the sleek actors and actresses that had filled the pages of January's *Photoplay* magazines. A few of the women even had cropped hair, cut short at the neck, in the style that January had once wanted to do hers, but hadn't the courage. January would have loved to see Atlanta now, with its lights and noise and energy and glamor. When Ruby thought of her friend, though, it felt as if she were choking. January would never make it to New York City. Never find her movie star husband and have a closet full of furs and send Ruby postcards with details of her big city life.

Ruby gritted her teeth and pushed herself away from the window, forcing herself to pace up and down the length of the room. She'd spent her life walking away from places she had thought to call home. The mountains. The Village. And now the carnival. It didn't matter that the Star Light was now nothing more than an expanse of ash. She had left it behind her. She would have to think like that or she would never get through it. When Hayden suddenly banged through the door, she was desperately relieved.

He set a large paper bag down on the dresser and began to pull out bread and sliced meat, but Ruby ignored the food and snatched up the newspapers. She spread them out on the floorboards and scanned the headlines: murder, prohibition, the price of cotton. Hayden stretched out across the bed with a sandwich in his hand and looked over her shoulder.

"How do you think you're going to find him that way?"

Ruby turned over a page and shook her head.

"I don't know. I guess I'm looking for something showing he left his mark, something like..."

"Like the fire?"

Ruby chewed on her lip and flipped more pages. Advertisements for shoes and automobiles. Articles on the upcoming election. Film stars.

"If he's here, wouldn't he have done something, I don't know, noticeable?"

She leaned back against the bed and looked over her shoulder at Hayden. He finished chewing and swallowed.

"Daniel was with the Star Light for two weeks before he did anything. And, well, that was different."

Hayden stopped himself and quickly looked away from her. She turned and glowered down at the floor.

"I know. I was there. And you've said it yourself. He was only there to kill me."

"We don't know that."

"I know that."

She heard the bedsprings squeak as Hayden moved around and then slid down to the floor next to her. She raised her eyes to him.

"Why else would he have done it?"

Hayden shrugged.

"I don't know, because he's a crazy mythical beast? Because he's not human?"

"He's partly human. He looks human."

Hayden kicked his feet out over the newspapers.

"So he looks human. We've worked with people who looked like monsters. Real, true monsters. That didn't mean they were. You, of all people, should know that appearances mean nothing."

She cut her eyes at him.

"So you're calling me a monster?"

Hayden groaned.

"You are not a monster. I know you feel that somehow you and Daniel are alike. You're pulled together by your tattoos. But you can't believe that. You're not like him. You're his antithesis, if anything."

Hayden crinkled the edge of one of the newspapers.

"And if you're determined to do this thing with Daniel, I'd like us to go ahead and do it now so we can see whatever lies on the other side. Maybe have a shot at being together and, oh, I don't know, maybe even being happy. Assuming I don't somehow manage to screw it up again. And assuming we make it out of this alive, of course."

He grinned at her and she rolled her eyes.

"You're taking all of this well."

Hayden took off his hat and spun it around on his finger.

"Ruby, you're telling me you want to fight a god. Demon, trickster, whatever the hell Daniel is. Do you hear how that sounds? You might as well be saying, 'Hayden, I'd like to go fight a dragon today.' How else am I supposed to handle this?"

"Fine."

She pushed away the newspapers and put her head in her hands, trying to think.

"He's got to be in the city. I just have no idea where to start looking."

Hayden stood up and lit a cigarette.

"Well, if you want to know what everybody's talking about on the street, it isn't a tragedy."

Ruby looked up sharply.

"What is it?"

Hayden walked over to the window with his cigarette and looked out.

"It's this new radio station."

"Radio?"

Ruby stood up and followed him. Hayden handed her the cigarette.

"I guess Atlanta's starting up its own radio station. Like they have up in Philadelphia. One that will have music and people announcing sports as they're happening. Everything. You'll be able to turn on a radio and dial up their frequency and get the weather report or the news, just like you would in the paper."

"Seriously?"

Ruby had heard about radios, of course. She'd just never seen one. No one she knew had. Radios were used on ships and in the War, that was all she knew about them. To be able to work some machine and hear music and voices from far away? She couldn't even begin to imagine. It was otherworldly.

"It's all anyone could talk about. First radio station in the South. It's going to be owned by the *Atlanta Journal*, so I bet there's something in the paper about it."

Hayden pushed the newspapers around on the floor until he found the *Journal*. He brought it over to Ruby and they looked through the pages together. The write-up was at the bottom of the second page, an announcement that the *Atlanta Journal* was going to be operating the first Southern radio station, WSB. The inaugural broadcast was scheduled for the next day. Hayden took the cigarette back from Ruby and handed her the paper. He leaned against the wall next to the window.

"It'll be on the front page tomorrow, I'm sure."

Ruby read the article again and then looked up at Hayden, startled.

"They're going to have a ceremony outside the newspaper office tomorrow morning when they air the first broadcast."

Hayden nodded.

"It'll probably be a big whoop-de-do. These sorts of things always are. A crowd of people all standing around to hear a bunch of speeches beforehand. When I was in Houston one winter, it seemed like it never stopped. Every inch of progress was celebrated with a ribbon cutting and a fight among the local elect over who got to do the honors. A mess of showing off."

Ruby folded the paper in half.

"He'll be there."

Hayden turned back to the window and looked out at the street again. It was beginning to rain.

"Daniel? Why would he be?"

For an instant, Ruby's mind flashed back to her walk with Daniel to The Rainbow Theater. His talk of cities and films, progress and the future. It could have all been lies, part of his act, but Ruby didn't think so.

"Trust me. He'll be there. I don't think he could resist it."

She watched Hayden's back, waiting for him to respond. She wasn't going to explain herself. She wasn't even going to offer to. When he turned around, he only nodded.

"Do you have an idea for how you're going to find out?"

"Not yet."

Hayden put his hands in his pockets and rocked back on his heels.

"Well, I do. We don't have to rush this. You want to trick Daniel, you want to catch him off guard, right? Let's at least make sure he's in Atlanta first. I'll go to the ceremony tomorrow and scout it out."

Ruby shook her head.

"No way."

"Ruby. Be smart. You are smart, so act smart."

She turned away from him. Ruby didn't want to be left behind, but she had to agree that Hayden had a point. She knew her limitations. She couldn't blend in. Especially in a crowd of high society socialites. She had very little on her side going up against Daniel, and surprise was one of the few resources she possessed. Showing up at the ceremony would blow that all to pieces. She'd have to act right then and that wouldn't work with the rest of her plan. Ruby turned back to Hayden.

"All right. But be safe. And don't let him see you."

Hayden crossed his arms and grinned at her.

"I wasn't planning on it. Come on, Ruby. If you get to slay the dragon, at least let me have a little piece of the glory."

TWENTY-FOUR

aniel stood amidst the gathered crowd on Forsyth Street and raised his gaze to the fifth floor of the *Atlanta Journal* building. Somewhere on that level there was a cramped little room filled with coils and tubes, batteries and generators, microphones, headsets, knobs and the almighty 100-watt transmitter. There were men haphazardly connecting exposed wires and laying out fruit jars filled with lead and zinc to produce enough voltage. There was sizzling, invisible energy just waiting to be harnessed and sent upwards to the antenna towering on the roof behind the *Journal* marquee and then back down to the awaiting receiver box on the stage. It was all about to happen and Daniel was there to witness it.

A round of polite applause echoed from the crowd around him and Daniel glanced toward the wooden stage set up in front of the soot-stained brick building. The railyard was not far and even now the air was tinged with a thin black dust that settled on the hats and shoulders of the onlookers. He watched as a man with gray hair parted slickly down the middle and a yellow rose in the button hole of his white suit jacket ascended the stage and began his speech.

"Today is a great day! Today is a monumental day that will go down in the history of Atlanta and the history of the South! Today is a day that makes me so proud to be your mayor!"

Daniel ignored him and made his way to the end of the stage where the equipment was set up. He effortlessly pushed past prominent local businessmen and their blue-blooded families who had been waiting out in the blazing sun all morning, vying with each other for the closest, and most attractive, spot from which to view the speeches. They wanted to see Mayor Key and Hoke Smith, the owner of the *Atlanta Journal* and now a state senator, standing proudly together on the bunting-draped stage, and they wanted to be seen. By Key and Smith, but also by the society columnists prowling through the event and, most importantly, by each other. Even as Daniel glided past them, futures were being decided for budding debutants and alliances made and broken that would shape the fate of the coming election. Daniel could care less. Cruising like a shark in his sharp black suit, he parted through the sea of Atlanta's elite and thought nothing of kicking mud onto their shoes.

Hands began to clap around Daniel as the mayor stepped back and the imposing form of Senator Smith took his place. For a moment, Daniel glanced up toward the man, red-faced and sweating in his checkered tweed suit. Daniel had half a mind to make the man fall over, tumbling like a bowling pin off the stage and into the ocean of lace and linen below. But then he would never hear the radio, and that was all that Daniel cared about.

"My dear Atlanta citizens! It is such an honor to be standing here before you and to have my very own newspaper, the *Atlanta Journal*, the flagship institution of modernity in the South, bringing you this immense accomplishment today. I hope that it will be forever remembered in history that we were the first. The *Constitution* receives its broadcasting license tomorrow, but ours has come through today. Hallelujah!"

Daniel slipped past one more row of sweating spectators and came to the side of the stage where the radio receiver was displayed on a low table, just about at eye level with him. A large sign proclaiming DANGER had been tacked beneath it. Daniel stared with wonder at the receiving box, open so that the power amplifying tubes could be seen. A tangle of wires, probably more than was needed, but which created quite an effect, led to the dish of the reflector and the large, ominous horn of the loud speaker. Daniel had no idea how the thing worked, and being mystified delighted him. He had been expecting something a little more grandiose in size, as he thought back to the marvelous demonstration on electricity, magnetism and phosphoresce he had once seen Nikola Tesla give at the Royal Institute in London, but he supposed that for being in the middle of Georgia, this would have to suffice. Senator Smith droned on from the center of the stage, but Daniel kept his eyes on the wires, coils and dials as he waited to be impressed.

"And so now, without further delay, and in the hopes that this great leap forward will always be remembered, I give you the first radio broadcast from a station in the South, our very own WSB, transmitting from inside this very building and received by this radio, right here on this stage. I say to you, as a beacon of what we will say to this great nation of ours, as our call letters ring out: Welcome to the South, Brother!"

A pattering of cheers rose up from the crowd and then all eyes turned to the gangly man with his tie half loosened who was now kneeling down amidst the mess of radio equipment. Atlanta's finest, panting in the heat, waited patiently while the awkward radio operator turned the dials on the receiver back and forth, trying to find the 620 AM frequency transmitting from the top of the building. Suddenly, a crackling leapt from the speaker and those close enough to hear it gasped. Daniel was staring intently at the horn, for once waiting with everyone else to see what would happen, and then a bolt of sound rang out. A man's foggy voice echoed over the silent, breathless crowd.

"...Afternoon. This is the Radiophone Broadcasting Station of the *Atlanta Journal*. Per the meteorological society forecast from Washington, we should experience temperatures in the low nineties with little chance of precipitation. There is a slight possibility of afternoon thunderstorms tomorrow. This is WSB, I repeat, WSB, signing off to resume again in one hour on frequency channel 620. Welcome to the South, Brother."

The radio crackled a few moments more and then went silent. The crowd slowly began to look at one another, some awestruck and some bewildered. Senator Smith stepped forward again.

"There you have it, ladies and gentlemen. The first broadcast of the South's first radio station. WSB will be airing the weather reports every hour and will be open for any emergency broadcasts."

Seeing the confusion on many of the faces in the crowd, the senator held out his hands and grinned widely.

"And don't you worry, folks! WSB should have live news and entertainment programs airing in the next few months. Just think! New York, Chicago, Philadelphia. They won't have nothing on us now. Not when they hear we have the Home Town Boys live in the studio!"

Smith enthusiastically clapped his broad hands and soon the crowd followed suit and the ceremony officially ended. Everyone began milling around, jockeying against each other, some rushing toward the shade of the storefront awnings while others began forming tight circles of commentary and influence. Daniel didn't move. He was transfixed by the wired box in front of him. A man walking with another man passed behind him and Daniel overheard him say that even Henry Ford was thinking of finding a way to put radios inside of his Tin Lizzies so people could drive and listen at the same time. The men chuckled about the absurdity of this, especially considering that at the moment the only folks who could pick up radio stations were tinkering kids with homemade crystal sets in the attic. Daniel looked after the men and then turned back to the stage. A motorcar with a radio. He was stunned. Could it be true?

Daniel laughed out loud, startling a group of women still standing behind him. If the world kept progressing at this rate, he wouldn't even need to meddle with humanity to get his kicks. He could just sit back and enjoy the show.

Hayden had been skirting around the fringes of the crowd, trying to peer over the wall of straw boaters and cloche hats to see into the heart of the gathering. After trying to jump and landing on the foot of a woman who responded to his apologies with a look of contempt that could whither a snake, he retreated to the edge of the street where he could safely wait until the crowd had dispersed. The ground was still muddy from the rain the night before and he dug the toe of his boot in the muck while he halfway listened to the speaker on stage. He had seen no sign of Daniel yet and still wasn't convinced this would be the best place to find him. Ruby had seemed sure of it, though, and he had nothing else to go on.

The crowd went silent around him and Hayden was suddenly startled by the piercing crackle reverberating from the stage all the way back to him. Like most people, he had never heard a radio broadcast of any kind. He looked down into the mud and strained to hear the scratchy, muffled sound. Hayden couldn't make out any of the words, but he'd heard the noise and that meant something.

He had heard the future. Just as he'd felt when he had first ridden in his visiting uncle's Model A at nine years old, he was now aware that something would be different from this day forward. Then, he had been conscious of the possibilities of being able to embrace speed and go in any direction at all, for as far as the road would go. Now, it was the same with sound, with voices and music and ideas. The thought ran a chill of excitement up his spine. He wished Ruby could have been there to hear it.

The sound soon faded out and the man came back on stage and promised something about music and news. The crowd was beginning to turn restless and Hayden moved in closer. Yet another round of clapping broke out and then it appeared that the ceremony was over. As people began to push past him, heading for the coolness of the drugstore and diner across the street, Hayden squeezed his way through the oncoming crowd, keeping his eyes open. He turned around in frustration and was shouldered on both sides by men striding past him with an air of importance and impatience. He was starting to think he should have gotten a better vantage point and tried to view the scene from a distance, when he saw a flash of black. In a sea of white shirts and the occasional beige or light gray jacket, a solid black suit shone out like a sliver of obsidian in the sun.

Hayden quickly darted around a group of women, all clucking about the approaching season and their respective daughters' chances. He trailed behind them and then cautiously looked over his shoulder. The crowd was thinning rapidly and now Hayden could clearly see Daniel, his pale face turned upwards and his slick black hair gleaming. He was standing right up against the stage and appeared engrossed in contemplating something in front of him. Hayden suddenly realized that the tangle of wires and the strange cone rising above it must be the famous radio receiver. Ruby had been right; Daniel was bewitched by it. Hayden edged his way around the lingering knots of chattering ladies and boasting husbands until he found a spot where he thought he could safely keep his eye on Daniel without being seen himself. He put his hands in his pockets, hunting for cigarettes, but realized he had left them at The Anchor with Ruby. Then, out of nowhere, one appeared before him. He jumped and turned to face a woman smiling and holding out a cigarette between lavender-gloved fingers.

"Want one?"

The woman was older than him, maybe in her fifties, and had too much powder pressed onto her damp face and too much rouge brushed on top of that, but she had a frank, inviting smile. Her voice was deep. Hayden smiled at her.

"Aren't I supposed to offer you one?"

She waved the cigarette at him.

"I'm sure you would if you could. As for rules of decorum, I tend to find those preposterous and tedious. Now, if you happen to have a light, I'd let you have the point for that."

Hayden pulled a squashed box of matches from the breast pocket of his vest and lit both of their cigarettes. The woman blew a stream of smoke out of the side of her crimson lips and looked toward Daniel.

"I don't know who was staring more intently. You at that man in the black suit or the man in the suit at the radio."

Hayden didn't know what to say so he just smiled weakly and smoked. The woman was quiet for a moment and then held out her hand.

"Anita Bosch, by the way."

Hayden turned from Daniel and took her hand. She had a firm grip.

"Hayden Morrow. It's a pleasure to meet you, Mrs. Bosch."

Hayden had no idea where the conversation was going, so he just shrugged inanely. Mrs. Bosch dramatically blew out another plume of smoke and gestured toward Daniel.

"Do you know him? The mysterious man in black?"

Hayden abruptly looked away from Daniel.

"No. I just thought he looked odd. Standing out here, all in black in this heat. I was just gawking, I suppose."

Mrs. Bosch frowned and absently fingered the long, triple strand of pearls cascading down the front of her dress.

"Pity. I've seen him in the dining room of the hotel where I'm staying. He seems such a character, all trussed up in that black suit of his no matter if it's breakfast or tea time."

She cocked her head thoughtfully.

"I wonder if it's the same suit every time or if he has a whole trunk of them. I was the lover of a man like that once. In Brussels. He had an entire wardrobe full of the exact same suits, all hung up together. Completely identical. Though they were all pale blue, not black. He was my husband's half-brother, if you really must know. Poor soul. Poor Ruben. He didn't make it long after the German invasion."

Hayden had stopped listening after the mention of the hotel. He couldn't believe his luck and had to force himself to speak calmly and casually. He tried to appear disinterested, but polite.

"The same hotel, you say? Which hotel might that be?"

Mrs. Bosch flicked her gaze up and down Hayden, taking in his rough appearance, and then she gave a little shrug.

"The Plaza, of course. It's really the only place in this city to stay. My daughter has just married her second husband, a wretched weasel of a man who has more money than God, and I was forced to come down here and meet him. I don't know how you people do it, living in this heat all year round. It's dreadful up in Boston, but this is almost unbearable. I constantly feel as if I'm going to faint and, trust me on this, I am not the swooning type. I usually summer up in the Catskills with friends, but no, Pricilla just couldn't wait. She's an absurd, spoiled woman."

Mrs. Bosch smiled broadly at Hayden again and reached out to touch his arm.

302

"But then, I suppose, so am I. Hayden, wasn't it?"

Hayden smiled back at her. He was trying to figure out how to steer the conversation back to Daniel. He was also worried that Daniel would turn around at any moment and see him. Daniel was standing with his head cocked, peering closely at the pile of wires, as if trying to figure out how the radio worked. Mrs. Bosch continued to prattle on beside him.

"Now, Hayden, I don't know if you're married or not, though with a face like that you should be, but there's something you need to know about women. We are all outrageous and fickle and it is better to just do what we ask than try to reason with us. Pricilla's poor weasel of a new husband, Ernest, is already finding that out. I can see the terror in his beady little eyes whenever she walks in the room. I tell you, it's best just to let us have our way and pay the bill later."

Hayden decided that just outright interrupting would be the best course of action. Mrs. Bosch could most likely go on for days if he didn't stop her. He nodded toward Daniel and then leaned his head conspiratorially toward her.

"That man. Have you spoken to him? At your hotel?"

She seemed to have forgotten Daniel and had to turn around and look behind her. Hayden's heart began to beat faster as he watched Daniel take a few steps back from the stage, taking in the view of the radio one last time. Then he turned and slowly began to walk away with his hands in his pockets, as if deep in thought. Hayden tried to turn so his back was to Daniel, but he didn't have to worry; Daniel was walking in the other direction. Hayden was at a loss as to whether or not to follow him, but he was hoping he could wheedle more information out of his new acquaintance, so he stayed put. Mrs. Bosch swiveled her head back toward him and raised both her painted eyebrows.

"Well, let me tell you. I haven't spoken to him yet, but Pricilla said that when she accidentally dropped her handkerchief near him yesterday afternoon out on the veranda, he walked right past it. Right past it. She said he must have seen it, but deliberately ignored her. I mean, the rudeness. The arrogance. Too proud to stop and help a lady. I don't think Pricilla has ever been treated that way by a man. To tell you the truth, I think she found it quite thrilling. As for myself, I can't wait to see how he acts at the ball tonight."

Hayden watched Daniel disappear around the corner, but he quickly turned his interest back to Mrs. Bosch.

"There's a ball tonight?"

Mrs. Bosch laughed.

"Of course there is. It's in all the columns."

She frowned, looking at Hayden's faded vest again.

"But then, maybe you don't read those."

Mrs. Bosch brightened up again, charmed by this.

"I mean, who does, really? Only old ninnies trying to spy on one another. Those ladies who don't have enough oomph anymore to go out and live life to the fullest."

Hayden nodded.

"The ball is tonight, you say?"

"Oh, yes. It'll be the talk of Atlanta. Senator Smith, that bore who was yapping away up there, is putting it on. And all of things, it's a masquerade. I mean, how very European! I didn't think the old stuffed-shirt had it in him to be interesting. You should see my costume. One of my companions, Gustave, oh, I don't travel anywhere without him, has been working on it for weeks. He's a true artiste. He has a vision of me as a sea queen and my dress and mask are just to die for."

She paused for breath and then gave Hayden a strange look. Mrs. Bosch handed him her burned-out cigarette and cupped his chin with her gloved hand.

"You should see it, you know. A costume like this only comes along once every decade or so. It's going to be quite magnificent.

Yes, you should come. I'll put you on my list."

She let go of his chin and slapped his face playfully. Hayden was stunned.

"Pardon? You want me to come to the party?"

"Yes, yes, of course. It'll be a gas. A hoot. You'll probably want to bring a girl, though. With your looks, the debs will be swooning all over you, and that's the last thing their mothers need. Rally up a girl and bring her on your arm so they won't have a fit and throw you out. Think you can manage?"

Hayden swallowed and nodded.

"Good. And now I better be off. That ferret Ernest has been standing over there waiting for me this whole time. Do you think he looks more like a ferret or a weasel? I just can't decide. Anyway, simply wonderful to meet you. Just say your name at the door and they'll let you in. And don't forget, you'll need masks. I'm not sure what you can scrounge up this late, but you look resourceful. I'm sure you'll work something out. And do remember to bring a girl. Even my Pricilla might be tempted otherwise, and we can't have that, now can we?"

She winked at Hayden before flouncing past him. He watched her walk away toward a man who did indeed look like some sort of rodent. Then he glanced around the empty ceremony area with wonder. Forget radios. Women like Anita Bosch were the true marvels of the modern age.

The plan all came together when Ruby pulled the mask out of the bag and held it between her hands. She ran her fingers along the feathered edges and smiled. Hayden chewed on the toothpick between his teeth and grinned.

"Well? What do you think?"

Ruby held it up against her face and looked in the mirror on the dresser.

"It's perfect."

She laid the mask down on the bed and stood back to consider it. Her mind was racing.

"There's another one in there, too, of course."

Hayden rummaged through the paper bag.

"And clothes. A dress, a suit."

Hayden dug all the way to the bottom of the bag and felt around.

"The man tossed in a sewing kit as well. We might have to work at it a bit, but I think we can pull it off."

Ruby put her hands on her hips and nodded.

"Really, it's perfect. Where did you get all this?"

Hayden sat down on the bed next to the mask and looked up at her.

"It wasn't easy. But there's a lot to Atlanta, if you start looking in the right places. Cleaned us out, though. I hope you're not hungry. Or can wait until we crash the ball."

Ruby frowned.

"You spent everything we had left?"

"Which, between the two of us, wasn't much. But hey, I figure we might as well. It could be the end of the world tonight. We might as well go out in style."

Ruby looked from the mask to Hayden. He was no longer smiling and his face had a tight, pinched look to it. She sighed.

"The world is not going to end."

Hayden shrugged.

"Sure. You're going to just waltz in, have a little chat with him, he'll say he's sorry, you'll forgive him, the balance will be restored to the universe and then we'll all raise a glass of champagne in the spirit of forgiveness and go home. Easy peasy."

"Hayden."

He rolled the toothpick along his bottom teeth and then spit it out on the floor.

"Or Daniel could see you, get angry and bring the entire hotel down around our ears. Start a fire. Kill everybody in it. Maybe he'll try something new. I'm sure he's full of surprises."

"That's not fair."

"I'm just saying that there are options."

Ruby bit her lip and looked up toward the ceiling.

"What do you want me to do, Hayden?"

"I want you to tell me that this plan of yours is going to work. That confronting Daniel is the right thing to do and that it's going to be worth it all. Everything that we might lose."

Ruby looked down at her hands. When she thought about Daniel, his hands on her hands, holding her wrists, that uncanny, almost maniacal look in his eyes, something inside of her began to burn. After her mother had died and she had felt nothing, nothing, for weeks alone on the side of the mountain, she had slashed at her thighs with her Barlow knife, to make sure she could still feel. The pain had been breathtaking, excruciating, and she had fallen back onto the forest floor and let the tears run down the sides of her face. They were not tears of tribulation, but tears of relief. The pain had meant that she was not a shade, as she had begun to fear. The pain meant she was still alive.

Hayden knew the plan, but he didn't know everything. He didn't know about the burning in her chest. He didn't know what she had felt in the geek tent, when Daniel had put his hands on her and she had let him in. He didn't know the real risk she was taking.

"You said you were with me. No matter what."

Hayden sighed and rubbed his hands up and down her arms.

"I am with you."

Ruby looked up at him.

"I can tell you that it's the right thing to do. I can't tell you if my plan will work and I can't tell you if it will be worth it in the end.

But I know it's the right thing to do."

Hayden pulled her to him and rested his chin on her shoulder.

"I can't stop you."

"No."

Hayden shook his head and let her go.

"No. This whole damn thing is absolutely insane. But when I said I was with you, I meant that I was with you."

He picked up the mask and held it to her face.

"Come on, Ruby Chole. We've got a party to go to."

TWENTY-FIVE

They were late. But not too late, Hayden hoped. As they climbed the white sandstone steps leading up to the broad veranda of the Grand Plaza, he tried not to think about what was actually happening. The absurdity of what they were about to do. Or try to do. Though the rest of the street was brilliantly lit up at ten o'clock at night, the lights on the hotel façade had been dimmed, giving it a hushed, mysterious feel. It was almost too quiet, as the usual line of cabs and chauffeured cars had come and gone and wouldn't be needed again for hours. No one was checking in or out until the morning.

Under any other circumstances, Hayden would have appreciated the sharply cut steps and towering mahogany doors, inlaid with gilt designs and held open to them by men wearing black tailcoats and purposefully vacant stares. Despite his nerves and ill-fitting tuxedo, he was determined to walk proudly, with

Ruby's hand resting lightly on his arm. He couldn't look at her, though, or the fist of dread that was already clenched in his stomach would twist and he would falter and drag her back down the steps and away from the madness she was walking into. But the time for doubt had passed. Hayden held his head up stiffly and escorted Ruby past the row of fluted columns and through the imposing doors, ignoring the doorman who cut his eyes at him with unconcealed disapproval, and into the reception area.

Though the doorman had been somewhat discreet, the head concierge made no secret of his appraisal of Hayden. His watery eyes traveled from Hayden's scuffed shoes, up the length of his trousers, hemmed only hours before, along the shiny seams of his worn tuxedo jacket and across his tanned face, all the way to the ragged haircut he had given himself in the hotel mirror. Hayden gritted his teeth and tightened his hold on Ruby's waist. When the concierge finally found Hayden's eyes, the contempt and disdain between them both was obvious and mutual. The man sniffed.

"This is a private party of Senator Hoke Smith's."

Hayden let go of Ruby and stepped forward slightly.

"I was invited. Check the guest list."

The concierge raised his eyebrows and his chin, looking down his narrow nose at Hayden.

"Oh really?"

"Yes. I am a guest of Mrs. Anita Bosch. My name is Hayden Morrow. She should have left word of me."

The concierge glanced over at Ruby and frowned. He languidly looked down at the list in front of him. His eyes slowly scanned the names and his frown grew even more pronounced when he came to Hayden's.

"It appears she has. A guest of Mrs. Bosch. Well, she does seem like the sort to require unusual amusement and diversion."

"Can we go in now?"

"You are late, you know."

Hayden only glared at the man.

"And this is a masquerade ball. Per Senator Smith's instructions, all guests must enter wearing an appropriate mask. As I'm sure you are aware, the senator is always very particular about his guests' appearance at these soirees."

The concierge's eyes flickered back to Ruby.

"She will do. But you?"

Hayden held up his simple black mask and dangled it before the man. The concierge's tone and expression did not change.

"Well. Put it on, then."

Hayden tied the strings of the mask around the back of his head and then gave the man a smile that let him know what he was going to do to him if he gave them any more trouble. The concierge sniffed at Hayden again, but pointed toward the lobby.

"Through there. The Grand Ballroom is on the left, by the Grand Staircase. I do hope you have a pleasant evening."

Ruby looped her arm through his and pulled him along. The concierge nodded curtly and Hayden let himself be led away. His anger soon subsided and he felt relieved as they stepped into the cool, silent lobby.

Ruby was a flame, but against the pale shimmer of the marble floor she burned even brighter. The dress he had procured for her was a viper shade of red and would have appeared almost scandalous on anyone else but her. Between the length and cut of the gown and the satin opera gloves, her tattoos were mostly covered and the red was such a distraction that the visible tattoos on her chest and throat almost seemed to fade away. And then there was the mask, the same shade of red, covering half of her face and surrounding it with a halo of brilliantly dyed feathers. She had pinned her hair so it fell along her jawline in soft waves and he was struck by how she was carrying herself. Certainly not like the girl he knew from the carnival, slouching with her hands in her self-sewn trousers or standing Amazon-like with her swinging braids and snakes. She was a far cry, too, from the ostentatious women he had seen at the radio broadcast ceremony, pert and preening in their gaudy finery. No, Ruby was empyreal, gliding across the reflective lobby floor like a creature from another world. A being wholly possessed of itself and its power. For a moment, watching her, he believed in what she was about to do. He believed she was a match for Daniel.

Ruby turned suddenly and caught him looking at her. A strange smile spread across her lips, and she came and took his arm again.

"This is the most beautiful place I've ever seen."

Hayden nodded in agreement, but was looking only at her. They walked across the lobby, past the stately columns and cream chaise lounges, past the potted palms and bronze statues, held up on slender alabaster pedestals. He glanced upwards to the arched glass ceiling, glowing down on them with the warmth of Atlanta's dazzling night sky. Hayden saw the entrance to the ballroom, guarded by two more stiff doormen, and stopped in front of the wide, curving staircase before they approached it. He turned to Ruby.

"You ready?"

The smile was gone and her jaw was tight and firm. They looked at one another through their masks.

"Ready."

The doors to the ballroom billowed open and they entered the masquerade. A few heads turned when Hayden and Ruby stepped into the room, but for the most part they slipped in unnoticed. Hayden immediately snapped up two glasses of champagne from a tray held out to them and followed Ruby off to the side so they could get their bearings. He raised his glass.

"I guess they haven't heard of prohibition here."

Ruby raised her glass to his, but the chime of their toast was lost in the cacophony of sound churning around them. The room was enormous, with high, vaulted ceilings reflecting back every echo. A ten-piece band was set up against one wall and half of the room had been turned into a dance floor. Men in tuxedos and women wearing every color under the sun clung together as they bounced through tipsy foxtrot steps. The other half of the room was crammed with rows of tables above which hung hazy clouds of cigar smoke. The guests not sitting or dancing had bunched up into raucous clusters, all laughing and shouting to be heard over the music and each other. Everyone had a glass in their hand and though waiters stalked through the crowd, whisking trays of champagne and gin martinis in front of anyone who was idle, two bars had also been constructed at the back of the ballroom. Spidery chandeliers on long golden chains hung down over everything, creating bizarre shadows. The room was at once arcane and bustling. Everyone was wearing a mask.

Hayden drained his glass of champagne and handed it off to a waiter gliding by. He immediately picked up another. The room was so full of people that he could barely see through the snarl of chaos. He and Ruby slowly drifted around the fringes of the party and did their best to blend in. The women all wore different dresses in a rainbow of colors and each had a mask of lavish, singular design. Hayden recognized Mrs. Bosch reigning over a crowd in the middle of the room. There were so many layers to her aquamarine dress that she did indeed seem to be enveloped in sea foam and her mask was a starburst of turquoise sequins. She was easy to identify. The men, however, all merged together in one uniform swath of black and white. A few had been caught up in the spirit and wore true carnival masks, with long beaks and curving horns, but they were the exception. For once, Daniel's signature black suit would not be giving him away.

The band transitioned into a slower song and dancers began to shuffle on and off the floor for a waltz. Ruby grabbed Hayden's arm and whispered.

"The bar at the far end. The man in black, do you see him?"

Hayden cautiously glanced toward the back of the room.

"All of the men are in black."

She brought her head in close to his, trying to steer him with her eyes.

"Near the end. Right under the chandelier there. It's a different sort of black. I know it's him."

People were milling around at the edge of the dance floor, blocking his view, but then his line of sight opened up again and Hayden saw him. Ruby was right; his tuxedo jacket was different from the other men's. Darker somehow, and brighter, as if jeweled. He was standing at the end of the bar with his back to the room and a definite space on either side of him. He was alone, untouchable. His black hair shone in the chandelier glow and when he turned his head slightly, Hayden could see he was wearing a simple black mask like his own. Ruby handed him her glass.

"Stay here and stay out of sight. If he knows you're here, he could try to use you against me."

"Ruby, wait."

He tried to reach for her, but she had already stepped away, blazing across the ballroom in her scarlet dress. The crowd opened up for her and then swallowed her whole. Hayden looked down at the two empty glasses in his hands. He wanted to smash them at his feet and run after her. Instead, he handed them off to a nearby waiter and picked up another. He had done his part, delivering Ruby to Daniel. Now, he could only hope that Ruby knew what she was doing. He could only trust her.

When Ruby was halfway across the room, the crowd peeling back around her in murmurs, Daniel turned at the bar and saw her. Ruby locked eyes with him, trying to judge the expression on his face. She knew she'd caught a glimpse of shock, if only for a moment, and she was pleased that, if anything, at least she had managed to surprise him. His look quickly morphed into one of intrigue, followed by a disconcerting carnality. He didn't move as she kept toward him and soon his face was restored to the smug smile he so often wore. His black eyes seemed to sparkle even more than usual and there was something about him that was at once vibrant and at ease. Ruby realized she was seeing Daniel in his more natural element. She had never considered the fact that she would now be facing him in his territory, not hers, but it suddenly occurred to her that this would be an advantage. Her lips curled up in a smile.

Daniel turned slightly, still following her every movement with his eyes as she came up to the bar and stood next to him. The bartender was poised to a pour a martini in the glass in front of Daniel, but stopped and looked questioningly at him. Daniel, with eyes still on Ruby, raised his fingers.

"Two."

The bartender quickly placed a long-stemmed glass in front of Ruby and began to pour more gin into the shaker. She watched him, aware of Daniel's intense gaze on the side of her face. She waited until the bartender, with a trembling hand, filled the glasses to the rim. When he retreated, she finally turned to Daniel.

"Got a cigarette?"

He narrowed his eyes at her and Ruby could tell he was trying to figure out what game they were playing. Her only card was that he couldn't. She knew she was unreadable to him. Daniel reached inside his tuxedo jacket and took out the silver case. He slid a cigarette from it and watched her as she slowly fit it to her lips. Daniel was staring at them as he sparked the lighter in front of her. She had painted her lips blood red to go with the dress. He clicked the arm of the lighter over the flame and Ruby blew a long stream of smoke toward her martini.

"So you recognize me? Even with the mask?"

Daniel picked up his drink and sipped it.

"Even with the mask. Which suits you, by the way. The color."

He set the glass down and turned to her, resting his elbow on the bar.

"How did you find me?"

"You destroyed my entire life. Did you think I wasn't going to find you?"

Ruby smiled at him.

"Or did you think you had destroyed me in the fire as well?"

Daniel cocked his head.

"I wasn't sure, actually. In hindsight, I think it was a sort of test. I was trying to figure you out."

"And have you?"

Ruby fingered the stem of her glass.

"Figured me out?"

She glanced up at him with a sly smile. Daniel tilted his head and narrowed his eyes.

"I know what you can do. Or, rather, I know what that can do for you."

His eyes wandered down to the tattoo on her chest. Then he abruptly looked away. The cigarette case was still on the bar in front of him and he tapped it with his long fingers.

"And I presume you think you know what I can do. Or who or what I am."

She didn't waver.

"Yes."

"Ridiculous."

"I know more than you think I do. I know you're not human."

"Good for you. Do you want a prize?"

Daniel laughed. The bartender looked up for a moment and then quickly turned back to the glass he was polishing. Ruby realized that the young man was scared of Daniel. As he should be. She stubbed out the cigarette in a crystal ashtray and picked up her martini glass, holding it just beneath her lips.

"I know you're ancient. I know you can read people's minds. I know you can make them do things they wouldn't otherwise."

"Yes, yes. How very right you are. How very perceptive."

Ruby refused to be deterred. She was getting to him, she knew she was, but she had to stay focused. Despite the patronizing, she kept her eyes locked with his.

"But you can't make me. You can't get into my head. You know this. And now I know this. Which is why we are able to stand here like friends and have a drink together."

"Is that what we're doing?"

"That's what we're doing."

The corners of Daniel's mouth turned down slightly.

"What are you getting at?"

Ruby smiled over the rim of her glass.

"Let's go back to the part about you destroying my entire life."

Daniel opened the silver case again, but only ran his fingers along the smooth, white cigarettes. He was smirking as he gazed at them.

"Oh, that. Do you want me to apologize? Is that what you're here for? Do you want me to say I'm sorry?"

Ruby finally took a sip of her drink and then carefully set the glass down.

"No."

"Then perhaps you're here to exact some sort of revenge?"

His grin grew wider, almost obscene.

"You want to throw yourself against me, try to hit me? Curse me? Maybe pull that little knife of yours?"

He turned to her. His eyes were as dark as his mask and his smile was wide and mocking. He pointedly looked her up and down.

"I don't know where you could possibly hide it underneath that dress, but I'm sure you could manage. Are you going to try to slit my throat?"

He drew his finger delicately across his neck. Ruby shook her head and decided it was the right moment to make her move. She had to take the chance and she spoke firmly, her eyes never leaving his, her voice never wavering.

"I want to give you what you want, Daniel. What you want the most. I'm the only one who can, and I'm here before you with the offering of it."

Daniel dropped his hand.

"What are you talking about?"

She leaned in close to him.

"You know what I'm talking about. Don't act like you don't."

Daniel looked away from her and picked up his martini, draining it completely. He pushed the empty glass away from him.

"I assure you, my dear, I don't. And I'm getting rather tired of this back and forth with you."

Daniel was turned away from her, but she could see his face in the mirrored wall behind the bar. His pale cheekbones were brushed slightly with color. She leaned toward him and put her hand on the bar, almost touching his arm.

"I know what happened to you when we were in the geek tent that night. When you put your hands on me."

"You know nothing."

Ruby leaned in closer.

"If my mind is a mystery to you, how would you know?"

Daniel wouldn't look at her, but she could see the tendons in his hands rising as his body grew taut.

"You don't know what happened. You don't know what I felt."

"Yes, I do. Because I felt it, too."

He turned on her suddenly, his eyes blazing.

"Oh really? You felt human? How very special for you."

Ruby had only a second to react.

"No. I felt like a god."

Daniel jerked away from her as if he'd been stung. His brows were knit together, his mouth slicing down in a sharp frown. His eyes were searching hers, searching for the lie in this, but Ruby had known it the moment the words escaped her lips. It was the truth. Now she knew what she had done to him and he had done to her. And everything fell into place. Everything she had felt with Daniel finally made sense. He raised his hand as if to place it over hers, but then he pulled it back, still frowning.

"That's impossible. You could never feel as I do."

"Just as you could never feel as I do? Daniel, we became one another. I don't know how or why. My tattoos, the symbol. It's almost like when we came together we reflected one another. I can't explain it. I only know what I felt."

She could see his shoulders curving inward slightly with tension. Ruby knew he was fighting himself. Daniel looked down at his hand as it lay on the bar next to hers and his voice came out as only a whisper.

"And you want to give this to me now? Why?"

Ruby felt herself walking on the edge of a knife.

"Giving it to you is giving it to me. I have nothing left. You took it all from me. You killed everyone I ever loved, you destroyed everything I ever knew. It's all ashes. Don't you see? You're the only thing I have left."

"But what I did to you…"

"Is insignificant compared to what you can give me now."

She edged her gloved hand closer and put her fingers on his bare wrist. He didn't move away.

"It is what I have longed for, for centuries. For millennia. To feel as you do. To know what it is to be one of you. But due to my nature, I have always been denied it. Even the gods have limits."

Daniel moved his hand slightly so that he caught two of her

fingers underneath his thumb. He looked down at her hand and then slowly raised his eyes to meet hers.

"As I suppose humans do."

Ruby didn't look away. She didn't falter.

"Until now. For us."

Daniel nodded.

"For us."

"There you are, my dear boy! I'm so glad you could make it! What do you think of my outfit? Isn't it divine?"

Hayden had slowly been making his way through the crowd, walking aimlessly while still trying to keep his eye on Ruby at the bar. The crush of people was overwhelming and several times he lost sight of her as the mass of the party opened and closed like clouds scuttling in a tumultuous sky. He'd finally found himself a good vantage point where, for the most part, he had a direct line of sight to Ruby. Incidentally, Hayden also found himself standing right next to Mrs. Bosch and her circle of cronies. He smiled politely and pretended to look at the different points of her dress as she held them out to him.

"Triple layers of crepe de Chine. This color doesn't even exist yet, but I'm wearing it. And this, a wave of mother of pearl. A wave! Can you imagine the hours of hand sewing? Of course, the entire dress is sewn by hand. Gustave didn't touch a machine. He never does. Do you, Gustave?"

He could see that Ruby was standing very close to Daniel now. Hayden was too far away to discern their expressions and it would have been too difficult with the masks anyway. He nodded at Mrs. Bosch.

"It's some dress. Truly. And thank you again for inviting me."

Hayden could feel the circle of men sizing him up. Gustave twitched his mustache like a disapproving otter. Mrs. Bosch made a show of looking to either side of Hayden.

"Oh my, I hope you didn't come alone. I told you not to. Couldn't you manage to wrangle a date?"

The short man standing next to Gustave barked out a laugh and then chomped on his cigar. The crowd shifted again and Ruby disappeared behind a wave of tipsy men, some now wearing their wives' brightly colored masks. Hayden turned distractedly to Mrs. Bosch.

"I did, she's here somewhere. I think she got caught up in a conversation somewhere over there."

Hayden gestured vaguely toward the dance floor. Mrs. Bosch craned her neck trying to see.

"I do hope it wasn't the Mathews. They're such bores and like to commandeer any poor thing that is polite enough to stand listening to them drone on and on about their house in Antibes. As if anyone would ever care! Did the man have a ridiculously large nose? Shaped exactly like the beak of a parrot?"

Hayden could see Ruby again. She had stepped back from the bar, but still seemed to be talking to Daniel. Hayden couldn't tell what was going on. Were they fighting? Had she already put the plan in motion? Was Daniel only moments away from sending a fireball blasting through the ballroom? Mrs. Bosch was standing at his shoulder now, waiting expectantly. Hayden didn't look at her.

"Maybe. I suppose, maybe."

Mrs. Bosch put her hands on her hips.

"Darling, what has captured your attention so fully? Is there some scandal in our midst that you're keeping from me?"

Hayden quickly turned to her.

"No."

He scanned the crowd and then nodded toward a sloppy couple sitting at one of the tables in the corner. The drunk man had his hand halfway up the woman's skirt.

"See for yourself. They don't look like a married couple."

Mrs. Bosch clapped her hands together in relish.

"Oh, no, not to each other, that's for sure!"

Hayden glanced toward the bar again, but Ruby and Daniel had vanished. A swell of panic rose up inside of him. Mrs. Bosch, oblivious, continued her chatter.

"That pretty young thing is the newly married Mrs. Delany. Pricilla plays bridge with her sister, Minnie. Mrs. Delany's been wed only four months now and I don't even think that's the same gentleman her husband caught her with last month."

Hayden's eyes were darting across the back of the ballroom, searching for a burst of red in the sea of black and white tuxedos. He couldn't see Ruby anywhere.

"And that man, now that I look closer at him, he could be Mr. Abbott. Of the Charleston Abbotts, you know."

Hayden gripped his empty glass tighter and his mouth went dry. He suddenly felt as if he couldn't swallow. He was about to break through the circle of sycophantic little men still gathered around himself and Mrs. Bosch and go charging to the back of the room. Daniel could have taken her anywhere, could be doing anything to her. He didn't know for sure that Daniel couldn't hurt Ruby. Hayden didn't know anything about him for certain. He wasn't even human, for Christ's sake. Hayden felt a hand squeeze his arm.

"Mr. Morrow, are you quite all right? You look dreadful. Do you need to sit down?"

Then Hayden caught sight of them. Ruby was leading Daniel by the hand, away from the bar and the crowd. She seemed in control of herself and the situation. Hayden wanted to call out to her and it took all of his willpower to stop himself. He watched them slip through a door at the back of the room. And then they were gone.

He turned to Mrs. Bosch who was looking at him with acute concern. She patted his arm.

"Too many drinks, perhaps? Do you need anything? Is there something I can do?"

Hayden stared at the door Ruby had walked through with Daniel.

"There's nothing anyone can do. Not now."

TWENTY-SIX

Ruby raised her head and gazed toward the glowing glass ceiling, arcing high above her. In all of her nights of staring up at the stars, she had never seen anything so sublime. If it was to be the last night sky she would ever see, it would be enough. She had Daniel's hand in hers and she led him out into the atrium. This late in the evening, with the hotel closed off for the party, the cavernous space was empty and full of echoes and shadows. They were behind the Grand Staircase now and with the walls curving around them and the glass bowing over them, Ruby and Daniel were in their own separate world entire.

Daniel suddenly pulled her toward him, whirling her around to face him. She forced her breath to even out, forced herself to stand tall and become the harbinger of her future. She now felt as if she understood so much more about who she was and who she could become. Daniel let go of her hand and untied his mask, gently dropping it to the floor at his side. His face betrayed everything she thought she knew about him. In the dim light, with the shadows glancing off his cheekbones and the curve of his mouth, with his eyes shining, he appeared vulnerable. In truth, not illusion, and this terrified Ruby. She knew now that to make it happen, to open the path between them, she would have to meet him as he was. She would have to surrender. Ruby would have to trust him, as she had done before. If he was offering himself up to her, she could not hold herself back. They would have to become mirrors of one another.

Daniel stepped closer and reached behind her head with both hands to untie her mask. His head was bent forward near her ear and she shut her eyes against the closeness. He was drawing her in and she knew it. She could feel herself on the edge of something dangerous. Primal. Familiar. Something she wanted as desperately as he did. If she let herself. Daniel lifted the mask from her face and flung it across the floor. He stepped back to look at her and she allowed him, meeting his hooded black eyes with hers clear and wide open. His voice was uncertain, almost like a lover's.

"This?"

Ruby could not back down.

"This."

She stripped off her long gloves and moved toward him. Daniel raised his hands and put both on her bare collar bone, spreading his fingers out. He slowly slid them up her neck and along the length of her jaw until he was holding her face in his hands. His fingers curved against the back of her neck and he brought his thumbs up to her lips. There was such hunger in his eyes, but such hesitation in his movements. She didn't have to fight him. She didn't need to. Ruby rested her hands lightly on the front of his suit. She leaned against him and then raised her hands to his face. His skin was cool, pearlescent, and shimmered beneath her fingers. Ruby knew this wasn't a trick of the light or the shadows. It was him, his true self. Daniel's fingers were in her hair now and he was drawing her closer. Before she closed her own eyes, she saw Daniel's flicker red and then she let herself go.

She wanted him. She wanted this. She wanted it all.

Daniel wrenched himself away. He careened forward and braced himself with his hands on his knees while he stared down at the marble floor, trying to bring it into focus. The world was spinning, racing in dizzying rings around him, and he had the strange sensation that he had been flung out into the cold depths of space and was only now drifting slowly back down, lured by the pull of gravity. He tried to catch his breath.

Touching Ruby again had felt the same as before, only infinitely more transcendent. It was as if she had completely given herself up to him, but not as the prey gives in to the predator. As a woman gives in to a man and a man to a woman. As humans do. It was a corporeal yielding, he was sure of it. In those moments, when he had reached out, when he had broken past the barrier with her, he had felt everything. A roaring passion ripping him apart. Pain. Tangible, physical pain in an agonizing burn down his spine. He had shivered and sweated. He was exhausted and wanted to sleep and he had been terrified of dying. He had felt himself at the enthralling edge of mortality. He had known he would not last forever and had been seized by the paralyzing grip of his limits. Limits! He had been contained, walled in by boundaries that were warm and close and kept him from feeling as if he were always exploding into a million tiny particles. He was no longer mere dust. He had felt a pure, raw lust for the woman he was embracing and then a startling rent in his stomach, an ache that seared throughout his entire body. He thought it could be love.

At this surge, Daniel had forced himself to pull away from her. It was overwhelming. Such a crest of fallible emotion. A galaxy of tiny nuances that he had only guessed existed. So many events he had witnessed over the centuries suddenly were illuminated. So many choices and decisions he had previously considered pathetic and dishonorable. Incomprehensible. The intentions and motivations had come forth to him with a shocking, trembling clarity. As the room around him slowly became fixed and the normal coolness of his being settled back over him like a mantle, it occurred to Daniel that he had just experienced something that none of his kind ever had before. He had passed through the threshold of the crossroads, if only for a moment.

Daniel stood up, his face wet with tears he hadn't even known he was able to produce. He touched his face and then examined the wetness on his fingers. He could feel the smile spreading unabashedly across his face. A genuine, unaffected smile. He slowly, shyly, raised his eyes to Ruby.

"Thank you."

Though he had just felt everything, everything he could ever have possibly hoped for, he still couldn't read her. Her eyes were bright, though, and her face radiant. Her hair had come loose and he moved toward her and pushed it back from her shoulder. It was so soft, so fine against his skin. He looked at her hair, caught in his fingers, and then at the curve of her neck, the terrible designs, yes, but also the warmth he knew was beneath them. Daniel stepped back, unsure of himself.

"How did you do that? How were you able to make that happen?"

Ruby caught her breath and smiled.

"I just let go. I trusted you and I trusted myself. I gave myself to you completely."

Daniel looked away from her.

"It was as before, in the tent. Only then it was just a hint. A glimmering of something more. And this, this was the more. But now there was a glimmer of something else."

He looked up at her sharply.

"Ruby, what did you feel? Just now?"

Ruby's mouth turned down slightly. If it was anything on the level of what he had just experienced, it would be difficult for her to put into words. She looked all around the room, everywhere but at him, and then her answer came haltingly.

"Guiltless. Free. Powerful. As if I could do anything and I would never have to care about the consequences. There was no regret. As if no one else in the world, in the universe, mattered. It was all laid out before me. It was all mine."

Daniel nodded.

"But you didn't feel me. You felt what I am, but not who I am."

Ruby tilted her head slightly.

"I don't understand."

Daniel took her hand and held it to his chest. The feeling he craved so badly was there, but it was fading. He needed her to make it happen. It was all Ruby.

"I felt what it is to be human. But I didn't feel what it is to be you. You, Ruby. The essence, the experience of one person. One person, who is everything."

Her eyes were wide.

"That is what you want?"

Daniel took her hand in both of his and raised it. He pressed it hard against his lips.

"That is what I want. And I want you to know me as well. Me. Can you do that?"

Ruby didn't blink. She was his, he knew this now.

"I can do that."

He drew her in again and this time, very gently, he touched his lips to hers.

It was a dark world, full of rushing wind and the sound of the stars grinding down into diamond dust. The first time Ruby could not see, but could only feel as the firmament beneath her rose up and the sky came crushing down and everything she had ever known was split into minute pieces and thrown asunder. Her body had burned and then been pierced with cold and then had left her altogether as she became filled with starlight. She was above everything, in a place where pain and sorrow and loss could not follow her. She could not be disappointed. She could not be betrayed. She could never have her heart broken, for she would never have to give her heart to anyone other than herself. No one could hurt her, no one could touch her. Yet the world was hers, blazing all around her; she need only reach out and take what she wanted. There would never be repercussions. There would never be second thoughts.

But this time, Ruby could feel Daniel in the wind, searching through the darkness for her. She let herself fall apart into those grains of stardust and be carried away, and though she knew the danger, the temptation, she finally went deep, so deep she could see. Only the eyes that Ruby opened were not her own.

It came at Daniel with a force he could not have imagined would ever be inside of one person. He opened his eyes and out of the ash and confusion, the moments began to assail him, one after another after another. He was alone in a forest with snow in his hair. He was surrounded by flames, screaming in anguish, a woman dying in his arms. He was standing behind a tent, trembling in a teenage embrace, he was aching as his body was scarred with a needle, he was drunk. He was laughing, he was abandoned, he was empty, filled with rage, self-loathing, he was reckless, he was helpless, he was ashamed. Brackish water from the bayou washed over him, sparks from popping colored bulbs rained down on him, faces in a crowd jeered at him, called out to him, lusted after him. A safe, warm embrace came around him. His stomach dropped as a Ferris Wheel lifted him high up into the sky. His heart fluttered at the scent of sweat and tobacco and charcoal on fingers. His breath was taken away.

Ruby was in a field strewn with the ravaged bodies of soldiers. Some were clutching spears, some swords, some rifles. Their cries were in a hundred languages. They reached for her, but Ruby felt nothing for them as she stepped through their blood and moved on. She was in a palace with light streaming across her face. She was under a white tree hung with fetishes and offerings. She was in a gilded room filled with beautiful men and women, their eyes glazed over with desire, looking only to her. She was feared, adored, envied. She was trusted. She was unquestioned. She was absolute. Ruby turned away and looked up to the heavens. The constellations were not abstractions, but her brethren. The creatures surrounded her, a rider on a horse with eight legs, a man with winged feet, a woman with a cloak made of eyes, and so many, many more all swirling around her, but she was not afraid. Some went back up into the sky, some went deep into the earth, some disappeared under the water. A few stayed to roam the twilit plains Ruby knew could be her home. Here she could stay for a thousand years, for more, and know that everything she touched, everything that came near her, anything she wanted at all, would be hers.

The expanse before her was fathomless, but she could see Daniel coming toward her, his hands in his pockets, a cigarette dangling from his lips. He stopped and smiled and Ruby knew that he was hers, too. All of this was hers, and with him at her side it could never be taken away.

But that was not why she had come. Ruby felt the essence of the gods coursing through her and knew she wanted it more than anything she had ever desired before, but no. It was not her Iku'anga. It was a path, yes, but it was not her path. Ruby closed her eyes and began to recede. She knew she could.

This time it was Ruby who pulled away first and the force of the release knocked her backwards. Daniel reached for her and they both stumbled to the ground, heaving and catching their breaths. He held her as she shuddered, gasping for air. Daniel's heart was pounding as he gripped her and ran his hands up and down her back, trying to soothe them both. She stayed in his arms a moment more and then Daniel lifted her up, helping her to stand. Ruby let go of him to brush the hair out of her eyes and wipe the tears from her face. She threw back her shoulders, raised her head and met his eyes. It was not what Daniel was expecting.

She was looking straight at him, her eyes twinkling, her mouth twisted in a cruel, mocking smile, and suddenly Daniel knew. A dark curtain fell between them, severing him from her. The look she was giving him was one that had been on his own face a thousand times before. Daniel had been tricked.

Ruby crossed her arms and held her head high as she watched Daniel try to compose himself. She watched as elation gave way to confusion and then to comprehension. Daniel smoothed down the front of his tuxedo jacket and straightened his cuffs. He ran his hands over his hair, laying it back perfectly again, but there was nothing he could do about the gray sheen of his skin. Daniel clasped his hands in front of him. He appeared steady, but his voice was shaky.

"So, what's this?"

Ruby smiled.

"You got what you wanted."

Daniel nodded slowly.

"As did you."

"I did. It's too bad it will have to be the last time."

Daniel's eyes blazed.

"What do you mean?"

Ruby stepped forward and leaned toward him. She was not anxious, she was not afraid. She was also not heroic. This was the moment she had come for and she was going to revel in it, no matter the consequences.

"I mean it's over. I mean it's lights out. I mean the show has gone dark."

Daniel's arm shot out and he grabbed her by the throat.

"That's not how this works."

"Oh, but it is."

She could see the tendons in Daniel's neck flexing, but she had closed the door against him. He could do nothing. Ruby raised her chin defiantly.

"What are you going to do? You can't kill me. We both know

that. And you can't force your way in. I gave you everything you ever wanted. And now I'm taking it away."

Daniel released his grip on her and stepped back, eyes flashing, teeth bared. Ruby felt a low gust of wind stirring the dress around her ankles. She didn't stop.

"I am taking it away from you. You will never feel human again, because I will never let you feel human again. I don't know how old you are. I don't know how many thousands of years you have stretching out before you, but they will be empty. They will be empty and taste only of ash and dust. Because you will always remember what it felt like when you put your hands on me. And you will always know that you can never feel such again. You, who have destroyed so many other lives, will now be haunted by me. I know who you are, Daniel Revont. I know the power at your hands, yes, but I know the loneliness in your heart, too. I know you, do you understand? I am the only one. And now I am shut to you. I will drive you mad."

The wind picked up and Daniel thundered at her.

"This means nothing! You are nothing!"

Ruby held her gaze steady.

"I am everything."

The room went dark and all Ruby could see were Daniel's eyes, glowing red. They held her for a moment and then the wind rose up again. With an animal howl of rage, Daniel shot upwards. He exploded through the ceiling, glass shattering in all directions, and then the roof came down upon her. She closed her eyes and felt the rain of glass and dust, small chips of bone, showering all around her, and then the soft fall of feathers, but she didn't move. Daniel was gone.

At the sound of the ballroom doors banging open and the gasps and shrieks of the party guests, Ruby opened her eyes. People had spilled out into the atrium, their mouths gaping wide as they looked at the floor, the hole in the ceiling and finally at Ruby, standing in the center of it all with her brilliant red dress and dark hair dusted all over with glass. She responded to them only with silence and a singular smile on her lips.

Hayden shouldered his way through the crowd, sliding on fragments of glass and twisted metal. When he made it to her, he seemed afraid to touch her.

"Are you okay? Are you hurt? What did he do to you? Goddamnit, what did he do to you, Ruby?"

He brushed some of the glass off her shoulder with the sleeve of his jacket while searching her body with his eyes. She grabbed his arms to steady him.

"I'm fine. I'm not hurt."

Hayden looked around the wreckage of the room in panic.

"And Daniel?"

Ruby glanced upwards. She had been so close. It had been so tempting. Wrenching herself away from Daniel had been the hardest thing she'd ever done. But she had done it all the same. Ruby looked back at Hayden.

"Gone. He's gone."

"So then it worked. You beat him at his own game."

Ruby nodded. Hayden took both her hands in his and looked down at them.

"And you came back to me. You went into the darkness, but you came back to the light."

Ruby waited until Hayden raised his eyes to hers.

"Yes. I came back."

Ruby fell into his arms. Hayden pressed his face against her, but Ruby raised hers toward the heavens. It wasn't about darkness and light. It was about existing in both worlds and navigating the space between them. Through the ragged, gaping hole above her, Ruby could now see the night sky. The stars were blotted out by the brilliant Atlanta lights, but she knew they were there. Miraculous. Looking down, watching over her. With her eyes fixed above, Ruby's voice was only a whisper.

"And I won."

CODA

1925

They say Hollywood is the place where all your dreams come true. Well, I don't know about that, but there are certainly enough young hopefuls lining the streets here to keep me entertained for some time. These farm boys and ingénues tumbling off the bus with only a suitcase and a pocketful of ambition. They are honest and fresh-faced and fall the hardest when reality sets in.

I do love this town, though. It is full of starlets, yes, but also backroom deals and palm-lined vistas, secrets and swimming pools and sun. I can put on my dark glasses and cruise down Hollywood Boulevard in my Austin Tourer without a care in the world. I can go to Café Montmartre and pretend to eat Spaghetti Tetrazzini while I watch careers being bought, born and broken at the next table over. I can leave one party and wander off to another. I can roll up my trousers and step into the ocean. I can look up at the enormous

HOLLYWOODLAND sign, blinking away in the night. It is perfect. For now, at least.

Are you surprised to find me here? Did you think perhaps that I had disappeared? Followed Loki and Hermes and Coyote, and fled to the West with my tail curled between my legs? I have gone west, of course, but I arrived here in style. Did you think anything less would do?

But let me guess. The one you really want to know about is the Snake Charmer, the woman who possesses the Eye of Kakarauri, who can walk through the twilight lands, the only one who has and will ever know my true self. Ruby. Did you think I had forgotten?

If I dreamt, she would be in my dreams. I see her in the night sky, on the long mountain roads, in the smoldering brush on the Santa Ana hills. If I try very hard, I can still feel the echo of her hand on my face. But that is all. I cannot conjure the exchanges between us, when I became her and she I, and we met on the hallowed plains. I cannot even remember them. They are like the faintest shadows of flitting wings, nothing more than a rustling in the garden. And yet, I would give all that I have, all that I am, for one more moment on the other side. One more moment with her.

She was right, you know. She will drive me mad. But at least in that madness, she will always remain. I will never lose her completely.

But what of her, you ask? Not of the madness, but of the woman?

The truth is, I have no idea.

The truth is, I may never know.

For you must remember, this is a story where no one wins. Not me. Not her. Bets may be placed and hands played. A die rolled, a card flipped, a trick performed. But the score will never be settled. The end will never come.

The game will never be over.

END

Acknowledgments

As always, thank you to Ryan Holt. You never stopped believing in my little carnival tale and now we have *Miraculum*. It's been a wild ride and I couldn't have made it without you.

Thank you, so many thank yous, to Janet Sokolay, who has been the champion of *Miraculum* since day one. I promise to do my best to bring Ruby, Daniel and Hayden to the big screen.

I owe so much to the following incredible people: Jason Pinter, Josh Getzler, Jeff Ourvan, Mimi Bark, Michael Connelly, Joe Ide, Aaron Mahnke, Anthony Breznican, Jill Breznican, Will Chancellor, Alexis Sattler, Josh Kendall, Patrick Millikin, Mika Elovaara, Kimi Faxon Hemingway, Phillip Sokolay, Alex Segura and Rob Hart. Thanks also to my Holt family and my Blake HS family. In ways large and small, you've touched this book. You are the stars that have brought it to life.

And thanks to Vito, sitting at my feet, grumbling for a snack, for over sixteen years now. Every step of the way.

Finally, thank you readers. You are everything. I hope you enjoyed the show.

ABOUT THE AUTHOR

Steph Post is the author of the acclaimed Judah Cannon novels *Lightwood* and *Walk in the Fire*, as well as Big Moose Prize finalist *A Tree Born Crooked*. She was a recipient of the Patricia Cornwell Scholarship for creative writing from Davidson College, and the Vereen Bell writing award. Her fiction has appeared in *Stephen King's Contemporary Classics* and many other outlets. Her story, *The Pallid Mask,* was nominated for a Pushcart Prize. She lives in Brooksville, Florida. Visit her at www.stephpostfiction.com or @StephPostAuthor.